Rita Bradshaw was born in Northamptonshire, where she still lives today. At the age of sixteen she met her husband – whom she considers her soulmate – and they have two daughters and a son and three young grandchildren. Much to her delight, Rita's first attempt at a novel was accepted for publication, and she went on to write many more successful novels under a pseudonym before writing for Headline using her own name.

As a committed Christian and passionate animal-lover Rita has a full and busy life, but her writing continues to be a consuming pleasure that she never tires of. In any spare moments she loves reading, eating out and visiting the cinema and theatre, as well as being involved in her local church and animal welfare.

By Rita Bradshaw and available from Headline

Alone Beneath the Heaven
Reach for Tomorrow
Ragamuffin Angel
The Stony Path
The Urchin's Song
Candles in the Storm
The Most Precious Thing
Always I'll Remember
The Rainbow Years
Skylarks at Sunset
Above the Harvest Moon
Eve and her Sisters
Gilding the Lily

GILDING THE LILY

Rita Bradshaw

headline

Copyright © 2009 Rita Bradshaw

The right of Rita Bradshaw to be identified as the Author of
the Work has been asserted by her in accordance with the
Copyright, Designs and Patents Act 1988.

First published in 2009 by
HEADLINE PUBLISHING GROUP

First published in paperback in 2009 by
HEADLINE PUBLISHING GROUP

5

Cataloguing in Publication Data is available from the British Library

ISBN 978 0 7553 4238 9

Typeset in Bembo by Palimpsest Book Production Limited,
Grangemouth, Stirlingshire

Printed in the UK by
CPI Antony Rowe, Chippenham and Eastbourne

Headline's policy is to use papers that are natural, renewable
and recyclable products and made from wood grown in sustainable forests.
The logging and manufacturing processes are expected
to conform to the environmental regulations of
the country of origin.

HEADLINE PUBLISHING GROUP
An Hachette UK company
338 Euston Road
London NW1 3BH

www.headline.co.uk
www.hachette.co.uk

This book is for our dear friends Peter and Dorothy, in memory of their beautiful, brave and very precious daughter, Lizzie.

The night the *Titanic* went down the sky was alive with shooting stars; the brilliant shooting star that Richard saw when Lizzie went home to be with her Lord was a word to those she loved that she's free from pain at last, wonderfully healed, and singing praises to the God she loved with all her heart and soul.

I know you, and Phil and Richard, miss her more than words can say. Clive and I continue to pray that the Lord Jesus will give you songs in the night and treasures in dark places, and that he will carry you when all else fails and grief is overwhelming. We love you very much.

Acknowledgements

There has been so much written, and have been so many films, about the terrible tragedy when the *Titanic* went down in April 1912. I wanted to portray the facts of that disaster which could so easily have been avoided as seen by someone who was on board ship, without being confused by the many myths and fables that can colour things over a passage of time. To this end I gathered together a great deal of research, but one book which stands out above all others for clarity and objectivity has to be *Unsinkable: The Full Story of the RMS Titanic* by Daniel Allen Butler.

'Every city or house divided against
itself shall not stand'

Matthew 12:25

Contents

Part One	January 1890	A Divided House	1
Part Two	May 1907	Sarah's Wedding	43
Part Three	February 1908	Trouble Begets Trouble	149
Part Four	June 1911	Choices	239
Part Five	April 1912	The *Titanic*	305
Part Six	May 1912	Breaking Free	383

PART ONE

January 1890 – A Divided House

Chapter 1

For a long time afterwards he asked himself how things would have panned out if he hadn't come home unexpectedly that sunny April morning. Would he have discovered the truth in time, or would he have carried on thinking he was the luckiest man alive to be married to Geraldine, even if she did pick fault with everything he did? But all that was relative. He *had* come home.

Stanley Brown pressed his lips together, his eyes narrowing on the snow-covered fields in front of him. It was bitterly cold. The heavy blue-grey sky threatened further squalls of blustery snow, but chilled to the marrow as he was he preferred the icy landscape to the warmth of his house in the heart of Bishopwearmouth's terraced streets. House . . . His wide mouth curled in self-derision. Two rooms, to be more precise. Rooms where at this very moment his wife was in the process of giving birth to a child who would be a sister or brother to their little Sarah.

Hunching his shoulders against the raw January

wind, he began walking along the Durham Road. He passed the north moor on his left. To the east of that was Silksworth Colliery but the mine would be silent today, it being a Sunday.

No one was about, but why would they be on a day like today? He smiled grimly. You'd have to be mad to be taking a constitutional in this weather. Mad, or so sickened by what was at home that anything else – even this piercing wind – was preferable.

He walked for over an hour before once again stopping to stand and gaze over farmland. The exposed blackened skeletons of a number of beech trees were being assailed by icy blasts but otherwise the normal laws of nature seemed suspended by the extreme cold of the January afternoon. There were no birds about, not even the odd seagull.

Resting his elbows on the drystone wall bordering the narrow lane he'd turned into a few minutes before, Stanley ran his fingers idly over the raised scar covering the bridge of his nose. The accident had changed his life for ever. Funny how a moment in time could do that. It had been his own fault though, he'd forgotten the cardinal rule of the shipyards which declared you couldn't afford to lose concentration for a second. He'd been working with a plater in the fabrication shed on a guillotine that chopped the steel plates. It had a little hand crane which you worked yourself and he'd got distracted. He hadn't realised his finger was on the button of the crane when the sling was going up. It had caught the guillotine and snapped, hitting him full in the face and breaking his nose.

He shook his head at his stupidity. They didn't call

Doxford's, where he worked, the blood yard for nothing, that and Thompson's Yard. They were the worst on the Wear for accidents. Only yesterday poor old Shane O'Leary had copped a load. Shane had been climbing a ladder between decks and his boot had got caught in the handle of his paint tin. He'd fallen on the tank top, landing on his hands and knees. The bones of his wrists had been sticking out through his skin when he'd climbed back up the ladder before passing clean out.

Stanley straightened, as though throwing something off. You couldn't dwell on what might happen though, you just had to get on with it. Mind, if he was being honest he wouldn't want to work anywhere else. From a bairn he'd been fascinated by the shipyards, probably because his da and his granda had been shipwrights. He'd absorbed tales of what went on with his mam's milk. Gantries collapsing, girders falling, men and boys losing fingers and eyes or having limbs sliced off. He'd heard it all long before he'd turned thirteen and started work as a rivet catcher boy. He'd thought he'd landed in hell that day. The deafening noise, the hammering and riveting and black belching smoke had made him all fingers and thumbs as he'd climbed the staging above the engine room. He'd looked down on the heaters' fires and it had reminded him of a picture the teacher at Sunday school had showed them, *Dante's Inferno*, he thought it had been called, by some French bloke. But he'd survived that day and the ones following it although two lads he'd started with hadn't been so lucky. The fatalities among catcher boys was high.

A gust of icy wind tried to snatch his cap and he

pulled it further down over his forehead, tightening his muffler round his neck. Slowly he began to retrace his footsteps to the town.

He'd broken his nose that April day because he had been worrying about Geraldine. For some weeks he'd had the notion there was something wrong with her but he hadn't been able to put his finger on it. Once the infirmary had patched him up and sent him home for the day with a thudding headache, he'd walked to their rooms in a house in Church Street West at the back of the cement works wondering how he was going to tell Geraldine he was losing a day's pay. In the event that had been the least of his troubles.

Sarah had been in her playpen in the kitchen when he'd let himself into the house the back way. She'd been crying earlier, if her tear-blotched face was anything to go by, although she had been sitting quietly with a rag doll his mam had made her when he entered the room. She'd raised her little head and seen him and immediately clambered to her feet, holding out her arms, in spite of his knocked-about face. He'd lifted her up and cuddled her for a moment or two before placing her back in the pen. With hindsight he knew that even then he must have suspected something, although what he didn't know. But something had been telling him not to make his presence known.

Sarah had settled down with her dolly again and he had carefully made his way into the hall. The upstairs of the house was occupied by an Irish couple who worked during the day. He had stood for a moment outside the front room which was their bedroom, Sarah's cot having been squeezed in next to their brass bed.

All was quiet and Geraldine could have been merely lying down for a rest. Maybe it was her changed behaviour over the last weeks that had alerted him but when he quietly opened the door and saw the two bodies lying among the ruffled covers, he found he wasn't surprised. Nauseated but not surprised.

They must have had their fun because they were lying entwined with their eyes shut, the man's white buttocks facing him. He hadn't reacted for a moment, he'd simply stared at them. Geraldine's hair had been in a fan on the pillow behind her and one full pink-tipped breast had been visible. That had perhaps enraged him more than anything else. Since the time they had found Sarah was on the way and had a hasty wedding, Geraldine had insisted on undressing in the dark. And this the woman who hadn't been able to get enough of him. And there she was, in the middle of the day, lying as exposed as one of the whores who plied their trade down by the docks.

The sound he'd made deep in his throat had brought them both jerking upwards seconds before his fists found their target. The fight had been short but savage and all the time Geraldine had been as silent as the grave, shrunk back against the bedhead clutching the sheet to her as though he'd never seen her naked before. The other man hadn't stood a chance. Not only had he been taken by surprise but his naked-ness, combined with the fact that he was slight and finely boned, had put him at a severe disadvantage.

If it hadn't been for the fact that the neighbours would have had a field day he would have booted him out of the house stark naked. As it was Geraldine's

7

fancy man had left fully dressed but looking as though he had been hit by a tram.

The snow he had been expecting all afternoon was beginning to fall, great fat flakes that whirled and danced in the icy wind. He had reached the outskirts of Bishopwearmouth now but he didn't hurry. His hands thrust deep in his trouser pockets, he walked steadily on, his mouth a thin line in his grim face.

And now his wife's bastard was being born and under cover of his name. Whatever Geraldine said, he knew it wasn't his. She hadn't let him near her for weeks before that April day and he hadn't touched her afterwards. Just the proximity of living in the same house sickened him these days. No, this baby was her fancy man's, all right. When he'd found out she was expecting a baby and done his arithmetic he'd told her to clear off to this fella and it had been then she'd admitted he was long gone, that he'd scarpered the day after he'd found them together. Should he have still thrown her out? Probably. But there had been Sarah. He hadn't wanted to lose his bairn.

The snow was fast becoming a blizzard but as he passed the grim confines of the workhouse its austere lines mocked what he was trying to tell himself. All right, so it hadn't altogether been his love for Sarah which had stayed his hand, nor the fact that with nowhere to go Geraldine might well have ended up in the workhouse. It had been the thought of folk knowing he'd been made a cuckold of he couldn't bear. The neighbours might have their suspicions because you couldn't so much as sneeze before the old wives knew about it, but suspicions were one thing. Fact was another. He'd always prided himself on being the big man, in deed as well as stature. Stanley Brown, who'd won Geraldine Preston as his wife and her the daughter of one of the big nobs in the town who had his own engineering works. Never mind her da had cut her off without a penny once he'd discovered she was pregnant by a common steelworker, it had been him Geraldine had been mad about. At least in those first heady weeks and months.

Pride goes before a fall. How often had his mam said that? But she was right. After her fancy man had limped off with his tail between his legs Geraldine had screamed at him that she hated the two rooms they were stuck in, hated having to wash and clean and cook from dawn to dusk, hated being a mother, hated *him*. Julian was the man she'd had an understanding with before she'd met him, the son of one of her father's wealthy friends. He could have kept her in the manner to which she was accustomed and he loved her.

Oh aye, he'd loved her all right, Stanley thought bitterly as he passed Millfield engineering works and approached the maze of streets close to the river. He'd loved her so much he'd high-tailed it off abroad leaving the thick, stupid, clodhopping husband to bring up his bairn. The words Geraldine had flung at him that night still rankled. And now the living proof of her betrayal was making an appearance.

He ground his teeth together as he stood at the top of Church Street West. How often in the last months

9

had he looked at his wife's swelling stomach and loathed her and the new life growing inside her? Times without number. Some days he'd been unable to think of little else. He knew his mam and da were worried about him. His mam never missed an opportunity to press him as to what was wrong but he'd rather cut out his own tongue than suffer the humiliation of revealing the truth.

The kitchen was empty when he walked in. Mrs McKenzie from next door had taken Sarah once it was evident the baby was on its way. He could hear Geraldine groaning in the bedroom and the midwife's voice. So, it wasn't over yet.

The kitchen wasn't as warm as usual, the fire in the range was low. After throwing some coal on, he lifted the kettle from its steel shelf at the side of the hob. It was empty. Walking through to the small back-yard which housed the privy and the wash-house, he bent over the tap. When he turned it only a thin trickle of water dribbled out. He knew the signs. Within hours the tap would be frozen and it would take umpteen bits of burning paper pushed up its spout to get it going. With this in mind he took the full kettle through to the kitchen and placed it on the hob. Then he returned to the yard and filled two buckets of water and brought them into a corner of the room for later.

Once the kettle was boiled he made a pot of tea and brought it to the kitchen table. At this stage of his Sarah's birth he'd been frantic. In fact, he'd been so beside himself the midwife had come out of the bedroom where she was seeing to Geraldine and given him a bit of a talking-to. 'Your wife's doing fine, man. This is perfectly natural after all.'

When he had protested Geraldine wasn't very strong and had a delicate constitution, the midwife had been even more forthright.

'She's stronger than she looks, Mr Brown. We all are. It comes from having to tend a family and do several things at once. I know your wife wasn't born round these streets' – this was said with a sniff and stated quite clearly the midwife was aware of Geraldine's parentage and furthermore, he'd suspected, had been the recipient of what he privately termed Geraldine's uppity side – 'but she's young and strong and healthy.' He had thought the midwife somewhat hard and unsympathetic. He had been a fool in those days. But no more.

He drank two cups of scalding hot tea straight down but still the chill inside him made his insides shake. Geraldine's pains had begun just after breakfast and, deciding he needed more than a bowl of porridge in his stomach considering it was nigh on twilight, he made himself a sandwich. The bread was fresh, Geraldine had baked the day before, but he found he had to force each mouthful past the constriction in his throat. He had just finished and was drinking his third cup of tea when the back door opened and his mother walked in.

'Mrs Stamp told me she's started then.' Ava Brown was a small plump woman, the very antithesis of her tall, lean son.

'Aye.'

Ava plumped down on one of the hardbacked chairs,

unbuttoning her coat. 'It's enough to freeze your lugs off out there. Bitter, it is. Is there another one in that pot, lad?'

Silently Stanley poured his mother a cup of tea and pushed it towards her. He was supposed to have fetched her once the baby was on the way; she had offered to look after Sarah and Geraldine each day till he was home from work. He didn't refer to this but his tone was apologetic when he said, 'I was coming to see you later.'

'Aye, well, I'm here now, aren't I, so I might as well stay put till she's had it. You had your tea?'

'I've just had some bread and cheese.'

'That's not a meal for a full-grown man. I'll get you something—'

'Leave it, Mam.' His tone had been too sharp and now Stanley moderated his voice as he said quietly, 'I'm not hungry, Mam, but thanks anyway.'

Ava looked at her lad. She still thought of Stanley as her lad even though he was twenty-five and had been married the last three years. He was her first-born and although another five bairns had followed him, of which only three had survived beyond their first year, she knew she loved Stanley differently to the rest. Possibly because, in spite of his being over six feet two, he had a vulnerability about him her two daughters and other son didn't have. Which was how that one in there had got her claws into him in the first place.

Taking a deep breath, her voice low, Ava said, 'What's wrong, lad? And don't say nowt. You haven't been yourself for months now. I know I keep asking—'

'And I keep telling you, I'm fine.'

'Aye, and pigs fly.'

'Drink your tea, Mam.'

Ava said no more. As she sipped her tea she glanced round the kitchen. The range needed blackleading, the floor was filthy and there was dust thick enough to write your name in on the dresser. She was no housewife, Geraldine. Always harping on about them being stuck in two rooms and she couldn't even keep them clean. Mind, she hadn't heard her complain the last little while, not in Stanley's hearing anyway. Minded her p's and q's now in front of him she did, which was better than how she used to talk, as though he was muck under her feet. And him, she'd never known such a change in a man. From worshipping the ground Geraldine walked on, he seemed sometimes as though he couldn't stand the sight of her. Could the gossip be true? Mrs McKenzie had been positive there'd been some man visiting when Stanley was at work. Could Geraldine have been carrying on and he'd found out? It would explain a lot.

Once she had finished her tea, she rose to her feet, saying, 'No doubt there's a basket of ironing waiting. I'll be getting on with that. What time is Mrs McKenzie bringing the bairn back?'

Stanley didn't question how his mother knew the neighbour had taken Sarah, it was the way things were. 'I'm to collect her when I'm ready.'

'Well, I'll do the ironing and a few jobs and maybe pop round meself.' Ava waved at the battered old armchair to one side of the range. 'Why don't you settle down and shut your eyes for a minute or two, you look done in, and you won't be getting much sleep with a new bairn in the house.'

Stanley did as his mother suggested without comment. He hadn't slept well for months and lately hardly at all. He had been dreading this day. He'd prayed the bairn would be stillborn more times than he could remember but he didn't expect God to answer his pleading. How could he if he was a holy God? But he still kept praying it nonetheless.

He had brought Sarah's cot out of the bedroom that morning and the small wicker crib he'd bought cheap at the Old Market in Sunderland's East End in readiness for Sarah's birth now stood in its place. Sarah would be sleeping in the kitchen from now on. He had already made up his mind that he would join her most nights whether or not she needed him to. His armchair was comfortable enough and infinitely preferable to sharing a room with his wife and her bastard.

'What's the matter, lad?'

Too late he realised his mother had been staring at him and he quickly wiped his face of all expression. 'Spot of toothache,' he said briefly.

Silence reigned in the kitchen, the only sound coming from the bedroom next door. At some point he was vaguely aware of his mother putting the ironing away and then the midwife coming in to ask for hot water, after which his mother went through to the other room with her, but then he must have fallen into a deeper sleep. When he next opened his eyes it was in response to a baby's cry.

He found he was wide awake, every nerve in his body sensitised, but he didn't move from the chair.

A few moments later his mother appeared in the doorway. They stared at each other and his mother's voice held none of the elation a new life normally brings when she said, 'It's another little lassie.'

He nodded. He would rather that than a boy who might resemble the slight blond man he'd seen just that one time but whose face was forever etched on his memory.

'She's nothing like Sarah was. Half her size for one thing, and this one's got no hair to speak of.' Sarah had had a mop of straight black hair that had stuck up comically over her forehead.

He nodded again. 'Every bairn's different.'

Aye, every bairn was different but she thought she had her answer as to what was troubling her lad. Did he know the bairn wasn't his? Then she answered herself with, Why ask the road you know? He knew all right. But of course she might be mistaken. She might be putting two and two together and coming up with ten. But every one of her other five grand-children, including Sarah, had the Brown stamp on them. The mass of black hair and high forehead and the fact they were all nine pounders and over when they were born. It was a family joke. But she didn't think there'd be much jesting over this little lassie. Flatly, she said, 'You can come and see her in a minute, the midwife's just tidying them both up.'

They were still staring at each other and her suspicion she now knew the reason for the dramatic change in her son strengthened when Stanley blinked, looking away from her into the fire. 'There's no rush. I've seen a baby before.'

As big and old as he was, Ava had the desire to go across to him and take him in her arms as she'd done when he was a bairn. There was no one better than her lad, no one, but hadn't she always been fearful this would end in tears? From the minute he'd let on he was seeing Mr Preston's daughter on the quiet, she'd felt in her water it would go wrong. He had been fair barmy about Geraldine but the lass had been in a different class to him with her da having his own business and them living in a fancy house Hendon way. She'd known what had attracted Preston's daughter, it had been her son's looks and his size. Ever since he was a lad Stanley had had the lassies falling over themselves to catch his eye. But she'd worried herself sick Geraldine would discard him when the novelty had worn off, and most likely she would have done if the bairn hadn't come along.

Ava stood a moment or two more. 'I'm going to get you a bite of supper.'

It was said with the air of one who had just thrown down the gauntlet and Stanley was aware his mother expected him to argue. Whether or not he would have done so Ava never found out because the next second the kitchen door opened and Mrs Boyce, the midwife, came in carrying the infant who was swathed in a blanket. 'Mrs Brown's asleep so I thought I'd bring this one in here for a bit, give her a chance to have a proper rest. Likely you want to see your new daughter?' she added cheerily and, without waiting for an answer, bent down and placed the baby in Stanley's arms which opened automatically to receive the bundle.

He felt rather than saw his mother's instinctive move towards him. He sat absolutely still and rigid, and as he stared down at the tiny little thing in his arms he saw his mother had not exaggerated. This child seemed half the size Sarah had been when he'd first held her. The baby had been sound asleep in the midwife's arms but now she stirred, opening her mouth and yawning before looking sleepily up at him.

'Shall I take her?'

His mother was at his elbow but he kept his eyes on the child. 'No,' he said numbly. What had he expected? Some kind of monster, probably, the way his mind had been the last little while. Certainly the swelling in Geraldine's stomach had taken on a devilish appearance to him; something foul, unclean. But this was just a baby, a tiny little girl with a sweet face who had been born into bitterness and despair. Because that's what he'd been feeling, gut-wrenching, blind despair.

He swallowed hard, horrified to find he wanted to cry. He couldn't break down now, not with the midwife watching. Forcing words past the constriction in his throat, he mumbled, 'She – she's very small.'

'Aye, she's a wee one, all right, but bonny and perfectly formed. There's nowt to worry about save she'll need feeding more often than most. Still, you're going to be looking after things for a week or two, aren't you, Mrs Brown?' the midwife added, turning her gaze on Ava.

'Aye, lass, I'll be here. Now can I get you a cup of tea?'

'No, I'll be away home, it's been a long day.'

Stanley looked up, nodding with his head to the mantelpiece. 'There's your money there, Mrs Boyce. Can you get it, Mam?'

The midwife took the brown envelope Ava passed her, saying, 'Thanks, lad. By, I wish everyone was like you I don't mind saying. I have to wait weeks with some of them and even then it comes in dribs and drabs. And I know for a fact more than one or two of the husbands wet the baby's head regular as clockwork, if you know what I mean. Any excuse with some of them, and the poor wives at home with next to nothing in the cupboards and the rent man knocking at the door. Pitiful, it is.'

Ava smiled at the midwife as Mrs Boyce put on her hat and coat. 'I dare say you see plenty with your job.'

'Oh aye, that's for sure. But I keep me own counsel.'

'Best way, lass. Aye, best way.'

Stanley was aware of the women's chatter as his mother saw the midwife out, but his whole being was taken up with the emotions tearing through his chest. He hadn't wanted to feel like this, damn it. He gazed down at the sleeping baby. The minute features were perfect – beautiful – and she had none of the red puffiness Sarah had had when she'd been born. This one looked like a little porcelain doll.

He swallowed again as his mother came back into the kitchen. The child in his arms was the only innocent one in this mucky mess, that's what he had to face up to. He should never have taken Geraldine down in the first place and then he wouldn't be in this position. No matter she had been brazen in her wanting of him and he had been dazzled by her. He should never have

18

begun anything with her and he had known it all along. He had been courting Sally Hammond from a few doors down, his childhood sweetheart, before Geraldine had beguiled him. He had broken Sally's heart and felt like the worst scab out but he still hadn't been able to give Geraldine up. Even when he'd discovered he wasn't her first lover it hadn't deterred him from seeing her again. It was like he'd been bewitched; that was the only way he could explain the madness to himself now.

'I'm going to nip back an' let your da know she's had the bab afore I get Sarah; do you want me to put her in the crib afore I go? I'll get your supper once I'm back.'

'No, she's all right with me.'

His mother came to stand by his elbow. 'Have you and Geraldine picked a name for the little lassie?'

They hadn't discussed names. They hadn't discussed anything since the night he had told his wife she could continue to stay under his roof on the understanding that she did exactly as she was told. Her days of being pandered to were over, he had said grimly. From now on she would toe the line and stop acting like Lady Muck or she could sling her hook. Frankly, it was all the same to him. He looked at his mother. Her second name was Lily and his maternal grandma had been Rose. 'Lily Rose.'

Ava's plump face flushed with pleasure and there was a smile in her voice as she said, 'That's nice, lad.' Pulling on her coat and hat, she eased her woollen gloves over chapped hands. 'Ta ta, then, I won't be two ticks.'

Once he was alone, Stanley put out a finger and

touched the silky smooth brow and then the wispy down on the tiny head. Lily. Aye, it fitted her. The wild lilies that grew in the fields Tunstall way had the same pure transparency and beauty. Unbidden, he felt the same fiercely protective love he had experienced when he'd held Sarah for the first time welling up inside him. There was none of the joy of that occasion, but, strangely, it made the feeling for the scrap of humanity in his arms stronger, if anything.

The pricking in his eyes became unbearable but he was alone now. As the tears flowed they rolled down his cheeks so fast they fell on the baby's face like raindrops.

Chapter 2

It was late the same night. Sarah had made no objection to the new arrangement whereby she slept in her cot in the warm kitchen and she was fast asleep. Lily had just been fed and settled down and Stanley was snoring gently in his bed. Only Geraldine Brown was wide awake. She was tired, but her mind was grappling with the events of the past hours, especially the moment when her husband had informed her, in a tone which had brooked no argument, that the new baby would be named Lily Rose. She had stared at him, wondering if this had indicated a softening in his attitude, but the same coldness as before had masked his face. And the bolster was still in place between them in the bed.

The light through the bedroom curtains from the street lamp positioned outside their window allowed her to see the contents of the room quite clearly, and she lay with her eyes open and her body taut. How she hated that bolster. Stanley had placed it in position shortly after he had found her with Julian and

21

the humiliation and rage she'd felt then had grown with time. The silent declaration that he wanted no part of her and could do without her had cut her to the quick and hurt her pride.

At first she'd told herself he wouldn't be able to keep it up, not wanting her as he did. From the time they'd bumped into each other in High Street West one Saturday afternoon when she'd been browsing for a new dress with a girlfriend, she'd sensed she could twist him round her little finger. He had been crazy about her, putty in her hands. The fact that she could engender such passion in the tall, handsome steel-worker had thrilled her. But the bolster *had* remained in the bed. As the weeks and months had crept by and her body had burnt for release from sexual frustration, so her humiliation had intensified. From the time she had returned home from the select private school for young ladies she'd attended till the age of seventeen and enjoyed her first sexual encounter with a boy after a dance at the tennis club, she had recognised the fires which burnt within her did not burn inside all women. And when she had set eyes on Stanley she'd known he could satisfy those cravings as few men could. And he had.

Geraldine shifted her body on the old flock mattress. It was lumpy and threadbare but had come with the bed and had been all they could afford. She'd got used to it after a while, but tonight her back was aching – not that this birth had been like the first, and for that she was grateful.

She hadn't expected her relationship with Stanley to last too long, just till she had got her need of him out of her system. After all, he wasn't of her class and she knew her parents would have a blue fit if they found out. But they had slipped up. And her father had further compounded the situation by washing his hands of her. She'd never forgive him for that, never. He'd consigned her to these two wretched rooms and a life spent working her fingers to the bone simply because she had gone against him. They'd had a maid and cook at home and although the house hadn't been large by some standards, she and her sister had had their own sitting room where they could entertain friends. And now Millicent, who wasn't half as pretty as her and who had no figure to speak of, was married to a country squire with a great deal of money. It wasn't fair.

Tears seeped from her eyes as she considered her lot. Who could blame her for having a bit of fun with Julian? He had been so sweet to her that afternoon when they had met in Mowbray Park when she had been walking Sarah in her perambulator. She had known Julian ever since they had been children and had always been aware he liked her; when their parents had made it clear the two of them should get married she had gone along with their wishes although he'd been a little too slight and almost feminine-looking to stir any real interest in her. They had been on the point of getting engaged when she'd discovered she was pregnant by Stanley. And then, much later, when they'd bumped into each other again, their assignations had given her something to look forward to, something to break the numbing monotony of her life in this horrible place.

Wiping her tears on the sleeve of her lawn night-dress, she turned over. Her feet felt like blocks of ice. Although Stanley had lit a fire in the small grate because of the baby, the room was still cold. It was always cold. More often than not a thin crust of ice covered the inside of the window in the mornings. She hadn't noticed the cold so much when she'd been wrapped in Stanley's arms and sleeping curled close to his big body.

This thought brought more tears. Stanley was cruel. She would never have believed he could be so cruel to her. No one understood what she'd had to give up when she had come to this place. Everyone was against her, everyone.

But he had named the child. She hadn't expected that. She had thought he would want nothing to do with the baby. It was a good sign. Perhaps now the child was born and she could regain her figure he'd want her again. She didn't believe he didn't love her. He was just angry she'd slighted him by going with Julian. He'd look on it as a slur to his manhood; his class was so provincial. Her lip curled. But now she was herself again she would bring him to heel. In the fullness of time she would make him suffer for his treatment of her but she would play the loving wife first. Now she wasn't encumbered by her shape that would be easy. She relaxed, slowly allowing the physical exhaustion to take over. And she would also make sure they did not live the rest of their lives in this hole. She wanted a house of her own, a place where she could close the front door and pretend the mean streets surrounding her did not exist. It would make being married to Stanley and living in this vile part of the town bearable.

It was a full three months before the incident occurred which told Geraldine her relationship with her husband would never resume its early pattern. It was the occasion of Lily's christening at St Andrew's church at the bottom of Church Street West.

The day had gone well on the whole. Stanley's parents, and his two married sisters and their husbands and children, along with his sixteen-year-old brother, Matthew, had come back to the house after the service to toast the baby and have a bite to eat. Geraldine had made sure she put on a good spread, and had cleaned the two rooms from top to bottom the day before. She'd dressed carefully in one of the good-quality day frocks she had brought with her when she had left her father's home. Although it was now past its best, the fine soft cloth in jade green showed off her red hair and hazel eyes to full advantage.

She had been bright and vivacious and on her best behaviour for the benefit of the company, satisfyingly aware she stood out from the other women present like a butterfly among moths. Having regained her figure and begun to take an interest in her appearance again, she had been working towards this day. She was determined to show Stanley what he was missing. He had been all hers till he had found her with Julian, she knew that, and such was her character that once he had shown her he could do without her, it made her want him as she had never done before. More especially, she didn't want any other woman to have him. She knew from experience Stanley was a man of deep and fierce passions. If he wasn't sleeping with her it stood to reason he'd eventually find release elsewhere, and that mustn't happen.

The kitchen had been crowded all afternoon but Stanley and the other menfolk, including Matthew, had left for the Shoulder of Mutton in Ropery Road. Jinny and Rachel, Stanley's sisters, had also left to put their children to bed, it being seven o'clock. Geraldine and Ava cleared up together, Sarah watching from her playpen and Lily asleep in her crib which now reposed in a warm corner of the kitchen. Since the baby had begun to sleep through the night after her ten o'clock feed, a couple of weeks before, they'd moved Sarah back into the bedroom. The little girl had been quite happy to sleep in the kitchen but had remained wide awake till they had left the room to go to bed, causing her to become a little fractious during the day.

Geraldine was not happy Stanley had gone drinking. The Shoulder of Mutton was one of several pubs serving the industrial workers of Deptford, and she knew he was bound to meet some of his shipyard cronies and only roll home once the pub closed. She had hoped after her triumph of the day that it would be just the two of them when the others had gone. She was sure he was beginning to mellow. Admittedly the bolster was still in place, but he treated Lily exactly the same as Sarah and since the baby had been born he had appeared less sullen at times. She just wished the children weren't so different; Sarah with her dark hair and stocky frame and Lily as tiny and pale as a fairy with eyes as green as grass.

Ava had been thinking along the same lines. Without looking at her daughter-in-law, she said, 'You couldn't get two sisters less alike than your two. Mebbe the bab's fairness runs in your side?'

Geraldine glanced at her mother-in-law who was busy scrubbing at a dish which had held roast potatoes. She neither liked nor trusted Ava, a feeling she was sure was reciprocated, but she needed to keep on Stanley's mother's good side if she was going to win her husband back. He thought a great deal of his mother, did Stanley. Curbing the tart retort which had sprung to her lips, she said flatly, 'My sister has fair hair.' Actually Millicent's hair was a horrible mousy brown but that was by the by and none of Ava's business, she thought irritably.

Ava nodded, keeping her eyes on the dish. 'Mebbe that's it, then. Breeding outs, one way or the other.'

Her remark could be taken two ways. Geraldine glared at Ava's back. She knew her mother-in-law had been wondering what was wrong between her and Stanley but she hadn't mentioned anything directly, not to her at least. Perhaps she had to Stanley but if she had, he hadn't confided in her. Geraldine found this encouraging. Deep down he must want to make a go of their marriage if he was averse to turning his mother against her.

She reached for a plate and began to dry it, hating the sight of her red chapped hands. They used to be so soft and pretty. But she'd looked bonny today, everyone had said so. Everyone except Stanley and his mother. As Ava placed the dish on the work table to one side of the washing-up bowl, Geraldine said, 'That's the last of it; you go now, you've done enough. I want to get Sarah to bed, she's overtired with all the excitement.'

Ava looked at the young girl in front of her. And that's what Geraldine was, she told herself. A silly young girl. She wished she could find it within herself to like her because, after all, she was Stanley's wife, but the older that wee bab got the more she was sure she wasn't a Brown. Still, as Albert kept reminding her, what went on between a married couple was their business and theirs alone unless one of them decided different. Mind, if he said, 'Least said, soonest mended, lass' one more time she'd hit him over the head with the frying pan.

Pulling off Geraldine's apron which she'd put on earlier to wash the mountain of dishes, she nodded to her daughter-in-law. 'Right you are then, lass. I'll leave you to it. An' it was a nice do, you did the little lassie proud.'

Geraldine smiled stiffly. These awful people. A nice do! Everyone hemmed in so they could hardly move and the men guzzling the beer Stanley had bought as though they'd never had a drink before. There had been enough to last them all night if Jinny and Rachel's husbands hadn't been such pigs and then Stanley would have had no excuse to go to the pub. The more she saw of her in-laws, the more she realised Stanley was a cut above most working men. He had ambition, that was the thing. In the early days of their relationship he had talked of bettering himself, becoming a gaffer, as he'd put it. And he could do that, he had both the determination and a way with people. Yes, he could do it and she would make sure he did.

Geraldine's face revealed a lot more than she thought it did and Ava kept her smile in place and her voice civil with some effort as she said goodbye and left. Once she was in the back lane she stood for a minute or two, breathing deeply and telling herself not to get riled. The April night was cold enough to quell the smell from the privies in the backyards and the twilight was thick, a lone blackbird digging frantically in a patch of dirt a little distance away for his supper. She watched him pull up a long fat worm and smiled to herself as he made short work of it before flying off. It was only then she moved; she hadn't wanted to deprive him of his meal.

She hoped she was wrong about the bab. She'd give all she possessed, such as it was, to be wrong and for her lad to have the old light in his eyes when he looked at his wife. And Geraldine was a bonny piece, there was no doubt about that. Whatever was wrong between them now she had turned his head at one time. Maybe she could do it again, as long as it wasn't . . . that. Because what man worth his salt could overlook the living proof of such carryings-on?

Ava continued to chew the matter over on the short walk home to the two-up, two-down terraced house in Charles Street, close to the old glass works. When she entered her kitchen by way of the tiny scullery she immediately stoked up the fire she had banked down before they'd left at midday for the church. Once it was burning brightly she put the big black kettle on the hob and made herself a pot of tea. She poured herself a cup before plumping down in Albert's well-stuffed armchair at one side of the range, her feet resting on the thick colourful clippy mat which covered part of the stone-flagged floor. After taking a sip of tea, she looked round the room.

She hadn't lit the oil lamp. From habit, when the bairns had been small and money had been tight, she rarely lit it till it was nearly too dark to see. Now, in the glow from the fire the kitchen appeared cosy and mellow. The steel-topped, brass-tailed fender, and the dresser with its blue and yellow crockery of which she was inordinately proud, twinkled as they reflected the leaping flames, and in the middle of the kitchen table stood a vase of bright yellow daffodils which Matthew had bought her that morning. He was a one for little gestures like that, she thought fondly. Stanley had been the same.

She settled herself further in the chair and took another sip of tea, sighing softly. On the morning he'd got wed Stanley had thought of her, even when he'd been so excited he'd appeared like a dog with two tails, bless him. He'd gone out first thing and come back to present her with a grand little pot of blue and pink hyacinths. They had scented the kitchen for weeks.

'For you, Mam,' he'd said thickly, and he had touched her face fleetingly, his eyes tender. 'If Geraldine is half the mother you are, she'll be doing all right.' And then he had rushed upstairs to get changed into his Sunday suit, eager to get to the church and his lass.

Quietly Ava placed the cup and saucer by the side of the chair and, burying her face in her hands, she let the tears flow.

Chapter 3

Stanley knew he was merry. Not drunk, he told himself as he laughed at some witticism from one of his brothers-in-law, but just merry enough for the lead weight which sat in his chest these days to feel lighter. He had consumed what was to him a vast quantity of ale, but most of it had come from a group of his shipyard pals sitting at a table in a corner of the bar who, once they'd learned of the occasion, had insisted on standing him pint after pint.

It wasn't long before closing when he saw Mr Hammond, Sally's father, making his way towards him. The smile sliding from his face, he waited for the older man to approach him. He had once counted Jack Hammond as a friend but after he had finished with Sally her father had let him know exactly what he thought of him. Stanley couldn't blame him. He and Sally had had an understanding and he'd played a dirty trick on her, getting mixed up with Geraldine. Well, if ever a man had been paid back in kind, he had.

'Stanley.' Jack nodded as he stopped in front of him. 'Celebrating the night, I hear.'

'Aye.'

'We're doing a bit of that ourselves at home. You heard about Sally?'

Jack knew he hadn't heard about Sally, it was clear in his voice. Stanley said nothing but his stomach muscles tensed as he waited for Jack to go on.

'Copped herself a real gent, Sally has. Tim Finlay, him that owns the ironmonger's in Fawcett Street. Fair barmy about her, he is. They're getting wed in the summer.'

Tim Finlay? Stanley knew the shop but he had thought the man who owned it was married with bairns.

'Lost his wife three years back, Tim did, round about the time you and Sally parted company. She's been acting as housekeeper for him and looking after the two bairns. Course, me an' the wife could see it coming. It was clear he was smitten, but being a *decent* bloke' – the word was charged with meaning – 'he waited a while before declaring himself.'

Stiffly, Stanley said, 'I'm pleased for her.'

'Aye, I thought you would be. I said to the wife, Stanley will be pleased to know Sally's done so well for herself. In clover she'll be from now on and no one deserves that more than my lass. She couldn't have done better, in my opinion.'

Stanley said nothing, there was nothing *to* say.

His eyes as hard as bullets, Jack nodded again. 'You're still in Church Street West, then? Two rooms, isn't it?'

Again Stanley didn't reply but now his temper was rising. The Hammonds lived a few doors down from his parents and theirs was a big family, consequently they were as poor as church mice. Many the time as a bairn he'd gone with Sally to the pawn shop with her mother's sheets and her father's Sunday suit so the family could eat in the couple of days before her father got paid. The bairns had always been clean but the lads had never had boots on their feet, even in mid winter, and they'd regularly scrounged bones from some of the kinder butchers at the end of a working day or foraged for droppings of spotted fruit under the market stalls. Jack Hammond had nothing to preach at him for.

'All right, Jack?' Albert entered the conversation with a warning hand on his son's arm. 'Can I buy you a jar?'

With some effort, Jack turned his eyes away from the younger man. 'No thanks, Bert, I'm on me way home.' He nodded to them all and then turned on his heel and walked out of the pub into the black night.

The group had fallen silent and Stanley knew what they were thinking, even Matthew. They'd never come right out and say it because family was family, but at bottom their sympathies were all with Jack Hammond on this. His family had thought the world of Sally. He drained his glass and wiped his mouth with the back of his hand. 'I'm off then. See you at the yard tomorrow.'

Once outside he stood for a minute in the bitingly cold air. So, Sally was getting married. He felt like he'd been punched in the stomach which was daft, stupid. Nevertheless, that's how he felt. Finlays was a big shop, impressive; he dare bet Tim Finlay didn't live in the gridiron acres of terraced housing behind the industrial riverside. Far more likely he'd have a house in one of the more spacious suburbs – Ashbrooke way or somewhere similar. Well set up, Sally would be.

He began to walk slowly, his hands thrust in his pockets. Deep down he was glad for her; if anyone deserved some happiness, Sally did, but his guts felt like a giant hand was clamping them at the thought of another man touching her. He shook his head at himself. If anyone had asked him yesterday, even an hour ago, how he felt about Sally Hammond, he would have told them in all honesty he wished the very best for her. And he did. After what he'd done how could he wish anything else? But suddenly he felt as though he had lost something irreplaceable and infinitely precious and it was only now, when it had been snatched away, that he realised how special it had been. Which, again, didn't make sense because he had lost Sally one sunny spring day over three years ago when he had first clapped eyes on Geraldine. If he had known then what he knew now, he'd have run like a bat out of hell.

There had been occasional sharp flurries of snow throughout the day. Winter didn't relinquish its grip without a fight in these parts. As he reached the top of Church Street West a few desultory flakes of snow fluttered haphazardly in the wind, for all the world like delicate May blossom. Stanley stood staring down the dark street. He was gripped by a sense of aloneness that was overwhelming.

He would give anything not to have to go back. He breathed in deeply, hunching his shoulders. His parents' house was only a couple of streets away but, poor as it was, it was a palace compared to what he and his family were living in. But they were stuck there for the time being till he could drag them out of the mire. And he would. Aye, he would. Not for Geraldine's sake. He was done with trying to please her. But his little lassies, that was a different story. He'd work all the hours under the sun to provide them with somewhere better than this.

He began walking, his eyes narrowed on the greasy pavement underfoot and the feeling of frustration gnawing at his vitals. He had to forget about Sally. She belonged to another lifetime. Likely she was aware where he was living and perhaps even feeling a sense of satisfaction at the difference in their circumstances. Well, all things being equal, he couldn't blame her for that.

Something in him baulked at entering the house by the back way. The middle classes used their front doors as a matter of course and one day he would do the same. And they'd have a garden. Not a yard where the stink of the privy prevailed but an area of grass and flowerbeds, somewhere for bairns to play in. Somewhere clean and sweet-smelling.

When he entered the house it was to hear the O'Flannagans going hell for leather at each other upstairs. They fought like cat and dog half the time; the other half the bed springs twanged like there was no tomorrow. Stanley was amazed there wasn't a tribe of little O'Flannagans but according to the neighbours' gossip there was something wrong with Mrs O'Flannagan in that department. Whether it was true or not he didn't know and he didn't care. He had enough problems of his own to contend with.

The kitchen was in darkness when he opened the door but he had expected that. What he hadn't expected was to see Sarah's cot standing next to the crib. He stared at the sleeping children for a moment. He wanted to make himself a pot of tea, and while Lily slept through anything once she was off, Sarah was a light sleeper. He stood undecided for a few moments and then took off his cap and coat and slung them over one of the hardbacked chairs. Pulling off his boots he placed them close to the range and then slipped out of his Sunday suit and folded that neatly along with his shirt and tie.

What the dickens was going on? Geraldine must have lugged the cot through to the kitchen, but why? Admittedly it was always warmer than the bedroom but he thought they had decided it was no good trying to make Sarah sleep in the evenings when they were still up.

The cold was getting into his bones so, clad in his vest and long johns, he closed the kitchen door gently behind him, and went through to the front room. As soon as he opened the door he saw Geraldine had the fire blazing high enough to set the chimney on fire. As his gaze swung to the bed he froze with his hand on the doorknob and the door slightly ajar.

'You've been long enough.' Geraldine's voice was low and throaty. She smiled slowly at the expression on his face. 'But you're back now.'

She was lying stark naked on top of the bedclothes, her hair spread out on the pillow in rippling waves. Her smooth arms were folded behind her head and her breasts gleamed like alabaster in the flickering light from the blazing fire. She looked for all the world like a beautiful marble statue, or perhaps a porcelain statue would be a better description because her white flesh seemed almost transparent.

Stanley stared at her and the reason for Sarah's banishment to the kitchen became clear. She had planned to seduce him. Her unshakeable belief in her power over him, even now after all that had happened between them, was truly astounding.

'Come to bed, Stanley.' She sat up, flicking her hair over her shoulders as her breasts swung provocatively. 'You must be frozen standing there and I can make you warm. We can make each other warm.'

The O'Flannagans had stopped arguing. In the next moment the bed springs above them began to twang and creak.

Stanley pushed the door to and as it clicked his mind was working again, coldly and without passion. He didn't fool himself it was him Geraldine wanted; any man would have sufficed. She had been denied sex for some time and the result was that she was like a bitch on heat. He had once thought she loved him but for a long time now he'd known she had never felt for him what he had felt for her. The words she had screamed at him the day he had sent Julian packing were perhaps the truest she had spoken and they had been degrading and raw. He had felt as though she had stripped him of his manhood that day, in every way.

She had used him as the farmers used a stud bull and with as little feeling, and had it not been for Sarah she had made it clear that she wouldn't have dreamed of sinking so low as to marry a man like him.

It had hurt at first. Hurt? It had nearly sent him mad. But strangely, and for no reason that he could understand, the moment he had gazed into Lily's tiny, perfect face he had felt a release. Certainly of the hatred that had been eating him alive and turning him into someone he didn't want to be. And with that release had come the knowledge that Geraldine couldn't hurt him any more. He was immune. Flatly, he said, 'Cover yourself.'

'Please, darling.' She knelt, holding out her arms like a supplicant at church as she pouted a little. 'I want to make it up to you. I was wrong, I know that, and weak, but he pursued me. He wouldn't leave me alone. It was only the one time, Stanley, I swear it, and I've learned my lesson. I want you, I've always wanted only you.'

'Don't.' He didn't want her to debase herself further. He just wanted to be left alone. 'Don't say any more because you'll regret it. It's over, Geraldine. Accept it.'

'No. How can I? I love you.'

He walked across the room to the rickety wardrobe and opened the door, taking one of her lawn night-dresses from the shelves at the side of the hanging space and throwing it towards her. 'Put it on and let's go to sleep.'

'Please, Stanley, you have to believe me.' She slid off the bed, leaving the nightdress where it had fallen. She was remembering how he could make her feel, the things he had done to her and in that moment she believed she meant it when she said, 'I love you.'

'But I don't love you, Geraldine.'

'You do, I know you do. You're angry and I can understand that, but we can go back to how we were if you let me show you how sorry I am.' She had reached him and as she twined her arms round his neck, pressing herself against him, she murmured, 'Anything you want I'll do. Anything, Stanley.'

When he reached up and unwound her hands, holding her by her wrists as he moved her away from him, she didn't understand what he was doing for a moment. Dispassionately, he said, 'Stop this.'

'I can't. I love you.'

She flung herself at him again and as he pushed her away so sharply she almost fell, he growled, 'Damn it, woman, stop this. I don't want you. I don't want you touching me, do you understand? Whatever was there, it's over. Finished.'

'You can't mean that. What about the rest of our lives? I need—' She stopped, licking her lips before she whispered, 'I need you.'

He stared at her, and his voice was guttural and his northern accent strong when he said, 'You don't need me, not me as an individual. What you need is mating now and again. But I'm not an animal, Geraldine. I need more than that' – he indicated her body with a wave of his hand – 'when I take a woman to bed. I'd as soon use the services of one of the whores down by the docks as sleep with you. That's the truth of it.'

Slowly the blood drained from her face. She swore,

an ugly profanity which shocked Stanley. He had heard such language in the yard but for a woman who had been brought up as Geraldine had been to know such words wasn't right. Then he realised he'd pushed her beyond breaking point when she flew at him, scratching and kicking and screaming. He held her off as best he could but it took all his might. She was like a woman demented and possessed of a strength that almost matched his.

It wasn't till she was finally spent and had dropped down to the floor in a shuddering heap that he let go of her. He walked over to the bed and picked up the nightdress. Dropping it at her feet he gathered up his working clothes and one of the blankets off the bed and left the room without another word.

Geraldine lay where she was for some minutes. Stanley's rejection had given her the biggest shock of her life. For a while she was incapable of moving and then she sat up, reaching for the nightdress. She pulled it over her head and slowly stood to her feet.

Once she was in bed she lay quite still, her eyes wide open. She hated him. For him to dare to sit in judgement on her, the mealy-mouthed upstart. What was he, after all? A common shipyard worker. Her father could buy and sell his whole family a thousand times over. She had been mad to take up with him in the first place but he ought to be down on his hands and knees thanking God she had looked the side he was on.

If only she hadn't given him the satisfaction of humiliating her like that. But she had. It was too late now.

She clenched her fists, the urge to hurt him rising up again. He was nothing, scum. Him and that mother of his.

She would make him pay for this night. She would devote the rest of her life to it. To getting her own back on him; the big fellow, the devoted husband and father.

Her eyes narrowed. Stanley thought a lot of Sarah, Lily too. She didn't understand that, not with him knowing what he knew. Nevertheless, it was clear his feelings for the baby were genuine. For herself, if she could walk out of here tomorrow and leave the lot of them, she would. But she had nowhere to go. There were more ways of killing a cat than skinning it, though; she'd seen Stanley's face today when he had been holding Lily at the font, and later when they were home and Sarah had clambered on his knee. He loved both little girls as his . . .

For once Geraldine was comfortable, the coal she had heaped upon the fire had made the room as warm as toast. The urgings of her body temporarily sated by the emotion and energy she had expended in the last half-hour, she snuggled further under the covers as her mind continued to consider Stanley's devotion to his children. He thought he could spurn her and get away with it, did he? Cast her aside and still continue to play the happy family man with Sarah and Lily? Well, she'd see about that. She was the one who was home with them all day, she had their ear. Who was to know what she whispered to them and fed into their minds? She would be subtle; she didn't want Sarah repeating anything to Stanley or his mother, but a steady drip, drip was powerful in its own way, especially with children. Oh yes, she'd get her own back on Stanley and it would be a revenge that would twist the knife every year the girls grew a little older.

Shortly after dawn when the lamplighter passed down the street with his long pole with a hook at the end of it and extinguished the lamp outside the house Geraldine had not slept. But she was no longer in turmoil. She knew now how she was going to make Stanley's life miserable, she thought, as she climbed out of bed and began to dress for the day. And it would be all the more sweeter because he wouldn't be able to prove a thing.

PART TWO

May 1907 – Sarah's Wedding

Chapter 4

When the murmur of angry voices downstairs woke Lily some time after midnight she lay quite still, willing the thudding of her heart under control. The third time this week, it was a bad spell.

'Mops? Are you awake?'

Her sister's voice came low and clear from the other side of the room and Lily breathed a silent sigh. She had been rather hoping Sarah would sleep on but she might have known. It was strange how they were tuned in to their parents' arguing; they always had been, right from when they'd been little bairns.

'You *are* awake. I can always tell.'

The whisper was an affronted hiss and Lily knew she'd have to answer. 'What's the matter?'

'You know what the matter is. They're going at one another again, listen to them. They make me sick, they really do. You'd have thought they could lay off the fighting for just one night, wouldn't you? It isn't every day one of their daughters gets married.' Sarah flung back the covers and padded across the room to perch on the end of Lily's bed. The curtains at the sash window were open and a full moon cast enough light for the sisters to see each other's outlines clearly enough. Sarah had always refused to sleep with the curtains closed. 'I'd be as pleased as Punch to be getting out of here if you were coming with me.'

Lily sighed again. She'd been waiting for Sarah to start. Her lips moved hard one over the other before she said, 'I'll be fine, lass.'

'You won't be fine and you don't have to put up with their carry-on.'

'Leave it, Sarah.'

'How can I leave it when you won't see sense? Ralph was all for you having the spare room when I put it to him, I told you that. You'd be welcome, more than welcome. And, frankly, a lodger would help with the rent.'

Sarah's face was in shadow but from the set of her sister's body Lily knew she had the bit between her teeth. It was the knowledge that Sarah was genuinely concerned for her that made her voice soft when she said, 'I've told you before there's no way I'd come and live with you and Ralph. It's a daft idea, lass, with you being newly-weds. I'd be in the way and even if I wasn't I'd feel I was. And you're not going to have that long on your own as it is.'

Sarah was silent for a moment. 'We're not bothered about being on our own where you're concerned, and with a baby on the way, money'll be tight.'

Lily doubted that. Ralph Turner worked at the docks but she knew from the odd thing Sarah had let slip in the past months that this was not his only income.

Sarah didn't seem to have any problem with Ralph handling the goods which regularly 'fell off the back of a lorry', and certainly Ralph had been generous enough in the nine months he and Sarah had been courting – buying her this and that and taking her places. Not that this or anything else could endear him to their mother, who considered the Turners far beneath them. When she had learned that Sarah was expecting Ralph's child and there was a necessity for an immediate marriage, the roof had nearly gone off the house. There had been bitter words exchanged that day and even now, some weeks later, mother and daughter were barely speaking.

In the quiet that had fallen the rise and fall of their parents' voices could be heard, the words indistinct but the acrimony undiminished by the journey through bricks and plaster.

'Hark at them.' Sarah's voice throbbed with resentment. 'I know you feel sorry for Mam and I did once, but I've seen another side to her the last few weeks. If Da's had to put up with some of what she's dished out to me all their married life, no wonder he can't stand the sight of her. I don't blame him.'

'She's upset, that's all.'

'She's not upset, she's spitting mad. And her main worry is the neighbours will find out I'm expecting.'

Lily said nothing to this. She knew Sarah was right.

'How are you going to stand it here without me, lass? We've always said it's each other that makes it bearable.'

'I know, and that was true when we were still bairns, but it is different now, Sarah. You know it is.

47

From when we both started work we could make sure we weren't in so much, and since you took up with Ralph I'm rarely back till just before bedtime. Molly and Bridget like me to share an evening meal with them once they've seen to Mr and Mrs Gray; I suppose it makes a change from just the two of them.'

'I've never understood why you didn't get a nursery-maid's post where you lived in. It would have been easier, wouldn't it?'

When Lily didn't immediately reply, Sarah nudged her foot. 'Mops?'

'I suppose I didn't want to leave you here by yourself.'

'There, you see? That's how I feel now.'

'Your situation's different. You're not going for a job, you're getting married, for goodness' sake; and with a baby on the way you had no choice about whether to go or stay.'

This time the silence stretched for longer. Sarah's voice was very low when she said, 'I – I feel awful.'

'Well, don't.'

'No, you don't understand. You know I told you me and Ralph had only done it the once when I'd had some homemade wine at his cousin's wedding? Well, that – that wasn't true. The truth of it is I knew he'd marry me if I fell for a bairn and . . . it was my ticket out of here. I – I wanted my own home, and I knew Ralph could afford to set us up, not like some of the lads round here.'

Lily sat up in bed. She was shocked to the core. Having a bairn when you weren't wed was the worst thing that could happen to a lass, and Sarah had done it on purpose? 'What if he hadn't married you?'

'I knew he would.'

'But what if he hadn't?'

'Look, I understand Ralph. In his own way he's as big an upstart as Mam, though he'd never admit it. Going out with me was a feather in his cap; that's how he looked at it. Us living here and Da being a manager at the shipyard . . .'

As Sarah's voice trailed away Lily screwed up her face in the shadows. Sarah had called their mother and Ralph upstarts, but what was she if she had used this thinking to her own ends? There had been a note in her sister's voice, something verging on gratification when she had spoken of how her soon-to-be husband felt. Flatly, Lily said, 'We live in a terrace same as the Turners.'

'You can't compare our house with theirs, Mops.'

No, she supposed she couldn't, but it didn't matter, did it? The Turners lived in the dense-packed streets sandwiched between the railway and the coastal industrial belt of docks, paper mills and gasworks in Hendon, known locally as Little Egypt. This was because street names such as Tel-el-Kebir Road and Cairo Street were popular when the British had occupied Egypt over two decades before.

West of the railway was a different story. Here the odd farm and grand manor house could still be found, intermingled with rows of new detached and semi-detached red-brick residences and large terraces. Some were set in enclosed parks and boasted indoor water closets with staff to see to the family's needs. Her parents hadn't been able to rise to those heights but their house off Mowbray Road in St Bede's Terrace was nicely situated in a tree-lined avenue which was quiet and pleasant.

She could remember clearly the day they'd moved in. She had been twelve years old and terribly excited. She and Sarah had explored the large terraced house, amazed at the spaciousness of the rooms and not a little overawed. The house hadn't thrilled her half so much as the fact that they had their own front garden, though, along with a small lawn at the back of the house. Beyond the lawn a privet hedge discreetly masked the privy and a large washhouse. There was a young cherry tree in the front garden and others in the street beyond. Birds gathered in their branches every morning to begin the dawn chorus. For a long time after they'd moved in she had awoken early every morning just to listen to 'her' birds. Her delight in her new surroundings had gone some way to make up for the fact that they no longer lived close to her Grandma and Granda Brown. She had found that hard at first.

Her mother's side of the family was never mentioned. She knew her mother was the daughter of the Prestons who had owned a prosperous engineering works in the town before they had sold up and moved down south somewhere. She understood there had been a falling-out before Sarah was born and her mother had never spoken to her family since. In view of this Lily found it even more contemptible that her father had treated her mother so shabbily when she had no kith and kin to talk to.

Gazing at the figure at the end of the bed, Lily said, 'Does Ralph know? That the baby wasn't an accident?'

Sarah snorted. She had a repertoire of such sounds which she'd used often in the last few weeks, mainly to irritate her mother. 'Course not. Ralph's like all men, he'll believe anything if you handle him right.'

Lily had thought she knew everything about her sister but this new side to Sarah was disconcerting. They had shared a bedroom all their lives and she would have sworn on oath they had no secrets from each other. Her voice low, she said, 'What if he finds out?'

'How can he? There's only you and me who know.' Sarah paused as they heard the staircase creak which meant their parents were coming upstairs. They slept in separate rooms and had done so since they had moved to St Bede's Terrace which, unlike their former homes, had three double bedrooms. She and Sarah had never minded that this meant they had to share a room; they would have chosen not to be separated anyway.

Sarah remained silent till they were sure their parents were in their respective rooms, then said softly, 'I really am sorry about leaving you in the lurch, but this place was stifling me. Do you know what I mean?' Without waiting for Lily to reply, she went on, 'I know Mam thinks our place is the pits but anywhere away from here is all right by me.'

Sarah was renting a two-up, two-down terrace a few doors away from Ralph's family. It had become vacant shortly before and the two sisters had spent hours scrubbing the house from top to bottom. It had been filthy, evidence of mice in the kitchen and bugs crawling under the damp wallpaper. They had stripped the walls bare, squealing when insects had dropped out, sometimes into their hair, then applied the special liquid Sarah had purchased from the hardware shop in town. This had smelt strongly of ammonia and other chemicals and had made their eyes water, but as the walls had begun to dry it seemed the house was disinfested.

'Sarah, you're getting married in the morning so go to sleep.' Lily bent forward and hugged her sister as she spoke. 'You want to look the radiant bride, don't you?'

'Do you think I show in the dress?'

Already a slight swell was evident in Sarah's stomach when she was undressed, but due to her sister's heavy build Lily could answer in all honesty, 'Not in the slightest. You look beautiful. Those extra gathers Mam put in under your bust hide everything.' Their mother had made Sarah's wedding dress and due to the fact that the Turner family consisted of nine children, two of whom were married and had children of their own, it had been decided it was fairer to have no brides-maids at all, especially with the haste in which the nuptials had been arranged. Geraldine had insisted the wedding take place at Christ Church which she and the girls attended every Sunday. The Turners had fallen in with this, even though the family were Methodists.

Once Sarah was back in bed she was asleep in minutes but Lily continued to lie wide awake, her mind chewing over all that had been said. She rubbed idly at her hands which had itched ever since the debugging operation. She hadn't minded the hard work, the mice and bugs, or the smell which had seemed to work its way into her skin, but every time Ralph had joined them she had felt awkward and on edge. It wasn't that he was unfriendly: just the opposite. She bit down on her lower lip. Aye, just the opposite. She could have coped with unfriendliness just fine, but the way he looked at her sometimes and the 'accidental' touching her whenever he could made her feel sick. If Sarah hadn't been in the family way she would have risked an upset and told her sister about her misgivings. But it was too late for that.

Lily turned over onto her side. She felt all at odds. The truth of it was Ralph Turner made her flesh creep the more she'd seen of him. Although Sarah had been going out with him for over nine months it had been on the quiet. Lily had known about the relationship but hadn't met Ralph till the night he had arrived at the house with his parents to discuss him and Sarah getting wed. She had expected he might be a bit sheepish, in view of the circumstances, but he hadn't appeared to be. That had been an awful night. Her father had been grim and upset and her mother had been beside herself with fury.

Lily turned onto her stomach. The pillow felt as though it had rocks in it tonight. She thumped it once or twice.

She couldn't help feeling sorry for their mam. She agreed with Sarah that appearances were everything to her, they would all be sacrificed on the altar of keeping face if it came to it, but she wouldn't have been that way if she was happy. And it was her father's fault that she wasn't. He had never treated her right. He had made her what she was, all she had was her house because she got no consideration or affection from him.

Lily did not question how she came by this knowledge, it would not have occurred to her to do so. It was something she knew without a doubt and believed utterly. All the problems in her parents' marriage were firmly at the feet of her father and that was that. He had always made, and continued to make, her mother miserable.

And now Sarah, who had pleased their mother by obtaining a good position in a high-class jeweller's shop in the town on leaving school, was having to get wed into a family their mother considered far beneath them. It had been a bitter blow. Worse, even, than when she herself had refused to attend the short-hand and typing course her mother had arranged for her and insisted she intended to work as a nursery-maid. Her mother had taken to her bed for a week but Lily had stuck to her guns, knowing it was what she wanted to do. It was the only time she'd ever opposed her.

Lily heard the old grandfather clock in the hall chime two o'clock. She was just mulling over whether to go downstairs and make herself a hot drink when she fell asleep. The next time she opened her eyes it was to a room full of sunlight and Sarah leaping about as though she was on springs.

Daylight revealed the spartan quality of their

surroundings. All three bedrooms were the same. The floorboards weren't relieved by even a rug or mat, and apart from their beds and a wardrobe, the only item of furniture was a small table holding a water jug and bowl.

Downstairs, where visitors to the house could observe what they did and didn't have, was a different matter. Here her mother had spared no expense to create what she considered a good impression.

The sitting room, or parlour, as her mother insisted it be called, was very well furnished. The sofa and two armchairs, large china cabinet, small upright piano and stool, and three occasional tables were in a dark wood, and stood on a deep blue carpet which stretched from wall to wall. A charming writing desk, with all kinds of little drawers and neat compartments and a treasured silver inkstand stood beneath the window. This was framed by heavy dark blue drapes and stiffly starched lace curtains. The dining room was furnished with an equal need to impress, along with her father's study. Lily knew her mother would rather cut out her tongue than admit most of the furniture downstairs had been bought second-hand.

It was the kitchen Lily invariably gravitated to, the room's homeliness a source of comfort in a house in which she had never really felt at ease. It reminded her strongly of her Grandma Brown's kitchen. From an early age when they had lived closer to their grandma's, she and Sarah had been in the habit of slipping in on their way home from school and spending some time with the woman who had always been more of a mother to them than Geraldine. This source of family warmth had come to an end with the move to St Bede's Terrace, although Lily made sure she saw her grandparents every weekend. The big coal-burning open fire range in the kitchen made it the heart of the house as far as Lily was concerned. It had an oven at one side and an oblong tank for heating water at the other, and was kept going night and day. The kitchen was the one place in the house that was always as warm as toast.

It was this which now made Lily say, 'It might be May but it's freezing in here this morning, let's get downstairs quick', as she swung her feet out of bed and reached for her dressing gown.

Sarah grinned. 'You need to get some flesh on your bones. A few plates of tripe and onion would stick to your ribs.' She knew her sister hated even the smell of tripe cooking.

'I eat plenty. You know I do.'

This was true, but whereas every bite Sarah had settled on her hips, Lily's sylph-like frame never gained a pound. And that wasn't the only dissimilarity between them by a long chalk.

Sarah's dark brown hair was straight and glossy; Lily's blond mass of curls had to be persuaded into the demure bun she wore for work. Sarah's blue eyes were round and she had the straight Brown family nose which sat well in her pretty plump face. Lily's clear green eyes were definitely almond-shaped and heavily lashed, her small nose adding to the overall impression of fragility. Sarah had once said she was sure Lily had been brought by the pixies. Lily hadn't minded that half so much as one of the wits she'd been forced to share a class with dubbing her the mop, because of her slender shape and abundant riot of curls. The nickname had stuck, but since she'd left school only Sarah called her Mops and Lily knew it was said with affection.

Halfway down the stairs, Sarah caught hold of Lily's arm. 'I have to ask one more time. Won't you reconsider coming to live with us? I'd love it, you know I would. I'm going to miss you so much.'

Lily smiled. 'I'll miss you, but I'm not coming.'

'It's Mam, isn't it? At bottom, you're staying for Mam. Can't you see she won't appreciate it? When all's said and done, she married him of her own free will.'

'It's not Mam. I've told you. A newly married couple shouldn't have to share their home with a third party.'

Sarah stared at her. 'Married.' She breathed out in a whoosh. 'I can't wait to be in charge of my own house and get away from the list of dos and don'ts here. I shall never make my bairns miserable, I've made my mind up about that. Whatever happens in the future with me and Ralph, my bairns won't suffer.'

Lily nodded but said nothing as they continued downstairs. She hoped it would work out between Ralph and her sister. She and Sarah had always known their parents lived one life in front of family and friends, and an entirely different one once they were alone: a bitter life full of angry arguments and long cold silences. And yet they must have loved each other once.

Lily glanced at her sister's face as they reached the hall. Sarah looked happy. She didn't seem to have any qualms about what she was doing. In fact, by her own admission, she couldn't wait to get married. But that was Sarah all over, she never thought too hard or long about anything.

For herself, Lily wasn't sure she ever wanted to take the step Sarah was taking today. There might be the odd couple like her Grandma and Granda Brown who were happy together, but there were lots who weren't. And the woman always had the worst of it. Like her mam.

'Come on, let's go and pretend we didn't know they were arguing half the night.' Sarah linked her arm in Lily's. 'I have to say, lass, I shan't be sorry it's the last time I have to do this. I wonder what they'd say if I asked them straight out why they hate each other?'

'Don't say that.'

'Why? You know it's true. And I tell you something else, like I said last night, I've seen another side to Mam the last few weeks and I feel sorry for Da. I do, Lily, and you needn't look at me like that. Some of what she's said to me is unforgivable.'

'She'll come round once you're wed and everything's settled.'

'I don't care if she does or not. You might shake your head but I mean it. Anyway, come on, I'm starving.'

When the two girls entered the kitchen their parents were sitting at the table. Stanley was hidden behind his newspaper.

'Good morning.' Sarah's voice was loud and she looked at her mother who inclined her head stiffly but said nothing.

Stanley lowered his paper. 'You've got a good day for it.'

Sarah brought her eyes from her mother. 'I know.' She grinned. 'The sun shines on the righteous.'

'And the unrighteous alike.'

They smiled at each other and Sarah plonked herself down, reaching for a slice of toast from the plate in the middle of the table.

Stanley glanced at Lily. She didn't meet his eyes. She never did. Slowly he raised his paper again. Geraldine had done a good job on the lass; she hated his guts. Sarah had been the same once but lately, since all the hoo-ha, he had sensed a change in her. He should be thankful for that. And he was, by, he was. Sally had always said the girls would come round one day.

Sally . . . The printed words in front of him faded away and in his mind's eye he saw Sally's bonny face. What would he do without her? Go stark staring mad. He'd been on the brink that day when they'd met up again, at the end of himself. It hadn't been long after they'd moved here, just a week or so. He had sat in this very kitchen and seen his life for what it was. Empty, pointless. He had faced the fact that Geraldine had alienated him from Sarah and Lily as completely as if he was dead. After years of sublimating every natural desire and need into working to provide them all with a decent home he had finally managed it, and what had it meant? Nowt. In the final analysis, nowt. He had nothing and no one. There wasn't one person alive who would mourn his passing should he be taken. Except his mam, bless her. But he had wanted, he had *needed*, more than a mother's love. He had looked down the years stretching in front of him and what he had seen had terrified him.

Sally always maintained it was God who had directed her to him the night he had walked to Wearmouth Bridge intending to throw himself off and finish it once and for all. He didn't know about that. He was no churchgoer but from the little he'd read of the Bible he wasn't of the opinion a holy God would countenance encouraging a man into committing adultery, however dead his marriage was. But if Sally liked to believe that, he didn't argue with her. What he did know was that she had saved his life that night. It had been the day the King had been crowned at Westminster Abbey and there had been all sorts of goings-on, street parties for the bairns and the like. It being a Saturday and a half-day for most industry, the shipyard had given their workers the morning off so families could make a day of it. Perhaps it had been that which had driven home to him how futile his life was; all the men with their wives and bairns, laughing, joking, joining in the fun and getting well oiled, some of them. He had watched it all but only as an observer, not a participator.

The August evening had been warm and muggy after the hot day and he had taken his time walking to the bridge once most of the jollifications were over. There had been no hurry, he knew what he was going to do now. He had stood looking down into the water, tight-packed with shipping, and had wondered how it had come to this. He couldn't blame it all on Geraldine; he'd made his mistakes too, the biggest one being breaking up with Sally Hammond all those years ago. He'd continued to think of Sally as he watched a three-masted sailing ship being towed in by a tugboat.

When he had glanced round him to make sure there was no one near enough to stop him when he climbed over the railings and she was standing not a yard away, he thought for a moment she was a figment of his imagination. Till she spoke. 'Hello, Stan,' she'd said quietly. 'You were miles away, I didn't want to interrupt.' He had forgotten what he'd said in reply, some inane comment, before falling silent, and then they had stood looking at each other. Her voice had been even quieter when she'd said gently, 'What's the matter?'

He'd known her husband had died five or six years before and that she was now comfortably off, having sold the business, but little else. He had opened his mouth intending to make some dismissive remark which would send her on her way, but to his horror he couldn't speak. Something was happening inside him, an overwhelming flood of feeling. He coughed and swallowed deeply, before bringing out in a cracked voice, 'Nothing.'

'You're ill.' Her quick movement was checked before her hand had touched him but now she was so close he could see the tiny dent in her small straight nose where she had worried at a chickenpox scab when they were bairns.

An elderly couple had walked past them and his gaze had followed the pair simply because he couldn't bear looking into the softness of her eyes a second more. The enormity of what he had thrown away had been with him for years but seeing her like this, face to face . . . He had to keep strong, he had to be a man. It would be the final humiliation for Sally of all people to witness how low he had fallen.

'Stan?' She had been gnawing on her lip when he had forced his gaze back to her. They hadn't spoken for a full twenty seconds or more, and then she'd said. 'Let's walk a bit, shall we? and he had guessed she'd got an inkling of what he'd been about to do.

He hadn't been able to speak but now the flood had risen up into his throat, his eyes, his nose and, turning blindly away, he had stumbled a few yards with his head down and his hand held out behind him, palm up.

'Here, here, it's all right.'

He hadn't been able to see her through his blurred, streaming eyes but he had felt her turn him into her, shielding him from any curious eyes. And she hadn't let go of him. He had mumbled his deprecation of himself in an agony of indignity and shame, hardly knowing what he was saying. How long they had stood there he didn't know, but when finally he had been able to gain control he had wanted the ground to open up and swallow him. The ignominy of her seeing him like this was more than he could bear. He had wronged her all those years ago and, deep down, however kind she was, she must feel a certain satisfaction in knowing how disastrous his marriage had been.

He had stood there, feeling as though he was shrinking into a tiny speck, nothing, and wiped his face with the sleeve of his jacket. When he had been able to look at her, her face had been awash with tears and what he had seen in her eyes had humbled him further, if that was possible. 'Don't you know?' she'd whispered brokenly. 'There's only ever really been you. Tim was a lovely man and we were happy in our own way, but compared to what I felt for you . . .'

He had stared at her, his heart pounding like a sledgehammer. He had wanted to ask a hundred questions but he hadn't dared. It might break the spell and she might walk away from him. 'I love you, Sally.' After what he had done she had the right to hear it. 'I never stopped loving you. The other' – he waved his hand, unable to put what he was really feeling into words – 'it was a kind of insanity, like when you have a fever and everything is distorted. I have no right to ask you to forgive me, I can't forgive meself—'

She had stopped the painful flow by putting her finger on his lips. And when he had looked into her face and seen the light that illuminated it from within, he had pulled her fiercely into him.

And that had been the start of it.

Chapter 5

'It couldn't have gone off better, don't you think? An' didn't your Sarah look bonny?'

Geraldine stared into the flat broad face of the small woman who had addressed her. Her eyes touched on the green felt hat which sat on the newly permed grey curls like a pancake before dropping to the garishly patterned turquoise dress. She paused a moment before saying, 'Yes, Mrs Turner. Sarah looked quite fetching.'

'Oh call me Nora, lass, everyone does, an' we're family now, aren't we?'

'Yes, I suppose we are.'

'I said to my Harold, you can't go far wrong with a summer weddin', six to one it'll be fine for 'em an' I weren't wrong.' Ralph's mother's voice was loud but it dropped a decibel or two as she added, 'Look at 'em, they make a right picture, don't they? Jack for Jill, all right.'

Geraldine's gaze followed that of the smaller woman's. Her face was blank but something of what she felt about Nora's son came across in her voice when she said, 'I'm sure Sarah will do her best to make the marriage successful.'

Uppity mare. Nora Turner stared at the well-dressed, elegant woman in front of her and the longing to slap her across the face was so strong she had to clench her teeth against it. That was all this wedding needed, a punch-up. That would crown it all. Her Harold would never forgive her if she let herself down like that, bless him. He didn't like it when the lads went in for a bit of rough and tumble, let alone his wife. Keep talking, Nora, she told herself. Don't let starchy-drawers get to you. 'It's always harder with the first one, you know.'

'I beg your pardon?'

'The first bairn to leave home, it always hits you hard. When our Cissy got married I was all of a dither for weeks before; drove Harold barmy, I did. But here she is, five years later, settled in a nice little home with a husband who thinks the world of her. You can't ask for more than that, can you? Two bairns they've got, an' another on the way.'

'Really.'

'An' then our Florrie wed her Neville two years ago. Little lad she's got. Bonniest baby you've ever seen. An' both the twins, David an' Francis, are courtin' strong an' them only just eighteen. I say to 'em, you want to be more like John. Plays it canny, does our John. He might be only twenty but he's got an old head on his shoulders. Wants to get on in life. Goes to night school, John does.'

Nora paused, waiting for a response to this wonder.

When none was forthcoming she sniffed before continuing, 'Mind, it'll be a while before the nest is empty. Our Robert leaves school in the summer but Hannah's got a couple more years and little Larry's not yet started. I can't say I'm sorry for it in spite of the noise an' mess my lot make. I was one of fifteen meself, an' we all live within a stone's throw of each other. You got any brothers or sisters, lass?'

'A sister.'

'Lives near, does she?'

'No.'

Hen's teeth, she'd cause a saint to swear, this one. It boded well for Ralph that Sarah took after her da rather than her mam. Stan seemed a good 'un from what she'd seen of him. He might be a gaffer at one of the shipyards and live in St Bede's Terrace, but he didn't come the old soldier like his lady wife. How he'd come to be landed with her she'd never know. And the other little lass seemed all right, all eyes and skinny with it, but nothing a husband and a bellyful of bairns wouldn't sort out. She'd been as thin as a pikestaff herself once, till she'd started having the bairns one after the other.

Nora sipped at her beer. They were holding the little get-together for family and a few friends at Harold's working men's club. Geraldine had flatly refused to host a reception at her house. It had been Nora and her daughters who had prepared the sandwiches and ham and egg pies and the rest of the food, and Nora was reminded of this as she glanced at Geraldine's soft white hands. Admittedly the Browns had stumped up for all the drink which would have come to a pretty penny, she couldn't fault them on that, but Sarah's mother had been determined not to help practically. She dare bet she never got her hands dirty if she could help it.

'. . . is it, Mrs Turner?'

Nora caught her name but she had been far away. 'What's that, lass?'

'I said' – Geraldine's tone verged on insultingly patient – 'this marriage is hardly off to the best start with only the kitchen and bedroom being furnished at home.'

'Don't you worry your head about that,' Nora said flatly, looking Geraldine straight in the eye. 'My lad will soon sort the house out. It won't do 'em any harm to build up gradual like, anyway, like me an' Harold did. I understand your man wasn't born with no silver spoon in his mouth if it comes to it.'

Geraldine's creamy skin took on colour. 'That is not quite the point, Mrs Turner.'

'Perhaps not. Aye, perhaps not. The point as I see it is that they're starting out with a bun already in the oven. That being the case, the pair of 'em will have to make the best of what comes along.'

'Please keep your voice down.'

Dear gussy, did she really think anyone was fooled by this show today? A few words by the vicar and a white dress couldn't put the pig back in the poke. 'Me voice is me own to do with what I want, thank you very much.'

'Sarah was a good girl before your son took advantage of her.'

Nora felt she would swipe her one and to hell with

67

it if she had any more of this. Drawing herself up to her full five feet four inches, she said, 'It takes two to make a babbie in my book, and while we're on the subject I haven't heard Sarah complainin' she was taken down against her will.'

Turning her back on Geraldine's outraged countenance, Nora stalked across the room, her plump cheeks fiery red. It was just as well she wouldn't be seeing anything much of that one after today because she wouldn't be able to keep her hands to herself. Just because she was old Preston's daughter, she thought herself the cat's whiskers, but she was nowt in her book. And if what she'd heard was true, Sarah was born a mite quick after her parents had got wed. Certainly something had happened to upset the apple cart because by all accounts Preston had had nothing to do with the pair of them after the marriage. Not that she was throwing the first stone, things happened when a man and maid were young and the sap was running high, everyone knew that, and many a couple had to get to the church on the run. Look at Sarah and Ralph. But for her to come the hoity-toity as though butter wouldn't melt in her mouth, that was something else.

'What's the matter with you? You look like you've lost a bob and found a farthing piece.' Harold had joined his wife, his walrus moustache showing evidence of the beer he had been imbibing. He was a small man, thickset and stocky, and his face was a dull shiny red. This was not as a result of his fondness for beer but because he had worked in the blast furnaces at the shipyard most of his working life.

'It's her, Sarah's mam. Havin' a go at our Ralph, she was.'

'Aye, well, likely she's feeling middlin' the day, lass. An' it's natural for her to want to blame our lad rather than Sarah. You'd probably be the same in her place.'

'I would not.' Nora reared up indignantly. 'I never would, Harold Turner.'

'Look, lass' – he bent nearer to her, so close his moustache tickled her cheek –'I don't like the woman any more than you do, if you want the truth of it, but keep your chin up, all right? Likely we won't see much of her, an' with Ralph an' Sarah being a few doors away from us, you'll be the one the lass comes to when she needs somethin' or a bit of advice. If you let Geraldine rile you now an' you lose your rag, it could put an obstacle between you an' Sarah an' you don't want that.'

No, she didn't. She liked her daughter-in-law. She nodded to her husband and he smiled at her, reaching for her empty glass. 'You stay put an' I'll get you another, lass.'

As he trundled off Nora watched him, smiling faintly now. She had met Harold a week or two after her family had moved south from Glasgow when she was a lass of fifteen, and she still reckoned it had been the best day of her life. He might not amount to much in the world's eyes, lacking any ambition or drive, but she knew she and the bairns came first with him and that was enough for her.

'What were you and Da talking so quietly about?'

Nora's hand went to her breast as she said, 'Oh our John, you made me jump.' John was Nora's fourth child and three years younger than Ralph. She loved him as she loved each one of her children, but John was the only one she didn't understand. The others were cut from the same mould as their parents, but she had always known John was different. From a little bairn John had wanted to know the whys and wherefores of everything he touched and saw. His teachers had all said he was very bright and had wanted him to try for a scholarship at some fancy school or other when he'd turned thirteen, but they'd needed an extra wage so John had had the choice of following his father into the shipyard or working at the docks with Ralph. A job had been going at the docks so that had clinched it. And then two years ago he'd announced he was going to night school in the town. Ralph had jibed him about that till they'd come to blows. It had transpired John had set his sights on becoming an accountant.

Nora smiled at her son, reaching out her hands and fondly straightening his tie. She'd felt funny about the night school but as the time had gone on and he'd remained the same old John she'd felt happier. 'It's her, Sarah's mam,' she said in answer to his question. 'Turning up her nose at us all.'

'Aye, I've noticed.' John glanced across the room, his brown eyes narrowed. He was a good head taller than his older brother but apart from that the two young men were very similar with black hair and fresh-looking skin.

'Ralph'll have trouble in that direction, you mark my words. Every time she opens her mouth poison comes out. Still, at least Sarah don't take after her mam.'

John said nothing to this. He did not envy Ralph his mother-in-law, but only time would tell if Sarah was as pleasant and easygoing as she seemed. One thing was for sure, many a lad would hesitate about taking up with one of the Brown sisters after clapping eyes on the mother. But then Ralph probably hadn't thought that far. His brother had always let what was between his legs rule his head and, furthermore, it appeared Sarah had been obliging in that regard.

Harold returned with his wife's drink. 'I've just been talking to Stan's mam and da. His da's in a poor old way. Can't work no more, apparently.' Harold worked in Austin's shipyard on the eastern side of town but all shipyard workers felt a kinship whatever yard they worked in. 'Mind, he was a welder so what can you expect? Times I've looked into a tank where three or four welders were working and you couldn't see the lights of the welding arcs for fumes. No wonder he can't get his breath.'

John looked across to where Stanley Brown's parents were sitting with the other sister, Lily. He had known she was there, he'd been conscious of her whereabouts all day, which had faintly annoyed him. He couldn't quite make her out, that was the thing. Physically she was almost shapeless in form, showing little evidence of either hips or bust and yet he understood she was only two and a half years younger than Sarah. And her face was unusual; bonny but definitely unusual. And her hair, he didn't think he'd ever seen hair like it. But it was the air she had about her which had irritated him; it was cool, withdrawn. She was definitely a chip off her mother's block.

71

Nora had followed his gaze. 'That poor little lass has been sittin' with her grandma an' granda all afternoon. Why don't you go across an' make yourself known?'

Poor little lass? Only his mother could refer to that uppish piece as a poor little lass. He drained his glass before he said, 'She's sitting there because she wants to, Mam. No one's forcing her.'

'Aye, but likely she feels she's got to keep the old couple company.'

'She doesn't want to join in, it's as plain as the nose on your face.'

'Not to me.' Nora's eyes were no longer soft on him. 'She's nowt but a bit of a lass an' she don't know folk, not our side, anyway, an' there's half a dozen of us to any one of them. Geraldine Brown already thinks we don't know how to conduct ourselves an' it's not helpin' with your head stuck in that glass.'

'There're plenty of other people who can talk to her. Why pick on me?'

If Nora had spoken truthfully here she would have said, 'Because you're bright and know about things the rest of us don't,' but this would have meant admitting she considered the Browns above them. Instead, she said, 'You were Ralph's best man an' if things had been different an' not so rushed, likely Sarah's sister would have been chief bridesmaid. It would have been your job to look after her then.'

For crying out loud! John recognised his mother had got the bit between her teeth. She didn't do it very often but when she did they all knew about it. He glanced at her face under the green felt hat.

The hat clashed horribly with her new dress, a dress she could ill afford, but she'd been as pleased as Punch when she'd got it cheap because it had a tear in the skirt. She'd sat all one evening mending it till it didn't show. He reached out a hand and patted her arm, his voice reflecting the tenderness he felt for this indomitable little woman. 'All right, all right, keep your wig on. I'll go and make small talk for a minute or two if that's what you want.'

'I should think so.' Nora hitched up her ample bust with her forearms, only partly mollified. 'You've never been shy an' the lassies have been after you since you were in short pants, but it's different for a lass like that one.'

He didn't see how, besides which he'd bet his last farthing Lily Brown didn't have a shy bone in her body. 'Aye, all right, I've said I'd go, haven't I? I take it I'm allowed to get myself another drink first?'

'Please yourself.'

'That'll be the day with you around.' He softened the words with a smile, drawing her plump little body into his side and hugging her for a moment.

Across the other side of the room with her grandparents on either side of her, Lily felt miserable. She was worried about Sarah, more worried than she had been earlier that morning because, now it was too late to say anything, she regretted not voicing her doubts about Ralph to her sister. But how could she have done? she asked herself for the umpteenth time. Sarah was having a bairn, she *had* to marry him. The shame of having a baby outside wedlock was unthinkable.

No, she couldn't have said anything but she felt awful nonetheless.

A gust of ribald laughter brought her head turning to where Ralph and a crowd of lads were standing. They were all three sheets to the wind, and since they had left the church and entered the club she hadn't seen Sarah and her new husband exchange more than a word or two. Ralph had been steadily knocking back the beer with his brothers and cousins, and Sarah had been going round the assembled company chatting to folk. It hadn't seemed to bother her sister, admittedly, but it wasn't right. It smacked of the sort of relationship so many people seemed to have round these parts, the man spending his free time at the local pub and his Saturday afternoons at the football match while his long-suffering wife stayed at home minding the bairns or went round to visit her mother.

Lily's eyes moved to Geraldine. Her mother was talking to the vicar's wife. Her granda had remarked earlier her mother was wearing a face like a smacked backside and he was right. She wasn't making any effort to pretend she approved of the marriage.

She looked to where her father was talking with several of Ralph's relations. As she did so, her father said something which provoked a gust of laughter. Her lip curled. Her father was acting a part as always. When they'd first found out Sarah was having a baby he had wanted to knock Ralph into next weekend.

Ava had followed her granddaughter's gaze. She was well aware of the gulf between Stanley and his daughters and it disturbed her greatly. She was in absolutely no doubt who was behind it, but on the rare occasions she'd felt moved to broach the subject with the girls they had closed up like clams. Quietly, she murmured, 'Would you rather your da spoilt Sarah's wedding day by being unsociable and causing waves?'

Lily's head shot round. She stared at her beloved grandma but said nothing. There was nothing she could say. She was being unreasonable, she admitted silently, but where her father was concerned she couldn't help it.

'He's doing what he's done since you an' Sarah were born, what he believes is the best for you both. I pray God you'll see that one day, lass.'

'I'm sorry, Gran.' She didn't want to upset her grandma, she had enough on her plate with Granda being poorly. A surge of feeling demanding she take the sad look from her grandmother's face swept through her, and quickly, with the lightest of kisses, her lips touched the faded, lined cheek. 'I love you.'

It wasn't often such things were said and Ava blinked before she smiled. 'I love you too, me bairn.'

'I'll get you and Granda another drink.' She gathered up the empty glasses and stood up just as John Turner reached her.

'Hello.' He nodded at Lily and then to the older couple. 'I'm John, Ralph's brother. I don't think we've been introduced properly.' He shook Albert's hand and then Ava's, exchanging a few words before he turned to Lily. 'Can I get those refilled?' He nodded at the glasses in her hands.

'No, it's all right.' He was considerably taller than his brother but the resemblance to Ralph was so strong it brought immediate antipathy. 'I need to stretch my legs.'

'I'll help you, then.'

'There's no need, really.'

'I'd like to.'

'I'm perfectly capable of getting the drinks myself.' Her voice had been too sharp and as she saw his face change, she added lamely. 'But thank you anyway.'

He turned from her without a word and she knew she had offended him. Staring after him, she could have kicked herself. What had got into her? She wasn't normally like this.

After fetching the drinks she told her grandparents she needed to get some fresh air. This was true. For the last hour or so she had felt stifled in the thick, stale atmosphere of the club. The cloying smell of cheap cigarettes and pipe smoke and beer, along with an underlying odour she couldn't put a name to but which was a composite of stale, unwashed bodies and old men's pee, was making her feel nauseous.

Once outside in the club's small yard it wasn't much better. The stink from the privy was overpowering and there was evidence of vomit in dried patches on the cobbles. For one of the rare times in her life she felt in tune with her mother about something: this was an awful wedding. Poor Sarah. Oh, she wished the day was over and she was back home. She'd have the bedroom all to herself now. This thought was not comforting, and she felt she was missing Sarah already.

Fighting back tears she made an effort to compose herself. Perhaps it would work out between Ralph and Sarah and at least Ralph's mother seemed nice. And the thing was done now, it was no use harking back to what she should have said or done. She gazed at the grey rooftops over the top of the yard's high brick wall. The endless rows of chimney pots beneath the blue sky were depressing and she lifted her gaze higher to where a bird – a lark, by the look of it – was soaring and swooping in the thermals.

She was still looking at it when a slurred voice behind her said, 'I thought I saw you come out here. Had a bit too much to drink, have you?'

Lily swung round. Ralph stood swaying within inches of her, a bedfuddled smile on his perspiring face. 'Of course I haven't; I just wanted a breath of fresh air, that's all.'

'"Of course I haven't."' The mimicry was soft but the teasing had an edge. 'Lily wouldn't drink too much, Lily's a good girl. Isn't that right?'

She stared at him, at his bloodshot eyes, his red complexion, the beer he had slopped down the front of his shirt. 'I'm going back in.'

'What's your hurry?' He was blocking her escape and he knew it. 'Can't you try and be civil for two minutes?'

'I want to go back in, Ralph. *Don't show him you're frightened, stand your ground.* 'Kindly let me pass.'

'Been avoiding me all day, haven't you? Oh I know, I know.' He tapped the side of his nose. 'And you haven't congratulated me yet on me wedding day.'

'Congratulations.'

'Not like that.' The waving movement of his hand slopped more beer down his shirt. He put the glass down on one of the beer barrels stacked to one side of the doorway. 'How about a kiss for your new brother?'

'You are not my brother.'

'Brother-in-law, then. Same thing.'

'Get out of my way,' she said stonily.

'Now why do you have to be like that, eh? You're not kind, you know, Lily. Not like Sarah. Now she was kind from the first time we went out together.'

He was so close she could smell the beer on his breath and his sweat. The small yard seemed to have shrunk further and it was pressing in on her. Would anyone hear if she screamed? But she couldn't scream. It would bring people to them and how would she explain this to Sarah? It was Sarah's wedding day. Keeping her voice low, she said, 'Sarah was kind to you because she loves you.'

He smiled. 'Give us a kiss an' you can go back in.'

He was looking at her in the way that made her feel sick. 'I'm not going to kiss you out here. I will when we're back inside with everyone.'

'Not good enough. I deserve more than a peck on the cheek.'

His voice was cold. It dawned on her Sarah's husband was not as drunk as she had supposed. He knew exactly what he was doing. Curiously she found the knowledge put iron in her backbone. Her next words wiped the satisfied smile off his face and caused him to stiffen. 'Let me make one thing clear once and for all. Sarah is my sister and I love her, and I'd no more do anything behind her back than fly to the moon. If you ever try this again I shall tell her immediately, and not just her. I'll broadcast it to your mam, your da and every member of your family and beyond.'

'You wouldn't dare.'

'No?' She glared at him. 'You don't know me very well if you think that.'

'You wouldn't want to upset Sarah.'

'Far better upsetting her if it came to it than letting her go on loving a man who isn't worthy to lick her boots.'

'You little—'

'Don't swear at me, Ralph. And I'm asking you one more time. Get out of my way.'

He remained planted in front of the doorway, looking at her with both hate and desire in his eyes, but he said nothing. After a full ten seconds, the longest of Lily's life, he stood aside and continued to watch her as she marched past him and back into the noise and laughter. It was only when she had disappeared from view that he began to swear, foul oaths that came out in a continuous string of profanity. Reaching for his glass he drained the last of his beer and wiping his mouth with the back of his hand, muttered, 'I'll see my day with you, you see if I don't. It might take time but you'll live to regret them fine words, m'lady.' And with one vicious movement he threw the glass against the wall of the yard.

On entering the club Lily stood in the passageway which led into the main room for a moment, her heart pounding and her hands clenched into fists at her side. He was disgusting and she hated him. Tears burnt at the back of her eyes but she blinked them away furiously. She was not going to cry over that despicable man, but oh, Sarah, Sarah, what have you done? To escape home you've tied yourself to him for life. This was her father's fault. If he'd treated her mother better and things had been different at home, Sarah would never have married Ralph Turner.

Worried Ralph might come up behind her she forced herself to enter the room and immediately a barrage of sound and smoke enveloped her. In view of her thoughts it was unfortunate that the first people she met were her father and John Turner who were standing by the door, drinks in hand, deep in conversation.

'You all right, lass?' Stanley's gaze narrowed on his daughter's over-bright eyes and the two spots of burning colour in her cheeks. 'What's up?'

'Nothing is "up" as you put it.'

Her voice had been a snap and as her father's eyebrows rose, John stared at her. It was clear what he was thinking. Stanley, aiming to pour oil on troubled waters, said quietly, 'Can I get you a drink?'

'Lily gets her own drinks. Isn't that right, Lily?'

John's voice was pleasant and his words could have been termed jocular, but she had seen the look in his eyes. Flushing still more, she said, 'Yes, that's right.'

'One of these suffragettes, are you?' John asked, his voice still deliberately amiable.

'What's wrong with the suffragette movement? Why shouldn't women press to have the vote?' She didn't actually belong to the movement but one of the members of the weekly reading and discussion group she belonged to at the local library did, and she had listened to Ellen Lindsay's views on the subject and agreed with them. 'It's our country too, isn't it?'

'I'll leave you to it.' Stanley had had enough. The whole day had been a nightmare and all he wanted to do was to leave as quickly as he could and get Geraldine home before he made some excuse to go out again. He needed to see Sally. Hell, how he needed to see her. He didn't know how much longer he could go on with this hole-in-the-wall affair.

'Well?' Lily didn't turn her head as her father left but kept her eyes on the man in front of her who looked so like his brother. 'Why shouldn't women have their say?'

John glanced after Stanley. When he looked at Lily again he didn't answer her question but said flatly, 'Do you always speak to your father like that?'

Totally taken aback, she stared at him. 'That – that's none of your business.'

'When you behave like that in front of me I think it is. I like your father.'

'Do you?' she said tightly. 'And you've known him . . . how long? Two hours, is it? Or three?'

'Meaning?'

'You work it out.' She wanted nothing so much as to go somewhere and have a good cry, but that luxury would be denied her for some time yet.

John found himself in the unusual position of feeling at a loss. This hadn't happened in a long time and he didn't like it, especially when he was being put in his place by a slip of a lass. He ran his fingers through his thick hair, reminding himself this was a wedding and things needed to be kept sweet, much as Nora had done earlier when she had been talking with Geraldine. 'I think I'm a good judge of human nature,' he said shortly. 'And your father is the sort of person who improves on acquaintance, unlike some.'

'Is that a dig at me?'

It hadn't been, but her tetchiness took the last of his patience. 'What is the matter with you?' He shook his head, signifying something between condemnation and pity which made Lily bristle still more. 'You're so damn sharp you'll cut yourself on your own tongue. This is a wedding, in case you've forgotten, and everyone's supposed to be all hail and well met. Your sister has married my brother. Accept it.'

'I wish I didn't have to.'

As she glared at him it struck John he'd never seen another pair of eyes as beautiful as hers. It wasn't just the pure clear green of them or that the fringe of thick, curling dark lashes were emphasised by her blond hair, it was the shape of them, too. And at present those same eyes were letting him know she thought he was something that had just crawled out from under a stone. 'You are like your mother, aren't you? You think Sarah's married beneath her and that Ralph's not good enough for her.'

That was exactly what she thought but not for the reasons he supposed. Not that she could go into that. She lifted her chin in an unconscious gesture of defiance but said nothing.

'Can't you bring yourself to put your prejudices aside and wish them well?'

'For the sake of the baby, you mean?' His eyes widened; she had shocked him by mentioning Sarah's condition, she thought, with some satisfaction. Her eyes holding his, she said quietly, 'The only reason two people should marry is because they love each other and I'm not sure your brother does love Sarah, if you want to know.'

'At the risk of sounding impertinent, what do you know about it anyway?'

She had really riled him but she didn't care. He was as arrogant and objectionable as his brother any day. 'Enough.'

'Oh no, Miss Brown, no clever cryptic monosyllables. You have just accused my brother of something and the least you can do is back it up.'

'That's where you're wrong.' John was standing with his back to the room but from her vantage point she could see her mother staring over at them with an annoyed expression on her face. Any minute now she was going to come across and break up what she clearly imagined was a tête-à-tête which would put the tin lid on things. 'I don't have to explain a thing to you.'

What did she know? John's mind was racing. Ralph was a fool, how many times had he told him he'd catch his toe with his messing around, especially since he'd been courting Sarah? He couldn't even keep his hands to himself on his stag night, he'd had to toy with that barmaid who was no better than she should be and her with a face like the back of a tram. Had Sarah's sister caught wind of that, or something else?

While he was still hesitating, Lily made to brush past him and it was only then he said, 'What gives you the right to look down your nose at anyone?'

Lily looked at him. The expression on her face convinced John she had something on his brother. They continued to stare at each other for a few moments more, and when she walked past him he made no effort to detain her this time.

Hell's bells. Should he say something to Ralph? Warn him? What if that one whispered what she knew in Sarah's ear? That'd be a good start to wedded bliss. He could brain their Ralph. He'd always been full of himself, swaggering about like a cockerel in a farmyard where the lassies were concerned. He knew for a fact that from when his brother had first got involved in knocking off the odd load from the docks he'd spent a good portion of the money in a certain whorehouse in the East End. No one could ever accuse Ralph of being too particular.

When the door a few yards in front of him opened and Ralph walked through, John saw his brother's eyes move swiftly round the smoky room before coming to rest on him. 'All right?' Ralph said airily.

'I want a word with you.' Moving quickly, John pushed the smaller man out into the passageway again, ignoring Ralph's, 'Hey, what you playin' at?' as he said, 'Shut up and listen. That barmaid from the Boilermakers' Arms, how far did it go with her?'

'What's it to you?' Ralph stared at his brother, belching a breath of stale beer. 'You mind your own business.'

That was twice in the space of five minutes he'd had that said to him and perhaps he should, at that. The last thing he wanted was to get caught up in any domestic rows. 'You didn't get back till gone three that night.' They shared a room with the twins and Robert and packed in like sardines as they were, Ralph had woken him up when he'd climbed over John's pallet bed to fall into one of the two three-foot single beds the room held. John preferred the hard pallet bed on the floor to top-and-tailing with one of his brothers. Their close proximity and the sounds and smells that emanated from their persons was bad enough as it was. 'And you left the rest of us at midnight.'

'So?' Ralph squared up to him belligerently. 'What are you, me keeper or summat? It's nowt to do with you what I do.'

Oh, to hell with it. Whatever Lily knew or thought she knew, they could work it out between themselves. Anyway, the lass might keep her mouth shut. 'Please yourself.'

'Aye, I will an' all.' And then with one of the quick changes of attitude that had always characterised their relationship, Ralph lightly punched him on the arm, saying, 'Come and have another jar and stop looking so miserable. You think too much, that's your trouble.'

'Good job one of us does.' It was the answer he always gave and had covered everything with his brother from his refusal to accompany him to the East End and 'have a bit of fun' to his insistence he wanted nothing to do with the thieving at the docks. Both these things, John knew, had offended Ralph, and his brother had made this clear by various forms of subtle torment for months after the event. And yet he knew Ralph loved him in his own way and he hadn't been surprised when Ralph had asked him to be his best man. With three years' difference between them there had been a time, when he had first started school, when Ralph had been his buffer against the inevitable bullying that occurred, a role Ralph had fulfilled to the letter. Ralph had often teased him unmercifully and pinched his Saturday penny, but if anyone else had so much as laid a finger on him his brother had been there with fists and feet. He was a funny mixture, was Ralph.

They walked back into the room together but after a while John made his way to where his mother was talking to Cissy and Florence at a table in a corner. Bending down, he said in her ear, 'This is going to go on for a while yet if I know Ralph and the others when they get started. I'm going to nip back and do a bit of work but I'll be back later, all right?'

'Aye, all right, lad.' Nora knew he had his 'homework' from his night classes, reams and reams of it which he usually did in the hallowed front room which up till the point he had needed a quiet place had only been used on high days and holidays. She was very proud of the fact that despite the hard times she had been able to keep her precious front room with its horsehair-stuffed suite and giant aspidistra intact. It had meant the lads being crammed into one bedroom and Cissy and Florrie sleeping in a desk bed in the kitchen and the youngest ones in with her and Harold, but it had been worth it. When the doctor or the minister called there had always been somewhere to receive them, even when there hadn't been a crust in the house and the bairns hadn't been able to go to school because they'd had no boots on their feet. But now John was doing his writing and reading in there, work which, God willing, would take him into the hitherto unreachable heights of a white-collar worker. It added a touch of reverence to her thoughts about the front room.

John straightened. As he did so his eyes were drawn to a splash of gold on the other side of the room. Lily was talking to Sarah but the conversation couldn't have been a deep one; Sarah was smiling and, as he watched, the two sisters embraced. So, it looked as though she was going to keep quiet. Ralph had got away with whatever it was he'd done once again.

Twilight hadn't yet begun to fall when he stepped out into the street. The club was situated in the warren of roads and alleys stretching south-east from Mowbray Park, and as he began to walk the faint smell of rotting garbage carried on the cool May evening.

He passed numerous children playing their games on the greasy pavements and in the gutters, and knew there would be still more in the back lanes. Here and there women stood gossiping on their doorsteps, shawls tucked into their long skirts and their arms resting on the mounds of their stomachs. John walked swiftly and without making eye contact with anyone, he'd had enough of passing pleasantries for one day. A couple of lads were swinging on a lamp post from a rope dangling from the iron arm which jutted out beneath the gas lamp. Neither had boots on their feet and above their dirty faces their hair was matted and clearly verminous. Spotting him in his suit, one of them called out, 'Spare a penny, mister?' as he landed at the side of him.

John shook his head. If he gave to one they would all be round him and he had learned from experience the more persistent would think nothing of following him home, chanting and name-calling.

The nearer he got to Canon Cockin Street the

more the smell from the chemical works and other industry lining the east side of Hendon made itself felt. He stood for a moment at the top of the street he had been born in as he was wont to do at times when the grind of constant studying got him down. It was identical to hundreds of others in the area, most of which were overcrowded, insanitary and unhealthy. It only needed a minute to convince him that whatever he had to do, however he had to struggle and however long it took, he'd make a better life for himself. And education was the answer. He wouldn't be a dock labourer all his life.

Becoming aware his hands had curled into fists, he slowly released his fingers before walking on, and he had almost reached his doorstep when one of the doors opened and a grey-haired woman stepped into the street.

'Ee, John lad, I didn't see you.'

'Hello, Mrs Craggs.' He liked this neighbour, she had been a good friend to his mother in her time. Smiling, he added, 'What have you got there?'

'Just a bite for poor Mrs Dodds. She's just had her second and there's Mr Dodds laid up after the accident.'

John looked down at the bowl of thin gruel and slice of toast. Mrs Craggs had lost her husband in a mining accident similar to the one which had crushed Mr Dodds's legs a few weeks back, and the family managed on the wages of the two teenage sons who had followed their father down the pit. With six bairns under the age of twelve, Mrs Craggs could ill afford to spare any food. Impulsively he reached in his pocket and placed a half-crown on the tray. 'Give them that from me for the bairn.'

'Aye, I will, lad. Ta ta for now then.'

Cissy had been at school with Elsie Dodds, although she had been Elsie Jefferson in those days. She had been a pretty girl, but even before her husband's accident she had been looking old and tired. The family lived at the 'poor' end of the street where several of the houses had one family to each room. He remembered Elsie had had light brown hair which had turned golden in the summer . . .

As he entered the house and the smell of last night's herrings assailed his nostrils he wasn't thinking about Elsie Dodds any more, but a slim finely boned wisp of a girl whose fair hair was so light it looked to have the texture of spun gold and whose green eyes had told him she wanted nothing to do with him.

Chapter 6

'Where are you going at this time of night?'

'Out. I've told you. I need some fresh air after being stuck in that club all evening.'

'Huh! Many's the time you've stood drinking in the Salutation or some other pub all night.'

Stanley turned from his wife and walked to the kitchen window, standing and looking out into the darkness. He didn't move from the window when he spoke, saying, 'Come with me, if you like, it's all the same to me, but I need some fresh air and that's the end of it.'

The 'huh' came again. They both knew she wouldn't take him up on his offer. 'Any normal man would sit and talk the day through when his daughter's just got married.'

'Why would I want to do that?' Now he did turn and face her, staring at her elegant shape in the expensive coat and dress which had cost him an arm and a leg. 'I know your opinion of the Turners.'

'And you think they're the bee's knees, do you?

That scum getting your daughter pregnant is all right with you, is it?'

Wearily, he said, 'We've been over this time and time again. What's done is done, Geraldine.'

'She's thrown her life away the same as—' She stopped abruptly.

'The same as you did,' Stanley finished for her. When she merely continued to glare at him, he smiled coldly. 'Like mother, like daughter, eh? But I think in Sarah's case she's decent enough to keep herself for her husband from now on.'

'Be quiet.' Geraldine pushed the kitchen door closed. 'Lily's upstairs.'

'And your role of the hard-done-by wife must be maintained at all costs, mustn't it?'

'I am hard done by. The way you've treated me over the years—'

'I've worked my fingers to the bone to get us where we are today and you know it,' Stanley cut in sharply. 'You've had my wage packet every Friday and not when I've drunk half of it away in the pub, like some.'

'I'm not talking about that.'

There was a short silence. Stanley had known what she was referring to and he also knew she had a point. For a woman who was built as Geraldine was it had been cruel to deny her the comforts of the flesh. He knew that, he had always known it, but from the day he had seen her spread out on their bed with her fancy man he'd known he couldn't touch her again. After he had taken up with Sally he had told himself he was a hypocrite and maybe that was true but, nevertheless, the thought of making love to Geraldine

91

disgusted him. It was as simple as that. 'I'm going out and I don't know what time I'll be back.'

'Go, then; you needn't come back, as far as I'm concerned.'

'Don't tempt me, Geraldine.'

As he opened the door leading into the scullery, she said, 'I hate you, Stanley Brown. You know that, don't you?'

'Yes, I know that.'

When the back door closed behind him Geraldine continued to stand for a few moments longer, then she whirled round and made her way into the sitting room. There was a fire burning in the grate which she had stoked up as soon as they had entered the house some minutes earlier, and now she walked across to the blaze and held out her hands to the warmth. *Did* he have another woman? It was a thought which had crossed her mind more than once in the last few years since she had noticed a change in her husband. She could pinpoint the time the change had occurred, it had been after the coronation of the King. In the weeks and months following this Stanley had been . . . odd.

Wrinkling her brow she stared into the red and gold flames of the fire. But no, she answered herself as on previous occasions. He was right when he said he gave her his wage packet each week. That had never varied, not even in their worst times. And the little he had back was only enough for the odd pint or two and his baccy. What woman would put up with being the mistress of a married man if he didn't make it worth her while? Besides which, Stanley didn't have the gumption to start anything with another woman. Her lip curled. He was too taken up with the idea of himself as the big man, the gaffer at the shipyard. She knew him through and through. His reputation was everything to him. Her life had been sacrificed to it, hadn't it?

Bending down, she reached for the tongs in the coal scuttle and added more coal to the fire, even though it didn't need it. She had never imagined he would be able to keep up his rejection of her; not him being the sort of man he was, passionate, full-blooded. And with each month, each year, he had shown he didn't want her, her loathing of him had grown. If he crawled the length of Sunderland on his hands and knees she wouldn't have him in her bed now.

As her body repudiated this thought, Geraldine turned sharply, the sound in her throat almost a groan. She glanced round the room that was her pride and joy but which held no satisfaction for her tonight. When the tears came they were scalding hot, burning her face, and they brought her no relief.

Stanley walked swiftly through the moonlit streets towards the west side of town. Here the air was thinner, cleaner, and the further he got from St Bede's Terrace the more energised he became. He was making for an area on the far side of Bishopwearmouth, not far from Barnes Park. Sally had purchased a small detached cottage there three years ago, shortly after the last of Tim Finlay's two children had married. The two-bedroomed cottage and quarter acre of ground was enclosed by a six-foot-high wall which guaranteed privacy.

When she opened the door to his knock, Sally's round plump face showed her surprise. 'I didn't expect you the night, not with Sarah's wedding and all.'

She was already attired for bed, her thick pink dressing gown doing nothing to hide her voluptuous curves.

'I needed to see you.' Once in the cottage, he took her into his arms. 'I don't think I can go on like this much longer.'

She melted into him but her voice was quiet and firm when she said, 'You know what we agreed, Stan. We wouldn't come out into the open till all the bairns, yours and mine, were settled. It's not fair. You know what folk are like.'

He knew she thought of Tim's bairns as her own but he was also aware of her longing for a child from her own flesh. It hadn't happened with Tim, nor with him, to date, and this surprised him. Sally's plump, accommodating body seemed tailor-made for babies. 'What if you fall for a bairn? What then?'

She moved in his arms so she could look up into his face and her expression pained him. 'I've given up hoping in that direction.' And when he was about to speak she put a finger on his lips. 'Anyway, you're enough for me, lad. I'm not greedy, I won't ask God for more.'

'Oh, lass.' Her love for him was humbling.

'And I'm no spring chicken. I'm on the wrong side of forty, don't forget.'

'That's nowt.' He traced the outlines of her eyes

and nose with his forefinger before kissing her. 'Lots of women have a bairn in their forties.'

'Not their first, Stan.'

Her words reminded him of the passage of time; he had been thinking a lot about that lately. He didn't want year after year of keeping Sally hidden as though she was good for one thing only. That wasn't how he felt. He didn't want her only in bed, he wanted to *live* with her. He wanted to wake up beside her in the morning, share her meals and every other thing. He wanted to be able to walk out with her and for folk to see them together. He wanted . . . he wanted it all. 'I love you, lass,' he said thickly. 'I let you down years ago and it sent us down paths we should never have gone down. It's my fault, all of it. I don't know how you can love me.'

'Stan, Stan.' She took his big face in her hands. 'Don't you know by now you're my sun, moon and stars? I loved you when I was a bairn and I never stopped loving you. I wanted to but I couldn't. I – I can't remember a time when I haven't loved you.'

He was holding her tightly and his voice trembled when he said, 'And me you. No, don't look like that, lass. It's true, I swear it. I might have been blinded for a time but that's all it was, like when you look at the sun and then try to see what's about you. You can't for a bit.'

'But now you do?' she said with a small smile, trying to bring some normality into the moment because she saw he was very upset.

He stared at her, his face serious. 'I could say that, in every way that matters, you're my wife, and it'd be true.

But I want it legal an' all, lass. I want to divorce her, I've wanted to for years, you know that, but seeing Sarah wed today it . . . well, it all swept over me.'

'What about your job? The scandal would—'

'*Damn my job.*' He pulled her into him, saying, 'I'm sorry, I'm sorry, but the job doesn't matter. Nothing does except you. We'll move away, start again, anything you like.'

'But your children? And I couldn't leave Alice when she's just got wed, and Howard's wife is expecting a baby soon. Tim would expect me to be there for them.'

'Then we'll stay here, I don't care. I just want to be with you properly. Let me tell Geraldine and have done with it.'

'It wouldn't be fair on Lily. You know that, Stan. She'd feel she'd have to stay with Geraldine, she'd end up an old maid. We've got to wait till she's settled, that's what we agreed. If she'd got a husband, everything would be different, however much criticism there is.'

'You're too nice, lass.' But his voice was soft. Then again they were kissing, hard and hungrily.

'How long can you stay?' she asked after a moment or two.

'For ever.'

'I was just going to get into bed when you knocked.'

'Sounds good to me.'

She lifted her hand and cupped his cheek. 'Come on then, I'll let you stay till midnight, how about that?' And together, holding hands like two young bairns, they went into the bedroom.

Chapter 7

'The children are asleep, ma'am, and I've left the night light burning in Master Edwin's room. I'm afraid he wouldn't go to sleep till I promised not to take it away.'

'That's all right, Lily. I'll see to it shortly.' Arabella Gray smiled at her nurserymaid. 'It's your evening at the library, isn't it? You run along now, you don't want to be late.'

'Thank you, ma'am. Goodnight, ma'am, sir.' After nodding at her employers who were sitting side by side on the sofa in the drawing room enjoying a pre-dinner sherry, Lily quickly made her way to the kitchen, divesting herself of her cap and apron as she did so.

The Grays lived in a substantial detached property in Ryhope Road. This was convenient on a day-to-day basis being only a moderate walk from St Bede's Terrace, but on the evenings Lily went to the town library she caught a tram so as to arrive on time. As she entered the kitchen Molly, the cook, raised her head from a fish dish she was preparing. 'You off, then?'

Lily nodded, pulling on her hat and coat and placing her cap and apron on a peg on the wall. 'It's my discussion group.'

'By, lass, I'd have thought you talked enough in the day with them three bairns.' This was from Bridget, the maid, who was Molly's sister and was sitting having a cup of tea at the kitchen table.

Lily smiled. She liked the sisters and they liked her, but Molly and Bridget were miles apart from her in their thinking. Although only in their thirties, both sisters freely admitted they had all they wanted from life with the Grays. They lived in, sharing a large room in the attics, had plenty of good food, kind employers who appreciated Molly's culinary efforts and Bridget's discretion and smooth handling of her duties. They did not want for a thing. Lily knew the sisters had been born in Fitter's Row in the East End, a place where foul language, brawling, thriftlessness and crime were rife and where every other building was a public house. Two of twenty children born to illiterate Irish immigrants, with a father who was violent and a mother who drank harder than any man, Lily could understand why Molly and Bridget never went home on their half-day a month off.

She had reached the back door when Bridget called after her, 'How's that sister of yours doing, lass? The bairn must be due soon.'

Turning, her hand on the door knob, Lily said, 'In three weeks, and she's doing fine.'

'You must miss her.'

'Aye, I do.'

'Bridget, let the lass go or she'll miss her tram.'

Smiling at them both, Lily called, 'See you tomorrow,' and made her escape. Once outside the grounds she stood in Ryhope Road for a moment, breathing in the air. It was a beautiful soft evening in late September. They had been enjoying an Indian summer and as yet the nip of autumn had not made itself felt. She had taken the three children for a walk that afternoon and Prudence, the eldest at seven, and Belinda, who was five, had galloped like ponies put out to grass in the park. Edwin, the baby at three, had found this vastly entertaining, laughing and clapping his hands. The girls had lessons each morning with a private tutor who was very strict, so in the afternoons, whenever she could, Lily took them for a walk so they could run wild for a time. She wasn't at all sure Mrs Gray would have approved of this, but the children had instinctively seemed to recognise they didn't discuss the nature of their 'constitutionals'.

Smiling to herself now, Lily hurried to the tram stop and within minutes it had trundled into view. Once on her way to the library, however, her thoughts turned to Bridget's last remark. She was worried about Sarah; her sister had lost her sparkle. Of course it could be her condition as, in Sarah's own words, 'she was as big as a house'. Ralph had seen to it that their home was kitted out, each room was now furnished and Sarah had told her he didn't keep her short of house-keeping money. She tried to avoid visiting Sarah when she knew Ralph would be present but on the few occasions he had been there, he hadn't put a foot wrong. She still didn't trust him – her brow wrinkled at the thought of him – but maybe he had changed his ways? But if so, what was wrong with Sarah? If something *was* wrong, of course.

So immersed was she in her thoughts that she almost missed her stop. It was only the conductor, a smiley middle-aged man, tapping her on her shoulder and saying, 'Don't you normally get off here, lass, on a Wednesday?' that brought her jumping out of her seat and scrambling down the steps to emerge in Borough Road. The library was situated in the Extension Park, just off Borough Road, and adjoining the rear of the building was a large conservatory, the Winter Gardens, which housed tropical plants, several cages of foreign birds and a pond well stocked with fat goldfish. The library was on the ground floor with an antiquities gallery and art gallery on the floor above, and as she hurried through the doors and joined the reading and discussion group sitting at a large circular table tucked away in a side room, she immediately sensed something was wrong.

'Lily, dear.' Beatrice and Quentin Cunningham, the founders of the group and the only members Lily did not like, moved from their seats on the opposite side of the table where they had been deep in conversation with their neighbours, to sit either side of her. 'I suppose you've heard?'

'Heard?' Lily looked into Beatrice's sallow face which had – unusually for her – a tinge of colour to it. 'Heard what?'

'About Bruce and that woman.'

'Do you mean Ellen?' Bruce McGuigan, a quiet

100

scholarly schoolteacher, had introduced Ellen Lindsay to the group at the beginning of the year. It had been at a time when Lily had been considering leaving, mainly because of the two on either side of her now. She had joined the group a few months before this, partly for something to do while Sarah was courting Ralph every night, but also because she had always loved reading and the thought of discussing various topics and themes had greatly appealed to her. She had soon discovered that Beatrice and Quentin ran things, and also that they were both patronising and pretentious. They were what her father would term upstarts. She knew that, but for the fact she lived in St Bede's Terrace and her father was a manager at the shipyard, they wouldn't have wasted the time of day on a nurserymaid. Ellen had breezed into the group like a breath of fresh air. She wasn't pushy, but when asked had no hesitation in declaring her views with an authority rarely found in a woman. The fact that she was Bruce's friend and, furthermore, a suffragette, had for ever damned her in Beatrice's eyes. Beatrice had always had a soft spot for Bruce, something everyone knew but didn't talk about.

'Yes, of course we mean Ellen.' Beatrice leaned forward, her pale blue eyes alight. 'Quentin and I always knew there was something funny about her. Didn't we, Quentin?'

'From the first moment.' Quentin nodded his bald head.

'Not that we suspected *that*, of course.' Beatrice paused, waiting for a response from Lily. When none was forthcoming, she bent even closer. 'Ellen Lindsay was detained by the police on Friday night on a charge of prostitution and apparently it isn't the first time.'

'What?' Lily sat back in her seat. 'I don't believe it.'

'It's perfectly true.' Beatrice's voice was heavy with self-righteous glee. 'My brother is an inspector, as you know – Lily said nothing, *everyone* knew, Beatrice made sure of that – 'and we had called in to the station on Friday night to report our neighbour. He became positively abusive to Quentin earlier in the evening because Quentin reprimanded his children. We know it was them who have been stealing apples from our apple tree but he wouldn't have it. Anyway – Beatrice took a deep breath – 'we were talking to Theobald when we saw Ellen at the sergeant's desk outside Theobald's office. Naturally I asked what was wrong.'

'And he told you?'

'He was surprised we knew her.' Beatrice sniffed at the disapproval in Lily's voice. 'He was concerned for our reputation. He told us about the previous incident and suggested we might like to distance ourselves from further contact.'

'So you don't know for sure why she was at the police station on Friday night?'

'Of course I do; it's obvious, isn't it?'

'Not really.'

Beatrice's expression changed. She seemed to increase an inch or two in stature as she stiffened in her seat. 'You're very young, Lily. You will fully understand the social implications of associating with such a woman in time. As it is, I felt it was my duty to the members to take measures to remove such an influence from our gatherings. To that end we have written to both Bruce and Miss Lindsay stating our position. Of course we have no doubt Bruce was totally unaware of the true position; he has clearly been duped, as have we all. There is no slur on his good name, none at all.'

'You wrote on behalf of us all, or just from you and Quentin?'

Beatrice's face became icy at Lily's tone. 'Does that matter?'

'I think so, yes. I would expect to be consulted if it was the former.'

Beatrice stood up. What she would have said at this point Lily was never to find out, because at that moment the door to the side room opened and Bruce stepped in, Ellen on his arm. The low buzz of quiet conversation froze. There were a few seconds of stunned silence before Beatrice stepped forward, her face a picture. 'This is too much. You know that, don't you, Bruce? This is too much. You dare to bring that woman here into the company of respectable people?'

'That's enough, Beatrice.' Bruce's voice was grim and his eyes were blazing. He didn't resemble the quiet schoolteacher they all knew.

'It isn't enough. It isn't nearly enough. This is an outrage—'

'The only outrage has been committed by you and your vicious tongue.'

Beatrice looked as though she was about to have a seizure. 'How dare you.'

'Believe me, I haven't even got started yet.'

'Leave it, Bruce, please. I will deal with this myself.' Ellen was as white as lint but quite composed, and anyone less like a woman of the streets it would have been impossible to imagine. Her dark hair was fastened in gleaming coils at the back of her head upon which her dainty hat sat and this matched her coat. Her clothes were smart with an expensive stamp about them but subdued, almost plain. She looked to be in her late twenties, her pretty face clear and unlined and her large blue eyes set under dark, curving brows. It was these eyes which betrayed her emotion; they were almost black with anger as she faced the woman who had maligned her. 'I think it is only fair to tell you that I have placed your letter with my solicitors.'

Whatever Beatrice had expected, clearly it wasn't this. Lily watched her mouth open and shut like a goldfish before she stuttered, 'Don't – don't be ridiculous. I – I've done nothing wrong.'

'Forgetting the nature of your letter for a moment, the fact that you have spread slanderous gossip which has no foundation in the truth is more than enough for my solicitor to be getting on with for now.'

Beatrice had recovered herself. Her sallow skin blotched with fiery colour, she glared at the woman she bitterly resented. 'Don't give me that. I know what I know. I have it on the highest authority—'

'No, you don't.' There was a note in Ellen's voice which caused Quentin's eyes to flash to his wife and then back to the woman standing within an arm's length of her. It was clear from his face that, for the first time, he suspected they might have got it wrong. 'I was at the police station on Friday night because I happened to be a witness to an attack on Mr Routledge, the watchmaker on the corner of High Street West

104

and York Street. Myself and another lady were asked to make statements to the police.'

'I don't believe you.'

'That is of no consequence, it's the truth.'

'But . . .' Beatrice was floundering. Aware of the hush in the room and knowing she couldn't afford to let Ellen Lindsay get the better of her, she said bitterly, 'Be that as it may, can you deny you were brought up before the law in the past?'

'I don't have to justify myself to you, but I will say my conscience is clear, Mrs Cunningham. Can you say the same?'

'What do you mean?'

'Simply that it ill behoves a married woman to make a nuisance of herself with another man. Everyone in this room is well aware of why you are determined to blacken my name, and it does you no credit.'

As Beatrice moved to smack Ellen across the face it was Lily who sprang forward to catch her arm before it made contact. She wasn't prepared for the way the furious woman swung round or the ringing slap on the side of her head. She fell sideways across a chair. About her pandemonium reigned, but Lily's first experience of physical violence and the force with which her head had hit the floor had rendered her dumb.

She was aware of being lifted and seated on a chair but her ears were ringing and she felt nauseous. 'Are you all right?' Bruce was kneeling in front of her. 'The woman's deranged, mad. She should be locked away.'

Someone thrust smelling salts under Lily's nose. The smell was so revolting she knocked them away, gasping.

'Here, drink this.' Ellen held a glass of water to her lips.

'I don't want it.'

'It will help. Drink a little.'

Rather than trying to find the strength to argue she took a sip or two and then leaned back in the chair. She felt very dizzy. 'I'm all right now.'

'You aren't, that was a nasty fall.' Ellen looked at Bruce as she said, 'She's got a bump the size of an egg on the side of her head. Look, feel that. I think we should get a doctor to look at it.'

'I don't want a doctor.' Lily was feeling acutely embarrassed. Now the dizziness was clearing she could see everyone was standing looking at her. Beatrice and Quentin were nowhere to be seen. 'I'll just go home and rest. I'll be fine.'

'Sit here while I go and find a cab.' Bruce straightened and glanced round at the others. 'I think the meeting's over, folks. We've all had more than enough excitement for one day.'

By the time Bruce returned, most of the group had dwindled away. Lily left the building supported on either side by Bruce and Ellen. She looked at the horse-drawn cab and said weakly, 'I would prefer not to go home like this. Is . . . is there somewhere I could go for a little while till I feel better?'

'I've rooms in Crowtree Road.' Ellen patted her hand. 'Would you like to come there and have a cup of tea?'

Lily nodded and then stopped quickly when it made her head swim again.

'Come on then.'

Bruce helped the two women into the cab and then climbed in himself. No one spoke on the journey and Lily sat with her eyes shut. She was beginning to feel slightly better but her head was pounding. She could hardly believe Beatrice had behaved in such an undignified way.

Ten minutes later she was comfortably at rest on the studio couch in Ellen's sitting room-cum-bedroom, her legs covered by a blanket. Ellen had two rooms on the ground floor of the three-storey property. Lily didn't know what the rest of the house was like but she was amazed when she looked about this room. Instead of the customary brown walls or dark wallpaper, the room was painted a light cream and a deep red carpet covered the floor. This colour was reflected in the thick drapes at the window. A tall bookcase filled with books stood in one recess at the side of the fireplace, and the other held a built-in cupboard in light oak. A charming writing-desk stood beneath the bay window and the only other items of furniture were a small occasional table, and two dainty cabriole-legged armchairs which Lily instinctively recognised as expensive period pieces. She had never seen a room furnished in such a way with no elaborate chair-backs, mantel-borders or the inevitable aspidistra, and she thought it beautiful, light and uncluttered.

Bruce had gone with Ellen into what was presumably the kitchen, and now the door to the front room opened again and they came in, Bruce carrying a tray. The closeness Lily had sensed between them before – a closeness which had clearly got under Beatrice's skin – was more apparent away from the library. There was an easy familiarity between them which suggested they could be very good friends.

'How are you feeling?' Ellen was clearly concerned.

'Much better.'

'I'm so sorry you got hurt because of me.' Ellen turned to Bruce who had set the tray on the small table. 'I told you we shouldn't have gone tonight.'

'Nonsense.' He glanced at Lily. 'I'm as sorry as Ellen for what happened, of course but' – he looked at Ellen then added – 'it was essential you showed your face there tonight and didn't hide away as though you had something to be ashamed of. That woman can't be allowed to get away with her lies. You do see that?'

'Oh, Bruce.'

'Don't say "Oh, Bruce" like that, Ellen. I mean what I say. The woman's poison.'

Ellen poured them all tea and handed Lily hers before she said, 'I knew something like this would happen one day.'

'And now it has and we go on from there.'

Lily had never realised Bruce was so assertive. He was tall and lanky, with sandy-coloured hair and gentle brown eyes, and she'd always had him down as a bookish intellectual whose head was somewhat in the clouds. Not so. And he clearly adored Ellen.

Ellen must have caught what she was thinking because she put down her cup of tea and said softly, 'We owe you an explanation, Lily.'

'No you don't, not at all.'

'Yes, we do. Anyway, I'd like to explain. Bruce and I have been seeing each other for quite a while—'

'A lot longer than you'd think,' Bruce cut in, 'but it was months before I could persuade her to be seen out with me.'

'For your sake.' Ellen's voice had been soft and now she turned to Lily. 'I was worried something like tonight would occur. Bruce is a schoolteacher; he can't afford any scandal attached to his name.' And at Bruce's impatient click of the tongue, she added, 'He could lose his livelihood.'

'I'm sorry.' Lily looked at them. 'I don't understand.'

Ellen took a deep breath. 'Part of what Beatrice said was true, Lily. Not about Friday night, poor Mr Routledge *was* attacked, but about the other part of it.'

Again Lily said, 'I don't understand.'

'Ellen came to Sunderland three years ago from the south of England.' Bruce took the initiative when Ellen seemed unable to go on. 'She was escaping a brute of a husband and she was six months pregnant. Her husband was well-to-do but when she arrived here she had little money and knew no one. She took lodgings in a house, just one room, but several other women appeared to live there and so she thought she would be safe. She was an innocent.'

He glanced at Ellen but her head was bowed.

'This house was of a type known to the police. Shortly after Ellen arrived there was a disturbance late one night which developed into something more. Neighbours called the police. One of the women's customers had proved difficult.'

109

Bruce raised his eyebrows and Lily nodded in answer to the silent question. She knew what he meant.

'Everyone in the house was taken to the police station. Because it was proved Ellen had only arrived a few days before she was not charged with the other girls, but this only came about by the police contacting her husband. The result of this was that he came to Sunderland.'

Bruce swallowed hard. 'She left him because she feared for the life of her unborn child with the beatings and other cruelties she had been subjected to. He inflicted what he termed punishment for her betrayal. She was in hospital for weeks and the child was stillborn. The only good thing in this story is that when he left Sunderland in a hurry, probably fearful of how far he had gone, he was involved in a train accident and killed. Ellen did not learn this for some time. His family fought to prevent her receiving a penny and the clever lawyer they had hired made sure the bulk of the fortune stayed in the family. Nevertheless, the settlement Ellen received when she left hospital enabled her to purchase this house and take in lodgers.'

Lily's head was reeling. She didn't doubt for a moment that the tragic story was true. She stared at the young woman she had secretly admired for her independent attitude and air of self-sufficiency which she now realised had come at such a cost. 'I'm so sorry about the baby, Ellen.'

'She was a little girl.' Ellen raised her head, her eyes dry but dark with pain. 'I only saw her for a few moments. She was tiny and beautiful and so perfect.'

Lily didn't know what to say. It was so terrible. 'Didn't you have any family down south who could have helped you?'

'We had been married for three months when Steven first beat me. He . . . he had been doing other things almost from our wedding night. I was black and blue and I went home to my parents. We were what I suppose you'd call middle class, my father was a professional man. Steven was very much the country squire and his family had connections with royalty. My parents had been beside themselves with pride when he had asked for my hand, I was their only child. When . . . when I explained to my mother what was happening she told me the beating must have been my fault and I must learn not to provoke him. She wouldn't let me tell her about the other things and when I tried to, she actually left the room. They called Steven and when he arrived to take me home they apologised to him for my behaviour. From that day I knew I no longer had any parents.'

'You have me.' Bruce reached across and took Ellen's hand. 'Now do you see?' he said softly to Lily.

She did see. Perhaps more than he had meant. She wondered how many times he had asked Ellen to marry him, and how many times she had refused because of her past.

'You couldn't have done anything other than go and show that woman — and the rest of them — that you're prepared to stand up to them,' Bruce said quietly. 'You know that, Ellen.'

'Perhaps.' Ellen gently extracted her hand from his. 'But I shan't go back there again. I have no wish to.'

'Nor shall I.' Lily looked at her. 'I was thinking of leaving before you came and now . . .'

'So you believe me?'

'Believe you? Of course I believe you. I never thought for one moment Beatrice was telling the truth. No one did.'

Ellen smiled. 'Thank you. I think that last bit is stretching the truth, but thank you for saying it.' And then she brought a smile to Bruce's face and made Lily laugh when in an exaggerated northern twang, she drawled, 'You're a canny lass, Lily Brown, and no mistake. A right canny lass.'

Chapter 8

'What's the matter with you, man? Are you seriously telling me you couldn't do with the money? I tell you, this is a one-off. Like I said, I'm in a bit of a fix an' you'd be doing me a favour and earning out of it. I can't say fairer than that.'

'How many times do I have to say it, Ralph?' John's voice was low and terse. 'I want no hand in that business. You'll catch your toe one day and then all hell'll be let loose. The dock police aren't as daft as you think they are.'

The two men were standing near the engine sheds in Hudson Dock North in the East End having finished their shift. The October evening was cold with a thin drizzle of icy rain making the grey twilight darker. The fine weather had broken three weeks before at the end of September with violent thunderstorms.

Ralph rubbed his hand round his jaw irritably. 'All right, all right. Fine brother you are. It's not like I ask you every week and I wouldn't be asking today but for the fact Wilf's laid low. But if you won't, you won't.'

'I won't,' said John grimly.

'How about if you take Wilf's takings from the last bit of business to him, then? He'll be needing it and I promised I'd drop it in tonight but now this other thing has come up I can't be in two places at once. I could be tied up most of the evening if I've got to unload by myself.'

John stared at his brother. He supposed he couldn't refuse. 'Where's he live?'

'Blue Anchor Yard, between High Street East and Low Street.'

'Aye, I know it.' The area was right in the diseased heart of the East End slums. Taking the brown packet Ralph held out to him John stuffed it in the pocket of his worn jacket. 'I'm only doing this the once, Ralph. I'm not your errand boy.'

Ralph grinned. He had known all along John wouldn't come with him, but if he'd asked him straight out to take Wilf's cut to him tonight likely his brother would have refused, knowing the money came from stolen goods. 'I know, I know, man. And thanks. Wilf needs it, you see. There's twelve of 'em now living at his place. He took his old mam an' da in a couple of years back when it would have been the workhouse otherwise. He's a good lad, is Wilf.'

John didn't comment. Wilf might look after his own, but he and Ralph were doing more and more business after dark with the ne'er-do-wells who ran the network of criminal activities which were rife in the East End. Look how Ralph had furnished his

114

house; you couldn't rise to that even if you took all the overtime on offer and then some. He knew his da had cottoned on, but his mam seemed to accept Ralph's explanation of doing extra shifts happily enough.

He turned and began to walk, raising his hand but not looking behind him as Ralph called, 'Tell Wilf from me to keep his pecker up. I'll see him all right till he's back on his feet.'

John didn't know exactly what had happened, but his brother had said enough to indicate that Wilf had met with a mishap whilst on one of their nightly excursions. The docks could be dangerous places at the best of times but when you were working quickly and in the dark, safety went out of the window.

It wasn't far to Blue Anchor Yard. He passed the rotting remains of a dead cat lying in the gutter and the stench made him swallow hard. All the East End was grim but this area was the worst.

When he reached the steep steps leading to the hotchpotch of housing in Blue Anchor Yard, a group of children were sitting huddled together in a corner. The oldest couldn't have been more than seven, and none of them were wearing coats, their bare feet showing evidence of smears of blood where their chapped skin had split. John spoke to the eldest lad whose hair was white-streaked with nits: 'Wilf Wright, which is his house?'

A pair of bright eyes weighed him up. 'What's it worth?'

'I only want to know where he lives.'

'Aye, I know.' The child wiped his runny nose on the back of his raggedy sleeve. 'What's it worth?'

John's gaze moved over the children. All had scabs round their mouths and a couple had styes on their eyes. Without letting his pity show, he said shortly, 'Penny each.'

'I'll show you.' The lad stood up, holding out his hand.

John stifled a smile as he deposited a penny in five little grubby paws that had shot out as their leader had spoken.

The child led him into the nearest doorway and thick darkness. 'Wilf lives at the top of the stairs.'

'Right, thanks.'

'You the new rent man?'

'What? Oh no, no, I'm not. I'm . . . a friend.'

'The old rent man was found with his head bashed in a few days ago.'

'Was he? Well, I'm not a rent man.'

The child disappeared outside again and John climbed the stairs that creaked and rocked ominously. Now his eyes had adjusted to the darkness he could see great holes in the skirting boards where rats clearly lurked and the rotten wall was crawling with lice. Dear gussy, the sooner he was out of here, the better.

On reaching the first-floor landing, which was filthy and strewn with rodent droppings, he saw the stairs continued upwards. Taking the child at his word he climbed to the next floor which he saw was the top of the building. There was an air of brooding decay but the floor showed evidence of being cleaned here. He could see two doors but one had a stack of crates piled against it. Stepping forward, he knocked on the other one.

It was opened immediately. 'Ralph, come in. Oh, you're not Ralph.' The woman in front of him peered at John. 'You look just like him. You his brother?'

'Aye, I'm John.'

'We were expecting Ralph, he said he'd call the night.'

'Something came up so he sent me instead.'

The woman had stood aside and now John entered the room. To his surprise it was spotlessly clean. It was clearly the living area, holding a table with two benches underneath upon which several children were sitting eating their evening meal. In the far corner of the room to one side of the fireplace, which had a crossbar jutting out from which hung a big black pot suspended from a thick chain, John saw a single bed. An elderly couple were sitting side by side eating bowls of soup. 'That's Wilf's mam an' da. I'm Maggie, his wife.'

John nodded. Propped against the wall in the other recess was a pallet bed with several blankets draped over it. He presumed this was where the children, or some of them at least, slept. Shelves holding pots and pans and crockery and items of food stretched along the wall above the old couple's bed, next to the one small high window in the room. A gnarled old wardrobe stood against the wall opposite Wilf's parents' bed, and now Wilf's wife stepped forward and drew aside a thick curtain which had been nailed to the wall beside the wardrobe. 'You'll want to talk to Wilf.'

John saw an entrance which was little more than a large rough hole which had been chiselled out between the two rooms. He had to bend almost double to scramble through. On straightening, he found himself in a smaller room but one which was again neat and clean. Wilf was lying in a brass bed which although being only three-quarter size took up most of the space, leaving just enough room for the cot beside it in which two young babies were lying fast asleep. 'The twins,' Maggie said as she joined him.

Wilf had been asleep but now he opened his eyes. 'John.' He looked behind him. 'Where's Ralph? Is owt wrong?'

'No, nothing's wrong. Ralph had a spot of business to do and so he asked me to come instead.' John was trying to hide his amazement that Wilf's wife had managed to create such a homely environment in such dreadful surroundings. 'He asked me to give you this.' He delved in his pocket and passed over the brown packet.

Wilf opened it, his fingers flicking the notes inside. John saw him visibly relax. 'By, your brother's a good 'un. Here, lass.' He threw the packet to Maggie who tucked it in the pocket of her voluminous skirt and, after smiling at John, disappeared through the opening into the other room. 'Ralph tell you I've done me back in?'

'He said there'd been some sort of accident.' John didn't want to stay and discuss things as though he agreed with what Wilf and Ralph were doing, but it would have been rude to leave immediately.

Wilf nodded. 'Me own fault. Still, the quack says it's nowt but torn muscles an' that as long as I stay in bed for a week or so I'll be as right as rain.'

'That's good.' John was feeling uncomfortable.

'Course it's made things a bit awkward for your Ralph, me being laid up.' As John opened his mouth to speak, Wilf held up his hand. 'Oh, I know you don't want nowt to do with it, lad. Ralph's explained. An' that's your call, every man to his own. I only know that without your brother we'd have been in queer street a long time ago. With eight bairns we'd never be able to manage on what I earn at the docks. Me poor old mam and da would have been for the workhouse without your brother, that's for sure.'

John cleared his throat. 'What will happen to your family if you and Ralph get collared by the law, Wilf? You ever thought of that?'

'I'd be lying if I said no, lad, but the way I look at it it's needs must. Anyway, the rich merchants and the shipping lines can afford to lose a bit, it's not like thieving from your own, is it?'

Maggie saved him the necessity of a reply by sticking her head through the hole and saying, 'I've just made a pot of tea, John. You want a cup?'

'No, thanks all the same, I need to get home for my dinner else my mam'll have my guts for garters.'

'Well, thanks for bringing it, and tell Ralph I'll be back at the docks as soon as I can.' Wilf moved very carefully on his pillows, wincing as he did so.

'I'll do that.' John just wanted to get away.

Once on the landing, he made his way down the shaky staircase. Two small girls were sitting on the gloomy stinking floor of the landing below and they both showed signs of suffering from St Vitus's dance, their jerky limbs stick thin and pitiful. He stared into

119

the small pinched faces which were in stark contrast to those of Wilf's children.

Feeling he didn't know which end of him was up, John continued down the stairs and out of the building. The drizzle of earlier had given way to hard driving rain and the group of children had disappeared. Walking swiftly, he turned into Prospect Row and then cut along by the side of the almshouses and orphan asylum at the side of the old town moor. He often caught a tram home when the weather was bad, but tonight he felt he needed to walk to clear his head.

He was soaked through by the time he reached the back lane of Canon Cockin Street. The mud was thick and he picked his way carefully, his cap pulled low over his eyes. As he passed Ralph's backyard he heard a voice call his name and he turned round. Lily was standing at the scullery door, beckoning him. He hadn't seen her since the wedding and as he opened the gate into the yard his heart began to thud. The last time he'd seen her he had been dressed in his suit and tie, what would she think when she saw him in his old working clothes? And then he berated himself. It didn't matter what Sarah's sister thought. She was nowt to him.

As he reached the back door he could see Lily was all of a flutter. 'What's the matter?'

'Ralph's not home yet. Do you know where he is or how long he'll be?'

As she stepped back for him to enter the scullery he stared at her in the dim light. Aware he was dripping on the floor, he rubbed his feet on the mat. Tendrils of hair had escaped the bun at the nape of her neck and curled round her head like a halo. Clearing his throat, he said, 'Ralph's doing a spot of overtime.'

'Overtime,' she repeated. Then, her voice conspiratorial, she whispered, 'Your mam's upstairs with the midwife; the baby's coming. This . . . overtime, how long is it likely to last?'

She knew. He supposed Sarah had told her about Ralph's nocturnal activities. 'I've no idea.'

The look on her face told him he had been too curt. Intensely irritated at the position he had been put in, John said, 'I'm sorry.' Taking off his sodden cap he ran his hand through his damp hair. 'Look, it's been a bad day. The truth is I don't get involved in Ralph's carry-ons. I don't know where he is or how long he'll be, only that he's got a bit of business to see to.'

Lily nodded. 'Sarah said your mam doesn't know anything about the nature of his overtime.'

'No, she doesn't, and I'd prefer to keep it that way for her peace of mind.'

'It was your mam who asked me to watch out for you when Ralph was late and Sarah said he'd likely be working an extra shift.'

John thought quickly. 'Tell her he's working on a boat that came in late but I don't know what one.'

She nodded again. 'I only intended to pop in for a minute or two on my way home, but apparently she's been having pains all day and didn't tell anyone. The midwife thinks it won't be long. Your mam's left the dinner in the oven and I said I'd come and dish it up once you were back. Shall – shall I come now?'

He was painfully conscious of his dirty jacket, his

121

old muffler and trousers and his big hobnailed boots. He couldn't explain to himself why he didn't want her to see him like this and that annoyed him still more. Breaking the unwritten rule which said a man never got involved in domestic difficulties, he said shortly, 'Don't worry, I'll see to it. I'll get Hannah to help.'

Lily looked at him. 'Your mam wouldn't have that. She said your sister's all fingers and thumbs.'

She was right. His sister was as skittish as a young pony. Knowing he was being unreasonable, John said stiffly, 'I didn't want to trouble you, that's all. Won't they be waiting for you at home?'

She shook her head. 'It's not like that in my house.'

She didn't elaborate, but the tinge of pink in her cheeks deepened. John knew he was staring but her face fascinated him. As her eyes dropped away from his he felt she was embarrassed, or maybe annoyed. Likely both. Calling himself every kind of fool, he said, 'Go and tell my mother Ralph'll be back once the job's done and that's all I know.'

'Yes, all right.'

'If you're coming round will you have a bite with us?'

'Thank you but I don't want to leave Sarah for too long.'

He could understand that. 'Have you contacted your mother?'

Lily hesitated. 'Sarah doesn't want my mother here. She can be – I mean she's not—' She stared at him helplessly.

Her discomfiture restored his equilibrium. 'Not

everyone can cope with these sorts of things,' he said diplomatically. 'We're all made different. Round these streets neighbours often tend neighbours so my mother's had plenty of experience, besides having nine bairns herself. Likely Sarah finds that reassuring.'

Lily nodded. 'Sarah loves your mam.'

He had noticed the slight catch of huskiness in her voice before, it was very attractive and added to her charm. The thought alarmed him. He did not find Lily Brown charming, he told himself with something approaching panic. Where the hell had that come from? This was the hoity-toity little madam who thought herself the cat's whiskers. 'Tell my mother I'll see the bairns get to bed on time if she's not back.' He stuffed his wet cap on his head. 'And give Sarah my best wishes.'

'Yes, all right. I'll see you in a minute.'

Their eyes held for a moment longer and then he turned and stepped into the yard, shutting the door behind him.

Ralph whistled to himself as he walked towards the dock gates. Tonight should be a nice little earner, he couldn't have let it pass him by. You only had to do that once or twice and the word was out you couldn't be relied on. It was a bit awkward with Wilf being laid up but nothing he couldn't handle, and maybe one of the blokes would give him a hand if he made it worth their while.

He was almost at the dock gates and just passing the yard of the sawmill when a dark figure stepped out of the shadows.

'Ralph? You by yourself?'

'Aye, Wilf's not too good the night.'

They walked together to the gates where the nightwatchman silently held out his hand. Ralph's companion reached in his pocket and notes changed hands.

'Mr Shawe wants a word with you before you start.'

Ralph stared at the other man. 'Owt wrong?'

'No, nothing's wrong. He'll tell you.'

Ralph felt prickles of unease in the pit of his stomach as he followed his companion into a large warehouse. Art Shawe was well known in the East End and further afield, having had his fingers in many pies for a number of years. The man at his side was one of Art's henchman and he had quite a few, great bruisers of fellows who were loyal to a man to their boss. Art never did any of his dirty work himself, but more than one body found floating in the murky waters of the docks had done something to offend him.

At the back of the warehouse a set of narrow stairs led to a small office. Several men were sitting at a table playing cards, an open bottle of whisky in front of them. The air was thick with cigarette smoke.

'Ralph, lad.' A thin foxy-looking man glanced up as they entered. 'Sit yourself down. I won't be a minute.'

Ralph sat. One or two of the men looked disinterestedly at him before concentrating on the game in hand. Five minutes crept by. Then ten. Ralph knew better than to interrupt or show any impatience.

It was fifteen minutes before Art finished the game by increasing the pile of sovereigns and silver in front of him. Ralph had the feeling he wouldn't lose too often.

'So . . .' Art sat back in his seat, his thumbs in the tiny pockets of his pearl-buttoned waistcoat. 'How goes it, Ralph?'

Ralph swallowed. 'Aye, good, Mr Shawe.'

'I'm pleased to hear it.' Art motioned to the henchman who had taken up residence behind Ralph's chair. 'Get Ralph a glass, man. Where're your manners?'

There were guffaws around the table as though Art had said something particularly witty, and Ralph smiled sickly. When the whisky was put in front of him he helped himself to a good measure. He felt he needed it.

Art watched him drink. Then said softly, 'Likely you're wondering what this is all about?'

Ralph nodded, replacing his glass on the table with a shaky hand. 'Aye, Mr Shawe. I hope everything's all right?'

'How long has it been since we first started doing business, Ralph? Six years? Seven?'

'Over seven.'

'Aye, I thought so. And in all that time you've not put a foot wrong. Unlike some.' The gimlet-hard eyes narrowed. 'I've been disappointed recently, Ralph. Very disappointed.'

'Oh aye?' He licked his dry lips.

'Let down. Now that's not a nice feeling, being let down. Especially when you thought you could trust someone. Still, there's no accounting for greed. I don't like greedy men. Do you, Ralph?'

Ralph shook his head. He could feel the sweat running down him despite the cold night.

'So I had to take measures.' The men at the table were completely silent, it was clear they knew what these measures had been. Ralph didn't doubt there would be a body floating in the murky water come morning. 'Measures to protect my own interests and that of my organisation. I have plenty of men looking to me for their livelihood, Ralph. Families to support. You know what I mean? Aye, course you do. You're a family man yourself. So, I'm left with a vacancy, as it were. And whose name popped into my mind?'

'M – mine?'

'Aye, yours, Ralph. Have another drink.'

This time he knocked it back in one. 'What can I do for you, Mr Shawe?'

'No, lad. It's what I can do for you. I've watched you over the last few years and like I said, you haven't put a foot wrong. Not taken on more than you could chew or got careless. You'd be surprised how many men in your position get careless. Or greedy. So, as far as the law's concerned, your nose is clean. You've got a steady job, a family. You're respectable, Ralph. Get my drift?'

He didn't think he did but he nodded anyway.

'And men like you are useful to me. Your predecessor owned a tidy little boatyard near the wharf brewery. On paper at least. In actual fact, he never put up a penny for it. But as far as the authorities are concerned, it's a respectable establishment and that's what matters. Nice big warehouse, it is. Know the one? Sort of place that can hold a lot more than the odd boat, and no one's any the wiser as long as a bit of work is done out front.'

Ralph's mind was racing. He meant Vickers's place. He knew Peter Vickers by sight, he'd seen him drinking in the Mariners' Arms in Custom House Quay and in the Earl of Durham a few times. He was a rotund little man who always had a smile on his face. A shiver passed over him. They'd done for Peter Vickers?

'Now before he was called away' – again the men at the table sniggered – 'the gentleman in question was persuaded to sign everything over to you, Ralph. My solicitor saw to it personally. All you have to do is sign this document – he tapped a large envelope at the side of him – 'and it's all legal and proper. I like things done legal and proper and I like to be generous to them that appreciate it. What I can't abide is sticky fingers but you're not like that, are you, Ralph?'

'No.'

'Good. Now you can get Wilf working alongside you but I don't want no one else sniffing about. All you have to do is keep your mouth shut and do what you're told. For that you come out of the docks and get nicely looked after. How does that sound?'

Ralph stared at Art. He knew the question was rhetorical. You didn't say no to a man like Art Shawe, not if you wanted to keep company with your kneecaps. For the first time it dawned on him where the path he'd started on seven years ago had led. Once he was on Art's payroll, Art would own him, body and soul. But he'd be set up for life.

A sliver of excitement made itself felt. Give it a few years and he'd be able to provide Sarah with a house to match her da's, probably bigger and fancier at that. That'd be one in the eye for her mam. 'It sounds fine to me, Mr Shawe.'

'That's me boy.' Art smiled, showing blackened teeth. 'You'll go far as long as you remember one thing. And that's where you've come from. You can just as easily fall back in the gutter if I give the nod. All right?'

Ralph nodded. 'Aye, yes, an' thanks. Thanks, Mr Shawe.'

Art's smile widened. Rising to his feet he leaned over the table and filled Ralph's glass himself. 'I've got a feeling you an' me are going to be all right, lad,' he said softly.

Sarah's baby was born just before ten o'clock. Nora and the midwife had thought it unseemly for Lily to be present, her being a mere slip of a lass, but in the last stage of delivery when Sarah had called for her Lily had marched into the room and remained at her sister's side. She was the first to hold her niece, a bonny big baby with a cry as lusty and loud as any male child.

'She's beautiful, Sarah.' After wrapping the baby in a shawl, Lily handed her to her sister. They were both crying, Nora too. Happy tears.

'Oh she is, lass, she is.' Nora sniffed loudly. 'Look at all that hair. You'll be after plaiting it, I'll be bound.'

Sarah was exhausted after the long twenty hours of labour but she was grinning from ear to ear as she looked down at the child in her arms. 'I can't believe she's mine,' she said softly.

'You soon will, lass,' Mrs Osborne, the midwife, said drily. 'She'll be waking you up umpteen times a night to prove it.'

'I don't mind.' Sarah stroked the baby's silky brow. 'She's mine and I love her.' Raising her eyes to Lily, she murmured, 'Do you think Mam felt like I'm feeling?'

Lily found she couldn't speak the truth. Instead she whispered gently, 'She loves us in her own way, Sarah.'

Sarah's snort wasn't as vehement as usual, and when she closed her eyes and tears seeped from beneath her lids again, the midwife said, 'That's natural, have a good weep, lass. "Weep when it's born, no more before dawn" that's what I always say. I'll be on my way but I'll look in come morning, all right? You looking after the lass, Nora?'

'Oh aye, I'll be here.'

Nora saw the midwife out, and once the two sisters were alone, Lily sat down on the bed and put her arm round Sarah's shoulders as they stared down in awe at the new little person in her arms. 'What are you and Ralph going to call her?'

'Imogen. Do you like it? Do you think it suits her?'

'Perfectly.'

'Imogen Sarah. If she'd been a boy, it would have been Henry Ralph.'

'That was nice too.'

Sarah twisted round to look at her. 'He's done the house out nice, Mops.'

'Ralph? Aye, he has.' Lily squeezed her sister's shoulder.

'He's not mean.'

'No, I can see that.'

'I have plenty of housekeeping and I only have to ask for extra and he gives it me, without wanting to know the ins and outs. An' he likes me to dress nice.'

'That's good.' Realising her voice hadn't been enthusiastic enough, Lily said again, 'That's good, Sarah.'

'Yes, it is, it is good.' Sarah turned back to look at the child in her arms. 'So why do I feel like I do?'

Lily bit her lip. It was a moment before she said, 'How do you feel?'

'Unsettled, like I don't really know him, not properly, not as a wife should know her husband. Oh, I don't know.' Sarah flapped her hand. 'Likely it's been my condition and everything. It wasn't the best start to a marriage, was it?'

Lily didn't answer this. What she did say was, and very softly, 'You've got a beautiful daughter now, the pair of you. You can build on that however it's been the last months.'

'I know.' Sarah nodded. And then as they heard a male voice downstairs, she said, 'Is that him, Ralph?'

'I'll go and see.' Lily reached over and kissed the baby's tiny soft forehead. 'And I'd better be making tracks now. I told Mam I'd be calling in to see you on my way home but she might start to get worried.'

'I wouldn't bank on it, the only person she worries about is herself.'

'She doesn't show her feelings, you know that, Sarah.'

'She showed her feelings to me in the lead up to me getting wed,' Sarah said drily. 'And she's been here once, that's all, and then only to pick fault.'

Nora came bustling into the room. 'John saw the

midwife leave and he's called round to see you home, lass,' she said to Lily.

'He needn't do that.' Lily stared in consternation at John's mother. 'It's not far.'

'Nevertheless, he'll see you back,' Nora said firmly. 'And I'll stay with Sarah until Ralph's home so don't worry about that.'

Lily had no option but to make her way downstairs and she found John waiting in the kitchen. 'It's a girl then,' he said, smiling. 'And bonny, Mam said.'

Lily nodded. He had an overcoat on now, not his work jacket, and it made his big frame look even bigger. His charcoal cap matched the dark off-black colour of the coat and his boots were shining. She hadn't allowed herself to think of him as handsome before, not when he resembled Ralph so strongly, but as he smiled at her now, she thought, he looks different when he smiles, not nearly so much like Ralph. 'They're going to call her Imogen.'

'Imogen?' He considered the name. 'Imogen Turner. Likely she'll be the only one in her class with that name but that's no bad thing. There were three more Johns alongside me.'

'Really? There was another Lily in my class too.'

'Be thankful it was just one. In the end we got labelled John one, John two and so on, in order of our surnames. I felt sorry for John number two. You can imagine some of the nicknames he got landed with.' He made a funny face and Lily giggled, just as the door to the scullery opened and Ralph walked in.

His gaze took in their smiling faces in the moment before Lily's straightened. He looked from one to the

131

other before eyeing his brother through narrowed lids. 'What's going on?'

'Sarah's had the baby, that's what's going on.' It was clear Ralph's tone had needled John. 'Lily called on her way home from work and went and fetched Mam. She's up there now with her.'

Ralph blinked. 'What is it?'

'A little lassie.'

'And Sarah's fine,' Lily put in tartly, pulling on her coat and hat.

As she looked at him he brought a smile to his face. 'Good, good. That's the main thing.'

'I'm taking Lily home.' John took Lily's elbow. 'We'll go out the front way, the back lane's a quagmire.'

'Aye, it is that, and thanks, thanks for helping out, Lily.' Ralph followed them into the hall. 'Come and see Sarah again soon, an' the babbie.'

John turned after opening the front door, obviously feeling he'd been too short with his brother. 'Congratulations, man,' he said, clapping him on the shoulder. 'You're a father.'

Ralph grinned. 'Aye, how about that.'

After shutting the door on them, Ralph didn't immediately run up the stairs to see his wife and child but stood staring down the hall, and he was no longer smiling. It was a full minute before he walked to the foot of the stairs and his jaw was clamped tight, his eyes narrowed slits.

Chapter 9

Lily and John walked in silence down the street. It had stopped raining but the night was cold and blustery, the pavements gleaming greasily in the dim light from the street lamps.

Despite his overcoat which, although bought second-hand, had the name of a London shop inside it and was clearly of excellent quality, John was feeling acutely uncomfortable. He had always told himself he could hold his own with anyone, high or low, but there was something about Lily Brown which took away his natural ease and self-possession. It annoyed and irritated him but the slender young woman at his side had a coolness about her which he found disconcerting. And yet she hadn't been like that with Robert and Hannah and little Larry earlier when she had come round to see to the dinner, he told himself in the next moment. He'd seen a different side to her then. She had laughed with Robert and Hannah and cajoled Larry into eating all his food when the toddler had whined for his mother. She had been all right with his father and David and Francis too, come to it. So he had to assume it was him she didn't like. And Ralph. She'd certainly weighed Ralph up and found him wanting. Perhaps she'd labelled him and his brother as birds of a feather?

He told himself to make conversation but for the life of him he didn't know what to say. When she had been in his mother's kitchen he had wondered what she thought of the general mess and untidiness. It was clean, he emphasised to himself in the next moment, as though someone had challenged this, but nothing like she was used to for sure. When he had first walked in after leaving Ralph's he had been about to try and tidy away before she came. Then he had stopped himself. They were as they were, he'd told himself, and he wasn't ashamed of it. Lily would have to take them as she found them and to hell with it.

Clearing his throat, he said quietly, 'Thanks again for seeing to the dinner. Larry kept asking for you when you'd gone.'

'Did he?' She smiled, clearly pleased. 'He reminds me of Edwin, that's one of the children I look after.'

'How many of them are there?' He didn't really have any interest in knowing but her voice had been warm and he wanted to hear it again.

'Three. Edwin, he's three and as bright as a button. Then Belinda's five and Prudence is seven. They're all lovely, not a bit spoilt, but that's down to their parents.'

He nodded. He had been surprised when he'd learned she was a nurserymaid. He'd put her down for something grander, something more in line with St Bede's Terrace. 'You've got a way with bairns.'

'They know I love them,' she said simply. 'They're so much nicer than adults.'

Her words seemed to agitate her, hot colour flooded her cheeks. He kept his eyes on her as he said, 'You don't rate adults much, then?'

'What? Oh yes, of course. Well, some.' She shrugged, her slim shoulders moving under the thick material of her coat.

He smiled. 'Forgive me for saying so but that didn't sound too enthusiastic to me.'

Lily shrugged again, smiling. 'Children are so honest, aren't they? If they want to be nasty they do it straight in front of you, no soft soap and no pretending. Usually, that is. Animals are the same. I like that.'

John nodded again. Reading between the lines from what he knew of her mother and father, and from the odd thing Ralph had repeated that Sarah had said, he could imagine the Brown household was not a happy one. And yet Ralph had also said that this sister was for the mother which he found difficult to comprehend, having met the woman. 'I know what you mean. I read something the other day about a forest fire somewhere abroad, I forget where now. Apparently when the birds have got young and they know the fire's coming they choose to stay with the fledglings, their wings spread over them to protect them. They know it means certain death for themselves but perhaps they hope their young will survive. I read that and then I looked at some of the bairns down near the docks where I work. Filthy, hungry, thrown out of the house from dawn to dusk to fend for themselves. It makes you wonder, doesn't it?'

'Yes.' Her voice was soft. 'It makes you wonder.'

'Of course the experts would say it's just down to instinct for survival of the species as far as the animal kingdom is concerned, but I don't altogether believe that.'

'Neither do I,' said Lily firmly. 'How does that explain a dog sitting by the grave of his dead master week in, week out, or even pining away? And cows trying to hide their calves because they know they're going to be taken away? Or magpies stealing bright pretty objects simply because they like them? And – oh, loads of things.'

'Exactly.' They smiled at each other.

They had passed the Villette Brick Works while they had been conversing and now as they made their way down Villette Road and into Toward Road, Lily said, 'Sarah tells me you take evening classes in accountancy?'

It was John's turn to flush. Did she think him an upstart? He'd had that thrown at him by more than one person since he'd begun. There were men he worked with, staunch union supporters who would back the working man getting his rightful dues to their last breath, who had taken it almost as a personal insult that he wanted to better himself. They hadn't come right out and said that a working man should always remain a working man and not aim for the white-collar fraternity, but that's what they thought. Rising up through the ranks to become a gaffer at the docks was all right, even if it took a man off the shop floor and into the offices, but not what he was doing. 'Aye,' he said shortly. 'I do.'

'You obviously like working with figures.'

He glanced down at her. The top of her head came to his shoulder, she was such a slender, wisp of a thing, and beautiful. Really quite beautiful. Ridiculously, he felt as though he wanted to say or do something to impress her, to make her look at him with new eyes. The last time he'd felt like that was when he was in short pants and showing off in front of Amy Mullen, a little lassie from a few doors down who had always had the whitest pinafore in the street and a mass of burnished ringlets. He'd come a cropper that day. In swinging round the lamp post higher and faster than anyone else, he'd catapulted off onto his head and promptly brought up his breakfast.

Reminding himself of the ignominy of that day, he said quietly, 'I understand figures, that's all. I always have. And you know where you are with them.' That sounded silly. Hastily, he added, 'They hold no surprises, that's what I mean.'

'I was awful at arithmetic.'

He couldn't imagine her being awful at anything.

'But I loved English, especially English literature. Books and poetry open up new worlds, don't they?'

John smiled. Almost apologetically, he said, 'I'm not much of a one for poetry.'

'You were probably made to feel poetry is for girls.'

He was about to deny this but then realised she was right. Any lad who'd expressed a liking for poetry in his class would have been goaded unmercifully.

'And that is such a shame,' Lily went on, holding onto her hat as a gust of wind threatened to whisk it off her head. 'As bad as the belief that needlework

137

and cooking are only for lassies, and carpentry and metalwork for lads.'

Startled, he said, 'You're not telling me girls would want to do carpentry instead of cooking at school?'

'Why not?' She stopped to face him.

'Because . . .'

They were standing regarding each other now, oblivious of the spots of rain in the wind. 'There, you see?' she said when he faltered. 'There's no good reason for it except that society has decreed men and women must be moulded in a certain way from birth. And if girls *want* to do needlework and cooking, that's fine, and I'm not saying the vast majority wouldn't. But for those who would rather do metalwork or carpentry, why shouldn't they be able to? Likewise, lads shouldn't be made to feel cissies if they've an interest in poetry or cooking or something like that.'

He stared at her. 'I'd be worried if a lad of mine wanted to do needlework.'

'But good tailors can earn plenty of money.'

'That's different.'

'How?'

Flatly, he said, 'This thinking comes from the suffragette movement.'

She gave an impatient exclamation and started walking again so he was forced to fall into step beside her. 'Don't tell me, you're against women having the vote.'

'Actually I'm not. I only think—'

'What?' Her deep green eyes under her felt hat held his. 'What do you think?'

Rattled, he snapped, 'That half of them wouldn't

have a clue how to vote knowing nothing about politics whatsoever. They would simply vote as their menfolk do which defeats the object, surely?'

He expected her to vehemently deny this and was visibly taken aback when she considered his words before replying, 'More than half probably. At first. But that's where education comes in. Once the average working-class woman realises what a precious right they'd have in being able to vote, things would change. *They* would change.'

Drily, John said, 'That's likely why they've been denied the vote so long.'

She surprised him yet again by laughing out loud, and in such a way it brought a smile to his own lips. Then, her face straightening, she said seriously, 'Would *you* feel threatened by women getting the vote?'

'Threatened? No. No, I wouldn't.'

'And do you think women are of inferior intelligence to men?'

They had reached the corner of Toward Road and Gray Road, and as they crossed the latter making for Mowbray Road, a fierce squall of wind almost lifted Lily onto the pavement, causing her to lose her balance. John's hands steadied her and for a moment she lay against his chest, his arms about her and his body shielding hers.

When he released her, her cheeks were pink. His voice gruff, he forced himself to answer her question as though the last moments hadn't happened. 'I think there are intelligent men and women at all levels of society as well as plenty who are not in either camp.'

Had she sensed it? They began walking again.

Had she been aware of that feeling of . . . He found he couldn't put a name to the emotion which had gripped him when he'd held her in his arms. He'd walked out with several girls in his time and a couple had allowed him liberties, but not one of them had induced the trembling excitement the brief touch of her body had. And all he'd done was hold her for a moment.

Lily's head remained down as they made their way along the street. He glanced at her, looking for some recognition of what had transpired, but she didn't raise her eyes. By the time they crossed into Mowbray Road, and St Bede's Terrace stretched before them, he was doubting what had occurred.

She stopped a little way down the street. The houses lay well back from the road and they all had neat front gardens. Although not far from Canon Cockin Street, they could have been in a different world. 'Thank you for seeing me home.'

She spoke like a bairn who had been schooled to be polite. Under any other circumstances it would have made him smile. 'You're welcome.'

'Goodnight.' She held out her hand as she looked at him.

After the merest hesitation he took it. 'Goodnight, Lily. I'm glad all went well with Sarah.'

She opened the garden gate and walked down the path, and he turned and walked a few yards before turning to make sure she was in safely. She was standing in the lighted doorway and she waved. He raised his hand uncertainly and then continued to to walk on, his steady measured pace belying the racing of his heart.

*   *   *

'Where on earth have you been and who was that man? Do you know what time it is?' Lily turned from shutting the door to see her mother walking down the stairs, her face tight.

'I've been with Sarah. She—'

'Don't give me that. I saw you with a man out there.'

'That was John Turner. He walked me home.'

'John Turner?' Her mother was far from mollified. 'Another of the Turners? I don't believe I'm hearing this. Have you gone mad, girl?'

'Sarah had the baby tonight.'

'What?'

'You are a grandmother.' Lily found a certain satisfaction in saying this; she had heard her mother say to her father on one or two occasions that she would not countenance being called grandmother. The child would address her by her name, she had stated. She would insist on it.

Geraldine stared at her daughter, her face working. After a full ten seconds, she said, 'What is it?'

'A little girl.'

'I see.'

Was that all she was going to say? Lily thought. Wasn't she going to ask any details or how Sarah was?

'And why did John Turner have to see you home?'

'He didn't have to. He offered and I accepted.'

'Of course he would offer, girl, don't you see? He's like his brother, trying to worm his way into this family. I don't want you to have anything to do with John Turner. It's bad enough your sister so far forgot herself as to take up with a docker, a common labourer.

141

Did anyone see you with him? Did you meet any of the neighbours outside?'

Quietly, Lily said, 'Don't you want to know how Sarah and the baby are?'

'I presume they are both well or you would have said. Now I repeat, did anyone see you with that man?'

Lily was saved a reply by the front door opening and her father stepping into the hall. His eyes flashing from one to the other, Stanley said, 'What's up?'

'I'll tell you what's "up".' Geraldine glared at her husband. 'John Turner has just walked Lily home. Bold as brass, they were. I saw them from the bedroom window. Thank heavens it's dark outside.'

'Sarah had the baby tonight.' Lily turned towards Stanley. 'A little girl. I called in to see her on my way home and then fetched Nora and the midwife. I stayed to help.'

'Help?' Geraldine's voice was high. 'How could *you* help?'

'Leave it, Geraldine.' Stanley's voice was brusque. 'How're Sarah and the baby?' he said, looking at Lily.

'All right.' Lily was suddenly aware of how tired she was. 'They've called her Imogen.'

'Imogen. There won't be too many lassies with that name, I'll be bound.'

'That's what John said.'

It was too much for Geraldine. 'It's John now, is it?'

Wearily, Lily said, 'It's his name, Mother.'

'Don't you talk to me like that, madam. I had enough of your sister's tongue when she was here. She thought herself a clever little piece too and look how she turned out.'

'I think Sarah's turned out just fine and she's got a bonny little daughter.'

'Born of a Turner.' Geraldine's voice was scathing. 'And she knew full well Mr Henderson had his eye on her because she told me so before she met Ralph.'

Lily pictured Sarah's former boss who was the son of the owner of the jewellery shop where she had been employed. Eustace Henderson could only have been in his twenties but his soft, portly body and white feminine hands emphasised the privileged, cosseted life he'd always enjoyed. 'Sarah would never have looked the side he was on and you know that. She used to laugh about him liking her but that was all. She found him repulsive.'

'The family are extremely well thought of in the town and have several servants.' To Geraldine, that said it all.

Lily caught her father's eye. They exchanged a look that was perhaps the first real moment of understanding between them. It threw Lily into a state of confusion and she got over what felt like a betrayal of her mother by divesting herself of her hat and coat and hanging them on the coat-stand in the hall, saying, 'I'm tired and I'm going to bed.'

She had reached the foot of the stairs when Geraldine's voice came, cold and commanding: 'I want you to promise me you won't have anything to do with John Turner, Lily. Do you hear me? We're already the laughing stock of all our friends.'

The sensible thing to do would have been to comply, especially because she had no intention of starting anything with Ralph's brother, even if John himself had wished it which he had given no indication of. She found John Turner too disturbing and she didn't think he even liked her, let alone anything else.

She turned to face her mother intending to smooth things over for the sake of peace and harmony, but then found herself saying, 'If any of our so-called friends feel like that, then they're hardly our friends, are they? What gives them the right to judge anybody by where they live or what work they do?'

Geraldine stared at her daughter. She was flabbergasted. She knew Lily had a mind of her own, her daughter's unfortunate obstinacy over the matter of her employment when she left school had proved that, but most of the time she knew Lily wanted to please her and therefore bowed to her wishes. This made her stand now even more alarming. 'I'm not prepared to debate things with you,' she said sibilantly. 'Do I have your word you will have nothing to do with this man or not?'

'Geraldine, this is not necessary.'

'Yes it is; it is necessary but as ever you are too stupid to see what is in front of your nose.'

The fury and bitterness in her mother's face as she glared at her father made Lily want to cry out she would agree to what she asked, anything to stop this argument from turning into something worse. But the memory of John Turner's voice as he had spoken about the mother bird and her young and the children he saw around the docks stopped her. Her mother had got the wrong end of the stick regarding herself and John, she could say that, though. Flatly, she said, 'I can assure you Ralph's brother is not going to ask me out but I won't be rude to him if I happen to see him at Sarah's. If the same sort of situation as tonight presented itself again and he offered to see me home safely, I would let him.'

'I see.'

Her mother twirled round in an angry flounce and disappeared into the parlour. Lily stared at her father. Stanley's voice was quiet when he said, 'Go upstairs, go on. I'll see to her. Don't worry about it.'

'He only saw me home to make sure I was all right. I think his mother asked him to do it.'

Stanley nodded. 'I'd do the same. Like I said, don't worry. You know this business with Sarah's got her all worked up.' Again they stared at each other for a long moment before Lily slowly turned and made her way upstairs.

Stanley watched her go, biting his lip. When he walked into the parlour, Geraldine was sitting stabbing at a piece of the needlework she liked to do. She didn't look at him as she said, 'Do you want Lily to be taken advantage of like Sarah? Is that what you want?'

He had his own ideas about what had transpired between his daughter and Ralph from one or two things Sarah had said when she had broken the news she was pregnant. It had been that which had caused him to stay his hand with the man. Rather than go down that road, he sat down in one of the big armchairs close to the fire and kept his voice calm when he said, 'I don't think Lily harbours any feelings for John Turner but if you keep on like this, that could change.'

'Oh really? And you would know, would you? You're so close to her after all.'

'You've seen to it that that's not the case as we both know. Nevertheless, I'm right in this.'

'But you think you're right in everything, Stanley. You always have. Saintly Stanley, champion of the high moral ground.'

Grinding his teeth, he waited a moment before he said, 'This isn't about us, Geraldine. All I'm trying to say is that if you're not careful you'll lose Lily like you've lost Sarah. Do you want that?'

'When has it ever mattered what I want?' she said coldly.

'For crying out loud, woman, listen to me for once. Cut the lass some slack. She's a different kettle of fish to Sarah, can't you see that? Sarah's way of coping with your' – he had been about to say control over her life but, realising this would add fuel to the fire, changed tack – 'with your fears for her was to keep quiet about what she was doing and who she was seeing. And we all know where that led to. Lily's different. If she takes up with a lad then she'll tell us about it.'

'I think I know Lily better than you do,' said Geraldine, her lips folding into a thin line.

Stanley had never had much patience. 'All right, then, have it your own way. Badger the lass to death and see what happens, but I warn you, you'll live to regret it.'

Geraldine continued to apply herself to the needle-work. 'I've regretted many things in my life, Stanley, but none so much as the day I married you.'

146

'Give me strength!' He jumped up, stamping across the room and out of the door.

He didn't slam it as Geraldine had expected. She listened to his footsteps going up the stairs as she let the needlework fall beside her on the sofa. Maybe she had been foolish to challenge Lily in the way she had but she would never admit it to him. But she could quickly gain lost ground with her daughter. She would squeeze out a tear or two tomorrow when she and Lily were alone. One thing was for sure, she thought, her mouth tightening, she would not tolerate another breath of scandal in this house. If there was anything going on with John Turner she would make sure it was swiftly nipped in the bud. She had worked too hard to become a member of the Ashbrooke bridge club and gain prominence in several little social happenings in the district to have it spoilt by another daughter making a disastrous match. She knew eyebrows had been raised by one or two of her acquaintances when Sarah had married a docker. It wouldn't happen again. Not while she had breath in her body.

Upstairs in her room, Lily had not begun to get ready for bed but sat with her hands in her lap staring across the expanse in front of her. She missed Sarah. How she missed her. But little Imogen was so bonny. Sarah was a mother now. She and Ralph had a daughter. Would that change him? Something needed to happen because Sarah wasn't happy.

Her thoughts continued to whirl and dance but after a few minutes she knew she had to face the thing she had been trying to keep at the back of her mind. John Turner had put his arms about her and held her close. All right, it was only because she had stumbled, but nevertheless it had happened and it had made her feel . . . odd.

Her cheeks scarlet, she shook her head at herself. She was daft, silly, it had only been for a moment and he clearly hadn't thought anything of it. Why would he? Sarah had told her he'd had lassies, likely he was walking out with someone now. He was a good-looking man, after all. And nice. Nicer than she had thought. But they seemed destined to forever rub each other up the wrong way.

He didn't like her. She jumped up and walked across to the window, staring out into the darkness. And that was her fault. They hadn't got off to a very good start at Sarah's wedding. She gnawed on her bottom lip for a moment before muttering, 'Oh, what does it matter anyway?'

It didn't matter. She wasn't likely to run into John Turner above once or twice a year, if that. This was the first time she had seen him since the wedding after all.

She stood for a little while longer before turning from the window, and when she walked across to the bed to begin undressing, the corners of her mouth were drooping.

PART THREE

February 1908 – Trouble Begets Trouble

Chapter 10

'I'm sorry, Bruce, but in this alone I do feel the end justifies the means. Of course I don't agree with violence but it's the authorities who provoke it every time. Look at the clashes with the police last year. Women were marching peacefully through the streets and mounted police rode into them, it's a wonder no one was killed. The Finnish parliament gave women the vote two years ago and now there are women MPs. It *has* to happen in Britain and America.'

'I couldn't agree more, but all I'm saying is that the cause isn't helped by suffragettes chanting slogans and hurling insults at Asquith and assaulting police and goodness knows what. They will simply be labelled hysterical females. You know that as well as I do.'

'But peaceful measures are getting us nowhere.' Ellen's voice reflected her frustration. 'And Emmeline Pankhurst is far from being a hysterical female, as you well know. She's a formidable and highly intelligent woman who is fighting for the right to have a voice in her own country. I wish I lived in London. I'd be right there beside her.'

'I'm glad you don't.'

Bruce's voice was so heartfelt, Lily had to smile. She had been listening to the heated exchange of views for some time, ever since Ellen had read out Emmeline Pankhurst's inside view of the misery of prison life. The leading suffragette had been imprisoned on charges of obstruction and given a six-week jail sentence, and in a letter from her bleak cell had written graphically on the meagre rations, the coarse clothing with its convict's arrows, the stark surroundings and the despair of her fellow inmates, 'all so weak and feeble and sad'.

Ellen, catching her smile, said forcefully, 'Don't encourage him, Lily. Bruce persists in thinking of me as the fragile little woman whatever I tell him to the contrary.'

'Not at all.' Bruce glared at the woman he loved with all his heart. 'No one could call you fragile, Ellen. You have a will of steel and a heart to match. I'm off home.' He stood up. 'And I still say your suffragettes are in danger of making themselves ridiculous. That last escapade of trying to enter the Commons by concealing themselves, Trojan horse-style, in a large furniture van was downright farcical and you know it. Goodnight, Lily.'

'Goodnight, Bruce.'

After Ellen had showed Bruce out and returned to the sitting room, Lily said quietly, 'You know he's fully in agreement with women having the vote, Ellen. Why do you rile him so?'

'I don't—' Ellen stopped abruptly, sinking down

into the chair she had vacated moments earlier. Shaking her head, she glanced at Lily. 'I suppose I think he's too good to be true.'

'Bruce?'

'Yes, Bruce. He's so gentle and kind and . . . and good.'

'But that's what he is, Ellen. Why can't you just accept he's a nice man?'

'I thought my husband was a nice man.'

Ever since the evening when Lily had come back to Ellen's house, thereby beginning a friendship which had strengthened week by week, Ellen had not spoken of her marriage again. Hesitantly, Lily said, 'Bruce isn't like your husband, Ellen.'

'How do you know? How does anyone really know anyone else? Steven appeared to be a caring, kind individual. Butter wouldn't have melted in his mouth before we were married.'

'Bruce really loves you, Ellen.'

'I thought Steven really loved me. Everyone said we were the perfect match, my parents were ecstatic, and all my friends were envious.' Ellen shook her head. 'I was so stupid in those days.'

'But you're not now.' Lily reached out and clasped her friend's hands. 'You were still a girl then, you're a woman now.'

Ellen smiled. 'There speaks Methuselah,' she said, but not unkindly. 'The thing is, I don't think I could survive another mistake, Lily. I'm more fragile than Bruce thinks. I can cope with people like Beatrice and Quentin being cruel, they don't matter, but Bruce . . . He does matter.'

'Bruce hasn't got a cruel bone in his body. You must know that? Must sense it?'

'My daughter was denied the right to live.' Ellen's voice was flat. 'She should be growing up, laughing, talking, learning new things. She should have had a mother to tuck her into bed at night and protect her, to keep her safe. But her mother let her down in the worst possible way.'

'You don't really believe that?' Lily was aghast. 'Ellen, you were totally innocent in all that.'

'I made a mistake in marrying Steven but it was my daughter who paid for it. I can still enjoy life, feel, see, hear, but she – she's in a little white casket under the ground –'

'No.' Lily shook Ellen's hands. 'No, she isn't. She's in a better place, Ellen. You have to believe that. And you'll see her again one day, you'll be able to hold her then, love her, kiss her.'

'I wish I could believe that.' Ellen gently pulled her hands from Lily's, standing up and walking over to the fire. 'I really do,' she said, staring down into the flames. 'I used to believe in heaven and hell before I got married. My parents were churchgoers. Every Sunday morning and then eventide we'd go to the Church of England church where all their friends went. I accepted it all without really thinking about it. I accepted a lot of things in those days. But after my marriage when I prayed and prayed for the beatings and other things to stop . . .' She lifted tragic eyes to Lily's. 'I think I lost my faith when I lost my daughter.'

Lily didn't know what to say.

'I suppose you've guessed Bruce has asked me to marry him?' Ellen went on, turning and staring into the fire again. 'But I couldn't, Lily. I shall never marry again. It's a farce. How could I marry in the sight of a God I don't believe in and why would I trust myself to any man like that again? I – I don't want to shock you but I've told Bruce he can have all the advantages of marriage but without formalising it.'

'You haven't shocked me,' Lily said quietly.

'He wouldn't hear of it.' Ellen shrugged. 'And so we go on as friends. I suppose one day he will meet a woman he can love who will feel the same way as he does about things.'

'I doubt it,' Lily said soberly. 'I think you under-estimate him, Ellen.'

'Perhaps, but far better that than finding out behind closed doors you've married a monster. I believe in me now. Only me.'

'Well, he's still around. That has to mean some-thing.'

'But for how long will he be around? He's a young man. It is only natural he'll want a wife and family eventually. I – I'm prepared for that, I've told him so.'

'What did he say?'

Ellen smiled sadly, turning to face Lily. 'He said he knows one day we'll stand before God and man and be pronounced man and wife. When – when I'm restored in spirit as well as in body. He said he has faith enough for both of us till then.'

'I think you're very fortunate to have the love of a man like Bruce.' Lily stood to her feet. 'I ought to be going too, Ellen. Thank you for a lovely meal.'

'You're welcome. I love cooking for the pair of you.'

None of them had returned to the discussion group since the day of Beatrice's outburst. Instead Lily and Bruce had an evening meal with Ellen every Friday. They discussed a wide variety of topics. Or perhaps it would be fairer to say Bruce and Ellen conversed most of the time, and Lily listened, feeling woefully inadequate to express a view on the majority of subjects.

But she was learning plenty, she told herself in the next moment. And certainly the talk in Ellen's little sitting room was franker and more impassioned than anything which had been said at the library. She'd never realised how blinkered she was about so many things till she had become friendly with Ellen. The fight of the suffragettes, wider issues of social injustice, the trouble in Ireland, and the traditional values and practices of the Church were just a few of the subjects which were regularly chewed over. Ellen and Bruce seemed to know so much about the arts too, including controversial individuals like Oscar Wilde and Bernard Shaw. Sometimes she felt her mind wasn't so much being broadened as inflated to bursting point.

After waving goodbye, Lily picked her way along the icy, frost-covered pavements, slipping and sliding a few times on the way home. She could have waited for a tram, the February night was bitterly cold and there was the smell of snow in the keen north-east wind, but she'd developed a muzzy headache during the evening and felt like a walk to blow away the cobwebs.

It was a relief to be able to walk freely without

wading through thick snow. All over Christmas and well into the New Year there had been snowstorm after snowstorm, but a thaw the week before had cleared the last of it for the time being. It had been a funny Christmas, Lily reflected, drawing the crisp, biting air up through her nose as if inhaling a scent. She had been glad the Grays had asked her to work on Boxing Day; usually she had two days off but they had been having a big party for friends and family and had needed her to take care of the children. Sarah had been invited to her in-laws and so she and her parents had spent Christmas Day alone, although her father had gone for a long walk after lunch and hadn't returned till late evening. Boxing Day had been very different; the Grays' house had been filled with noise and laughter.

On New Year's Eve she had called to see Sarah but had only spent an hour or so with her sister and niece. Ralph had been there, and John and the rest of the family had arrived as she was leaving. She had only said a couple of words to them as she'd been anxious to get away. Ralph had been acting the big fellow now he had taken over Vickers's boatyard and his talk and boasting had sickened her. She had gone to see her grandma and granda Brown and had spent the evening with them. She knew the old couple had appreciated the company but part of her mind had kept returning to Sarah's; to her sister's strained face and brittle cheerfulness, Ralph's bumptiousness and the look in his eyes every time they'd met hers, and then there had been John. If she was honest, seeing John again had bothered her the most.

Lily walked steadily on, taking care not to turn her ankle on the white frosty pavements. She couldn't afford to be laid low at the moment. Mrs Gray had just discovered she was expecting another child in the autumn and was relying heavily on her. This pregnancy was not going well and some days the sickness was so acute Mrs Gray could barely get out of bed.

By the time she reached Mowbray Park her head was clearer. Because she was concentrating hard on where she trod, Lily only raised her eyes to give a cursory glance at the white frozen trees in the park as she walked along the perimeter path. Consequently she was unaware of the male figure standing deep in the black shadows at the end of the park and had passed where he stood to cross the road which led into St Bede's Terrace when a voice behind her brought her swinging round.

'Well, well, well. Fancy running into you the night.'

Ralph was standing a few yards away, his long dark overcoat and matching cap making him almost impossible to discern till he stepped out into the light of a gas lamp. Lily drew in a deep breath; he had startled her and her heart was racing. Aiming to keep any trace of how she was feeling from her voice, she said quietly, 'Hello, Ralph. I didn't see you.'

'You ought to be careful, wandering about by yourself late at night. Where have you been, anyway?'

She stared at him. She hadn't told anyone she had stopped attending the discussion group at the library. Quite why, she wasn't sure. No, that was silly, she was sure, she corrected herself. With her parents it had been to prevent the host of questions which would inevitably lead to her mother forbidding her to see Ellen, once she knew of Beatrice's accusations. She hadn't mentioned the matter to Sarah because she didn't want Ralph knowing her business. It was as simple as that.

She was still wondering what to say when he spoke again. 'Oh, I forgot.' He smiled, taking a step or two towards her. 'Friday is your night at the library, isn't it?'

He'd known that all along. He wasn't here by accident. He had been waiting for her. How long had he been hiding in the shadows?

'Good meeting, was it?' he drawled softly.

Again instinct warned her Sarah's husband knew she hadn't been at the discussion group. Which could only mean he had been there, or had at least been waiting outside for her to leave. As the knowledge hit her, she forced herself to shrug nonchalantly. 'I didn't go to the meeting tonight as it happens.'

As she was speaking a tram trundled into view, stopping close to where they were standing. She realised from his position in the shadows he would have been able to see anyone leaving the tram without them seeing him. A shiver snaked down her spine.

A man and woman exited the tram and walked off in the opposite direction. Lily took the opportunity to say evenly, 'Goodnight, then. Give my love to Sarah.'

'Not so fast.' As she began to walk he fell into step beside her. 'You didn't answer my question. Where have you been?'

It was on the tip of her tongue to tell him to mind his own business, but she didn't want a row if it could be avoided. Aiming for a normality which pretended they had just happened to bump into each other, she said, 'With a friend.'

'A friend.'

She was now just yards away from home. It gave her the confidence to say coolly, 'I do have friends, you know.'

'I bet you do.' Before she could retort, he added, 'Male or female? As if I didn't know.'

She wasn't having this. The desire for pacification went out of the window. 'That's nothing to do with you.'

'I think it is. I'm family, remember?'

'You are Sarah's husband, related by marriage only.'

'Don't look at me like that.' He gripped her fiercely by the shoulders. 'I'm every bit as good as you.'

Lily stood perfectly still. 'Let go of me,' she said icily. Anger had replaced fright. In fact, she couldn't remember ever being so angry in her life. There had been a girl at school who had tried to bully her and she had reacted in the same way then. It had resulted in a wild, feral fight but although Fanny Kirby had been bigger and heavier than her, she had held her own and the girl had never touched her again.

Ralph stared into the furious green gaze. Reluctantly he released her. He was breathing hard, his eyes had narrowed to slits and his chest was moving up and down as though worked by bellows. 'Who were you with?' he said again. 'What's his name? I know it wasn't our John because I've been round there this evening and he's at his books.'

She said nothing, staring at him defiantly. Now he

had let go of her she had begun trembling, but she was determined not to let him see it.

Suddenly, his whole manner undergoing a rapid change, he said, 'Lily, Lily, I'm sorry. Look, I can't help it. You've got under me skin somehow, from the first moment I laid eyes on you . . .' He drew in a succession of short, sharp breaths. 'If I'd seen you first, if me an' Sarah hadn't been in a fix, would you have gone out with me? I need to know.'

Lily couldn't believe her ears. She had the urge to turn and run from him, to fly into the house, but she knew that would serve no useful purpose. This thing wouldn't be dealt with by showing weakness. 'No, I wouldn't.'

'You're just saying that because of Sarah.'

'Your wife is my sister.' Her voice was rising and she checked it. 'She deserves so much better than you. And I wouldn't have gone out with you if you'd been the last man on earth.'

'Shut up.' His voice came in a low growl from between his tightened lips.

'No, I won't shut up. You've got the best wife in the world and a bonny daughter, and yet you can say what you've just said to me. You're scum, pure scum.' As he raised his fist, she stood firm. 'You dare, you just dare and I'll have the law on you. I swear it.' She returned his glare without blinking, her body as straight as a die.

After a long moment his hand dropped back to his side. 'I'll see me day with you, Lily Brown.'

'I'm not frightened of you but I tell you this, you try something like tonight again and I'll go to Sarah and your mam and da and everyone else. I swear it.'

'You're all wind and water.'

'Try me. Just try me.'

His eyes were like chips of black lead but she didn't falter. It wasn't till he turned and began walking away that she felt her legs were going to give way. She stood quite still till he had turned the corner and disappeared. Her limbs felt heavy, almost as heavy as her heart which was crying for her sister. They had been everything to each other throughout their childhood, supporting each other through thick and thin and creating their own little world which their parents couldn't impinge on. And now Sarah had gone from the frying pan into the fire because anything, *anything* else would have been better than her marrying Ralph Turner.

Slowly she made her way home, her eyes dry but every pore of her body weeping. It wasn't till much later she recalled Ralph's mention of John and when she thought about it, that disturbed her more than ever.

Chapter 11

Nora Turner sat back on her heels and surveyed her handiwork. She had just finished cleaning and black-leading the kitchen range with the blacklead which came in blocks like soap. She kept it in a jam jar, pouring water over it and working at it to produce a paste which she brushed on the stove, polishing it till it met with her satisfaction. It was a messy job and one which she often put off. When Cissy and Florence had been at home it had been one of their Saturday morning chores to blacklead the range, but although Nora had attempted to pass this task on to Hannah, the result was so poor she usually ended up doing it herself when she had a little spare time.

Shaking her head now at the thought of her youngest daughter, whom Nora considered as skittish as a newborn lamb and with as little sense, she began to polish the steel-topped and brass-tailed fender. That finished, she rose to her feet, and once the fire was blazing put the big black kettle on the hob for one of the count-less pots of tea she consumed throughout the day.

Once the tea was mashed she poured herself a cup, sitting down at the kitchen table and rubbing her knees which were aching. It was rare she had a few minutes all to herself, but with the rest of the family at work or school, Larry having started after Christmas at the Methodist infants', the place was quiet for once.

Outside the house was a white, hushed world. It had begun to snow the day before and hadn't stopped since. Still, she comforted herself, it was April now; they wouldn't have more than a few weeks of it even if it was bad. It wasn't like it was November and they had the whole winter stretching in front of them. She hated the winters. It wasn't so much the snow and cold; when it was really frozen she could stand that, in spite of having to go to bed with layer upon layer on and being unable to see out of the window for the thick ice coating it. No, it was the slush and mud that came with the frequent brief thaws that drove her barmy. The back lanes made their way into her kitchen however much she told her lot to wipe their feet in the scullery.

She was on her third cup of tea when she heard the back door open and a voice call, 'Hello, Mam.'

'Sarah.' As her daughter-in-law opened the door from the scullery, Nora rose to her feet, her arms reaching for the baby in Sarah's arms. 'By, lass, what are you doing out the day? It's enough to freeze your lugs off out there.'

'I wanted some company. You don't mind?'

'Mind, hinny? You know me better than that. Sit yourself down and have a cup of tea, an' there're some fresh teacakes in that tin.'

As Sarah took off her hat and coat and sat down at the table, Nora divested her granddaughter of her little coat and woolly bobble-hat, talking to her all the time. Imogen gave one of her toothless smiles in return. 'She's a bonny babbie, lass, an' those eyes of hers. Our Ralph'll have to fight the lads off in droves when she's older, you mark my words.'

Sarah smiled, but it was a strained smile. Nora waited a moment till her daughter-in-law had poured herself a cup of tea, then said quietly, 'You all right, lass?'

'Me? Aye, yes, I suppose so.'

'I'm not convinced.'

'Oh we've had a couple of bad nights with Imogen, I think she's teething. Ralph – well, he gets a bit impatient with her when she can't sleep but it's not her fault. Normally she's as good as gold.'

'Oh aye, I know. He ought to have had one like our John. Three or four hours a night was all he needed, right from when he was born. It wasn't so bad once he could read, mind. He used to go through umpteen candles, reading to himself in bed when the rest of us were asleep. I should have known then how bright he was going to be. It's not many bairns that can read before they're five, is it? Not round these doors, leastways. Always had to be reading or drawing or doing something, our John. Drove me scatty, he did, little devil.'

Nora's tone couldn't quite conceal the pride she felt in her offspring. Sarah smiled. She had come to love this little woman in a way she never had her own mother. But Nora's unswerving loyalty and affection for her own was the very thing which made it impossible for her to confide in her mother-in-law now. Her fingers unconsciously touched the bruises under the sleeve of her blouse. Ralph's violence when he had gripped her and almost thrown her out of bed the night before, demanding she shut Imogen up, had both frightened and shocked her. She knew he could be rough at times, and since their marriage she had learned he had little patience, but last night he had been different. He had acted as though he hated the pair of them.

The tears she had shed all morning pricked behind her eyes again, and quickly she said, 'She's been trying to sit up by herself; I think she's going to be ever so forward, and she smiles all the time.'

'Aye, you do, don't you, me bairn.' Nora beamed at the baby. 'And why wouldn't you, eh, with a lovely mam an' da an' a grand little home like you've got? I tell you, lass' – she turned to Sarah – 'our Ralph won't rest till he's got you a place like your da's but in the meantime he's turning that house into a palace. I know for a fact no one else hereabouts has got a proper carpet in their front room and a brand new three-piece an' china cabinet an' all. Picture, your house looks.'

There wasn't a trace of jealousy in Nora's voice. Sarah stared at the homely lined face that bore evidence of the countless sacrifices her mother-in-law had made for her family through the years. Ralph had told her his mother had taken in washing all her married life to make ends meet, as well as doing cleaning a few days a week at some of the big houses in Ryhope Way. It had only been when the twins had begun work that some of Nora's load had been lessened. Ralph's mother couldn't be more different to her own, Sarah thought. Impulsively she leaned forward and kissed Nora on the cheek. 'I don't know what I'd do without you,' she said softly.

'Aw, hinny.' Nora was both embarrassed and pleased and, to hide both emotions, she passed Imogen over to Sarah, saying, 'I'd better get started on the dinner. If I know anything about it they'll all come in with their stomachs thinking their throats have been cut.'

'Can I help?'

'No, lass, no. You sit an' take the load off for a while. We'll have another pot of tea once I've got the cow heel pie on. Lovely bit of black pudding I got to put with the cow heel and stewing steak. Do you put a bit of black pudding in yours?'

'I have done since you told me.' Nora had told her so much about so many things right from the first day of her married life. Sarah hadn't realised how ignorant she was about running a home. Hers had been such a cold, sterile upbringing in comparison to Ralph's; here love and warmth oozed out of the very bricks. She had said the same to Ralph a few nights ago when he had been derogatory about his former home. She hated it when he talked that way, but he was doing it more and more since he'd taken on the boatyard. Oh, that boatyard . . .

The kitchen was warm and cosy, the glow from the fire giving the room a rosy softness. The leaden sky and snow outside had made it darker than usual but Sarah knew her mother-in-law wouldn't light the gas for some time yet.

She watched Nora transfer the stewing steak and the cow heel — now devoid of all bones after its boiling the day before — to a pie dish, thickening the gravy and then adding three slices of black pudding before putting in a pastry funnel and covering the dish with pastry. Although her eyes followed her mother-in-law's deft movements, her mind was miles away.

Ralph had insisted he had bought the boatyard outright, he had shown her the documents with his name on it, but she still could hardly believe he'd had enough salted away for it and not let on to her. When she'd got upset, he'd admitted some business he'd been involved in after work had come up trumps. She knew what that meant and had said no more. It was only a small boatyard, with repair shops and woodyards and other equally modest businesses running alongside it, but he intended to build it up, he had told her. And already he seemed to be doing well, so well there were more notes being added weekly to the old oak trunk under their bed. And week by week he had got more full of himself and what he was going to do, more overbearing and testy.

Imogen had fallen asleep and unconsciously Sarah stroked the baby's velvet forehead, listening to Nora's chatter and putting in the odd word now and again when it was required, but with a part of her mind functioning on a different plane altogether. Marriage wasn't what she had thought it would be. *Ralph* wasn't what she'd thought he would be. And she didn't know what to do. Before last night she would never have thought she'd actually be frighened of Ralph . . .

When Hannah and Larry came bursting into the

kitchen from school they woke Imogen up, and after a few minutes Sarah stood up, putting on her own hat and coat and then dressing the baby. 'I need to put the pot pie on,' she said to Nora when her mother-in-law tried to persuade her to stay a little longer. That was true enough, but for some reason the normal sense of comfort and belonging she got in Nora's kitchen was absent today. This feeling was intensified when, as she left, her mother-in-law pressed a piece of seed cake on her.

'Put that in Ralph's packin' up tomorrow, lass. I know he likes a bit of seed cake, bless him. He's such a good lad.'

'I will, Mam.' How could she ever confide her fears to Nora? She couldn't. And with this realisation the weight on her heart became heavier. Nora, loving Ralph as she did, would have been the only person she could talk to because she wouldn't have felt she was betraying Ralph to her, but it was that same love Nora felt for her son which prevented her saying anything.

When she walked into her own kitchen she placed the baby in the wooden playpen they had bought a little while ago, propping her up with cushions and giving her a rattle to hold. She had prepared the pot pie before she had left earlier, and now she put it on to steam and then sat down at the kitchen table. Her eyes wandered round the room which was as bright as a new pin. Everything in the kitchen was new; in the last months since he had bought the boatyard Ralph had replaced anything they had bought second-hand when they had married. A dark wood dresser held their crockery which now all matched and had an attractive blue willow pattern painted on it. Two fine china dogs graced either side of the mantelpiece above the range, and in the middle of these a sturdy wood and brass clock ticked away the minutes. Two armchairs with plump red and blue cushions sat either side of the range and between these a blue and red rug – a thick shop-bought rug, not a clippy mat – reposed. Everything looked bright and cheerful, from the spotless white-painted walls to the pretty curtains at the window which were gathered and tied cottage-style. And so it was through the rest of the house, even Imogen's room had a large square of carpet on the floor and a new wardrobe and chest of drawers.

She was lucky. Sarah fought back the desire to lay her head on her arms and cry again. She was very lucky. She had to remember that.

A knock at the back door followed by her father's voice calling her name brought her head turning. Since Stanley's first tentative visit on his way home from work one night just after she had got married, he had taken to dropping in at least once or twice a week, something they both enjoyed. It had shocked Sarah to discover she hadn't had any idea of what her father was really like all the years she had lived at home. Her mother had called at the house just once, shortly after Imogen had been born. The visit had not been a success.

'Hello, lass.' Stanley's smile hid the fact he was worried about his daughter. She wasn't the happy-go-lucky girl who had lived under his roof, nor the feisty young woman who had been determined to marry

Ralph, come what may. Having lived in a state of misery with Geraldine for so long he thought he knew where Sarah's problem lay, but he had hesitated to do anything to spoil their burgeoning relationship by rushing in where angels feared to tread.

'Da.' Sarah had sprung up and now she said, 'Come and warm yourself by the fire while I get you a cup of tea. It's bitter out, isn't it?' She fussed round him, taking his coat and cap before putting the kettle on to boil.

Stanley had reached down and picked up Imogen, who had gurgled at the sight of him, before sitting in one of the armchairs with the child on his knee. 'She gets more bonny every time I see her. You're going to be a beauty like your mam, aren't you, hinny?' he cooed to the baby. 'Bonny as a summer's morning.'

It always brought a funny kind of ache into Sarah's chest when she saw her father with his grandchild. He clearly had a way with children and little Imogen adored him, and yet he had been such a distant figure when she and Lily were growing up. But she knew who she had to blame for that, she thought grimly. She'd had her eyes opened with a vengeance the last twelve months.

The thought prompted her to say something which had been on her mind for some time. 'Why did you marry Mam, Da?'

'What?' Stanley looked at her with startled eyes.

'Mam. Why did you marry her? I can't imagine she was so very different to what she is now. She's led you the life of a dog from the word go from what I can make out.'

Stanley didn't know how to answer his daughter. After a moment or two, he said, 'There're faults on both sides, lass. Make no mistake about that. I'm no saint.'

Sarah shrugged impatiently. 'I'm not saying you are. Who is? But she – she's cruel.'

'There're all different kinds of cruelty, lass, and I'm guilty of that an' all.'

'Oh, don't try to stick up for her.' The kettle was boiling and Sarah turned sharply, reaching for the big brown teapot which she had placed to warm on the steel shelf by the hob. Her movements jerky, she measured three spoonfuls of tea from the caddy into the pot and poured on the boiling water, taking it across to the table to mash.

Stanley had stood up and placed Imogen back in her play pen. Now, as Sarah went to move to the dresser for cups and saucers, he stopped her by putting his hands gently on her shoulders. 'What's the matter, hinny?'

The warm northern endearment coming from his lips was too much for Sarah's shaky equilibrium. To the surprise of both of them she burst into tears. For a moment Stanley hesitated, wondering if she would push him away if he attempted to comfort her. Growing up, Sarah and Lily had been stiff and un-responsive if he had attempted to hug or kiss them and for years he hadn't tried. Diffidently he put his arms round his child and when Sarah fell against him, her arms going round his waist, he took in a long, slow breath. 'There, there, lass. It's all right, it's all right. Come on, hinny, don't cry like that. Nothing can be that bad.'

'I've made a terrible mistake, Da.'

He didn't try to prevaricate. 'Do you want to talk about it, lass?' he said, as she drew back to look up at him.

Sarah gulped, her face awash with tears. 'It won't do any good. I've made my bed and I've got to lie on it, isn't that what they say?'

'Whoever "they" are, they're talking out of their backsides.' He made himself say the thing that had been on his mind for weeks. 'Does he hurt you, lass? He hasn't started knocking you about, has he?'

She shook her head. She could say in all truthfulness he didn't do that. 'No.' She leaned against him again. 'No, he's never hit me. I suppose most people would say I don't know when I'm well off. He's earning more than anyone else around here and he doesn't drink it down the drain like some. And he's ambitious, he's set his mind on rising in the world. I – I don't want for anything.'

'But you're not happy.'

'No, I'm not happy.'

As her shoulders began to shake again, Stanley pushed his daughter down onto a chair then knelt in front of her, taking her hands in his. 'Tell me,' he said softly.

Sarah looked into the kind blue eyes. For years she had been made to believe this man was a monster and she hated her mother for that. 'There's not much to tell,' she said weakly. 'Like I said, he provides for us well and I only have to ask for extra housekeeping and it's there. But . . .'

'But?'

'He's hardly ever here, for one thing. There seems to be business going on at the yard most nights till the early hours. And he's changed over the last months, Da. He's got cocky and awkward and so cold. He's not interested in Imogen. Maybe if she'd been a boy it would be different, I don't know. If his mam's here he'll play happy families, but it's all a front. Sometimes – sometimes I think he wants shot of us.'

'Look, lass, it's early days after Imogen. Your mother was low for months after you.'

'Oh, Mam.' Sarah shook her head. 'She's never known when she's well off. If Ralph was like you I'd be counting my blessings.'

Stanley felt as though he'd just had burning coals heaped upon his head. He didn't want to do anything to jeopardise his child's changed feelings for him, but he knew he had to come clean. If Sarah found out at a later date about Sally it would be ten times worse than telling her now, face to face. Standing up, he said quietly, 'Sit there, I'll get the cups and we'll have a sup. There's something I need to explain to you, lass, and now is as good a time as any.'

Sarah sat quite still as he began to talk and by the time he had finished Stanley had succeeded in taking her mind off her own troubles. She stared at him without speaking for some moments, her mind trying to assimilate what she had been told. 'You – you say things weren't right between you and Mam from before Lily was born; what went wrong, exactly?'

'I can't tell you that.' He had made the decision he would never breathe a word of it to anyone but Sally. 'But it was no small thing and all I can say is that I don't believe it was my fault. I've made lots of mistakes with your mother since then, lass, I hold my hands up for that, and maybe I should have asked for a divorce as soon as Sally and I got together, but you and Lily were young lassies by then and the stigma . . .'

Divorce. Sarah's eyes widened for a moment. She didn't know anyone who had been divorced, it just didn't happen. It would be as bad as a lass being taken down and bringing a bastard into the world. 'Does – does Mam know about her?' She couldn't bring herself to say the woman's name. Not that she blamed her da in a way; she didn't, how could she, knowing what her mother was like? But still . . .

Stanley shook his head, his eyes fixed on Sarah's face. 'I don't think so. Times I've wished she'd suspect something and ask me outright, but no, I don't think she rates me highly enough to have another woman in love with me. And it is love, Sarah. Whatever you might be thinking, I love Sally and she loves me. I was bedazzled by your mother and cast Sally aside and for that I'll be sorry to me dying day because we should have been wed all along. She – she's the other part of me. That's how it is.'

A mixture of emotions held Sarah silent. When Stanley dropped his head, looking down at his big hands on his knees, and said, 'I'm sorry, lass. Not about Sally, exactly, she's the light of my life and I'm not ashamed to say it, but to have to tell you this, me own daughter. I know it's not right. If – if you can't forgive me I wouldn't blame you.' She drew in a long shuddering breath. When her hand came out and covered one of his, Stanley lifted his eyes to her face. 'I'm sorry,' he said again, his voice thick.

'It's all right, Da.' It wasn't all right; she was feeling as though nothing would ever be right again. As her father had talked about this other woman and the depth of his feeling for her, she had known her own marriage had been a sham from the start. She didn't love Ralph, not in the way her father loved this Sally, and he didn't love her. She knew that now. In fact, she didn't think he even liked her these days. But they would remain married. Suddenly the years stretching ahead of her seemed unbearable. And when she found herself in her father's arms again, she didn't know if her tears were for him or for herself.

A week later she found she was pregnant again.

Chapter 12

The summer was a long hot one. For some time after the acrimonious scene with her brother-in-law, Lily found herself frequently looking over her shoulder. This passed, but the nasty incident had put her on her guard. She no longer walked home alone but made sure she travelled by tram. When she thought about it, it rankled that she felt obliged to do this, but she told herself she had to be sensible and it would be sheer foolishness to purposely put herself in possible harm's way.

She had continued to visit her sister but had only seen Ralph once or twice. According to Sarah, Ralph almost lived at his boatyard these days. More by what her sister didn't say than what she did, Lily felt things were not good between the couple. When she tried to talk to Sarah about the situation her sister refused to be drawn, only once saying enough for Lily to suspect Sarah was resigned to her lot. Lily was worried about her sister but she surmised if Sarah was expecting another baby the relationship with her husband couldn't be all bad. And Imogen was a happy, healthy child who grew more like her mother every day. With Sarah seemingly determined to make the best of things, Lily felt she could do nothing. Certainly she had more than enough to occupy her time. It had transpired Mrs Gray was expecting twins and the pregnancy was a difficult one. Consequently the Grays relied on her more heavily than before and she didn't want to let them down.

In June, Ellen, accompanied by a determined Bruce, travelled to London to attend the capital's largest ever suffragette demonstration. Huge crowds jammed Hyde Park and two hundred thousand supporters turned out. Ellen returned home flushed with enthusiasm to further the cause in the north-east. The long hours Lily worked prevented her from attending many meetings of the Sunderland branch of the Women's Social and Political Union, but on the few occasions she went along with Ellen she was amazed at the passion and resolution of those present. Throughout the summer constant clashes between the suffragettes and the police and those in authority in the capital were reported, and the women's fight for recognition was a topic on everyone's lips. In view of this it was perhaps not surprising that one evening in late October Lily found herself standing in front of Mr and Mrs Gray defending the cause. When she thought about it afterwards, she realised it was more surprising the matter had not reared its head before that day.

The conversation had begun innocently enough. She had gone to the drawing room to report that the children were asleep, as she did every night before joining Molly and Bridget in the kitchen, sometimes just to change into her outdoor things and leave for home, but other times to share an evening meal with the two women. After knocking on the door and having been told to come in, she heard Mr Gray reading an article from his newspaper to his wife who had her swollen legs up on the chaise longue. The twins were now a week overdue and Arabella Gray was finding each day a trial.

'Imprisoning them again is just making them martyrs,' Norman Gray said irritably. 'Why can't the Government see that?'

Arabella did not reply to this, turning her head to Lily who was standing just inside the door. She smiled as she said, 'Mr Gray does not agree with the verdict regarding Emmeline Pankhurst and her daughter, Lily. I dare say you are aware of the case?'

Everyone was aware of the case. The trial of the two women had been sensational and had even seen two cabinet ministers in the witness box for the defence at Bow Street Court. Emmeline and Christabel had been charged with conduct likely to cause a breach of the peace by inciting the public to rush the House of Commons, but even the two reluctant witnesses from the cabinet – the Chancellor of the Exchequer and the Home Secretary – had attested to the order-liness of the night of 13 October, as had a succession of others. One woman had said she'd been more jostled at society weddings. Mr Gladstone, however, had adamantly resisted the women's pleas that they be treated as political prisoners.

'Disgraceful, the whole business.' Norman Gray did

not wait for a comment from his nurserymaid but again addressed his wife, his handsome face flushed with righteous indignation. 'Don't know what the country's coming to when educated, well-bred women like Emmeline behave in such an undignified fashion.'

Lily swallowed. She knew she was not expected to proffer an opinion. The Grays were kind and quite liberal employers who took an interest in the welfare and happiness of their servants, but, nevertheless, the dividing line between those who served and those who were served was very clear. 'I – I think Mrs Pankhurst has always conducted herself with the utmost propriety.'

If she had suddenly taken all her clothes off and danced the fandango she couldn't have surprised them more. She was aware of Mrs Gray sitting up straighter but it was Mr Gray who fixed her with his eyes. 'You aren't telling me you approve of all this, Lily?' he said in a tone which left her in no doubt as to how he expected her to reply. 'Not a sensible girl like you.'

Lily stared at him. She wasn't sure if by 'all this' he meant the suffragettes' constant clashes with the police and those in authority which were becoming more bitter and fierce by the day, or the more relevant issue of the vote for women. 'I think if you spoke to any suffragette she would say the last thing she wants is violence of any kind, sir,' she said quietly, her heart beating hard beneath her demure uniform.

'And do you? Speak to these suffragettes, I mean?'

'I have friends who support the fight for women to have the vote, yes, sir.'

'As you do?' As she opened her mouth to reply, he

held up his hand. 'Think carefully before you reply, Lily. I consider this a most serious matter. You have responsibility for my children for large parts of the day, you are in a position of trust in my home. The disgraceful things we have heard and read about over the last years concerning the women mixed up with this fanatic, Emmeline Pankhurst, disturb me greatly. Women submitting to – nay, being directly the cause of – this unladylike force-feeding in prison and other indelicate procedures, let alone the militant and dangerous destruction of property and attacks on others, fills any decent soul with abhorrence.'

A log in the roaring fire crackling in the ornate marble fireplace shifted slightly, a shower of red and blue sparks flying up the chimney, and outside somewhere a dog barked briefly before becoming silent. Lily was aware of these things on the perimeter of her mind but all her senses were taken up with Mr Gray. She knew what he was telling her. If she didn't toe the line over this she could expect to be out on her ear, probably without a reference, too. That would mean the chance of securing another post working with children would be nigh on impossible. Without a reference to her good character she would be hard pressed even to get shop work or anything similar. It would have to be something like the kipper-curing factory or the jam factory, or even working as a menial at the Northern Laundry. Even in those places, without a reference, she would be doing the jobs no one else would do, and would be doing them for a pittance.

All this flashed through her mind and the beating of her heart now threatened to suffocate her, but the months spent with Ellen and Bruce, months when she had learned to put her thoughts in order and put forth a reasoned argument now came to the fore. 'I personally don't approve of violence in any shape or form, sir,' she said steadily. 'However, I do support wholeheartedly the right for women to have the vote and be heard as individuals in this country. England is a great nation but there are terrible injustices in her streets and all too often it is the bairns and women who suffer most. These are my private thoughts, however, and I wouldn't dream of mentioning them or anything else regarding such matters to your chil-dren. I am employed to take care of their physical needs and create a happy and safe environment for them; it is for you and Mrs Gray to shape their opin-ions and minds. Having said that, in my free time I shall continue to attend meetings of the Women's Social and Political Union when I can, which isn't often, and talk with friends of a similar persuasion.'

Arabella had swung her feet to the floor and was leaning slightly forward, clearly agitated. Her eyes had been flashing from one to the other and now she said, 'But, Lily, you must see that chaining themselves to railings and harassing prominent politicians and destroying property is no way for decent women to behave?' There was almost a pleading note in her voice. 'The Prime Minister himself said the women's suffrage societies have made out a conclusive and irrefutable case but that they must be patient, didn't he? He has tried to be fair. And Mrs Pankhurst's answer to that was to tell a rally later the same day that they'd been patient too long as it was.'

Lily looked into the pretty gentle face of her employer. Arabella Gray had been born into a privileged world and brought up by doting parents before they had given her into her husband's fond care. The women of her class were as far removed from the match girls working sixteen hours a day in the sweat shops of the East End, or a miner's wife bringing up umpteen bairns in two rooms and sharing a privy and washhouse with ten other families, as the man in the moon. She was a nice woman and a good wife and mother, but had probably never had occasion to think for herself in the whole of her life, other than to instruct her servants on the daily running of the household. 'When that conversation was reported in the papers two years ago, there was little mention that a petition had been handed to the Government by the societies forty years ago, ma'am. I have to agree with Mrs Pankhurst; they have been waiting too long for the Government to act.'

'Is that true?' Arabella turned to her husband. 'Has all this been going on for forty years?'

'I think we are digressing, m'dear.' Norman Gray rose to his feet as he spoke, standing with his back to the fireplace. 'The point here is that I had no idea you were involved with this movement, Lily. And I'm disappointed, very disappointed that this is the case. Rather than behaving in such a thoroughly reckless and unladylike way, those women would be far better employed in the home seeing to their husbands and children and letting matters take their course. I shall need to think very carefully about what has been said here tonight and whether I think you are a suitable person to take care of my children. Have I made myself clear?'

Lily had gone very white. 'Yes, sir.'

'And in view of what I have just said, you do not feel you could see your way clear to avoiding attending such meetings in the future?'

She felt sorry she couldn't agree to what he asked. In so many different ways she felt sorry because she didn't want to leave Mrs Gray and the children and Bridget and Molly, and if she had to work in a factory or something like that she'd hate every minute of it. There would be the stigma of losing her job and not being given a reference . . . Her thoughts tumbling over themselves, Lily stared at Mr Gray. Her mam would go mad, too. Life would be unbearable all round.

But Mr Gray wasn't just asking her not to go to the meetings, he was asking her to deny what she believed in, in a roundabout way. He probably didn't see it like that, to be fair to him, but that was what he was doing. And there were women, brave women going to prison for the cause and suffering goodness knew what. And look at Ellen; everything had been weighted on her husband's side and she'd had no real rights, no one to help her, no say in what happened in her marriage . . . 'I'm sorry, sir, but I think if matters are left to take their course like you suggest women will still be asking for the vote in another forty years.'

Norman Gray blinked. He saw little of his nursery-maid and was used to her flitting in and out of the room to say goodnight like a golden-haired shadow. He would never have dreamed in a hundred years she had opinions and such controversial ones at that.

His face stiff, he said, 'Very well. I shall speak to you tomorrow, Lily. Goodnight.'

'Goodnight, sir, ma' am.' Lily inclined her head at them and walked out of the drawing room, shutting the door carefully behind her. She crossed the hall and entered the kitchen where Molly was stirring a large pan of soup at the range and Bridget was sitting putting the finishing touches to a chocolate gateau her sister had baked earlier. The cake was a vision with delicate wafer-thin chocolate leaves and spider's-web-thin strands of chocolate decorating it, but for once the sight of one of Molly's creations didn't make Lily's mouth water.

She stood fighting back the tears but her face must have revealed plenty because both women stopped what they were doing and were at her side in an instant. 'Whatever's happened? Is it one of the bairns?' Molly asked in concern, before adding, 'The mistress isn't took bad, is she?'

Lily shook her head but still couldn't speak.

'What, then? You look like death warmed up, lass.'

'I – Mr Gray –' Lily shook her head. 'Can – can I have a cup of tea?'

'Aye, aye. Sit yourself down, lass. Bridget, pour her a cup, that pot's still half full. Ee, what now?'

The sisters stood over her while she began to drink the strong brew they favoured, then Molly returned to the stove and Bridget plonked herself down opposite Lily. It was a full minute before Bridget, who clearly couldn't contain herself any longer, burst out, 'Lass, if you don't tell us what's put that look on your face I'll disappear up me own backside. What's happened?'

Lily took a deep breath. She knew they wouldn't understand how she felt or why she had taken the stand she had. With regard to the latter she didn't fully understand it herself except she knew she wouldn't have been able to lay her head on the pillow and sleep at night if she had done any different. Haltingly, she told the two sisters what had occurred, word for word.

They surprised her. There was a brief silence when she finished speaking, then Bridget said, 'They'd be cutting off their nose to spite their face if they got rid of you for this, an' I shall tell the mistress so if it comes to it, lass. I shall, straight. I've no real under-standing of what it all means, the vote an' such, but me an' Moll know what our da was like an' what our mam had to put up with. By, no wonder she drinks. It was that or her topping herself years ago. I'm not sayin' there's not good 'uns out there, course there are, stands to reason, don't it? But there're more than a few like our da an' all. An' what can a woman do if even the law of the land don't take her view as worth owt? No, I can see things need to change, lass, an' it's women like you who'll make it happen. Me an' Moll'll never be any good at trying to get over what we feel; they talk about the Irish having the gift of the gab but it passed us by, but we know what we think nonetheless. Isn't that right, lass?'

Bridget glanced at her sister, who nodded. 'But you need to say you want to stay here an' how much you think of the bairns an' all, lass. You didn't say that, did you?'

Lily shook her head.

186

'That'll carry some weight with the mistress – him an' all. I've known him longer than you, lass, an' he's got a soft centre, has the master. Not like some of the gentry who'd wipe their feet on you, given half a chance.'

Lily finished the last of her tea. 'I'm not going to beg.'

'I'm not saying that. Just say how you feel. That'll be the truth and nowt else. All right?'

Lily nodded. She would never be able to make them understand how much their encouragement had boosted her morale when she had needed it most, but she said softly, 'Thank you. You two are the nicest people I know, and I mean that.'

'Aw, go on with you.' Molly flapped her hand and Bridget grinned.

'Go now,' Bridget urged. 'Likely they'll be mulling it over the night an' it won't hurt to put your two pennyworth in last thing.'

'Do you think I should?'

'Aye, I do.'

'It might be better in the morning.'

'No, they'll have slept on it by then. Anyway, you want to catch 'em together an' the master might leave early like he does sometimes. If the last thing they hear from you is you sayin' how the bairns come first with you, it won't do no harm, lass.'

Lily nodded. They were right, but she really didn't want to face Mr Gray again so soon. Squaring her shoulders, she stood up. 'If I'm not back in ten minutes send in the cavalry,' she said with a weak smile.

'You'll be all right. Just say your bit an' then leave, don't start going over old ground again.'

She nodded at Molly's well-meant advice as her stomach turned over. Straightening her cap and smoothing down her apron she looked at the sisters one more time before leaving the kitchen. Once in the dimly lit hall she saw a chink of light from the drawing room door and realised it was slightly ajar. Mrs Gray must have gone up to kiss the children as she did every night once they were asleep, it was a little ritual she never missed. She stood hesitating, wondering if Mrs Gray was still upstairs but then the sound of voices came to her.

'I'm not saying I *want* to get rid of the girl, Arabella. I like her as much as you do. But you have to consider the children—'

'That's exactly my argument.'

'Look at this dispassionately, m'dear.'

'Dispassionately?' There was a snort which could have come from Sarah and which caused Lily to freeze within a foot or so from the door.

They were having an argument, she thought, horror-stricken. And here she was outside the door listening. But she still didn't move.

'If there is one area where passion and emotion need to come into play it's with the children, Norman. Lily has proved herself to be a loyal and hardworking girl who is wonderful with the children; they all think the world of her and she handles them perfectly. Furthermore, she has been a rock to me over the last few months and done far more than I could have expected. You know that as well as I do.'

'M'dear—'

'And for you to insinuate you're thinking of giving

her notice simply because she's in favour of the vote for women, I can't believe it. I don't care if she wants the vote for dogs and horses too, it has no effect on how she conducts herself in this house on a day-to-day basis.'

'Now you're being silly.'

'I am not being silly, Norman. I'm being passionate and emotional but I've always been that way where my children's welfare is concerned. And any day now I shall give birth to two babies. Have you forgotten that?'

'Of course I haven't forgotten.'

'Then how could you consider for one moment letting Lily go?'

'I'm not suggesting we don't replace her immediately.'

It was the wrong thing to say. Lily heard Mrs Gray's voice go up a few decibels as she said, '*Replace* her? Like a sofa or a broken piece of crystal, you mean?'

'You're upsetting yourself, Bella.'

Lily almost had it in her to feel sorry for Mr Gray. The soothing tone to his voice had an edge of desperation to it now.

'*You* are upsetting me, Norman. You are not here all day like I am. You leave this house in the morning and return in the evening and expect it to be a haven of peace and contentment. And that is fine, that is your right. But it doesn't happen by itself. In the same way that Molly and Bridget do their part to enable things to run smoothly, so does Lily. More so. I have seen some of our friends' children's nurserymaids and nannies and I wouldn't want them for Edwin and the

189

girls. Lily suits me and she suits the children. I thought you knew that. I'm not looking forward to the next few weeks and only the thought that Lily will be here to take care of the children and help me with the babies is keeping me calm.'

'I told you I think we should get someone else in to help Lily.'

'And I told you we will if it becomes necessary but I prefer things to remain as they are. You were brought up by a host of servants and you told me yourself you were closer to your nanny and the nurserymaids than you were your mother. It wasn't like that in my home and I don't want it to be like that now.'

'All right, all right, don't cry. Look, I like Lily, you know I do, and I want to keep her as much as you do. We'll forget all about this now. I only wanted to impress upon the girl that I don't want her discussing such things with the children.'

'She wouldn't. How can you say such a thing? I know she wouldn't do that.'

'Well, as you say, I'm away all day. I'm sure you know her far better than I do, Bella.'

There was the sound of rustling and then Mr Gray's voice came softer, saying, 'There, there, a storm in a teacup, my precious. All right? You know your happiness is my only concern and always has been. Of course Lily shall stay with us.'

Lily backed slowly towards the kitchen but once having reached the door she stood outside for a moment. Who would have thought it? She had always assumed Mr Gray had the last say in everything that went on in the household and that Mrs Gray deferred to him without question, but she'd had him eating out of the palm of her hand. And Mrs Gray was for her. She really was. Which was nice, lovely, to know. Her face split into a grin. She had always known Mrs Gray liked her, you sensed things like that, but she hadn't realised she was actually needed, *valued*.

A warm glow spread through her and she told herself she'd do anything for her mistress. She'd work her socks off once the babies came to make sure they didn't have to have anyone else coming in. She didn't want someone to help her in the nursery, she liked things as they were. And Miss Belinda and Miss Prudence weren't babies any more, and Master Edwin was growing up fast.

She suddenly realised how devastated she would have been to leave this house and the children. They were like her family, which was silly because she was only the nurserymaid, but that's how she felt. And still grinning like a Cheshire cat, Lily opened the door into the kitchen.

The Grays' identical twin boys were born early the next morning after a short labour which nevertheless left their mother white and limp and completely exhausted. The babies were healthy, and weighed just over six pounds each, but it soon became apparent that most of the responsibility for their care was falling on Lily. Arabella had suffered a haemorrhage in the hours after the birth and in the days following she was too weak to raise her head off the pillow. By the time the family doctor sent his patient into hospital for 'a little operation' Lily had temporarily moved into a bedroom adjoining the nursery suite and remained there when Arabella came home.

This temporary arrangement lasted a full three months till both babies had cut out their night feeds, and at the end of this time Lily had given her heart away. The boys had been named Nicholas and Adam. They had silvery fair curls, round little faces and bright blue eyes, and their sunny natures and toothless smiles were enchanting. Everyone loved them, even Edwin, who at first had been a bit put out at the arrival of two other boys in the family.

Sarah's second child, another little girl whom they had christened Felicity Nora, had been born early on the morning of New Year's Eve. The Grays had insisted that Lily spend the day with her family and although she had protested at first, secretly feeling she'd rather be with the twins and Edwin and the girls, she was glad in the circumstances that she'd gone home. She had arrived mid-morning just as her father was leaving to go and visit Sarah and, after he had told her the news, they had gone together. They hadn't been able to persuade Geraldine to accompany them; she had retired to her room with one of her headaches.

On the way to Sarah's house, Stanley had told her it had been John Turner who had called to inform them they were grandparents once again and that Geraldine had barely been civil to him. He had tried to set things right as John had left but he feared some harm had been done. Although Lily stayed on with Sarah after her father had left, John had not made an appearance before she'd had to leave to return to the Grays. Ralph had offered to see her back but her refusal had been so swift and vehement that he hadn't pressed her. Nevertheless, there had been something in his face which had caused her to run all the way to the house in Ryhope Road, feeling as though the devil himself was on her heels. Even when she was safely indoors and sharing a bottle of Molly's potent cherry wine with the two women as the kitchen clock chimed in the New Year, the prickly sensation in the hairs at the back of her neck hadn't gone away.

It was now the middle of February; a bitterly cold February with driving snow and high winds that cut to the bone. At the beginning of the month the old pattern had been resumed and Lily had begun to go home each evening. To her surprise it had felt like an alien place. She found she missed her little bedroom off the nursery suite, missed being with the children twenty-four hours a day and sharing her meals with Molly and Bridget. She had slipped into the routine of living full time with the Grays as though she'd always done so. She knew from the odd thing that had been said, by Mr Gray as well as his wife, that the couple would have been happy for the temporary arrangement to become a permanent one and for her to take up residence with them for good.

And it was tempting, she admitted to herself as she walked down the path to the front door late one Friday evening after an evening spent with Ellen and Bruce. Especially with the weather so bad. Every morning she had to leave the house before it was light and battle her way to Ryhope Road, and more often than not her hat and coat had only just dried out by the time she was ready to go home, once again in the dark.

But how could she leave her mother? Her brows drew together and she paused on the doorstep before turning and glancing behind her. For once in the last couple of weeks it wasn't snowing and the cold white world stretching in front of her had taken on a frozen, sparkling beauty that caught at her senses. She couldn't abandon her to living at home with just her father, day in, day out. It had been different when Mrs Gray had been so poorly and the twins had needed her, but she had no excuse now.

Did she want an excuse to leave her mother?

The answer to this caused her to bite her lips hard as the guilt rose and, as always when thinking of the woman who had given birth to her, she told herself, it's *his* fault. It was he who had made her the way she was. And her mother did love her in her own way, Sarah too. She just couldn't express it, that was all. Was it any wonder, with what she'd had to put up with all her married life? Only that very evening, when discussing the court ruling made in London last week that a wife was not entitled to divorce, even if her husband had deserted her, Ellen had said that England's laws were made by men, for men, and till women got the vote it wouldn't change, and she was right. She was so, so right.

Swinging round, she was about to insert her key in the lock when the door swung open and her mother stood there. Lily could see immediately she was in a temper.

'Where have you been?' In contrast to her flushed

face, Geraldine's voice was glacial as she stood aside for Lily to pass her. Shutting the door, she said again, 'Where have you been tonight?'

Lily stared at her mother. 'With friends.'

'Friends?' Geraldine drew the word out. 'At the library?'

So that was it. Somehow her mother had found out she had left the discussion group without telling her. Taking off her coat and hat she hung them on the hall coat-stand before she said, 'No, not at the library. I haven't been there for some time.'

'So I understand, and not just in the last little while when you were staying with the Grays. That's right, isn't it?'

'You obviously know the answer to that, so why ask?'

'Don't take that tone with me, madam, don't you dare.'

To Lily's surprise her mother gripped her by the arm and hauled her into the sitting room with a strength that belied her thin frame. When they were standing in the middle of the room, Geraldine brought her face close to Lily's and demanded, 'Is it true one of these friends of yours is a woman of the streets? A common prostitute?'

'Let go of me.' Shaking herself free and her body bristling at her mother's rough handling, she flung back her head.

'Don't look at me like that. And I want an explanation from you, girl. I received this in the morning post' – Geraldine reached into the pocket of her skirt and produced an envelope which she waved under Lily's nose – 'and it's very specific about your activities.'

'Who's it from?'

'Never you mind, but think what would happen if Amelia Shelton or any of my other friends at the bridge club got to hear.'

'Amelia Shelton is a poisonous old hag and while we're on the subject of friends, I don't appreciate one of mine being maligned. Who wrote that letter? I've a right to know.'

Geraldine made a sound in her throat and then hissed, 'Is it true that a woman called Ellen Lindsay resided in a brothel which was raided by the police, and that that same woman was again taken into custody for a similar offence some months ago? *Is it?* And she, and the man she has her hooks into, caused such a scene at this ridiculous discussion group you attended that the police were again called to take her away?'

'What?' Lily couldn't believe how the truth had become so distorted. 'No, that's rubbish. It wasn't like that.'

'And you, *my* daughter, were involved in a brawl, a common brawl.'

'That's not true.'

'You weren't a party to physical violence?'

'I tried to stop Beatrice hitting Ellen, yes, but—'

'Ah, now we have it. And since that time you have seen this woman and her friend, and others of her like, no doubt, on a regular basis. Don't deny it.' Geraldine was fairly spitting in her rage. 'I know what I know so don't deny it. You could make me a laughing stock, do you know that? You could drag our name through the mud more effectively than your sister's done with her unfortunate marriage. What are the Turners, bad as they are, compared to this?'

'Are you going to listen to me?'

'Listen to you?' For a moment Geraldine stared at her daughter and such was the expression on her mother's face that Lily took a step backwards in spite of herself. 'Why would I do that? I've heard enough lies from you over the last few months, girl. All the time you were supposed to be at the library you've been consorting with the lowest of the low, scum even the Turners would turn their noses up at.'

The Turners again. Her mother was obsessed with the Turners. Lily took a deep breath, her voice trembling but low as she replied: 'Ellen Lindsay was never what you and others accused her of being. She's decent, more decent than Amelia Shelton and the like. When she first came to Sunderland to escape a violent marriage she inadvertently took lodgings in a house where certain women lived, yes, but she was never one herself. She was expecting a baby for goodness' sake. It was all a mistake. She didn't know.'

'You mean she didn't know she was a common whore?'

There was silence. Lily looked at her mother, her gaze taking in the screwed-up eyes blazing with fury and the bitter, scornful twist to her mother's mouth. It took every scrap of control she had left to say quietly. 'I've told you, she's a good woman and I'm proud to have her as my friend.'

'You little fool. You don't see, you really don't see what you've done, do you?' Geraldine's voice was rising

197

almost to a scream now. 'How can I hold my head up if this gets out? Two daughters and both drawn to the scum of society. I could understand it with Sarah, she's every inch her father's daughter and blood will out. Isn't that what they say? And take the lowest denominator at that. But you!'

Lily's brow wrinkled. Uncertainly she said, 'What do you mean?'

Maybe if Stanley hadn't chosen that moment to open the front door and appear in the sitting room doorway, saying, 'What's going on? I could hear you outside, woman,' Geraldine might have been able to control herself, furious as she was. But the sight of the man she blamed for all her problems, the man she believed had ruined her life and whom she hated with the very core of her being was too much. All day after receiving the letter she had paced the floor and worked herself up into a frenzy, and now the flood of rage that consumed her swept away the last fragments of reason. Suddenly Lily was out of the equation and all she wanted to do was to hurt Stanley. If she had had a knife in her hands she would have used it at that precise moment. As it was she used a more potent weapon. Her eyes on her husband but speaking to Lily, she ground out, 'I mean *your* father wasn't some big, blundering, coarse lump of nothing; he was a gentleman. A gentleman whose lineage had royalty in it. He was the man I should have married—'

'That's enough.' Stanley's voice was like thunder.

As he advanced towards Geraldine, she straightened up and held her head high. 'Go on, hit me,' she said defiantly. 'You've wanted to for years, haven't you?'

Whether Stanley would have been provoked to do just that was uncertain, but when Lily caught at him, saying, 'She's telling lies, isn't she? She's being spiteful because she's angry with me. That's it, isn't it?', he stopped in his tracks.

'You're not his.' Geraldine was looking at her daughter now. 'Tell her,' she said to Stanley. 'Tell her she's no relation to you.'

'So help me I swear I'll swing for you if you don't shut that evil mouth of yours.'

'You? Huh! You're all talk, Stanley. That's all you've ever been.' Geraldine's triumphant gaze swung back to Lily's white face. 'And what are you looking like that for? You've never liked him, have you?'

Lily wanted to be sick, she needed to sit down. Weakly now, she murmured, 'It's not true.' But even before her mother repeated flatly, 'It is true, you're not his child,' she knew it was. She didn't look like Sarah or any of her cousins, she didn't resemble anyone in the family. She had always been different. She had always *felt* different. And now she knew why.

Stanley stared into the great green eyes and nothing in his life thus far had pained him like the look on his daughter's face. And she *was* his daughter, he told himself fiercely. In everything that mattered. Ignoring Geraldine, he said softly, 'I am your father, lass. I'm the one who held you when you were born and loved you from the first moment I saw your little face. I named you, I've worried about you and fed and clothed you. Those are the things that make me your da, not an accident of birth.'

'An accident.' Lily turned to her mother. 'Who is he?

Do I know him?' She could hear herself speaking but inside she was screaming. If her da wasn't her da, then her Grandma and Granda Brown, her cousins, her aunties and uncles, they weren't her family either. And Sarah wasn't her sister, not properly. She was her step-sister or half-sister or something.

'No, you don't know him,' Geraldine said tightly. 'He left long before you were born. He' – she inclined her head at Stanley – 'made sure of that.'

'Does he know about me? That I'm his daughter?'

'No.' For the first time Geraldine was feeling fright-ened at what she had done and she didn't elaborate further.

'It'll be all right, lass.' Stanley gently put his arm round Lily's shoulders but she could have been made of wood. 'Nowt's changed, not really.' It was a stupid thing to say in the circumstances, the look in her eyes told him so. 'I mean, you're still the same person you were this morning, and so am I, and your mam.'

'All these years you've lied to me.'

'Not really. Like I said, to me you've always been mine just as much as Sarah is.'

'You'd like to think that, wouldn't you?' Geraldine's spite overcame her fear. 'The big man, the gaffer.'

'Shut up.' Stanley didn't shout but such was his voice that Geraldine's thin lips clamped together.

'Did you know? Before I was born, I mean? Did you know all along that I wasn't yours or was it because of how I look?' It was hurting that he wasn't her father, that she had no claim on him or he on her, and she didn't understand that. They had never got on, and she knew that was her fault, not his, but the loss of him was a physical pain in her chest. He had always been there, a solid reliable figure in the background, and she hadn't realised how much she had depended on that till now. All she had ever done was push him away, but she had always known he would be there for her and Sarah if they needed him. But everything was a lie, everything.

'I knew. I – I found them together, and when it became apparent your mother was expecting a child it was impossible for it to have been mine. I'm sorry, lass, but that's how it was.'

'Does Grandma know?'

'No one knows, lass. No one has to know unless you decide different.'

'Of course no one must know.' The reality that she had opened a can of worms was dawning on Geraldine. 'We none of us want that.'

Lily's heart was thumping so hard she gulped for breath a number of times before looking at her mother and saying, 'Don't tell me what I want, and don't preach at me about someone like Ellen Lindsay, not after what you've done. You're disgusting, do you know that? And all these years you've blamed Da for how it's been in this house. All this must have happened just after you were married, when Sarah was just a little baby. How could you?' Before Geraldine could open her mouth Lily shook Stanley's arm away, rounding on him, as she said, 'And why didn't you do something? How could you pretend and lie and let me believe I belonged to you and Gran?'

'You do, lass, you do.'

'I don't.'

Her eyes, bright and glittering, were looking straight into his and he searched for something to say that would lift the terrible hurt. 'I love you every bit as much as Sarah, lass, I always have. You're both mine in all that matters. And I know your gran and granda would say the same. You're you. Nothing can change that.'

'But who am I?' Lily drew back from them both, her face chalk white but for two spots of bright colour burning her cheekbones. 'I'm not Lily Brown, am I? I have no right to that name, not really.'

'Don't be ridiculous, of course you do.' Geraldine's voice was sharp but now both Stanley and Lily could hear the fear in it.

Like an animal sensing a way to wound a more powerful predator, Lily's eyes fixed on the woman in front of her. They moved slowly over the immaculate hair, carefully made-up face and beautiful clothes. 'I hate you,' she said slowly and clearly. 'For years I've made excuses for you in my head, and to other people – oh yes, other people too. But no more. Sarah's seen through you for a long time but I wouldn't listen to her. I felt sorry for you.' She made a strange sound in her throat. 'Imagine that, me feeling sorry for you! But I did.'

Unblinking, Geraldine returned her glare before saying, 'Pull yourself together.'

'I'm not going to pretend for you, Mother. I shall leave here tomorrow and I shan't be coming back, and when people ask me why I shall tell them.'

Geraldine shook her head violently. 'Oh no you won't.'

'You can't stop me.' Never in her life had she imagined she would talk to her mother like this or take a savage satisfaction in seeing the alarm and panic now registering on the smooth face. She didn't know herself, she thought numbly. It wasn't just her parentage that was in question, it was her, herself. 'I shall go and see Sarah tomorrow and tell her myself; she deserves to hear it from me.'

'You most certainly will not! I won't have the Turners discussing our affairs. I forbid it, Lily. Do you hear me?' Geraldine paused to catch her breath. 'Tell her, Stanley.'

'Lily has the right to do as she chooses.'

'Oh you!' Geraldine's hands clenched into fists at her side. 'You haven't got the guts you were born with. But have you considered this won't stay in the family, not if Ralph Turner and his crew get hold of it. *Have you?* And where will your precious reputation be then, eh?'

Stanley's voice carried a deep weariness as he replied, 'Are you really so blind and wrapped up in yourself that you can't see we've gone beyond that?' And then, as Lily turned, he caught at her arm. 'Don't go like this, lass. Let's talk.'

'I don't want to talk.' Ignoring her mother's command to stay, she left the room. She heard a scuffle as she reached the hall and her mother's voice saying, 'Take your hands off me, I won't allow her to threaten us.'

'You, Geraldine. She was talking to you. And she wasn't threatening anyone. She was making a clear statement of what she intends to do. You started this.

You started it umpteen years ago and you compounded things tonight. What possessed you? What possessed you to tell her?'

'You don't know what she's done. She's been associating with common prostitutes. And don't raise your eyebrows at me. It's the truth, I tell you. It's here in black and white. Here, read this.'

Lily had paused outside the door, her hand at her throat. There was a moment's silence, and then Stanley said, 'This letter is anonymous. The writer hadn't the courage to sign his or her name. How can you credit such a letter? And even if what it says is true it doesn't excuse your actions tonight.'

'I might have known you would say that. Your precious Lily and Sarah. They can do no wrong, can they? They could commit murder and you'd still be on their side. And yet I fall from grace once and there's no way back.'

'You brought your lover into *our* bed and you expected me to turn a blind eye?'

Lily had heard enough. With her hands over her ears she ran up the stairs to her room, locking the door behind her. She sat down on the bed, her heart racing. She could hear them shouting and carrying on downstairs and with her arms crossed under her breasts she swayed back and forth. When at last she became still it was to stare blankly across the room till, a full hour later, she rose and took off her clothes, slipping into her nightdress and sliding under the covers. Still she hadn't cried.

Chapter 13

When Lily came downstairs at half past five the next morning she was carrying all her worldly possessions crammed into her big carpet bag and a smaller cloth bag slung over her shoulder. Stanley was sitting at the kitchen table drinking a cup of tea and he didn't look as though he had slept a wink. Neither had she.

He stood up as she entered the kitchen, taking the carpet bag from her as he said, 'Sit down and have a cup of tea, lass. You look like death warmed up. No, don't argue. You're not leaving without something warm inside you and your mother won't be down for a good hour yet.'

When she was seated and he had poured the tea and put it in front of her, he said quietly, 'You're going without saying goodbye to her?'

'I think all that could be said was said last night.'

'You're sure you won't regret it?'

Lily looked at him. 'I don't care if I never see her again.'

'You might feel like that now, and it's understandable,

with the shock an' all, but likely you'll have second thoughts in a week or two. If you go like this there'll be no way back, you know what your mother's like. She can bear a grudge better than most, lass.'

Lily looked towards the kitchen window. It was still dark outside and snowing heavily, but inside the kitchen it was warm and cosy, the glow from the range and the soft plop, plop from the gas mantle familiar and soothing. It was all at odds with the way she was feeling inside. She had spoken the truth when she'd said she didn't care if she never saw her mother again. Through the long night she had looked back over her life and for the first time had seen her mother exactly as she was, without the foolish emotions of pity and tender-ness getting in the way. And they were foolish emotions where her mother was concerned, she realised that now. She knew she had never liked her mother but she had loved her, even if the main ingredient of that love had been a mixture of duty and compassion. 'I can bear a grudge too,' she said quietly. 'I discovered that last night.'

'Don't talk like that, lass.'

'Why not? It's the truth. Not that the truth has ever had any place in this house.'

'I'm sorry, lass.'

'No you're not, not really, or you wouldn't have let her be the way she is all these years. You both lied to suit yourselves. All my life, Sarah's too, she taught us to hate you. Did you know that? But of course you did, you must have done. But you didn't step in and stop her or try to make this into a proper home. When you found her with her fancy man, why didn't you throw her out?'

Stanley blinked rapidly. 'There was Sarah.'

'Grandma would have taken her or looked after her in the day for you.'

'It wasn't as easy as that, Lily.'

'It could have been. But you didn't want anyone to find out, did you?'

He swallowed hard. 'No, I suppose I didn't.'

'And then when I was born you pretended you were my father for the same reason.'

'Hang on a minute, you've got the wrong end of the stick there, lass. I told you how it was last night and I meant it. I loved you from the minute you were born.'

'You couldn't have, not knowing I was his. Every time you looked at me, when you look at me now, it must remind you of what she did. Did you love her? Before you found them together, I mean? Did you love her?'

'Before I answer that I want to set the record straight once and for all. You might not believe me but I've loved you the same as Sarah and I still do.'

Lily shook her head, lowering her eyes to the cup in her hands. 'I'm sorry, I can't believe that.'

'Then that's a shame, lass.'

There was silence for a moment. Then Lily said, 'Did you love her in the beginning? Up till you knew what she was doing?'

The clock on the mantelpiece above the range ticked some seconds away before Stanley said, 'I was crazy about her, I think that's a better way to put it. From the time we met till I found her with her fancy man I was blinded by my obsession with your mother.

207

It ate away at me every minute. I wasn't happy unless I had her in my sight but when I did she had the capacity to turn me inside out till I didn't know what I was doing.'

Lily had finished her tea while he had been speaking and now she rose to her feet. 'I'm going to the Grays, I know they'll have me. And I shall go and see Sarah before Ralph gets home later. If – if you see her before me, don't say what's happened. I want to tell her myself.' He stared at her, and she said sharply, 'She doesn't know, does she?' She knew Sarah and her da – she checked the thought, Sarah and her mother's husband – had got close over the last few months because Sarah had told her so.

'No, of course not.'

'What, then?' Something had put that funny look on his face when she'd said she was going to see Sarah.

'I need to tell you something, Lily. Look' – he stood up – 'I'll walk with you to the Grays, carry your bags.'

'I can carry them myself and I'd rather be alone.'

Her chin had tilted as she'd spoken and he bit his lip. Proud as punch. What had all this done to her? Damn it, he could kill Geraldine. 'I can understand that, but if you're seeing Sarah she might well tell you something I told her a while back. And I don't want that. Just as you need to tell her yourself about all this, I need to tell you something face to face. It probably isn't the right time the way you're feeling, but needs must.'

She said nothing for a moment and then nodded. 'I'll get my hat and coat.'

★   ★   ★

It was seven o'clock the same morning and Stanley was sitting in Sally's small sitting room, having gone straight to her house when he had left Lily at the Grays' garden gate.

'And she didn't say a word all the way? She made no comment at all when you explained about us?'

'No, I told you.'

'Don't you think that's strange?'

'Lass, I don't know if I'm on foot or horseback, so don't ask me what's strange or not.'

'And she's really moved out? She won't reconsider?'

'Not in a month of Sundays. If you'd seen her face this morning . . .' He shook his head, rubbing his hand across his face in a scrubbing motion. 'I've lost her, Sall.'

'Don't say that, Stan.'

'Perhaps it's daft, because I've known she's never had any time for me, her mam saw to that, but while she thought I was her da . . . Well, you know.'

'Oh lad, don't take on so. You don't know what she's thinking, now then. The poor lass probably doesn't know herself right at this minute. Things need to settle down for a bit.'

'I know what she's thinking and I don't blame her. I was gutless in the beginning; I should've thrown Geraldine and her fancy man out on to the street that first morning, just as they were, and claimed Sarah as mine. Mam would have had her, like Lily said.'

'You were too kind, that's your only mistake.'

'No, lass. Let's face facts. We've always spoken the truth between us. I didn't want anyone to find out she'd made a monkey of me, that's all I was thinking of then. And after, once the bairn was born . . .'

'You loved her.'

'Aye, I did. I do.'

'Oh, Stan.' Sally put her small hands on his, pressing them as she said, 'I wouldn't have you any different, lad.'

'You can say that? After the mess I've made of everything?' Again he shook his head. 'Hell's bells, I can't believe how everything's changed in a few hours and all because that one's temper got the better of her. I couldn't believe what I was hearing when I first walked in. All them years of keeping quiet and then it was her who let it out, and not in a quiet, shame-faced way. No. Yelled it from the rooftops like she was proud of it. I could've throttled her when I saw the look on that bairn's face, I could straight.'

'I'm glad you didn't. There's laws against such things.'

They exchanged weak smiles and then Stanley straightened up, moving his hands from under Sally's to take hers and grip them hard. 'This is the end of me living with her, Sall. With Lily gone there's no need to keep up a front any more.'

'You need to think about this.'

Stanley looked at her steadily, his blue eyes dark with emotion. 'Do you think I haven't? I haven't thought of anything else all night, and not just this last night either. Ever since we got together I've known what I wanted, you know that. It's been you who's put obstacles in the way. Don't get me wrong, I'm not saying you weren't right and true, the bairns should have come first, yours as well as mine, but it's not like that now.' He paused. 'Don't you want me with you all the time, lass? You can say, it won't make no difference to the way I feel.'

'Oh, Stan, it's not that. You know how I feel, how I've always felt.'

'What, then?'

'I — I don't want you to leave her because of me. What I mean is, I know you're mine. Every bit of you. And if we have to carry on as we are till our dying day, so be it. Knowing how you feel is enough for me.'

'Well, it isn't enough for me, lass. It never was. I'm going to tell her I want a divorce and if you'd been there last night you'd understand. She went at Lily hammer and tongs and she said what she said to hurt and wound, me as well as the bairn. After Lily had gone upstairs she carried on, without a shred of remorse for what she'd done to her own daughter. I told her she'd lost 'em both and do you know what she said? "I never wanted them in the first place, so don't expect me to cry any crocodile tears." She's not human, Sall. Straight up, she's not.'

Sally let out a long breath. 'When are you going to tell her?'

'When I get back lunchtime.' Saturday was half-day at the shipyard.

'Then I'll have dinner ready for later.' She smiled softly. 'And one side of the wardrobe cleared out for you.'

Stanley said nothing but drew her into his arms, holding her tightly for long moments.

It was Sally who eventually drew away, saying, 'You'll be late for work, you'll have to go,' pretending not to notice the tears he wiped from his face. She accompanied him to the front door and it was there she said, 'Who do you think sent the letter?'

He shrugged. 'Search me. Geraldine's upset a lot of folk in her time.'

'But how would anyone in the circles she moves in find out about this woman Lily's befriended? It seems odd to me. And wouldn't they tell her face to face? You don't think it's someone who wanted to hurt Lily rather than her mother?'

'Lily?' He stared at her in astonishment. 'Not a chance. The lass has got no enemies, how could she have? Whereas Geraldine! That letter was spiteful and I dare say among her highfalutin so-called friends at the bridge club and the like there're one or two who would like to bring her down a peg but without soiling their dainty mouths in the process. No, it was sent by someone in her circle to upset the apple cart, I'd stake me life on it. I don't know how they found out she wasn't still going to this discussion group and all the hoo-ha that'd gone on, but you know what people are like, Sall. And no one can ever keep anything quiet for ever, things always come to light in some way or other. I'm just amazed she hasn't found out about us before now from some kind soul or other who got wind of it.'

He took her face in his big hands, kissing her hard before he said, 'I shall call in on me mam an' da on the way home from work and put them in the picture before I tell Geraldine. I think Mam's always had her suspicions that Lily wasn't mine.'

Sally was silent for a moment, then said in a low voice, 'I don't know what they'll think of me when you tell them.'

'Same as they've always thought of you. That you're

212

a fine lass and I should have married you in the first place.'

Sally said nothing to this. Stanley's parents might, just might be that generous, but to everyone else she would be known as a shameless hussy who, having lost her own husband, had beguiled someone else's and further compounded that wickedness by enticing the unfortunate man to live in sin with her. And the feeling against her would be all the fiercer because of her rise out of the streets into which she was born. Those same old wives who had oozed sympathy when she had been left high and dry by Stanley and had congratulated her on making a fine match when she had accepted Tim, would be the first to call her an upstart and worse. Oh aye, much worse. They might not throw muck at her when she showed her face like they did to such women who still lived in the warren of streets in the depths of the town, for her having this fine little house and enough money never to want for anything again had taken her up and out of such overt condemnation, but their gossip would be all the more vicious because they would not dare to give physical expression to their hostility.

But she would have Stanley. She looked at the man she had loved unquestioningly all her life. They would wake up in the morning together, eat together. It would be her he returned home to every night, his slippers warming in front of the fire and his pipe and bowl ready for when he'd finished his evening meal. For this she would brave anything. She touched his big, rough face tenderly with the tip of one hand and then gave him a little push. 'Go on, you'll have to run all the way as it is.'

He smiled but didn't immediately do as she said, taking her in his arms one more time and kissing her till she was breathless. 'I love you, Sally, more than life itself. You're my next breath, my reason for living. You know that, don't you?'

Wordlessly, she nodded, her eyes full of tears.

'I'll be back later with me things, lass, and then we'll start the rest of our lives. All right? And as soon as I get my divorce we're getting wed legal and proper, but I say this to you now: I've been more wed to you since the day you took me back than I ever was to Geraldine, and no bit of paper will make any difference to that.'

She did not answer but leaned against him and his arms tightened about her.

Her mam and da and the rest of the family would think she was mad, and she didn't know how Alice and Howard would take the news she was going to live with a married man. Howard was very strait-laced, like Tim had been. He might disown her, but she would cross that bridge when she came to it. For now it was enough that they were going to be together all the time because, in spite of what she'd said to Stanley down the years, it was what she'd yearned for. And she wasn't daft, she wasn't going into this with her eyes shut. She knew everything in life had to be paid for and from what she knew of Geraldine Brown she would be sure to make them pay all right; she'd want her full pound of flesh. But again, they'd face that when they had to. Together.

★   ★   ★

'Don't be so ridiculous. This is your little gesture, isn't it? Your way of punishing me for telling Lily yesterday. You're trying to punish me by frightening me. Well, I'm sorry, Stanley, but I know you too well and it's pathetic. Divorce, huh! You would no more consider enduring the scandal and ridicule a divorce would bring than I would.'

'I mean it, Geraldine. I want a divorce.' She had been out when he had got home from seeing his parents at lunchtime. He had used the time till she returned to pack his clothes and any other belongings he wanted to take with him into two huge wooden boxes they'd used when they had moved into the house and which had been stored in the loft for years. These were standing just inside his study, the door closed. He had arranged for a taxicab to call at the house at four o'clock and it was now ten minutes to. He had been getting anxious, worried Geraldine wouldn't come home before he had to leave. He had wanted to get it over and done with this afternoon and not to have to return once he had gone to Sally's. But then he had heard her key in the lock. The thought of Sally emboldened him to say, 'I have wanted a divorce for years but with the girls still at home I felt I couldn't leave. It's different now. Last night changed everything.'

'Oh, for goodness' sake, stop dramatising.' He had met her in the hall and now Geraldine slipped off her coat, flinging it on a chair and unpinning her hat. 'You're worse than any woman for playing to the gallery.'

'There's someone else. We love each other and she

has been patient long enough.' He watched the cold hazel eyes narrow and her jaws tighten. 'I'm moving out today.'

'You're lying.'

'I wanted to tell you face to face. I felt I owed you that.' He could see she was struggling to take in what he was saying, disbelief warring with a dawning incredulity. He waited for the explosion which would surely come, bracing himself for the onslaught.

'You say you've met someone? Who? When?'

Her voice was flat and thin. He had expected her to shout and scream and go for him. 'It's Sally; Sally Hammond as was, the lass I was courting when I met you. She was widowed some years back and we met up again and, well' – he shrugged – 'we realised we both felt the same.'

'And you've been consorting with this woman for how long?'

'Since just after we moved here.'

'Who knows? Have you visited her openly? Where does she live?'

Stanley stared at his wife. Her voice had turned into a hiss but still the scene he had expected was unforthcoming. Again he shrugged. 'No one knows.' He knew he couldn't drop Sarah in it by admitting he'd told their daughter. 'Sally's husband left her nicely off and she's got her own place on the outskirts of town. It's very private.'

'How convenient.'

'We love each other, Geraldine.'

'Don't give me that!' She took a step towards him, spitting the words between her teeth. 'You dropped her like a hot potato when you met me, you couldn't give a hoot about her. Oh, I don't doubt when you met up again you tried your luck and probably she was ready for someone in her bed, having been widowed. It's the perfect scenario for her, isn't it? Living her own life without being at anyone's beck and call but having someone to warm her bed when she feels like it. And you, Saint Stanley.' She thrust her lower jaw outwards. 'You dare to preach at me and all the time you've been servicing some little trollop from the backstreets.'

'She's no trollop and it's not like that.'

'Of course it's like that, you stupid man. You don't think you're the only gentleman caller to her door, surely? What woman would put up with what you're suggesting? It suits her to have you on a string she can tighten now and again.'

Her hair was swept back from her temples in elaborate curls and waves and on the clear, virtually unlined skin a vein stood up like a piece of thin blue wool. She was getting older. It might not show much at the moment, but age was encroaching nonetheless. He, too, when he looked in the mirror, saw the steady advance of age spots and grey hair. But he had his Sally. Quietly, he said, 'I won't try to make you understand because I realised a long time ago you haven't got the capacity to love another human being, but Sally and I love each other with the sort of love that only comes once in a lifetime, and then if you're lucky. But for her insisting the bairns, hers and ours, were settled before I did anything to upset the apple cart, I'd have left you years ago, Geraldine. The day after I met her again, in fact. But your spite has secured my freedom earlier than I thought.'

'You're not free.' Her voice was shaking with fury, as was her whole body. 'And if you walk out that door I'll see to it your name and hers are blackened all over this town, you mealy mouthed hypocrite, you.'

'I don't doubt it. And I don't care. Do your worst.'

Knowing her as he did he should have seen what was coming but her apparent control had lulled him into a state of false security. As he turned from her and walked to the study door, intending to drag the boxes into the hall ready for the taxicab which was due any second, the glass vase holding the bunch of hothouse blooms Geraldine insisted on buying every week hit him on the back of the head. He stumbled against the wall, covered in water and flowers as the vase smashed at his feet.

It was at this precise moment the front doorbell sounded. The sound checked Geraldine who had grabbed a glass ashtray with the intention of sending it the same way as the vase. They stared at each other as the bell chimed merrily again: Stanley's gaze was dazed and blinking; Geraldine's was alive with hate.

She didn't move when he made his way to the front door, one hand pressed against the wall as he walked to steady his steps. She didn't move when the taxi driver, at Stanley's request, dragged the boxes from the study to his cab. She still hadn't moved when Stanley shut the front door on her furious face. As he climbed up beside the driver – the boxes having taken up all the space within the cab – the man stared at him.

'You all right, mate?' The taxi driver didn't attempt to move. 'Only you're bleedin'.'

'Am I?' Stanley put his fingers to the back of his head. He felt sick, dizzy. When he saw the red on his fingers he reached into his pocket for his handkerchief and held it to the gash. Weakly, he said, 'We had a row.'

'I'd worked that one out for meself. Handy, is she?'

'I'm sorry?'

'Her indoors. The wife's sister's the same. They have a row an' anythin' she can get hold of flies his way. He was in hospital for a week before Christmas due to the chamber pot knockin' him out. I said to the, wife, I hope it was empty at the time. Now, where are we goin'?'

Stanley gave him the address and then leaned back in the narrow seat as the horse began to clip-clop its way down the street. *He had done it.*

Chapter 14

Ralph Turner sat eating his dinner. He deliberately kept his face blank as he listened to what Sarah was saying but inside he was jubilant. When he'd sent that letter he'd never in his wildest dreams imagined it would have such an effect. He'd known it would put the cat among the pigeons for Lily with Lady Muck, who would be sure to clip her daughter's wings, but this? This was wonderful. Her a bastard; who'd have thought it?

'Lily was so upset, Ralph, it was awful. As soon as she came in I knew there was something terribly wrong, but then when she told me' – Sarah gulped and shook her head – 'I still can't believe it.'

He finished chewing a large piece of kidney, swallowing it and then wiping his mouth with the back of his hand before he said, 'I'm not surprised. As skeletons in the cupboard go, this one's a corker.'

'That's not a very nice thing to say.'

'Look, I'm not going to pretend I've ever had any time for your sister. Now if it'd been you I would have been upset.'

The stiff look left her face and for a moment he thought she was going to burst into tears. Instead she nodded, biting her lip. 'At least she was more like herself with me by the time she went. When she first came in she wouldn't hug me or anything, it was like we were almost strangers.'

'Well, you're not sisters, not in the way you thought you were, anyway, are you?'

'We're half-sisters.' It was indignant. 'It's only our fathers who are different, we've got the same mother. Such as she is.'

This last comment was so bitter it surprised Ralph. 'So how did your da react to the news?'

Sarah stared at him. 'He – he knew. That Lily wasn't his, I mean. He knew even before she was born, apparently.'

'And he did nowt about it?'

Defensively now, Sarah said quickly, 'Of course he did. He wouldn't have anything to do with Mam from when he found out but, because of me, he stayed with her. Then when Lily was born he accepted her as his own.'

'Another man's flyblow? He's barmy.'

'He loves her like he does me.'

Unknowingly, Ralph repeated Lily's words. 'I can't believe that.'

'It's true.'

'So you mean to tell me he's lived with your mother knowing what he knows and brought up another bloke's bairn and asked for nowt in return? He's either a saint or there're things you don't know about your da, take it from me.'

'He's not a saint.' Sarah hesitated, and then said in a rush, 'Oh, you'll find out anyway. He told Lily he's leaving Mam and going to live with his woman friend.'

'*Woman friend?*' Ralph forgot all about his dinner and leaned back in his seat, his face a picture. 'Your da's got a fancy bit on the side?'

'She's not a fancy bit, she's the woman he was with before he met Mam and he's always loved her. He – he's divorcing Mam.'

There was a moment of silence. Pushing his plate aside, Ralph said, 'Start at the beginning and tell me it all. All, mind. I'm your husband, I've a right to know. This is going to affect everyone. We'll all be tarred with the same brush.'

Sarah took a deep breath. 'Her name's Sally and she and Da grew up together . . .'

It was a few minutes before Sarah finished talking. She couldn't gauge the expression on her husband's face but it had had the effect of making her gabble the more she had revealed.

'And your mam an' da an' Lily had the nerve to look down on *me?*' he said after a long moment. 'To treat me as scum?'

'They didn't. At least Da and Lily didn't, you know they didn't. Mam, well, you know what she's like.'

'Your mam had a fancy man when she'd only been married two minutes, a man who gave her a bastard; your da's had a bit on the side for umpteen years and your sister's friends with a whore who's been in trouble with the police, and they thought *I* wasn't good enough for *you?*'

222

She could see he was angry. Nervously, she repeated, 'Da and Lily didn't think like that, Ralph.'

'Your sister – your *half*-sister,' he emphasised slowly, 'left me in no doubt as to what she thought of me. An ignorant nowt, less than the muck under her boots.' The rage that had consumed him when he'd made it his business to find out where she went on a Friday night once and for all burned again. He'd followed her to a house in Crowtree Road and after waiting for a while had gone into a pub across the road and asked a few questions. He hadn't got anything more than the name of the woman who owned the house at that point. He'd been surprised it was a woman; he'd been expecting Sarah's sister had a man friend, but still something hadn't sat right. On impulse he had made his way to the library and had gone into the room where the discussion group was held, introducing himself and making out he'd been sent with a message to tell Lily her mother had been taken ill. What had followed had been informative, very informative. He hadn't trusted himself to go back to Crowtree Road. If he had seen her that night he would have killed her. The conniving little slut.

'Lily is just reserved,' Sarah was saying. 'She's always been like that, it's nothing to do with you. She used to get teased a lot at school because she wasn't like everyone else, what with her hair and all. We looked so different—'

'And we know why now, don't we?' He reached for his cup of tea and took a long drink. 'So this friend of hers who's on the game. Got Lily interested in some easy money on her time off, has she?'

It took a moment for Sarah to understand what he meant. Then, hot colour rushing into her face, she said, 'Of course not, how can you think that even for a second? Lily wouldn't do anything of that nature. She's never even had a lad.'

'How do you know? Strikes me you don't know much about your family and her in particular. Oh, she's very good at being the lady and turning up her nose at all and sundry, but scratch the surface and what do you get?'

'Ellen, her friend, has never done . . . that. It was all a mistake, Lily told me. She said Ellen's a lovely woman.'

'Well, she would, wouldn't she?'

Sarah stared at him. 'Don't be like this. I wanted – I *needed* you to understand.' Her voice sounded flat.

'I do understand. It's making you understand that's the problem.'

Sarah continued to stare at him for some moments more. Then she rose to her feet. 'I'll check the bairns are asleep.'

'The bairns are fine. Sit down.'

'Ralph—'

'*Sit down.*'

He was so ferocious that Sarah visibly jumped. 'What's the matter with you?'

'You ask me that?' As she sank into her seat, he fixed her with granite eyes. 'Look, I don't know who Lily's father was, but by your own admission he went with a married woman in her own home when she'd got a young babbie. And then there's Lily consorting with prostitutes.' As Sarah started to speak he held up his hand. 'Water finds its own level and it's a case of like father, like daughter, if you ask me. Likely it was any woman at any time for him, and genes will out. They will, I'm telling you. I don't want her in this house contaminating my wife and children. Do you hear me? She'd better not come here again or there'll be trouble.'

The colour had left Sarah's face. Now it was chalk-white. 'You can't mean that.'

'Trust me, I do.'

'She's not just my sister, she's my best friend, too.'

'Half-sister, Sarah. Half-sister.'

'She's had a terrible shock, you must see that? How would it appear if I said she couldn't come round here any more after she's just found out about her father? She'd think I didn't want her because of that, it would be too cruel.'

Ralph half rose, the palms of his hand flat on the table and his face pushed towards hers. 'Cruel or not, I don't want the likes of her setting foot in this house again. And that goes for your da an' all. If he's going to disgrace the lot of us by living with his fancy woman I won't be seen giving my approval to it. I wasn't going to tell you till it was settled but there's a house come up on that new little development off the Queen Alexandra Road, the Ryhope end. Bonny, it is, four bedrooms and an indoor privy and a garden for the bairns. We're going up in the world and I won't allow your family to drag us down. You're a Turner now and you'd better remember it.'

He was actually enjoying this. Sarah's heart seemed to move upwards towards her throat as the truth dawned. The talk about Lily contaminating her and her da bringing disgrace on their heads, it was a front. Behind the self-righteous claptrap he was loving every minute of it. Had her mother's denunciation of him and his family really hurt him so much that he could take pleasure in their change of circumstances? She had a great desire to cry, but knowing from past experience it would only irritate him, she controlled it. 'I can't stop Lily and my da coming here to see me and the girls,' she said steadily, 'but I will make sure there's no possibility you'll run into them.'

His lips scarcely moving, he ground out, 'Are you deaf or just plain stupid?'

The trembling in the pit of her stomach increased but it wasn't evident in her voice when she said, 'Neither, as it happens,' with a touch of the old Sarah's feistiness.

The flat of his hand across the side of her head caught her totally unawares. But for her bulk, which had increased with each child, she would have been sent spinning off her chair. As it was, she merely reeled back, but the pain in her ear was excruciating.

Her head swimming, she looked at him through pain-blurred eyes, one hand pressed to her right ear. A part of her registered that she hadn't reacted by going for him tooth and nail as she would have done if he'd attempted such a thing when they were courting or first married. She didn't ask herself why, she didn't have to. She hadn't been afraid of him then.

'You'll talk to me with respect; I'm having none of your lip in this house. Your da might be as weak as dishwater but not me. By, when I think of what I

226

was put through with your lot when we wanted to get wed and all the time there was this muck under the surface.'

Sarah said nothing. It wasn't till he turned away and reached for his cap and jacket that she said, 'Where are you going?'

'To my mam's to tell 'em what I've married into. And I shall tell her what I've told you. Your da and Lily don't set foot over this threshold and I shall expect her to tell me if she sees owt.'

He glared at her one last time and then stamped out of the kitchen. Sarah heard the back door bang and then his shape pass the kitchen window. She didn't rise from the chair but, her arms crossed over her waist and her hands gripping her pinny, she swayed back and forth, the tears streaming down her face as she muttered, 'What am I going to do? Oh, Da, Lily, what am I going to do?'

Lily was sitting in the nursery on a chair between the sleeping twins' cots and she was asking herself the same question. It was a refrain which had repeated itself constantly over the last twenty-four hours, even though she knew there was nothing she *could* do. She couldn't change what was fact. Her da wasn't her da. Her Grandma and Granda Brown weren't her grandparents. Everything, her whole childhood, had been a lie.

Her eyes felt gritty, as though they had dust in them but she had no desire to cry. Tears couldn't ease what she was feeling.

She glanced across to the window; it was still

snowing, great fat flakes falling in their thousands. It had been snowing when she had nipped out earlier to see Sarah. Mrs Gray had been so good about that, her employers had been good about everything. When she had arrived at the house that morning with her belongings and explained a domestic crisis had made it impossible for her to continue living with her parents, they had asked no awkward questions, and had merely stated that she had a home with them for as long as she was in their employ. Bridget and Molly had been less tactful but they had been satisfied with her explanation that her father and mother had had a huge row and she no longer wanted to be piggy in the middle.

'Lass, we couldn't wait to get out of our place,' Bridget had said, patting her arm as they sat at the kitchen table drinking one of the endless pots of tea the two sisters enjoyed every day. 'Away from the fighting and screaming and carrying on. Folk don't realise what a blessing peace and quiet is unless they've never had it.'

She had nodded and said something, she couldn't remember what now. In fact, most of the last twenty-four hours was lost in a blur, the one thing which was crystal clear being that she was all alone, she had no one who was really hers. Sarah had hugged her and cried for her but she had found it a strain just being there, and, to her shame, she'd found herself resenting her sister. Sarah had the right to call her grandparents Grandma and Granda, she had a father, she even had bairns of her own. She knew all that wasn't Sarah's fault and she'd felt guilty at feeling the way she did, but, nevertheless, she couldn't wait to leave and be on her own.

Lily looked down at her hands in the dimly lit room. They were her fingers. When she looked in the mirror the same reflection she had always seen stared back at her. But who *was* she? Her mother hadn't wanted her, she hadn't wanted Sarah either; her da had admitted that morning that but for Sarah being on the way her mother would never have married him. No, not *her* da. She bit the inside of her lip so hard she felt the salty tang of blood in her mouth. She couldn't call him her da any more, she had to remember that. And he had this other woman, this Sally, who was the love of his life, the woman he should have married all along. The woman he'd gone to today.

She shut her eyes tightly for a moment and then stood up. She had been up here for ages, she'd have to go down to the kitchen for her evening meal. Bridget and Molly would be waiting for her.

Adam stirred in his sleep, giving a little mew of a cry before settling down again. She reached down into the cot and stroked the silvery curls from his velvet forehead, breathing in the baby smell of him, before doing the same with Nicholas. She wished she could stay in this room for ever with the babies. She wished she never had to see another living soul except her precious boys and Edwin and the girls. They loved her and their love was real. She didn't describe it to herself as unconditional. Just real.

It had stopped snowing the next day and the world outside Lily's bedroom window was clean and white, every tree and bush in the Grays' garden was lost under a mantle of sparkling diamond dust. A winter's dawn was bathing the sky in mother-of-pearl when she drew back her curtains, and for a moment she stood looking out. The purity of the scene pierced her through, producing a physical hurt that made her chest ache.

She felt dirty, she admitted to herself. Unclean. Ashamed. And she was angry they'd made her feel that way but the more she thought about her beginnings the more the feeling grew. People would look at her differently if they knew she was a bastard.

It was the first time she had made herself face the word but now she repeated it out loud. 'Bastard.' Her parents hadn't been married to each other. There had been a girl at school, Myrtle Woodrow, who hadn't had a da. She had lived with her grandparents and mother three doors down from Lily's Grandma Brown, and one day she remembered a group of children had surrounded Myrtle in the playground and chanted the word at her till she had run home crying. Sarah, being over two years older, had explained what the word meant on the way home that day and when they'd told their mother about the incident her only comment had been, 'I don't want you playing with that girl any more, she's a troublemaker.' Lily had been surprised at that because she had thought it was the other children who had caused the trouble. It was from that day she had realised Myrtle was never invited to any parties the children in the street had, or to tea with anyone. It had always been the case but she had never noticed it before.

She wished she hadn't told Sarah now. She should have kept quiet like her mother had demanded. Then no one would've known.

No. No, she shouldn't. Another voice, a stronger voice, drowned out the first. Her chin rose as her eyes narrowed. She wasn't going to be like them, lying, pretending, having secrets.

Why didn't you tell the Grays, then? And Molly and Bridget?

She answered the first voice out loud. 'Because it was none of their business. It *is* Sarah's business. She has a right to know.'

Nonetheless, she knew that wasn't the whole answer.

After Mr and Mrs Gray had left for church with Edwin and the two girls later that morning, Lily fed the twins their bottles of milk and then settled them down for their morning nap. She continued softly humming lullabies in the quiet room long after the babies were asleep, not because she was worried they would wake up – the two little boys slept like logs – but because she needed to be with them.

At eleven o'clock she went downstairs to the kitchen for her mid-morning cuppa with Bridget and Molly. Molly's delicious girdle scones tasted like sawdust in her mouth but she forced herself to eat two, liberally covered with butter. She had eaten so little the day before that she had felt faint first thing and she couldn't afford to be ill on top of everything else. She had just finished the second scone when the three women heard a knock at the back door.

'It can't be one of the tradesmen, not on a Sunday.'

Molly rose as she spoke, bustling through into the scullery. Lily and Bridget heard voices and then Molly reappeared in the kitchen doorway. 'You've got a gentleman caller,' she said to Lily, her brown eyes bright with curiosity. 'A Mr John Turner.'

The lurch her heart gave was so violent it must have shown in her face, because Bridget reached out and took her arm. 'What's the matter, lass? What's wrong? Who is he?'

'He . . . he's my sister's brother-in-law.'

'Oh aye?'

Thinking quickly she found herself doing the one thing she had determined not to do. 'I hope he's not bringing bad news. My sister hasn't been well.'

'Ah, so that's it. We wondered why you had to go and see her yesterday, but we put it down to you moving out of your mam's.'

'It was about that but . . . because she'd not been well I wanted to tell her myself. Explain properly.' Lily was horrified how easily the lies were tripping off her tongue. She looked towards the scullery. 'I'll talk to him outside.'

'Nay, bring him in, lass. It's bitter out there.'

'No, I'll talk to him outside. I don't think Mrs Gray would approve of him coming in.'

Molly and Bridget said nothing to this but when Lily stood up and went into the scullery they exchanged a glance which stated that they knew there was more to this than met the eye.

John was standing just outside the back door looking towards the garden when Lily saw him. She didn't doubt that Ralph had told his family all the ins and

232

outs of what had occurred and again she found herself wishing she hadn't told Sarah anything. She should have thought of all the repercussions before she had spoken, she told herself. Especially of John knowing. Somehow that was worse than anyone else. But she hadn't been thinking straight yesterday. She probably still wasn't, she admitted, because some of the thoughts in her head were so terrible she couldn't be in her right mind. Not to want her own mother dead.

John turned as she reached the open door. He was wearing the overcoat and cap he'd worn the night he had seen her home after Imogen was born and he looked very big and very handsome. They looked at each other and when she saw his face was evincing a feeling she termed pity, she bridled. Aware Molly and Bridget were straining their ears, she said coolly, 'Hello, John. This is a surprise. I trust Sarah and the children are all right?'

She saw her manner had taken him aback but he recovered almost instantly. Quietly, he said, 'Hello, Lily. Sarah and the bairns are well as far as I know, although I understand she's somewhat upset.'

Glancing swiftly behind her, Lily stepped outside, closing the door. They were standing on an area of stone slabs which were devoid of snow; clearly Bridget had been out earlier with her broom. Aiming to hide her crippling embarrassment but painfully conscious of her burning cheeks, she said stiffly, 'I don't understand why you are here.'

He didn't understand why he was there himself. He felt the colour sweeping over his face as she eyed him, much as one would look at something unmentionable on the bottom of one's boots. 'I'm sorry, I shouldn't have come.' His voice had been as cold as hers but then something in the luminous green eyes, something she couldn't quite hide, loosened his tongue. 'I know I shouldn't have come,' he said again, 'but I just wanted you to know I − all of us − didn't believe a word of what Ralph said about this pal of yours being a − a loose woman. That's all.'

Lily stared at him. He'd mentioned only Ellen, but he knew the rest. She could see it in his face. She'd seen it in his face when he had first looked at her. Praying the ground would open up and swallow her, she nodded jerkily. 'Ellen is a lady. If you met her you would know that.'

'The fact that you're her friend is enough for me.'

Her neck muscles were tight with the effort of keeping her head up, and her throat was so blocked with the emotion his kindness had caused that she couldn't get out the dismissive words she wanted to say. She couldn't bear him feeling sorry for her, not him.

John cleared his throat. 'My mother wants you to know you are welcome to meet Sarah and the bairns at our house any time. She sent Ralph home with a flea in his ear when he said he'd told Sarah you couldn't call at theirs.'

He realised his mistake immediately. The green eyes widened and the colour drained from her face, leaving it a sickly white.

'You didn't know.' It was a statement, not a question. 'Oh hell.'

'It's all right.'

'It's not all right,' he said. Her voice had been wooden but his was as sharp as a blade. 'The hell it's all right.'

'If Sarah doesn't want to see me—'

'Don't talk daft, of course Sarah wants to see you. She's half out of her mind with worry about you.'

Lily felt a moment's warmth.

'We — we all are,' he said, his voice soft now.

Pride returned in an overwhelming flood. 'There's no need, as you can see. I'm perfectly all right.'

John looked at her without answering.

Lily swallowed, a lump in her throat. 'I have to get back to the twins, they're probably awake now.'

'Don't let it make any difference to you.'

His speech had been rushed, the words falling over themselves, and his brown eyes held hers so she found she couldn't look away. She knew he was here because he felt sorry for her and more likely than not so did his mother. In fact, it was probably Nora Turner who had made him come to see her this morning, but the kindness in his face was her undoing. It cut through the barrier she'd erected and the resolve to stay cool and distant and show them all she didn't care. Her voice low and rapid, she said, 'What part of "it" do you mean? My mother going with another man and my da not being my da? Him having another woman for years and years, a woman he's now openly living with? The divorce? The lies, the deceit? I've been trying to remember when my mother ever put her arms round me or said she loved me, and do you know what? She never did. Never. In fact, I don't think she even likes me. Or Sarah. She never wanted us.

235

But Sarah's got a father who loves her and grand-parents and' – she closed her eyes, shaking her head violently – 'she knows who she is.'

'So do you.' He was now holding her hands between his own and he shook them slightly to emphasise what he was saying. 'So do you, Lily. This has been a shock but when it wears off you'll still be the same person.'

'I'll never be the same as I was before.' She couldn't explain to him – least of all John somehow – how desolate she felt, but she knew the sense of aloneness that had come upon her yesterday would always be with her. He came from a big, warm, rumbustious family who knew everything there was to know about each other. They were aeons apart. Disengaging her hands from his, she said, 'Please thank your mother for me and tell her I don't want to lose touch with Sarah, but perhaps it would be best to let things settle for a few weeks, then I'll be in touch.'

'Will you, Lily?' he asked meaningfully.

She flushed. 'I don't want to cause trouble with Ralph.'

'Damn Ralph.' He stared at her for a moment, his face straight, then said, 'I meant what I said, Lily. We were all worried about you.'

She had dropped her gaze and didn't see the message in his eyes. All she heard was the throb of what she termed pity in his voice. 'Thank you,' she said flatly, turning and putting her hand on the latch of the back door. 'I really must go. Mrs Gray will be back from church soon.'

'I wanted to ask—' he began.

The back door creaked as she opened it. She turned in the doorway. 'I'm sorry?'

There was a long pause. 'Nothing,' he said quietly. 'It will keep. Goodbye.'

'Goodbye.' She watched him as he made his way to the back gate which the tradesmen and tinkers used, his tall, broad-shouldered frame in the thick overcoat very big and dark in the white, sparkling surroundings. She didn't wait to see if he would stop at the gate and turn round and speak or wave. She shut the door and leaned against it, her heart thudding. Not for the world would she have admitted to herself that she wouldn't have been able to bear it if he hadn't, that she'd taken the coward's way out.

PART FOUR

June 1911 – Choices

Chapter 15

It was over two years since the fateful night when Geraldine had spat her venom and changed the lives of everyone in the Brown family. Stanley's departure from the marital home and his living openly with another woman had caused shock waves which had reverberated around the community for some time, till another scandal had taken its place. Once the divorce was through he had married Sally in a simple ceremony at the local register office. Only his parents and the bride's stepchildren had attended.

Geraldine had presented herself as the brave, betrayed wife from the day the news had broken and Stanley had not challenged this. He had chosen to walk away from the marriage without a penny which had secured his divorce earlier than it might have done, leaving Geraldine with the house and their nest egg in the bank. Geraldine had sold the big terraced property for a great deal more than Stanley had paid for it, moving to a smart little apartment overlooking Barnes Park. She had discovered one of the leading lights of the bridge club and the Women's Guild who'd recently been widowed lived in the same development.

Lily had not set eyes on her mother or Stanley since the weekend she'd left the house in St Bede's Terrace. She had gone to see her Granda and Grandma Brown shortly after she had talked to Sarah, and they had been adamant that as far as they were concerned she was still very much their precious granddaughter. For their sake she had started visiting them once a month on a Sunday afternoon, and Sarah had made the effort to be there at the same time with the children. At first Lily had found these afternoons extremely painful and awkward, but as the months had gone by, they were less so. Nevertheless, she had made it clear to Sarah that she couldn't see her sister at Nora's house as had been suggested. She had explained she felt it was better to let the dust settle, especially as far as Ralph was concerned. She didn't want to come between man and wife, nor did she want to cause problems for Nora with her son. This wasn't the whole truth. In her heart of hearts she knew it was John she couldn't face.

He had come to the house again a week or so after his first visit, enquiring after her well-being. She had been deliberately cool with an aloofness which had bordered on rudeness. He had not called again.

For a long time she had centred her life around the Gray children and especially Nicholas and Adam, rarely leaving the house except to visit her grand-parents. She had even curtailed her visits to Ellen to once every few weeks. It had been all she could cope with. For many months she had been unable to sleep at night or eat or deal with even the slightest deviation in the routine. Although on the surface she had strived to appear as normal, she had known it was a veneer. Inside she had felt like a small child shut in a dark room, frightened and bewildered and wanting to call out for someone to help but knowing no one was there.

Slowly she had pulled herself out of the maelstrom of emotion. She had begun to sleep properly and her appetite had returned. She had known she was more herself when she'd begun to see the beauty in a crisp frosty morning or a lovely sunset once more. She had weathered the storm, and yet, not quite. She had changed. She knew she'd changed and there was a part of her that was deeply saddened by it but she couldn't trust folk in the same way she once had.

She bumped into Nora one cold bright winter's afternoon in February when she had taken the twins to Mowbray Park. Sarah was with her mother-in-law; she and Nora had been sitting on a bench watching Sarah's girls playing with their hoops when Lily walked by. Nicholas and Adam had fallen asleep and when Sarah pressed Lily to sit with them for a while she reluctantly agreed, feeling acutely embarrassed and wondering if they were going to skirt round the past.

Nora being Nora, however, she came straight to the point. 'Ee, lass, I'm right glad I've seen you.' She patted Lily's hand. 'The times I've said to Sarah to bring you round ours. You'd be more than welcome, hinny. You know that, don't you? It don't make no difference to us what's happened.'

'Thank you, Mrs Turner.' Lily could feel the hot colour seeping up from her neck. 'But with Ralph feeling the way he does . . .'

'Don't you worry your head about him, lass. It's my house an' me an' Harold say who's welcome. Anyway, there's no chance you'd see him these days, is there, Sarah?' She didn't wait for her daughter-in-law to comment, continuing, 'Wouldn't be seen dead slummin' it nowadays, not since he moved to Sea View Road. Not good enough for the big man, we're not.'

Sarah wriggled on the seat and Nora turned to her. 'You know I'm only speakin' the truth. You're a good lass, none better, but I know what I know. I never thought I'd live to call one of me own an upstart, but if the cap fits . . . He used to be on at our John for wantin' to better himself, but John would never be ashamed of his beginnings, however high he rose.'

Nora's brusque tone couldn't hide the deep hurt and Lily impulsively squeezed her arm. 'I'd give the world to have you as a mother,' she said simply.

'Aw, lass.' Nora blinked rapidly. 'Then you'll come and see us some Sundays? When you're not at your gran's? Sarah comes every week. He' – this was said with a sniff – 'is always at the boatyard or tied up with paperwork. Isn't that right, hinny?' Again she didn't wait for her daughter-in-law to reply before she said, 'Come, Lily, please. It's worried me, you going into yourself like you have. Course, I understand it, it's natural, but you need family round you in times of trouble and with Sarah being your sister, I feel you're family.'

She hadn't been able to refuse in the face of such

kindness, but during the next months Lily had often wished she'd never run into Nora that day and begun something it would now be very difficult to get out of without offending Sarah's mother-in-law. It wasn't so much the chance of Ralph turning up at his mother's one day as John's brooding presence that had her on edge and made her uncomfortable every Sunday afternoon.

The small terrace was always packed to the hilt. Cissy and Florence and their husbands and families, together with David and Francis – both recently married – and their wives usually made an appearance for the ritual Sunday get together. Robert was now a young man of eighteen and his girlfriend, who was also a friend of Hannah's, was usually present, along with Larry who was now quite grown up at eight years old.

The children were usually shooed out into the back lane or, if it was too muddy and wet, into the street to play, but even though the men often stood in the hall or the backyard smoking their pipes and quietly talking, there was still normally only standing room in Nora's small kitchen. Not that anyone seemed to mind this, the Turners were a jolly lot on the whole. Copious pots of tea oiled the conversation and platefuls of bread and butter and Nora's fruit cake disappeared like the mist on a summer's morning.

And yet through all the noise and laughter and hullabaloo Lily was acutely aware of John every moment. She knew when he was chatting with the other men in the backyard, when he was playing with the younger children and pretending to be an ogre to send them scattering into the back lane screaming their heads off, or – most disturbing of all – when he stood silently leaning against the wall, his hands in his pockets and his handsome face sombre and far away.

He had been polite and non-committal when they had met again, seemingly unaware of the excruciating embarrassment which had turned her creamy skin bright red. Neither he or anyone else had made any reference to her long absence or the reason for it. Everyone had acted as though she had always accompanied Sarah on a Sunday afternoon. Nevertheless, each time she caught sight of his tall figure her heart began to thump like a piston engine and she found herself becoming tongue-tied and flustered.

Nora had told her with transparent pride that John was on the verge of finishing his studies at long last. 'Takes his final examinations in the summer and about time too.' She had pulled a face to hide her gratification at what to her was something verging on a miracle. 'He can start work as an accountant then, if he can find a place, of course.'

Lily had wanted to ask him about that. To wish him well, to talk to him, but . . . she couldn't. And yet she could talk to the others quite naturally after the first Sunday. This state of affairs ended abruptly on the evening of the day which saw George V crowned 'King of the United Kingdom of Great Britain and Ireland and of the British Dominions beyond the seas, Defender of the Faith, Emperor of India'. Throughout the country the coronation was celebrated by street parties for the children and much revelry, the towns and villages swarming with people as most shops and factories closed either for the whole day or at noon.

The Grays had been invited to spend the day with Norman Gray's family who had a large country estate on the outskirts of Newcastle. To Lily's surprise, Arabella had informed her she needn't accompany them but could treat the event of the King's coronation as a little holiday.

A shy June sun was forever popping in and out behind grey clouds as Lily made her way to Ellen's after lunch. But the weather held and after an early tea, Lily, Ellen and Bruce went for a walk. The side streets were packed with folk, adults organising games for the children before the bonfires all over the town were lit once twilight set in. A sense of gaiety and excitement pervaded the streets, and homemade banners and Union Jack flags were fluttering above every door.

Lily was listening to Ellen and Bruce having one of their discussions which bordered on argument as they strolled into the centre of town.

'I'm not saying people haven't got a right to celebrate, Bruce.' Ellen was on her high horse, her pretty face flushed and intense. 'But why all this talk about George V heading the largest empire in the world as though it's something to be proud of when the King and government can't even look after Britain? You know the state of the tenements here. You know how many men, women and children – yes, children – work seventy and eighty hours a week for a pittance. And yet today it's all forgotten.'

'People are proud to be British, that's all.'

'Proud?' Ellen glared at him. 'Really, Bruce, I can't believe you at times. We've got violence erupting every few months in the coalfields because the owners are squeezing the last drop of blood from the miners. Are you proud of that? Or the way the bosses locked out the dockers and iron workers to force them to accept cuts in rates of pay last year?'

'Of course not.'

'Women are being thrown into prison and treated abominably just because they want a say in their own country; doesn't anyone stop to think that we can't make a worse job of it than men have, and we might do a far better one?'

'I'm sure they do, Ellen, which is precisely why there's so much opposition.'

'But you can stand there and tell me you're proud to be British.'

'I actually said the folk celebrating tonight are proud to be British,' Bruce said in his customary mild manner. 'But if you are asking me, yes, I am, and I'm not about to apologise to you for what I think.'

'Why would you? You're a man.'

'It's very nice of you to have noticed.'

Lily giggled. These two friends of hers would never know how their unstinting support and understanding had helped her over the last couple of years. They had been upset and angry for her when she had first told them what had transpired in the traumatic weeks following her leaving home, then caring and encouraging as time had gone on. Slipping her arm through Bruce's and gesturing for Ellen – on his other side – to do the same, she said, 'That's enough, me bairns.

248

Be good now and I might treat you both to a bag of roasted chestnuts later.' She felt happy tonight, she realised with a little dart of amazement. She'd forgotten what it felt like. But something in the jubilant bright faces all around her was infectious. It wouldn't last, life would get in the way of it tomorrow for her and the thousands of others letting their hair down, but that didn't matter tonight.

Bruce laughed, his mouth wide. 'Roasted chestnuts, is it? I always said you were a canny lass, Lily Brown. And might there be a tot of something to go with it?'

She opened her mouth to speak but the laughing retort was never voiced. There, standing not a yard from her, was John. She stopped dead, her arm falling from Bruce's, but Bruce and Ellen took a few steps before they realised and turned. She was aware of this on the perimeter of her mind but her whole being was taken up with the tall dark man in front of her.

'Hello, Lily,' said John quietly, not taking his eyes from her face. 'I was wondering if I'd see you tonight.' That was a damn silly thing to say, he told himself in the next moment. It was the truth, but it was still a silly thing to say to her. She wasn't to know he thought about her all the time, seeing her face a hundred times a day in this woman or that. But tonight he hadn't imagined it. She was here, in front of him, staring at him with those great green eyes of hers.

He watched her blink, as though awaking from a dream, and her voice was as low as his had been when she said, 'Hello, John.' Bruce and Ellen had joined them, their faces still smiling but faintly wary, and as if suddenly remembering their existence, Lily said quickly. 'John, this is Ellen Lindsay and Bruce McGuigan, friends of mine. Ellen, Bruce, this is John Turner, Sarah's brother-in-law.'

'Pleased to meet you.' John reached out his hand and shook Bruce's before nodding to Ellen, but his gaze immediately returned to Lily. Seeing her like this, unexpectedly, her loveliness hit him afresh. For no reason he could understand he felt a constriction in his throat and he had to swallow hard before he forced his eyes from her and let his glance sweep over the three of them. 'Are you off to the fair?'

'The fair?' It was Bruce who replied. 'I didn't know there was a fair.'

John nodded. 'In one of the fields at Thornhill Farm off Thornholme Road.' His gaze returned to Lily as he said, 'My mother and Hannah took Larry and a couple of his pals earlier and they came home full of it.' He smiled. 'You know what bairns are for fairs.'

She smiled back but said nothing, it was as though her brain had ceased to function. Desperately she sought for something to say to ease what had become a strained moment, but it was Ellen who laughingly said, looking up at Bruce, 'Not just bairns, I hope. I'd like to go.'

'Then we shall. All right with you, Lily?'

She nodded. 'Of course.' She looked at John to say goodbye but something in his face, a kind of lost look, caused the words to stick in her throat. To her horror, she heard herself say, 'I suppose you're off to meet someone?'

'No. No, I'm not. I'm at a bit of a loose end actually. I'm usually studying at this time of night but I took my final exams a couple of nights ago and so all that's finished with. For the present, at least.'

'You did?' She forgot her embarrassment. 'Oh John, how did you do?'

'I won't know the results for some days but I think I did all right.'

'I'm glad.' She could hear the warmth in her voice herself and the pink in her cheeks grew deeper. To hide her confusion she turned to Ellen and Bruce who, she noticed, were now staring at them with some interest. 'John has been studying to be an accountant in his spare time.'

'Really?' Bruce gave John his full attention. Mathematics was his favourite subject. 'How did that come about, if you don't mind me asking? Have you got a day job?'

'In the docks.' John shrugged. 'I'd have liked to have stayed on at school but family circumstances didn't permit.'

'And so you've been studying at night?' Bruce's voice expressed his admiration. 'That can't have been easy.'

As the two men began to talk Ellen raised her eyebrows ever so slightly at Lily. Lily knew what the look meant. Who *exactly* is this man and why haven't you mentioned him before? Pretending she hadn't noticed, Lily pulled her straw bonnet more firmly down on her head and prayed her cheeks didn't look as burning hot as they felt.

She had gained her aplomb by the time there was a lull in the conversation. When John turned to her, his voice quiet as he said, 'Well, I'd better let you get on,' she thought her voice was remarkably steady when she replied, 'If you're at a loose end, as you said, you're more than welcome to join us.'

He didn't reply immediately and for a heart-stopping moment she thought he was going to refuse. Then she saw him breathe out slowly and his shoulders relax and realised that in spite of the air of self-assurance that sat on him like a mantle he was as tense as she was.

'Thank you,' he said softly. 'There's nothing I'd like more.'

It was a magical night.

By the time they arrived at Thornhill Farm a soft summer twilight had begun to fall, the smoke from the chimneys of the gaily painted Romany caravans curling to hang in the still air. They stopped at the far edge of the field, gazing over the canvas booths, roundabouts, chairboat swings, shooting galleries, coconut shies and sideshows for a minute or two. People had come in such numbers that the din from the piped music of the elaborately decorated steam organs could barely be heard above the shrieks and laughter.

Bruce eyed the crowds warily. Tucking Ellen's arm through his, he said in a tone that brooked no argument, 'You make sure you keep your arm locked in mine, all right? It will be easy to get separated in this lot.'

'Lily?'

John offered her his arm, and as she slid hers through his, his other hand came out to cover her fingers. She felt herself start to tremble but not through fear, at least not the kind of fear she had experienced when his brother had tried to press his attentions on her. This fear was a composite of how much she wanted this evening with him and of her feelings which had always been there, under the surface, for this man.

The four of them had a wonderful time. They rode on everything, watched the contortionists, visited the bearded lady's booth and some of the other sideshows, and ate roasted potatoes and bags of chitterlings followed by ice-cream and sticks of sugar. Bruce almost had his pocket picked, and they were all jostled and bumped, but Lily didn't care. Somehow, impossible though it would have seemed only that morning, she was with John. A day that had been ordinary – in spite of the coronation and all the shenanigans – had turned into something extraordinary.

The night was dark and all the stars were out when the four of them left the lights and music of the fair. At the end of Thornholme Road they stopped, and it was here John said, 'I'll see Lily home.'

Bruce and Ellen glanced at Lily who nodded her agreement. The two women hugged and Bruce and John shook hands, Bruce saying he hoped the four of them could get together again soon, to which John quietly replied he would like that very much.

As the two couples separated the old shyness swept over Lily again. She and John had been talking and laughing most of the night but now she felt constrained in his presence. They walked along the pavement side by side but without touching; now the crowds were left behind there was no longer any reason for her to be pressed close into his side, her arm in his.

253

Only courting couples behaved like that. She found herself wondering if he thought she had been too forward that night. Knowing what he did about her, would he expect her to be on the brazen side? And then she checked herself. No. No, he wouldn't think like that, not John. If she knew anything about him, she knew that much.

Would he ask to see her again? Did he *want* to see her again? She hadn't been very nice to him in the past and half the time she hadn't known why. Her thoughts were still racing when she glanced at him as he cleared his throat. He rubbed his hand tightly across his mouth and then brought her to a standstill by putting his hand on her arm and turning her to face him. 'I'm not much good with words, Lily. Give me figures any day.' He smiled with wry self-deprecation as he shook his head at himself. 'But I just want you to know this, if I haven't made it clear enough already. I like you, no, more than like. I always have. We got off to a bad start at Ralph and Sarah's wedding and it seemed to go downhill from there, but it didn't alter the way I felt.'

She stared at him. 'You never said. I don't mean at the wedding, but when we met afterwards.'

'We never stopped arguing and fighting for long enough.'

It was said with another faint smile but her face was straight. 'You always acted as though I annoyed and irritated you.'

'Not irritated. You maddened me at times.'

'You did me too.'

'I know.' He wetted his lips; then, his voice thick,

he said, 'I was going to say all this and ask, well, if there was any hope for me, I suppose, when I came to the house after you'd left your mam's.'

'Why didn't you?'

'You didn't give me a chance.'

No, she supposed she hadn't, looking back. But it wouldn't have been the right time the way she was feeling. 'I didn't know where I was then,' she said softly. 'I was all at sea.'

'And now?'

She knew what he was asking but she had to make sure. 'Are you asking me to walk out with you?'

He took both her hands in his and now there was no vestige of a smile on his face. 'I want you for my lass, Lily. I always have. Oh, I can't pretend there hasn't been the odd girl in the last few years, I'm no monk, but I have to say to my shame that they didn't mean anything. From when I first saw you I knew how I felt. I fought it because you'd made it clear you didn't want to know, but tonight I thought – no, I hoped – you might be changing your mind. Are you, Lily? I need to know once and for all. If you tell me I've misunderstood then that's fine. I promise you I won't bother you again. We – we can be friends.'

There had arisen in Lily a lightness. It was like the feeling you get before you laughed, but she didn't want to laugh. In fact, she felt more like crying but with regret at all the time they had wasted. But she had to say one last thing, to bring it into the open before she gave him her answer and she wanted to be looking into his face when she asked him. 'People know about my father leaving my mother for another woman, about the divorce and everything, but not – not about my beginnings. What if that were to become public? What if folk found out my da isn't my da, that I'm . . . illegitimate? It doesn't seem likely, but it might happen. They'd look at me differently, you know they would. They might not say anything about it, but they'd think it.'

There was silence between them for a moment but his grip on her fingers tightened. Then, his voice low, he said, 'If you want the truth, I don't give a monkey's what people think except for the way it might make you feel. And anyone worth their salt wouldn't think any the less of you anyway, like Ellen and Bruce and my mam, folk like that. The rest of them – well, the way I see it they aren't worthy to lick your boots, lass.'

'Your brother doesn't feel like that.'

'Like I said, he isn't worthy to lick your boots.' He shook her hands impatiently. 'I don't want to talk about Ralph, Lily. I want to know how you feel. Is it, yes, John, I want to be your lass, or no, John, you've got it all wrong?'

She stared straight into his eyes as she answered, 'It's yes, John. Yes, please. It's been yes for a long time but I wouldn't let myself believe you liked me.'

'Like you?' His voice dropped to a mere whisper but it made her tremble. 'Like doesn't begin to describe what I feel about you, Lily Brown.' He pulled her closer, his voice even quieter when he said, 'Don't be frightened of me. I'd never do anything to hurt you.'

She couldn't explain that her trembling had nothing to do with being frightened. She watched his face

256

come closer and then his lips were on hers, urgent and hungry as he crushed her into him. The kiss only lasted a few moments and then he let her go, his voice rueful as he said, 'I'm sorry, I'm sorry, I'm like a bull in a china shop. So much for me not frightening you. But I've waited so long for this, dreamed of it more times than I can count.'

She smiled a little shakily, privately amazed at the response she'd felt in her body as their mouths had merged. She had never kissed a man on the mouth before.

He reached for her once more but only to draw her arm through his as they began walking again, entwining his fingers through hers and holding them close to his jacket.

She was John Turner's lass. The wonder of it made her want to shout and jump but she walked on sedately. He cared about her. Really cared about her and he didn't mind about her da and any of that. And his mam and da and the rest of them liked her, she knew they did.

And Ralph? She felt a cold prickle at the base of her spine. It didn't matter what he thought, he couldn't hurt her; besides, she'd seen neither hide nor hair of him for a long time. He was taken up with his boat-yard these days. Nevertheless, the thought of John's brother disturbed her. He was the antithesis of John, predatory and cruel. She was in no doubt that the only reason he had banned her from visiting their house and forbidden Sarah to have anything to do with her was spite because she had rebuffed his advances.

'Penny for them?' John's voice intruded and she glanced up at him. The dark brown eyes were waiting for her response and they were smiling. The look on his face reminded her of a little boy on Christmas morning who'd received everything he'd ever wanted.

'I was thinking how fortunate it was you decided to go for a walk this evening,' she said softly, relaxing against him. They walked on in step, their hips moving against each other and their hands clasped tightly together.

Ellen waited till they were out of earshot before she said quietly, 'Well? What do you think?'

Bruce did not prevaricate. 'He seems a nice young man, certainly a go-getter. She could do a lot worse.'

'Yes. Yes, I suppose so.'

'Why that note in your voice?' They had been walking arm in arm without looking at each other, but now Bruce stopped, forcing Ellen to meet his gaze. 'Don't you like him?'

'It's not that.'

'What, then?'

'His brother is married to Sarah, Lily's sister, and in the past I've got the impression all's not well there. Lily's said her sister is unhappy but there's more to it than that, I'm sure of it. Lily seems almost . . . frightened of this man.'

'Lily? Frightened? I don't think Lily would be frightened of anyone. She's like you in that respect.'

Ellen did not reply to this immediately but began walking on so he fell into step beside her, her arm once again through his. She knew Bruce loved her but when he said things like this it brought home how little he understood her, and that disturbed her greatly. For how could he really love her if he didn't know what she was like inside? How she felt? But then again she had to be honest with herself and admit that was because she only let him see what she wanted him to see.

She was aware of Bruce giving her a long, scrutinising look before he said, 'What's the matter?'

'Nothing.'

'What have I said?'

'I told you, nothing's the matter.'

'Ellen.' He stopped and pulled her to face him again, and this time not gently. 'We've had a lovely evening and everything was fine till a minute ago. Right? Now we're standing here all night if needs be till you tell me what's put that look on your face.'

She knew he meant it. On the rare occasions he asserted his authority he never backed down. She shrugged her shoulders under her thin summer coat. 'I can get frightened sometimes, Bruce.'

'What?'

It was clear from his expression that whatever he'd expected it wasn't this. For a moment she felt slightly ridiculous. 'You said you didn't think Lily would be frightened of anyone and that she was like me. Well, I'm frightened sometimes. That's all.'

His brow had wrinkled. 'Of what or whom?'

She could have said she was frightened of her feelings for him, but that would never do. 'Nothing specific, I suppose. I'm just not some kind of wonder woman. Sometimes I think you attribute qualities to me which make me seem . . . unfeeling.'

He did not immediately deny this which surprised her. Her heart began to beat faster. More than once she had remarked to Lily that she was waiting for the day when Bruce would get tired of her and the more her dread of this day grew, so did her resolve not to accept his proposals of marriage. He already had too much power over her and he must not know this. The day she had left the hospital, her stomach flat and her arms empty, she had promised herself she would remain single for the rest of her life. Never would she become subject to a man again or allow one to have dominion over her. When she had cowered under Steven's last beating, curled up in a ball on the floor as she endeavoured to protect her stomach from his fists and feet, something had broken in her. Not physically, but in her spirit. Maybe if her daughter had lived it would have been different, but the suffering and humiliation she'd endured that night, the terrifying feeling of being helpless under his merciless attack, was still with her. It would always be with her. As a reminder of what she must not allow again.

'I don't think of you as a wonder woman, Ellen. Merely a wonderful woman, but one who is held by the past in some dark place I can't enter. Because you won't let me in, will you? The last five or six years since we met I've tried to show you who I am but it's always one step forward and two back. You make sure of that.' He smiled grimly. 'And you can be formidable.'

She stared at him. His eyes were kind but sad. 'I don't mean to be formidable.'

He shook his head. 'Yes, you do.'

Pride rose. She stepped back a pace, her voice cool as she said, 'Then why do you put up with me? I've told you before you're a free agent, I have no hold over you. I expect nothing from you.'

'And therein is the crux of the problem.'

'I can't change the way I am, Bruce.'

'I know that. That's why I've stayed around so long.' For a moment she stared at him uncomprehendingly. 'The real Ellen is the woman I love,' he said quietly, 'and I don't want her to change. And one day I shall break into that dark place and bring the light, and you won't be able to hide any more.'

Her face looked pinched and white in the dim light from the street lamp they were standing under and he could see the panic in her eyes his words had provoked. He swore softly, taking her arm as he said, 'We've talked enough for one evening and it's late. Come on.'

They walked to Crowtree Road in silence and once outside the house Bruce let go of her arm. 'Goodnight, Ellen.'

'Aren't you coming in?' He always came in for a hot drink.

'Not tonight.'

He sounded weary and again her heart began to thud painfully hard. She was losing him, she knew it. So why didn't she do something, say something? When he turned from her without kissing her goodnight she almost called out to him. Almost. Instead she watched him walk away and when he didn't turn at the corner to wave or see if she was still there but simply disappeared from view, her soft mouth hardened. So much for caring for her. He could just walk away without a backward glance.

She let herself into the house and once inside the front room drew the curtains and made up the studio couch as she did each night. That done, however, she did not begin to get ready for bed but found herself pacing the floor.

What was wrong with wanting a life free of emotional commitment, devoid of the physical and mental battles she'd endured in the past? Battles she could never hope to win? She had been honest with Bruce; from the first she had been absolutely above board as to what he could expect and what she was prepared to give. He couldn't say she'd played games or tried to fool him. On the contrary, her truthfulness had been the cause of many difficult moments but she'd been straight with him nonetheless. She sat down with a bump on the couch.

After she had been widowed she'd looked back on her life before she had married Steven and realised her sheltered upbringing had in no way prepared her for the outside world. She had been a true innocent, a perfect victim for a man like Steven, which was no doubt why he had chosen her as his wife. But in the years following her daughter's death she had rectified that. She knew what she did and didn't believe in now, she was able to stand on her own two feet and be beholden to no one, man or woman. Steven had swept her off her feet with his protestations of love and desire;

she had been a stupid young girl who had loved blindly and adoringly and she would never love like that again. She wouldn't let herself.

She stood up and began to undress, glancing round the quiet room, the only sound the steady ticking of the small marble clock above the fireplace. For the first time since she had got her home together, the tasteful, pretty surroundings did not soothe her; an emptiness akin to desolation swept over her. She went across to the writing desk by the window. It had three small drawers underneath, the middle one of which she always kept locked. Opening it, she stared down at the beautifully painted portrait it contained.

He had been so kind, the young painter she had found. He had spent hours listening to her and altering a brush stroke here and another there till she was satisfied with the likeness. Gently she lifted the white-framed painting and carried it over to the bed where she sat gazing at her daughter. She had been so terrified she would forget each detail of her tiny, perfect face; the button nose, rosebud mouth and downy hair that had curled in a wisp over the minute forehead. But here it was captured for ever. It was all she had, and it wasn't enough. Tonight, especially, it wasn't enough.

Chapter 16

'*John?*' Sarah stopped dead, her voice high and her round, plump face stretched in amazement. 'You're joking! You don't even like him.'

The two sisters had met at the corner of Ryhope Road and Regent Terrace as was customary on a Sunday afternoon when they were going to Nora's or to visit their grandparents. Lily had been standing waiting for Sarah and her nieces and she'd imparted her news as soon as Sarah had arrived. Now she continued walking, holding Imogen's dimpled little hand in hers, Felicity being fast asleep in the baby carriage. 'I do like him. I have for some time,' she said over her shoulder.

Sarah hurried to catch her up. 'But you never said. Why didn't you tell me?'

'There wasn't anything to tell before Friday night. I didn't even think he liked me.'

'I can't believe it. Not John.'

Lily looked hard at her sister. 'You don't sound very pleased.'

'Oh I am. If you like him and he's your choice, of course I'm glad for you. Haven't I been saying for ages you ought to have a lad? Especially with you being so bonny an' all.'

'What's the matter, then?' Lily asked quietly. 'Because something is. I can always tell with you.'

Sarah hesitated. She couldn't say she wished Lily had picked anyone but John. Not that he wasn't nice enough, he was, and from what she could see he wasn't a bit like Ralph inside, where it counted. But he *was* Ralph's brother and she knew her husband would go stark staring mad once he knew about this. Since that anonymous letter had put the cat among the pigeons and the truth about Lily's beginnings along with the talk of Ellen Lindsay had come to light, he'd been so nasty about her. Fortunately, none of the family had let on about Lily joining them on a Sunday afternoon although she knew that eventually it was bound to come out. Not that he could stop his mother having whomever she liked in her own home, of course, but he'd have blamed her, Sarah, not his mam. She and the bairns couldn't do anything right as far as he was concerned, and she was as sure as she could be he was carrying on with someone else. Why else wouldn't he want it from her? And the cheap scent she'd smelt hanging about him more than once wouldn't have come from any respectable woman.

'Sarah? What is it?'

Lily's voice brought her back to herself and as she glanced at her sister, she shrugged. 'Nothing really, except . . . well, I hope John turns out to be like he

265

seems. I thought Ralph was all right once but it was the worst day's work I ever did, marrying him.'

Sarah hadn't spoken about her marriage so openly for a long time. 'Oh, Sarah.' Lily didn't know what to say. She thought the signs about Ralph had been there from day one but it wouldn't help her sister to point that out now. 'I'm sorry, lass.'

'I hate him, Mops.' Sarah's voice was quiet and slow. 'He's a vicious man underneath, you've no idea, and he's got worse the more he's got on. And I tell you something else' – she leaned closer to Lily as they walked although there was no one else about apart from a group of children swinging round a lamp post a hundred yards away – 'this boatyard isn't all he's involved in, that's for sure. Once or twice he's let something slip and the people he's mixed up with are villains. I mean real villains, you know? The sort who'd think nothing about cutting someone's throat if it suited them. I've prayed one of them will cut his before now and I've meant it.' She raised her chin defiantly. 'That shocks you, doesn't it? Me own husband.'

Lily did not reply to this. What she did say was, 'Have you told Nora how bad things are?'

Sarah shook her head. 'If he knew I'd talked to anyone he'd kill me,' she said simply. 'You've no idea what he's capable of.'

Lily felt sick, really sick. She knew Sarah hadn't been happy for a long time, but this? This was something else.

'Don't look like that.' Sarah reached out and patted her arm. 'Most of the time I don't see much of him, which suits me down to the ground. I've – I've told Da a bit of how things are, but not much. I was scared he'd come round to see him and then there'd be murder done.'

Lily met Sarah's eyes. She knew her sister saw Stanley on the quiet because Sarah had told her so shortly after the balloon had gone up and he'd gone to live with his Sally. On that occasion she had made it clear she didn't want his name mentioned between them again and to give Sarah her due she'd stuck to that. Hurt and pain rose in a flood and the words were out before she could stop them: 'Well, he's *your* father, isn't he? Of course he'd be worried about *you*.'

'He worries about you an' all. He loves you, lass. I know you don't believe that but he does. As far as he's concerned he's got two daughters and nothing will alter that. If you don't speak to him to his dying day it won't make no difference to how he feels.'

'Don't, Sarah.'

'It's the truth, Mops.'

'Truth? Neither he nor Mam would know what the truth was if it rose up and bit them on the backside. No, don't, Sarah' – as her sister went to speak, Lily stopped her with a raised hand – 'don't stick up for him. He pretended to be my father to save his face, that and that alone is the *truth*. I don't want anything to do with him or Mam.'

'I can understand it with her. If the devil himself had to choose a mother he'd baulk at ours. Looking back I don't think she could ever stand either of us. It was one of nature's bad jokes, her falling twice. And then there's someone like Sally who'd give the world

267

for her own bairn and she can't have one.' Sarah stopped abruptly, aware of how Lily was staring at her.

'You haven't, our Sarah? You haven't met her?'

'Aye, I have.' Sarah tossed her head. 'And she's nice, lovely, and bonny with it, but not what you'd think. She's homely, motherly.'

In spite of herself Lily's curiosity got the better of her. 'I thought she'd got two bairns?'

'They were her husband's. He was a widower with two young 'uns when she married him. She thinks of them as her own and they think the world of her too, but it's not the same, is it, not when they can remember their own mam. Sally says she never set out to take their real mam's place anyway.'

Unconsciously Lily repeated Sarah's earlier words. 'You never said you'd seen her. Why didn't you tell me?'

'You said I couldn't even mention Da's name,' Sarah said reasonably.

Lily nodded, then glanced down at Imogen trotting by her side and whisked the little girl up into her arms, running with her a short way to make her squeal and laugh. She concentrated on her niece for the next minute or two and Sarah was wise enough to take the hint and say no more.

When they turned into the road which led to Canon Cockin Street John was standing at the corner. He raised his hand, his face lighting up, and began to walk towards them. 'By, lass, he's keen,' Sarah murmured on a smothered giggle, before raising her voice and saying, 'Look, Imogen, who's this? It's Uncle John, come to meet us.'

John made a fuss of Imogen when he reached them

but when Lily went to walk on with Sarah, he caught her hand. 'We'll be along shortly, Sarah. Tell them, would you?' he said, and without waiting for an answer he pulled Lily along the pavement in the opposite direction, crossing the road and not stopping till they were in the grounds of the old glassworks which had been disused for some time. 'I want a minute with you on our own without all that lot,' he said softly, his eyes warm on her flushed face. 'How have you been?'

'All right.' She didn't know why she was whispering, it just seemed right.

'I've missed you. Have you missed me?' His eyes had been roaming her face as he'd spoken but now they remained on her lips. Before she could answer his mouth was on hers and he was kissing her hungrily and she was kissing him back. When they finally drew apart they stared at each other for one moment before he laughed out loud, lifting her right off her feet and swinging her round and round in his arms till she was dizzy and begging for mercy.

'I can't believe you're mine,' he muttered as he set her down on her feet but still within the circle of his arms. 'You are mine, aren't you, Lily?'

'You know I am.'

He trailed a blond curl that had escaped the bun on top of her head through his fingers. 'You're beautiful, Lily. So beautiful.'

She didn't deny this as she would have done if anyone else had said it. Instead she lifted her fingers and touched his face, privately amazed he felt so strongly. 'If you think so that's all that matters.'

'Everyone thinks so.' He grinned at her. 'Mam was bowled over when I told her we were courting. She thinks you're a grand lass.'

Nora's approval was warming. Her voice soft, Lily murmured, 'I like your mam, John, I always have. She was so kind to me when I met her in the park that day.'

'How could anyone not be kind to you?' He kissed her again and they clung together for long moments before he straightened, tucking her arm in his. 'Come on, we'd better go and join the menagerie. Cissy and Florence and the rest of them were arriving as I left, no doubt Mam's told them the news by now.'

Lily felt suddenly shy.

'Don't look so nervous, I won't let them eat you.' He smiled at her, his dark brown eyes glowing. 'Although I feel like eating you up myself.'

He looked so tall and handsome standing there, the sunlight bringing out chestnut streaks in his black hair. And she was his lass. The wonder of it swept over Lily again. Everything had been so horrible for so long but now the world seemed a wonderful place where anything could happen. The fact that she was John Turner's lass was proof of that. And the summer was in front of them. Long evenings when she could slip out of the house once the bairns were asleep and now he wasn't studying they'd be able to see each other often.

'What?' He'd watched the way her thoughts were mirrored on her face. 'What are you thinking?'

'Just that we've got the summer together.'

'The first of many, I hope.' Again he swung her

round a few times before they started walking back the way they'd come. 'I heard about my exams today, by the way,' he said after a moment or two with deliberate casualness.

'You did?' It was a squeal. 'That's early, isn't it?'

He nodded, and then looked down at her, his face alight. 'I passed, Lily, with distinction.'

She beamed up at him. 'I knew you would.'

'I'm going to make myself known to all the accountants in the town and ask them to bear me in mind for when a vacancy comes up. I want to get out of the docks as soon as I can.' Just before they left the grounds of the glassworks he stopped, moving her to face him once more. 'I'm looking to the future, lass. I want to be in a position to provide well for a family.'

She blinked, her heart beating faster.

Then he laughed again, a joyous sound, and lifted his gaze to the blue sky. 'I'm on the up and up, lass. I can feel it in my bones. Everything is going to work out from now on, and do you know why?'

She shook her head, smiling at his enthusiasm.

'Because you're my girl. This time last week I didn't think I'd got a hope with you, but now? Now I could conquer kingdoms, that's how I feel.'

His boyishness was endearing and another quality to the personality she was fast realising was a complex one. Her father had used to say that still waters ran deep and that was true with this man. Her da . . . Sarah's words had been in the back of her mind like a constant refrain. *But he wasn't her da.* She shook herself mentally, putting that problem aside. She was with John and she wasn't going to think of anyone or anything else.

Throughout the long hot summer, a summer which saw thousands die in a record heatwave that baked the back lanes to dust and dried up rivers, Lily lived in a state she likened to heaven on earth. And this in spite of the mounting trouble and unrest in the country in general and the north-east in particular.

A shipping strike in June escalated in July to include railwaymen, and in Wales nine people were killed in a night of furious rioting, three by soldiers' bullets and six when burning trucks, filled with railway detonators and bottled carbide, exploded in their midst. Things worsened still more in August when the country was brought to a standstill and armed troops patrolled the streets in all the big cities. With the temperature soaring to ninety-seven degrees Fahrenheit in the shade, and the country forced to live on food reserves while a famine was predicted, the mood was ugly.

But none of this could puncture the bubble of happiness which encircled Lily. She only lived for the moment she saw John each evening, merely existing in the hours between.

Shortly after the dockers came out on strike and the industrial unrest spread like wildfire, John was offered a post as junior accountant in a long-established firm in the town, a job he accepted with alacrity. It was the best of times and the worst of times for him to leave the docks. With the unions locked in a battle with the Government, families were existing on subsidies which amounted to next to nothing, but in spite of the fact John's old dock colleagues knew he'd been studying and working to that end for years, some of them saw him as a rat leaving the sinking ship. And an upstart rat at that. One of them, a foul-mouthed bruiser named Archy McHaffie, had even gone so far as to spit in John's direction when he and Lily had been walking home from an evening at the picture house at the end of August. It had taken all Lily's strength to hold onto John when he would have gone for the man.

Once they were alone she had questioned him at length and he had finally admitted that there had been threats and intimidation from some quarters over the last weeks.

'But why didn't you tell me before?' She was horrified this had been going on and he hadn't mentioned it.

'Because most of the blokes are fine, it's just the odd hothead ones like McHaffie who spout off, but he's all wind and water. Don't worry' – he took her face in his hands, kissing her lips – 'it means nothing. He'd have been the same whenever I left; he was always jibing at me for wanting to better myself. He was one of Ralph's mates and when Ralph used to wind me up about the studying and all, he'd join in. He's as thick as two short planks.'

Lily stared at him. McHaffie might be thick but there had been something vicious in the man's little piggy eyes as he had stood there laughing at John's efforts to disentangle himself from her grip. She'd hung on like a limpet, though, determined not to let go.

As tall and fit as John was, the other man had been built like a brick outhouse. 'Be careful,' she said flatly.

'I told you, don't worry.' He kissed the tip of her nose. 'Like I said, he's one of Ralph's mates and he wouldn't want to get on the wrong side of him by hurting me.'

'But you never see Ralph these days.' And she was thankful for it. 'Your mam said none of the family have seen anything of him for months.'

'That doesn't mean he isn't still around and McHaffie knows it. He's a funny bloke, Ralph, and he's got funnier as he's got older, I'm not denying it, but him and me have always been all right in our own way. He always looked out for me when we were bairns.'

Lily lowered her head in case he could read what she was thinking. Ralph might have played the big brother when they were young but they weren't bairns any longer. And John might think he knew his brother but he didn't, not the side she had seen on occasion anyway. None of the family did. Only she and Sarah had experienced it in their own ways. It had been over two years since she had last seen him but he still featured in her nightmares now and again; a dark, ominous presence without a face, but she knew who it was all right. Even in that chimeric world of the subconscious she recognised Ralph Turner.

Perhaps it would be better when she actually met him face to face again? It was a thought which had occurred more than once over the time she had been seeing John. He'd have to find out about John and herself at some point, it was a miracle he hadn't already.

Only the fact that he spent every minute at the boat-yard, sometimes – according to Sarah – not going home for days at a time, had prevented it to date. But sooner or later there would be a family occasion that he'd attend and then he would know.

A chill flickered down her spine but then it was dispelled as John pulled her close, wrapping her in his arms. 'I like it that you worry about me,' he murmured into the soft curls of her hair, 'but I promise you I'll be all right. As long as I've got you, that is.'

She smiled up into his face. 'For ever and ever,' she said lightly.

He didn't smile back. 'I know we've only been seeing each other for a little while but we've known each other far longer, even if we did fight like cat and dog most of that time,' he said quietly. 'What I'm trying to say is, I know how I feel, Lily. This is no passing fancy with me.'

There was a question hidden in the low tones and she answered it. 'Me neither.'

'I'm on what they call a trial period at Sheldon & Todd's. Six months. Once that's up my wage will nearly double.'

He had told her this before when he'd taken the job but she knew this was different.

'If they take me on permanently it'll mean I'm set up, not like the docks where the foreman can cut your shifts and play silly devils at the drop of a hat. At Sheldon & Todd's I've got security.'

She nodded, her eyes soft on him. 'You could be prince or pauper and I'd feel the same.'

'Aye, I know that,' he said a trifle impatiently, 'but

275

what I'm trying to say is once I know for sure I'm in then all the plans I've got in my head for the future can become a reality. And . . . and you feature in them, you know you do. Will you wait till then? Till I'm free to say what I want to say?'

She wanted to tell him he could speak now, that she didn't care about his wage or the lack of it, but knowing him as she did she knew it wouldn't do any good. She nodded. 'I'll wait for ever, there could never be anyone else for me.'

'Oh, Lily.' He cupped her face in his big hands. 'I love you so much I ache with it, do you know that?'

She had been waiting for him to say it. He had expressed his love in a hundred and one ways but he had never said the actual words and she hadn't felt she could say them first. Now she took his hands from her face, pressing her lips to one and then the other. 'And I love you, more than you can ever know.'

It was exactly a week later, after a freak September storm that had seen torrential rain run off the baked fields and lanes and flood numerous dwellings, that Sarah came to the Grays' house. It was just on eight o'clock and Lily had been ready to leave to meet John at the end of the road when her sister knocked at the back door. As soon as Bridget ushered Sarah into the kitchen where Lily was adjusting her bonnet in front of the old speckled mirror and Lily saw her sister's face she knew something was terribly wrong.

'What is it?' The bonnet forgotten, she leapt across the kitchen and clutched Sarah's hands. 'What's the matter?'

'Oh, lass, lass.'

'It's not the bairns?'

'No, no.' Sarah took a deep breath. 'It's John. He's all right, I mean, he's still alive, but he's been beaten something awful. Oh, sit down, lass. I shouldn't have told you like that. I'm sorry, me and my big mouth.'

Lily had gone as white as a sheet and but for Bridget's stout grip would have crumpled to the floor. Once she was seated and Sarah was beside her, Molly bustling about getting a cup of tea and Bridget holding her hands, she said, 'Tell me.'

'I don't know much. It happened on the way home from work, apparently, not far from the house. He was in the habit of taking a short cut through that waste ground at the back of the synagogue, that's where he was found by one of their priests, rabbis they call 'em, don't they? Anyway, this rabbi saw two men kicking another who was on the ground and called out to them and they ran off.'

'Where is he?'

'In the infirmary.'

'I must go to him.'

As Lily made to rise, Sarah pushed her back in her seat. 'In a minute or two, lass. Have a cup of tea first. His mam an' da are with him and they're only letting two at a time at the bedside. He's out of it, anyway.'

'He's unconscious?' she asked faintly.

'Not exactly, I didn't mean that; Robert said they'd given him something for the pain that had made him so he didn't know what day it was.'

'When did you hear about it?'

'Robert came to tell us what was what just a few

minutes ago and I've come straight round here. Mam said she wanted you to know. Look, lass, I – I had to tell Ralph you were seeing John. He wanted to know why you had to be told. But he was all right about it.'

Lily didn't care about Ralph. She didn't care about anything but John, hurt and lying in a hospital bed. 'Is he going to be all right?'

'Aye, course he is, but it's as well the rabbi came by when he did, by all accounts. They think he's got a couple of broken ribs and he's black and blue from head to foot and with concussion an' all, but they'll know better tomorrow.' Sarah stared at her sister's chalk-white face. She didn't dare repeat what Robert had said about the men using John's head as a foot-ball. Robert had said his mam had collapsed at the first sight of John.

'I don't know what things are coming to when decent men and women can't walk the streets in broad daylight.' Molly put two cups of tea in front of Lily and Sarah. 'Here, drink that, lass.' She patted Lily's shoulder helplessly. 'It's got four spoons of sugar in it. There's nothing like hot, sweet tea for shock and if you're going to see him the night you'll likely need it.' As Bridget frowned at her sister, Molly said, 'What? What have I said now?'

'He – he told me one or two of the men he used to work with in the docks didn't like him leaving. There was a man, McHaffie, I think his name was, he tried to start a quarrel with John a few days ago when I was with him.' Lily rubbed her hand across her wet eyes, gulping hard. 'I told John to be careful but he wouldn't listen.'

'Aye, well, happen John'll be able to tell them tomorrow who it was,' Sarah said quietly. 'Now don't worry, Mops, he's in the best place and they'll look after him. He'll be out in no time, you know how strong and big John is. Likely the law'll be on to whoever had it in for him.'

Lily had drunk her tea, scalding hot and disgustingly sweet as it was. She stood up, reaching for her coat. 'I'll go now.' She turned to Molly and Bridget. 'Would you leave the key under the flower pot when you go to bed in case I'm late?'

'We'll be waiting up for you, lass, whatever the time is.' Then Molly added, somewhat naively, 'You'll feel better when you see him. The imagination is always worse in things like this.'

Molly's words rang in Lily's head as she stood gazing down at the still figure in the narrow hospital bed. It was barely recognisable as John and he was much, much worse than she could have imagined. It wasn't just that his head and face were swollen and his hair matted with dried blood, he was covered with cuts and abrasions and every inch of his flesh seemed to be bruised and turning a bluey-black.

'Who would want to hurt my lad like this?' Nora's face was puffed, her red-rimmed eyes peering out under swollen lids. 'He's as gentle as a lamb, my John.'

'I know, Mrs Turner. I know.'

The two women were standing with their arms round each other, Harold having stepped outside to make room for Lily. John was in a small side room off the main ward and it had taken some persuasion from Lily for the sister to allow her to see the patient. Only the fact that Nora had heard her voice and come out to add her weight to the urging had got Lily inside, and then the sister had been adamant that either the patient's mother or father would have to wait outside. 'You must understand, he's a very sick man and must not be disturbed,' the sister had said frostily, 'and visiting time is over as it is.'

'I'll only stay a minute, I promise.' Lily had been all eyes, her face as white as lint.

For a moment the sister's severity had softened. 'Very well, but five minutes maximum,' she said in the manner of one bestowing a great favour. Which indeed it was.

Nora wiped her eyes for the umpteenth time. 'There's been them that's jealous of him getting on a bit, he's told me about them, but to do this. That's something different, don't you think?'

Lily nodded. 'He – he will be all right, won't he?' she whispered through the tears that were threatening to choke her.

Nora gulped hard, trying to control herself. 'They think so, but the next forty-eight hours'll tell; they're not makin' any promises but then they never do, do they? I tell you, lass, I've been thankin' the good Lord for sendin' that rabbi along when he did. Mind, I wish he'd sent him a mite earlier,' she added with unconscious humour, 'but if he hadn't seen what was happening I reckon them blighters would have done for him.'

John was still asleep when Lily rejoined Sarah in the main ward. Sarah and Harold had been sitting quietly talking, and as John's father stood up, Lily noticed that for the first time since she had known him he looked an old man.

Once outside the tree-lined grounds of Sunderland's Royal Infirmary Lily stood for a moment, trying to compose herself. Sarah hadn't asked her any questions, she had just taken her arm and led her out of the building. Now she said, 'Is he bad, Mops?'

Lily nodded, unable to speak.

'Oh, lass.' Sarah hugged her tightly. 'He'll be all right, I know he will, even if he has to stay in for some time. He's a fighter, is John.'

They walked slowly through the town in the warm September darkness but even though Lily responded to Sarah's conversation her mind was working on a different plane altogether. What would she do if anything happened to John? She wouldn't be able to bear it, she wouldn't. But he *was* a fighter, Sarah was right. Nora said the police had come to the hospital earlier and asked a few questions of the rabbi who had accompanied John and remained with him till Nora and Harold had arrived. He hadn't been able to help them much. Apparently his eyesight wasn't too good. His description of the two men had been so general it could have fitted almost anyone. They were pinning their hopes on John being able to give a better description of his assailants once he was able to speak to them. She had told Nora about McHaffie and John's mother had promised to pass the information on to the police. But what if John was unable to tell the police who had attacked him, what then? Even if he recovered there would still be the possibility the same men might try to hurt him again. Nora was convinced that without the rabbi's intervention there would have been murder done and next time — if there *was* a next time — there might be no good Samaritan around.

Sarah insisted on seeing her home to the Grays' back gate and once inside the house Molly and Bridget clucked round her like two hens with one chick. She appreciated everyone's efforts on her behalf but what she really wanted was to be alone so she could face this fear that was paralysing her: the fear that John loving her, and her him, and their being together in the future had always been too good to be true.

Once upstairs she checked on the sleeping children as she did every night before retiring, lingering in the twins' bedroom and gaining some measure of comfort from the sight of the two little boys fast asleep under their coverlets.

What happened to turn little boys like these into men who would attack another and beat him to the point of death? she asked herself wretchedly. What rage had possessed them that they could inflict such injuries simply because John had attempted to pull himself out of the mire and aim for something better?

Leaving the bedroom quickly she went to her own room, where she gave way to the storm of sobbing which had been building up all evening since Sarah had walked into the kitchen.

Chapter 17

It was two weeks later, and Ralph was whistling to himself as he strode along the Durham Road and turned through the open gates of the Royal Infirmary. He continued to whistle, but under his breath, till he reached the ward where his brother was. John had been moved from the little side room after three days when he had been pronounced out of danger and since then had made remarkable progress, according to the sister. Only yesterday she had told Nora and Harold that the doctor was confident John would be home by the weekend and ready to go back to work within a little while. Fortunately, Mr Sheldon and Mr Todd had been extremely sympathetic and understanding about his misfortune, sending word that he would continue to be fully paid and that his job was waiting for him as soon as he felt fit enough.

John was in the end bed by the window and looking towards the door as he entered the ward. Ralph raised his hand and John waved back, and as he reached his brother, Ralph said laughingly, 'Strikes me you're skiving now, man. There don't look a thing wrong with you.'

John grinned. 'It only hurts when I laugh.'

'Aye, and the rest of the time an' all, I bet. Cracked ribs are the very dickens till they heal. You'll be strapped up for a while, no doubt.'

'Maybe, but as long as I can get back to work and into the swing of things I don't mind. It's driving me mad in here. Mind, as Mam keeps telling me, I'm lucky. It could have been a lot worse.'

'Aye, you're right there, man.' Ralph plonked himself down in the chair next to the bed, throwing a box of chocolates into John's lap. 'Mam reckons you need feeding up so I thought these might help the process, and aye, I'll have one if you're going to open 'em.'

They talked of this and that for a few minutes, dissecting Sunderland's progress in the football league before Ralph gave a blow-by-blow account of a boxing match he'd recently gone to, but after John had looked towards the door for the twentieth time, Ralph said, 'Stop whittling, man. She'll be here soon.'

John smiled sheepishly. 'I don't know what you mean.'

'Aye, an' pigs fly.'

John stared at his brother and then seemed to come to some sort of decision. Leaning forwards, his voice low, he said, 'I've been meaning to say this for the last few days, since I came back to myself, that is. I appreciate you coming in every day, Ralph. We hadn't seen much of each other for months and well . . . I appreciate it. And the way you've been about me and Lily an' all.

I know you were upset when all that about her mam and da came to light but it was nothing to do with her after all.'

Ralph said nothing for a moment, then rubbed his mouth as though in embarrassment. 'It wasn't that, the lass's background, man. It was the business with that friend of hers, the one who's on the game.'

'She isn't.'

'All right, all right, don't bite my head off.'

'Ellen's a nice woman. I've met her and she's not like that. In fact, it would be hard to find someone who is less like that. She's a lady.'

'I don't want to argue with you and you probably know a lot more than me about it, but her running her own place and renting out rooms doesn't seem . . . suspicious to you, then? In view of her past?'

'Ellen hasn't got a past, not in the way you mean. It was all a mistake, that business with the police. Lily explained it to me.'

'And you were satisfied with that? You're sure Lily's told you the truth?' Ralph asked mildly. 'You don't think there's more to this than meets the eye? I'm not saying there is, mind. Hear me right on this. I'm just asking.'

'I trust Lily implicitly.'

Ralph held his brother's gaze as he sat back in the chair. 'Then that's good enough for me. Look, John, I just don't want you let down, that's all. I know I've been tied up with the boatyard the last couple of years. Hell, I hardly see Sarah and the bairns these days. But you're still my kid brother, OK? I care about you. You know that, don't you?'

John relaxed back against his pillows. 'Aye, I know that.'

'Good.' Then as John almost bounced up in the bed again Ralph turned his head and saw Lily walking towards them. He stood up immediately. 'I'll be going, then.'

'You don't have to.' John spoke to him but his eyes were on Lily. 'Two visitors are allowed at any time.'

'In this case, I get the feeling two's company, three's a crowd,' Ralph said easily. 'Anyway, I've things to do and people to see.'

Lily had reached the bed and walked round the opposite side to where Ralph was standing, taking John's hand as she said, 'How are you?'

'Never better.'

She glanced at Ralph, her face straight as she nodded in answer to his soft, 'Hello, Lily.'

'See you tomorrow.' Ralph looked straight at John now. 'Anything particular you want me to bring in?'

'A ticket out of this place would be nice.' John smiled at his brother. 'But no thanks, Mam's on the case as you can imagine.'

Ralph laughed. 'She's on a mission now. She'll fatten you up like a turkey for Christmas if you're not careful.' His nod took in the pair of them and then he turned and walked down the ward, his eyes on the polished floor. He didn't turn round at the doors but continued out into the corridor without a backward glance.

Lily walked round the bed and took the chair Ralph had vacated, drawing it closer so she could hold John's hand when she sat down. Smiling, she said, 'You're looking better every day now the swelling's gone down, even if you're still black and blue.'

'I feel fine, I really do.' John hesitated. 'Lily, can't you try and get on with Ralph? Let bygones be bygones? I know he upset you over the thing with Ellen and all but he's sorry about that. It was a gut reaction, a wrong one, but that's typical of him. He always acts before he thinks.'

Her smile faded. She didn't think Ralph was impulsive, just the opposite, and there was still that something in his eyes when he looked at her. Smothered beneath the big-brother act, but still there. Quietly, she said, 'He's not good to Sarah, John.'

'Not good to her? Look at the house they're in and the clothes she wears, and the bairns want for nothing.'

'I don't mean like that.'

'But anything else is between them, surely? And don't forget you only get Sarah's side of anything. What's she been saying, anyway? Does he knock her about?'

Now it was Lily who hesitated. 'She's hinted at it.'

'Hinted at it,' John said flatly. 'Well, I'm sorry, but if he was physically hurting her, don't you think she'd do more than hint? And I can't believe that of Ralph. He's got his faults but haven't we all? The thing is' – he stopped, his voice gentling – 'you've never liked our Ralph, have you?'

The breath caught in her throat. For a second words trembled on her tongue. Words that, if voiced, would cause reverberations that would echo round the family and cause untold damage. For Sarah, for Nora, all of

287

them, and most of all John. If he thought Ralph had ever tried it on with her he wouldn't stand for it, she knew that. It would be the finish with his brother. Nora's heart would be broken if the family was split and how would Sarah feel, knowing her husband had behaved like that with her own sister? She swallowed hard. 'He's not like you,' she said weakly.

'We're all different, it's what makes the world go round. And Sarah apart, I know he upset you over Ellen, but, for me, won't you make an effort with him?'

'All right.' Her voice was a mere whisper.

'That's my girl.' He squeezed her hand. 'Give him a chance, that's all I'm asking, and you might even find he's more like me than you thought.'

He was grinning at her and she forced a smile, even as she thought, he's not like you. He's not like anyone in the family. The Turners were nice, normal people, friendly and warm. And Ralph? She wouldn't like to delve into what John's brother was.

When Lily left the infirmary it was dark and spotting with rain. Her coat collar was pulled up and her hat was low over her eyes, so she didn't see the broad figure step out of the shadows and begin to follow her. She made her way along the New Durham Road before turning into Vine Place and then Crowtree Road where Ellen lived, and once she had disappeared inside the house the figure stationed itself in a black doorway out of sight.

At just after nine o'clock the front door opened and Lily was silhouetted in the lighted doorway for a moment before she stepped down into the street,

Ellen continuing to wave to her from the doorstep till she had turned the corner. The storms of recent days had broken the hot spell and now, with the capriciousness of English weather, it was unseasonably cold for mid-September.

Lily had just reached the tram stop when a sixth sense alerted her to the fact someone was behind her and she turned quickly, her start of surprise immediately brought under control.

'Hello again.' Ralph's face moved in a mirthless smile. 'I think it's time we had a little word, don't you?'

'No.' It was steady. 'You and I having nothing to discuss.'

'I wasn't asking permission. My days of asking permission of anyone are long since gone.' He squared up to her, pushing his shoulders back and drawing his chin in. 'I thought your goose had been cooked a couple of years back and you'd have the sense to lie low, but you've bounced back again, haven't you? Brazen as they come.'

Lily glanced quickly up and down the street. There were one or two people in the distance, near enough to hear her if she called out. 'I have no idea what you're talking about.' She had felt in her bones this moment would come. She had seen John's brother once or twice in passing at the hospital and he had always been on his best behaviour, but she had *known* it was an act.

'Then let me make it clear for you, m'lady. There's no way you're thumbing your nose at me by taking up with my brother.'

'What?'

'You heard me.'

His effrontery was staggering. Did he really think she was with John just to spite him? 'Don't be ridiculous.' The tone was scornful. 'In no way did you feature in my decision to go out with John. We love each other, it's as simple as that.'

If Lily had searched all night for a better way to touch him on the raw she couldn't have found it. The disdain with which she'd always treated Ralph Turner was palpable, her distaste so caustic it felt like a slap round the face to the man standing in front of her.

It had been a long time since he had allowed her to rile him. Writing the letter and watching what it had accomplished had satisfied the canker of hate and desire for a while, and he had found release for his body by visiting a particular dockside dolly who would allow him to do anything to her for the right price and who didn't mind being called Lily while he did it. But from the moment he had bumped into Archy McHaffie in the Shipwrights' Arms and listened to him laughing about John's fiery little piece with blond hair and green eyes, he'd been consumed with fury. They'd all been in on it – Sarah, his mam and da and the rest of them. It had been a conspiracy, he'd seen it straight away. But he'd played it canny. He'd laughed along with Archy and said nothing to Sarah and then made his plans.

He brought his face close to Lily's. 'I can see you haven't grasped what I'm saying so let me spell it out for you. You'll tell John you want nothing more to do with him, that it was a passing fancy. You'll make it very clear it's the end, all right?'

'I will *not*.' She could see the tram coming, hear it trundling towards them.

'Because if you don't,' he continued, as though she hadn't spoken, 'the next beating he gets will be his last.'

Lily's mouth was open, her eyes stretched wide. 'You – you didn't!' She couldn't form the words.

The muscles of his face twitched into what could have passed for a smile but the veins in his neck were standing out like cords, betraying his rage. 'Why do you think he didn't recognise the men who were waiting for him, eh? The police suspected he was scared to name 'em, that they were old mates from the dock, but the police were wrong. He didn't know the blokes because they had no connection with him except through me; they aren't even Sunderland-based. They were brought in special to do a job and then they disappeared again, like magic. Untraceable. Beautiful, don't you think?'

The tram stopped and two women got off. The conductor hung out of the door for a moment, looking their way and seemed about to speak. Ralph glanced at him and the man took himself back inside the tram which drew away.

'I'll . . . I'll tell John. And the police, I'll go to the police.'

'Oh aye? And you think anyone will believe you?' He laughed harshly. 'John knows you resent me because I objected to your whore friend and right now I'm in the middle of a card game and there're ten witnesses who'd swear to it. And even if anyone did take you seriously, which I doubt, I can give the order any time

291

from anywhere and they'll see to John. I've got power in this town, that's what you don't understand. Real power. When I say jump, people jump.'

Lily was staring at John's brother as if hypnotised. The two women were far away now and the darkness of the night was all around her. She didn't doubt at this moment he was behind the attack on John, she only wondered why the thought hadn't crossed her mind before, but then who would think a brother capable of trying to kill another brother because he objected to his choice of girl? 'You . . . you tried to murder him.'

'Not me. I was nowhere near the synagogue when it happened. And the men had orders, so far and no further. With or without the rabbi stepping in, they would have stopped. But next time it'll be different. So, the choice is yours.'

'He's your *brother*.'

'Some brother.' His voice was derisive, his dark eyes gleaming black like cold granite. 'Having you behind my back.'

She stared at him as the knowledge swept over her that she was utterly unable to reason with him. He was unhinged, he had to be. 'Why John?' she whispered faintly. 'Why not me?'

He didn't answer her for a moment, then, his voice thick, he said, 'Lily . . .'

The inflection he gave her name was enough to jerk her backwards. 'No.' Her lip curled back from her teeth as though she was viewing something putrid. 'Stay away from me.'

'I'd be good to you. Haven't I proved what I'd do

for you, how I feel?' His voice dropping to a whisper, he muttered, 'You're in my head an' my bones, that's how I feel. The thought of anyone else laying their dirty hands on you—'

'*Stop it.*' She was backed against a row of railings which fronted a yard of front garden. 'You're mad, insane.' But he wasn't and that was more frightening than anything. He was cunning and scheming and if he was mad it was the sort of madness that couldn't be pinned down by any doctor.

Ralph remained silent for a moment. 'I might be at that, aye, I might be,' he said softly. 'Where you're concerned, at least. But remember this, if you carry on with John his blood will be on your hands. I only have to lift my little finger and it'll be done and that's no idle threat. And next time they won't stop till the job's finished, rabbi or no rabbi.'

'I hate you.'

'I couldn't put a name to what I feel for you,' he said thickly, his voice holding a quiver which made her feel sick. 'I never have been able to. I don't know if it's love or hate, I only know I want you so much I can taste it.'

'You're disgusting.' From somewhere she found the strength to bring herself up straight and look him in the eyes. 'John is everything you're not.'

'Then if you think so highly of him I take it you don't want him to end up as a piece of meat on a mortuary slab, because I tell you this, I'll be damned if I'll stand by and see you make a monkey out of me with him. You could have picked anyone, *anyone*, but no, it had to be my brother, didn't it? I'd have left you alone if you'd laid low but you had to go and rub my nose in it.'

A young couple were approaching the tram stop arm in arm. Ralph glanced in their direction before bringing his eyes back to her ashen face. 'Like I said, the choice is yours. You could try repeating our little talk to John or the powers that be, but you won't get very far. They'd want to know why you didn't mention our past little run-ins, don't you think?'

'That was to save Sarah finding out what sort of a man she had married.'

'Noble, very noble, but do you expect anyone to buy that? You can't prove a word of it. And the final line is, when all the dust settles there'll still be the sword of Damocles hanging over John's head.'

'If I told the police what you'd threatened and something happened to John they'd know it was you.'

'Lily, Lily . . .' He shook his head, his voice soft. 'You've no idea what you're playing with, have you? There are a hundred and one ways a man can have an unfortunate accident and with the means at my disposal I can make sure it's an absolute certainty no one would suspect a thing, whatever you say or do. You yourself told folk about the incident with Archy McHaffie and how John's been threatened, which takes care of this last lot.'

The young couple were coming within earshot and now his voice changed, becoming jocular when he said, 'It was nice to bump into you, lass, and you tell that brother of mine to be careful, all right? He's fast becoming accident-prone and we don't want that, do we?'

She watched him walk away, becoming indistinct

in the shadows till he walked under a street lamp and was clearly outlined for a short while. The young couple were talking quietly together but once or twice the girl glanced her way. Lily got the impression if she had returned her glance she would have spoken; she must be looking bad. She felt bad. She felt she had been looking into the face of pure evil and she wasn't exaggerating or dramatising. What was it he'd said at the beginning? Something about her goose being cooked and her lying low? Could it be, was it possible that Ralph had sent the letter to her mother which had done so much damage and blown their family wide open? She had always assumed the letter had been directed primarily at her mother. Her mother had upset so many folk in her time and she could imagine someone from her circle could get pleasure from trying to make her squirm, but now . . .

Lily shook herself mentally. All that didn't matter. Why was she even thinking of it now? What mattered was John and he was in danger. And Ralph was cunning. She hadn't a shred of proof to support what she said if she spoke out, and even if anyone did believe her, without something concrete Ralph couldn't be touched. That would mean the threat to John would still be there, waiting for the right moment to strike.

Her head was whirling, the rattling of another tram as it lumbered up the street barely registering. When it stopped and the young couple turned to her, clearly waiting for her to board first, she forced herself to walk forward. Once seated on the long wooden bench she began to tremble and bent forward, fiddling with the row of small buttons on one of her boots to hide her shaking. What was she going to do? What *could* she do? She didn't doubt Ralph was capable of anything.

She got off the tram at her stop and walked the few yards to the back gate of the Grays' residence. She pushed it open and was about to pass between the tall thick privet hedges on either side which shielded the grounds from the road, when a figure loomed out. She screamed, she couldn't help it, and then a familiar voice said, 'Lily, it's me, lass. It's me. I didn't see you there. I've been waiting inside with the two lassies but I thought I'd better be making tracks home.'

'Da?' In her fright the word came naturally.

'Aye, it's me,' Stanley said again. 'Me an' Sally have been away for a few days and I've only just heard about John. It must have knocked you sideways. It's a nasty business. Have they got anyone for it yet?'

Lily had stepped back on to the pavement when he'd startled her. Her heart racing, she gazed at the man whom for most of her life she had thought of as her father. She hadn't seen him in over two years and he had changed. He looked younger, or perhaps it was just the darkness? No, he *did* look younger.

When she didn't speak he bit down on his bottom lip. 'I'm sorry, I shouldn't have come.'

Slowly she removed her hand from her throat where her fingers had been clutching her flesh. She had thought it was Ralph hiding in the shadows. Silly, because he couldn't have got here quicker than the tram, but for a moment she had thought it was him. 'You – you made me jump,' she said weakly.

'I'm sorry but I was worried.'

'You needn't be.' She tried to pull herself together. 'John's doing so well they're letting him home soon.'

'That's grand, he's a good lad but, to be truthful, it was you I was more worried about, lass.' They stared at each other. 'Have they got who did it?' he asked again.

She shook her head. Nor would they. But she couldn't tell him that. *She would have to give John up.* As she looked at him the knowledge swept over her in a flood of pain. She had known all along John loving her and their being together was too good to be true.

'They want stringing up by their thumbs, whoever it was, to do that to a nice young lad like him.' Stanley paused, rubbing his mouth in a gesture she remembered from the past. 'Lily, I've wanted to come and see you umpteen times but Sarah said to keep away. She said you didn't want to see me.'

She knew it was a question but she was unable to speak.

'Your mother and I made terrible mistakes,' he said huskily. 'When I look back now —' He shook his head. 'But I can't do anything about that. But I want you to know one thing. To believe one thing and I swear to you this is the truth. I loved you from the moment I held you when you were first born and it was a love that took me completely by surprise. When your mother was pregnant I was angry and hurt, devastated. But then you were born.'

Her eyes, huge and glittering in the shadows, were looking straight into his but still she said not a word.

Stanley took a slow, deep breath. 'I can't expect you

to understand, not till you have children of your own, but it isn't only the act of procreation that makes a child yours. I have always felt I'm your da in the real sense of the word, in the only sense, and if I could have protected you from being hurt I would have done so. I thought that was what I *was* doing but I was wrong.'

'You should have made her let you share our lives.'

'Aye, I should.'

She stared into his big face in which she could see no part of herself. 'Do – do I look like him?'

A sixth sense told him to lie and to do it convincingly. 'No,' he said quietly. 'In fact, you look more like a picture of my grandmother when she was a young slip of a thing. She was a bonny lass with a mind of her own an' all, apparently.'

Lily nodded. She thought she remembered her grandma showing her the little portrait of her own mother which Ava kept wrapped in a handkerchief in a drawer because it was so faded. The girl in the picture had been young and slim but apart from that she didn't think there was any resemblance, so perhaps he was being kind. Because he *was* a kind man. She had gradually come to realise over the last two years when she'd considered her childhood and her life at home that he must have been acutely lonely for much of that time, and yet he had always been kind and gentle to herself and Sarah. And now he was here in front of her she knew she had been secretly hoping he would come and seek her out one day. It was a step that for a whole host of reasons she knew she had been incapable of, it had had to come from him.

How strange that it had happened on the day she had lost John.

A little sound halfway between a sob and a moan escaped her lips and as she fell against him his arms went round her and he held her tight, muttering over the top of her head, 'Oh, hinny, hinny, I'm sorry. I'm sorry, hinny, I am, I am. I'll make it right. Somehow I'll make it right, you'll see.'

And when she cried all the harder it was because she couldn't tell him that the one thing in all the world she wanted making right he couldn't do. No one could.

'I don't understand.' John felt as though he'd been punched in the stomach. He'd expected her to be as pleased as Punch when he'd told her he was going home in the morning and he'd known from her flat reaction then that something was wrong. But this? Where had this come from? 'You can't mean it.'

'I do mean it.' Lily's hands were joined together, her knuckles showing white as she stood by the hospital bed. 'I don't think we should see each other any more.'

'What's the matter?' His eyes narrowed on her tense face. 'What's happened?'

'Nothing.'

'Lily, yesterday you said you loved me and today you're telling me it's over so don't expect me to believe nothing's happened.'

She had expected this. She had known he wouldn't accept it, she wouldn't have in his place. She breathed in deeply through her nose and forced herself to meet his eyes as she said the words she had practised during the long night hours when she hadn't slept a wink: 'It's Mr and Mrs Gray.'

'The Grays? What have they got to do with you and me?'

'They're going to America next year.'

'So?'

'They're visiting a branch of his family in New York and they're planning to be away for all of the summer. They – they want me to go with them to look after the twins.' This had the advantage of being true but when Arabella Gray had put the proposition to her a few days ago once they knew John was on the mend, Lily had known her employer had expected her answer to be that she had to remain in England. As it had been. And to give Mrs Gray her due she had said immediately that she understood, although she was sorry Lily would miss such a wonderful opportunity to see something of the world. But Lily hadn't wanted to see the world, she'd just wanted John. And even if it meant leaving the Grays and Nicholas and Adam, she had known that would happen one day when she and John got married.

John was staring at her. 'And you want to go?'

'If I don't they'll get someone else in my place and I've been with them so long . . .' She gulped hard. 'Nicholas and Adam wouldn't understand,' she added, dropping her gaze.

A silence grew between them and then John said quietly, 'I won't pretend I don't want you to go but I'm more disappointed you've made the decision without even mentioning it to me. But if it means so much to you then I won't stand in your way. It's one summer out of our lives, that's all, and I'll be waiting for you when you come home.'

This was worse than she had imagined. She couldn't carry on with this, she couldn't. She had to tell him the truth and take whatever came. She raised her eyes and looked at him, at his dear face. It was still puffy and bruised, and he had so many cuts and abrasions it was difficult to find any unblemished skin. They'd had to cut away some of his hair over his right ear to stitch the gaping wound which had stopped at his eyebrow, and it gave his face a lopsided look. And his body was worse. Nora had said he'd had the imprint of a big boot in the middle of his back where his shirt had been torn off. A quiver passed over her face. 'I think it would be better if we were both free. A summer's a long time and it would put too much strain on us both. It wouldn't be fair.'

She wanted to be rid of him. Bile rose bitter in his throat. He would have staked his life she'd meant it when she'd said she loved him but here she was saying she wanted to be free. 'Fair on whom exactly?' he asked coldly.

'Don't make this more difficult than it need be.'

'*More difficult?*' He took a deep breath, wincing as the pain in his injured ribs cut like a knife. Aware of interested glances from the visitors at the next bed, he glared at them before fixing his eyes on Lily. 'I love you,' he said, lowering his voice, 'and I thought you loved me. Now you're telling me it's over, and for what? So you can be free to dally with some rich American you might meet over the ocean?'

'It's not like that.'

'No? I think that's exactly what it's like.'

'Then perhaps it's better we're finishing now. All the time I was away you'd be suspecting I was carrying on, I can see that.'

'For crying out loud.' Rage and frustration were uppermost. 'Don't you turn this round on me. I said I'd wait for you and I meant it. You only have to say the same thing and that's the end of the conversation. What more do you want from me, anyway? I've said you can go with my blessing, I can't do any more than that.'

'I know.' Her voice was small now as it came, saying, 'But it would be months, it's too long a time.'

'Is this some sort of test?' Dark brown eyes held green. 'Are you trying to see if I'd let you down like your father did, is that it?'

'Of course not.'

'Then what?' he asked tersely, his face darkening.

'I've told you.'

'Don't do this, Lily.' His words seemed to come from deep in his throat. 'If you walk away now I won't come after you. I mean that. I won't beg and plead. I love you and I want us to be together, but you have to want it too.'

Her lips were trembling, her eyes were moist as she looked at him; part of her was on the brink of telling him every word Ralph had said, the other screamed at her that she couldn't be responsible for his death sentence. She had to be strong, she had to do what was best for John. There was a long pause and when she broke it by whispering, 'I'm sorry, I think it's better this way,' he didn't move a muscle. 'Goodbye.' She turned blindly away.

He watched her go, unable to comprehend fully what had happened in the minutes since she had first entered the ward. He wanted to call to her but he didn't. In those last moments he had seen what was in her eyes. She meant it. It was over. And so he sat quietly till the doors had closed behind her, an agony in him that was worse than anything he'd endured during and after the beating.

PART FIVE

April 1912 – The *Titanic*

Chapter 18

Nora gazed at her son, exasperation in every line of her weathered face. As if things weren't bad enough, what with the coal strike having wreaked havoc in the shipyards and Harold and Robert out of work and that after the worst winter in living memory, now here was John talking about moving down south. And she knew why. He might be trying to make out he fancied seeing a bit of the world but she wasn't daft. Since him and Lily had called it a day he'd been a different man. For two pins she'd tell him to clear off to London and be done with it, although how they'd manage without what he brought in she didn't know. Hannah's wage and the bit she earned taking in washing wouldn't go far.

As though John had read his mother's mind, he said, 'I'm not talking about right away, mind. I'd wait till Da and Robert get set on again before I do anything.'

'Oh aye, and you know when that'll be, do you?' Nora said tartly. 'There's no end to your talents these days.'

'Don't start, Mam.'

'Don't start, he says.' Nora appealed to the empty kitchen. Harold and Robert had gone to a union meeting, Hannah was at work and Larry had finished his Saturday chores and was making the most of the change of weather with his friends in the back lane. After the big freeze in February which had seen the temperature drop to as low as -35F, spring had come early to a hungry, strike-torn north-east. Hedgerows were in leaf, cherry trees in blossom, and daffodils and narcissi nodded their bright heads in the gardens of the well-to-do. 'Here's me tryin' to make a penny stretch to two an' tearing me hair out most days worryin' about the rent man, an' you come in an' tell me, cool as a cucumber, you might be takin' off so I've somethin' more to lie awake whittlin' over. I won't rest not knowin' if you're all right or not. There's not one of the family livin' more than a mile or two away and you want to skedaddle down south.'

'I've told you, not yet.'

'Aye, but you're thinkin' about it, aren't you?' Nora fixed him with her glare. 'An' I know you, m'lad. If you've spoken of it it's because your mind is made up. Am I right?' When John said nothing Nora sighed deeply, her body seeming to deflate, and then came and sat by his side at the kitchen table. 'Why don't you go and see her?' she said quietly. 'Swallow your pride.'

John bowed his head, his voice terse when he said, 'Leave it, Mam.'

'"Don't start, Mam. Leave it, Mam."' Nora stood up, walked over to the range and lifted the big brown teapot that had been standing on the hob. 'Do you want a cuppa?'

'Aye, I'll have one.'

Nora returned to the table and poured them both a cup of tea that was as black as tar. 'You're miserable, lad,' she said softly after she'd sat down once more. 'An' from what Sarah says, so is Lily. Whatever the row was about it can't be so bad that it can't be sorted out.'

'I've told you, there was no row.'

'Aye, an' that's all you've said. One minute everything in the garden was lovely an' the next it's over. I don't understand you, lad.'

'Me?' John was at the end of his tether. In the weeks and months since he and Lily had parted he'd been to hell and back umpteen times a day. His mother talked about swallowing his pride. Well, he'd done that all right, he'd swallowed so hard it had damn near choked him. He'd written to her at first, several times, and received no answer. Then at Christmas when Sarah had told his mam – who of course had told him – that Lily was a shadow of her former self, he'd gone to see her. And come away with a flea in his ear. After that he'd determined no more. He wouldn't beg any more. He'd told her that the night she'd finished with him but now he meant it. Enough was enough. She was set on going on this jaunt across the Atlantic and she didn't want to be tied to him when she went. Fair enough.

'It's a Saturday afternoon. Go and see her.'

'I can't.'

'Aye, you can. It's different for a lass, the first move has to come from you.'

John looked at his mother and what he saw in the wrinkled face melted the barrier he'd set round himself. His voice low, he said, 'It was her who finished it, Mam, and she wouldn't listen, not when I sent her letters or went to see her. She's determined to go on this trip and even when I said she had my blessing and I'd wait for her it wasn't enough. All right? There, you have it all now.'

'Oh, lad.'

'In a few days she sails on the *Titanic* for pastures new and who am I to try and stop her? Likely she'll make a match with some rich American and stay in New York.' He knew he couldn't go and see her again. His self-esteem would never survive it. 'Whatever, it's over. I don't like it but I've accepted it. So should you.'

'There's somethin' fishy here, John. I know that little lass, an' this is all at odds with how she is.'

He took a deep breath and fought to control his temper. 'Mam, leave it. Please.' He swigged his tea and stood up. 'Some things in life are meant to be and some aren't. It's as simple as that. I'm going for a walk.'

Nora watched him walk out of the backyard, her brow furrowed. Sarah said Lily was as thin as a rake and hadn't a smile in her these days. Was that a lass who was looking forward to a great adventure and getting herself a rich husband? She didn't think so. She'd been expecting the pair of them to get back together before this, she had to admit it, and with the strike and all she had let John's problems drift to the back of her mind, but the lass was due to leave for the journey to Southampton with the Gray family in the next day or two according to Sarah. Time had run out. She sucked in her lower lip. Something would have to be done because, say what you like, something smelt as bad as the fish quay when they'd been gutting.

An hour later Nora was experiencing a little of the bewilderment and frustration that had assailed John for the last months. When she had knocked on the kitchen door of the Grays' residence she had been invited in by the cook, but when the cook's sister had gone to fetch Lily, the girl who walked in with her wasn't the girl she remembered. This one's face was set and stiff and there was no sparkle in her eyes. She had asked if she could speak to her privately and the two of them had stepped outside the back door, but the last few minutes she'd felt as though she was talking to a brick wall. 'I don't understand, lass,' she said for the umpteenth time. 'I thought you an' our John were fair set. Now I know he'd have you back quick as lightnin' an' you can't tell me you're happy. Won't you at least talk to him afore you leave?'

'There's no point, Mrs Turner.'

'He's got the idea you're after a rich husband across the sea but it's not that, is it?'

It was a statement, not a question but, nevertheless, Lily said flatly, 'There's always that chance, of course.'

'Don't give me that, lass. I weren't born yesterday an' I haven't got so long in the tooth without knowin' a thing or two. You're a good lass but somethin' made you drop our John like a hot potato. I saw you in the

311

hospital when he was bad, I know how you feel about him. So what's the matter?'

'Nothing, Mrs Turner.'

'An' I'm a monkey's uncle.'

With a touch of desperation, Lily said, 'I've got to get back indoors, I'm in the middle of packing the children's clothes and there's so much to see to.'

'He's thinkin' of leavin' Sunderland, leavin' the north, an' for good. Did you know that?'

Lily's heart jerked and raced. Without considering her words, she blurted out, 'Perhaps that would be a good thing.'

'Would it now?' Nora's eyes narrowed. 'Why is that?'

'I – I don't know.' Lily swallowed. 'The jobs are better down south for someone like him, aren't they? More – more opportunities.'

Nora never knew afterwards why she said it, perhaps it was because of the look in Lily's eyes, but she found herself saying, 'These blokes who worked John over? You know owt about 'em?'

Lily's mouth opened and shut. She was several moments too late when she said, 'No, no, of course not,' and they both knew it.

'What's goin' on, lass?' Nora's mind was racing. 'Someone frightened you? Is that it? You worried what happened to John might happen to you?'

'No.'

'That's it, isn't it? Someone's threatened you an' told you to stay well clear or else. Are they goin' to have another go at my lad?' In her agitation, Nora caught hold of the sleeve of Lily's dress, shaking her arm. 'Tell me, lass.'

Lily wrenched herself free. 'It's not like that.'

'What is it like, then? You tell me or so help me I'll be back in the mornin' an' I shan't come to the back door neither.'

'Listen. Listen to me.' Suddenly Lily was the one in control. 'I can't tell you anything except John is perfectly safe so long as we don't see each other. That's the truth.'

'What?'

'I can't explain. I would if I could but it's impossible.'

'You don't have to worry, lass. Our John wouldn't let anyone hurt you.'

'It's not me they'd hurt.' The two women stared at each other and Lily could almost see the cogs of Nora's brain whirring. Quickly, she said, 'If you told him anything of this it would be his death sentence, Mrs Turner. I mean it. These – these people are bad, really bad.'

'By all the saints, lass. What have you got yourself mixed up in?'

It hurt, she didn't want John's mother to think ill of her, but better that than the truth. Her voice low, Lily said, 'It will be all right if things are left as they are, you have my word on that. But if not they'll – they'll make it look like an accident. You mustn't say anything, do you understand?'

Nora was a sickly grey. 'Lass, whatever it is, however bad the trouble you're in, make a clean breast of it and go to the police. I'll come with you, if you like.'

Lily shook her head. 'It wouldn't do any good. Not for John. The best thing all round is for me to go away for a time. He'll – he'll meet someone else . . .'

The wind had been taken out of Nora's sails. The terror she was feeling was reflected in her voice when she whispered, 'He wouldn't survive another beating like that, lass.'

'He won't have to. I promise you he's perfectly safe but that's why we can't see each other. Understand?'

'I don't understand any of this.' Nora pulled back from her and stared into Lily's face. There was a short silence before she shook her head, muttering, 'I thought you were a good lass an' he worshipped the ground you walked on. Do you know that?'

'I'm sorry.' It was all she could say.

'I'd best get back, there's the dinner to see to.' Nora spoke as if in a daze which in truth was how she felt. What she'd imagined was a lovers' tiff had turned into something much darker. This morning all she'd had to worry about was where the rent money was coming from and whether she could eke out the housekeeping for another week; now she didn't know which end of her was up. She was halfway to the gate when she turned. Lily was standing where she'd left her. 'Does Sarah know owt about this?'

'No, she doesn't.'

Nora inclined her head, her eyes no longer friendly as she looked at the lass she'd thought would be her daughter-in-law. When she walked out of the gate she banged it shut.

Lily stood for some minutes more before she went inside although a hundred and one things were awaiting her attention.

She felt bereft and physically sick at the thought that Nora must now despise her, hate her even, and hold her accountable for the attack on John. She hadn't realised how much she had valued Nora's good opinion of her till it was gone.

Could she have said anything else? Done anything else? She stared wide-eyed into the blue sky, the scent of May blossom from the trees surrounding the garden mocking her misery with its sweetness.

No, she couldn't. Perhaps it hadn't been wise to say what she had and if she'd had more time to consider her words she might have been able to guide the conversation differently, but Nora had taken her by surprise.

She watched a bird circling high above as the leaden weight of aloneness made her feel very small. She wished she was leaving today. She wished a vast continent was already between her and everyone here. And perhaps she wouldn't come back. No one really cared whether she did nor not, no one except John. Oh, John, John.

Chapter 19

Lily stood amid the bustling chaos in Southampton's harbour surrounded by the Grays' luggage as she kept a sharp eye on the twins. The April day was bright and clear and the sky blue, but it was the towering, cliff-like ship at the White Star Line's Ocean Dock which held their attention and that of everyone else. Plumes of smoke were wafting from the *Titanic*'s four funnels, her white upperworks shining and her enormous hull dwarfing every other ship. An endless stream of people were walking up the gangways and disappearing from view, and every now and then an ear-splitting blast sounded from the ship's mighty steam whistles causing Adam and Nicholas to scream with excitement. A maiden voyage was always a cause for elation in a seafaring town and friends and families of passengers as well as those of the hundreds of crew members, along with crowds of sightseers, packed the docks.

In spite of herself and the desolation she was feeling Lily's spirit was stirred. The north's industrial cities with their endless factories, mines and steelworks belching black smoke, the filthy warrens of slums where disease flourished and illness and starvation crippled countless bodies and minds, all seemed a million miles away. The clean salt air, the procession of passengers – some of whom were clearly extremely wealthy, judging by the size of their retinues – and not least the stunningly beautiful *Titanic* herself, created the notion that she had stepped into another world.

She glanced over to where Mr and Mrs Gray were standing, each with a hand on Edwin's shoulders and with Belinda and Prudence at their side. Their faces reflected the same awe she was feeling. Arabella caught her eye and motioned to her to join them.

'The luggage will be taken care of,' she said just as a group of deckhands came over to it. 'Well, what do you think, Lily?'

'I can't believe it's so big, ma'am.' She hesitated and then voiced the question the twins had asked her earlier. 'Is this ship really unsinkable?'

Mr Gray smiled. 'God himself couldn't sink this ship,' he said, earning a reproving glance from his wife in the process. 'She's built to carry more than three thousand people. I've just been chatting to one of the officers and he tells me they've loaded forty tons of potatoes alone, along with two hundred barrels of flour and goodness knows what else.'

'There are electric lifts,' put in Edwin who was fascinated by the new up-and-coming phenomenon of electricity. 'And a gymnasium, squash courts, Turkish and electric baths and a swimming pool. Father and I are going to try them all, aren't we, Father?'

'To try anything we need to board first.' Arabella was not a good traveller and the journey from Sunderland had tired her. They had broken it into two days, spending the night with friends in London before getting the boat train from Waterloo Station at nine-thirty in the morning. Lily had found the deep blue broadcloth-upholstered cars with their gold-tasselled trim and mahogany woodwork luxurious in the extreme, but the Grays hadn't been impressed. Or if they had been, they hadn't voiced it.

Once on board, the first stop for the first- and second-class passengers was the Purser's Office to have their tickets processed. At the head of the third-class gangways a team of surgeons conducted an examination of each steerage passenger attempting to board. The immigrants were checked for signs of trachoma, a highly infectious and potentially blinding disease of the eye. American immigration laws forbade admission of anyone with trachoma into the country. Another requirement of American law which Mr Gray explained to the children on the way to Southampton was that locked barricades would be set up between steerage and the other passengers to prevent the spread of any disease the third-class folk might have. They must not remark on this, their father had cautioned. It would be bad manners.

As Lily had listened she'd wondered if her employer realised that, in the normal way of things, she'd be one of the third-class passengers. As it was, as a personal servant of first-class elite, she apparently had a place in a separate promenade and dining room reserved exclusively for the maids and menservants of the upper class. Belinda and Prudence had guilelessly told her some weeks ago that their wealthy New York relatives who had amassed a fortune in the fur trade were paying for the trip, and it was clear they hadn't stinted in arranging for the crossing to be a comfortable one. The suite of rooms they were shown to by their attentive steward were magnificent, holding full-sized, wrought-iron bedsteads and washstands with hot and cold running water. The sitting room, three bedrooms, wardrobe room and bathroom and lavatory were decorated in the Jacobean style, and even her bed, tucked away in an alcove of Belinda's and Prudence's bedroom, was made up with the finest linen and held feather pillows.

Adam and Nicholas having settled down for their late-morning nap, Arabella asked Lily to escort Edwin and the girls round the ship while she and Mr Gray had refreshments in the sitting room and the steward unpacked their belongings.

They got lost several times, but by the end of the expedition had seen most of the first-class public rooms. The beautiful reception room, lounge, reading and writing room, smoking room, lending library, verandah cafés and palm courts and many other facilities, were wonderful, and when they peeped into the first-class dining saloon which seated five hundred and ran the full width of the hull, the vast expanse of dazzling white tablecloths, sparkling crystal and gleaming silver caused them all to gasp. But it was the Grand Staircase which really took Lily's breath away. It descended with regal magnificence through four decks to the first-class dining saloon and had been fashioned to be the centrepiece of the ship, the Louis XIV balustrade a perfect touch.

The four of them were retracing their steps to the suite when the ship's whistle gave a series of short blasts warning friends of passengers and other visitors to make their way ashore. Edwin was desperate to watch the harbour tugs move into position with his father – they had discussed the procedure many times in the lead-up to the trip – and once back in the suite Lily stayed with the sleeping twins while the rest of the family made their way to the first-class promenade. She did not mind missing the departure and when at noon exactly one long, deep-throated blast signalled they were about to move, she shut her eyes tightly.

He hadn't come to say goodbye, but then, why would he? She had made it clear she wanted nothing more to do with him. She had spent an evening with her grandparents at her father's house and had met Sally, whom she'd liked very much, for the first time. She had met Sarah for a cream tea at Binns and had a tearful goodbye, and Ellen and Bruce had taken her out for a slap-up farewell meal, but all the time, what-ever she'd been doing, she had been thinking of John. Wondering if he'd try to see her, one last time. Dreading it and yet desperate for him to come.

She was glad he hadn't. She nodded fiercely, as though someone had contradicted her, resisting the desire to lay her head down on her arms and cry and cry. She had to put all that behind her now. It would be months before she returned to England, if she did decide to return, that was. America was supposed to be the land of opportunity; look at all the people in third class who were leaving everything to make a better life for themselves across the Atlantic. For weeks now she had been thinking she couldn't continue to live in the same vicinity as John; the thought she might catch sight of him was a constant fear and longing. And what if one day she saw him with another girl? She'd make a fool of herself. She knew she would.

But John might not be in Sunderland when she got back from America, he might have moved down south as Nora said he intended to do. She chewed on the end of her thumb. Did that make the prospect of returning home worse or better? She didn't know. In fact, she felt she didn't know anything any more. One moment she was absolutely sure she had done the right thing in keeping quiet about Ralph, the next all kinds of doubts assailed her. She was a mess, that was the truth of it.

She knew the huge liner was slowly moving and for a second panic hit. What was she doing leaving John like this? Going to the other side of the world in this floating town with its stained-glass windows, chandeliers, rich carpets and fine furniture? This was too final, too far away. She should never have agreed to it.

By the time the others came back, the children full of the fact that there had nearly been a terrible accident when the powerful suction of the *Titanic*'s wake snapped the lines mooring two smaller vessels, drawing one, the *New York*, dangerously close to the *Titanic*'s hull before Captain Smith took the action which averted a catastrophe, Lily was herself once more.

Adam and Nicholas had awoken and, as ever, dealing with her two small charges had restored her equilibrium. She was able to smile and nod as Edwin gave her a minute-by-minute account of the rescue of the *New York*, the moment the *Titanic* passed the Royal Yacht Squadron at West Cowes, when she had dipped her colours to the squadron of destroyers anchored at Spithead, the dropping of the *Titanic*'s pilot at the Nab lightship and, finally, the thrilling moment she had turned towards the English Channel and open sea.

This was her family, Lily thought, glancing round at the children's bright faces and Mr and Mrs Gray's smiling ones. And the feeling she had for little Adam and Nicholas couldn't be put into words. She was valued here, wanted. She was lucky. She was, she was very lucky; so many people had so little and here was she off on the adventure of a lifetime.

The ship's orchestra was playing in the first-class Dining Saloon as the ship's bugler sounded the call for luncheon, and it set the pace for the first day at sea. The sun was sinking low on the horizon when they approached the chalk cliffs of the French coast to pick up more passengers in the late afternoon, but long before they left France at nine o'clock the twins were tucked up in bed fast asleep along with Edwin, who was exhausted by the excitement of his first day at sea.

Arabella had developed a persistent headache during the afternoon and so she and Mr Gray dined early, returning to the suite before the ship's orchestra began playing the nightly after-dinner concert on A Deck. Once Lily had supervised the girls getting ready for bed she went along to her dining room, dressed in one of the plain but good dresses Mrs Gray had bought her for the trip. When she entered it was half full, and a waiter appeared immediately at her side, ushering her to a table where two other women were sitting quietly eating their meal.

Lily felt completely out of her depth. The lovely surroundings were one thing, but the waiter was acting as though she was one of the paying passengers rather than a servant. Once he had taken her order, one of the women leaned across and grinned at her. 'Takes some getting used to, doesn't it?' she said in a broad northern twang. 'Being treated like one of the nobs.'

The other woman at the table frowned. 'I don't see why,' she said coolly. 'I'm sure these people realise our status is special. Speaking for myself I am indispensable to my lady.'

The first woman pulled a face at Lily who smiled weakly. 'I'm Tess,' she said, holding out her hand. 'Pleased to meet you. And this is Miss Graham. Miss Graham is Lady Lyndon's personal maid.' She winked at Lily, the slight emphasis on the Miss making it clear how she viewed the other woman's manner. 'I'm maiding Lady Lyndon's eldest daughter.'

Lily nodded. She got the feeling Miss Graham wouldn't think much of Mrs Gray if she admitted she was the nurserymaid and Bridget was back in Sunderland, and, feeling curiously defensive of her employer, she said, 'I'm with Mrs Gray,' and left it at that.

Tess was a chatterbox but a bright and friendly one, and as the meal progressed Lily warmed to her new friend. It was at the dessert stage Tess bent closer and murmured, 'Did you see that business with the *New York* earlier? Don't bode well, does it? Not after that other mishap.'

'Oh for goodness' sake, Tess. Don't start that again.' Miss Graham's voice was sharp as she stood to her feet. 'I'm going back to the cabin, don't be long. Miss Wilhelmina will need your services and she'll probably retire early tonight. It's been a long day for someone of her delicate constitution.'

'Delicate constitution, my backside,' Tess whispered under her breath as Miss Graham disappeared. 'Miss Wilhelmina is as strong as a horse. She won't be back for a long while yet, especially as there's plenty of men for her to flirt and carry on with. One of the reasons Lady Lyndon has brought her on this trip is to get her away from an unsuitable admirer. She's been getting a bit of a name for herself, has Miss Wilhelmina.'

Lily didn't comment on this. 'What did you mean? About the other mishap?' she asked curiously.

'You don't know?' And when Lily shook her head: 'There was a man killed at the launch of the *Titanic* nearly a year ago. End of May, it was. Some poor bloke got crushed when they were knocking out the shoring timbers holding the hull in place. It was in all the papers at the time. Some say it was an omen.'

'An omen?'

'Aye, you know, a warning like, blood being spilled on the day she took to the water. And then with all that today . . .'

'But no one was hurt today, were they?'

'No, but it was a near thing.' Sensing Lily didn't

see eye to eye with her on this, Tess added airily, 'That's what them who are superstitious are saying, anyway, although I think it's all a load of hogwash. Everyone knows the *Titanic's* unsinkable, don't they? Anyway, I'd best get back or Miss Graham will let me have it. Thinks she's the cat's whiskers, she does. I'll save a place for you tomorrow, in case you get away the same time as us again. All right?'

'Aye, all right.' Lily smiled and nodded, but as she sat finishing her coffee she thought about what Tess had said. She hoped Mrs Gray didn't get to hear such silly gossip. Her employer didn't enjoy any form of travel, partly because it usually made her feel quite unwell, and talk about omens and such like might unnerve her.

Late the following morning Lily was reminded of Tess's words. They'd dropped anchor two miles off shore in Queenstown harbour in southern Ireland, allowing a handful of passengers to disembark and over a hundred new passengers — young Irish men and women — to come aboard for the journey to a new life in America. The tenders drew alongside the ship and began transferring passengers and mail, and a small fleet of little boats filled with vendors of various sorts intent on hawking their wares to wealthy passengers followed in the tenders' wake. For an hour or so promenade deck became an Irish market selling fine lace, linen, ceramics and porcelains.

It was as the tenders drew alongside that the incident occurred which made children scream in fright and more than one lady clutch at her husband's arm.

A black disembodied head suddenly appeared out of the fourth funnel, grinning widely.

Mr Gray, who had written to the White Star Line months before to find out everything he could about their new flagship to satisfy Edwin's endless – and often unanswerable – questions, was quick to reassure the family the funnel was non-functional and used only for ventilating the engine room. 'It's someone's idea of a practical joke,' he assured Arabella who had nearly fainted on the spot. 'And one in poor taste, m'dear. The man is covered in soot, that's all.'

'I'd like to horsewhip the blighter,' someone grunted behind them. 'The ladies don't need another upset, not after what happened yesterday.'

Lily turned to see an elderly gentleman who was supporting his equally elderly wife. She was nearer to them than anyone else and it was only she who heard the lady murmur, 'I told you, Sigmund, it's another warning. We should get off the ship now before it's too late.'

'Nonsense, Enid. You'll laugh about this when you're in America with Cathleen. And you want to see your new grandchild, don't you? Come along, m'dear. Come and choose a nice lace shawl for Cathleen's little one.'

Lily looked at the woman's face as they passed her. She didn't think the husband was right. His wife would never laugh at what had happened, she didn't think anyone would. It had been too upsetting.

Once the last passenger was on board, the *Titanic*'s whistles gave the warning for the tenders and small boats to stand clear. Within a short while the ship was clear of the Irish coast and on her way, her upperworks shining in the cool April sunshine. Many of the Irish immigrants gathered on the stern for a last goodbye to the land of their fathers, one of them playing the haunting 'Erin's Lament' on his pipes as the ship ploughed on through the Atlantic ocean. Lily found herself shivering as she listened but not from cold; the pipes seemed to be expressing what she was feeling but could never have put into words.

'Goodbye, John.' It was the faintest of whispers and even Adam, who was snuggled in her arms, couldn't have heard her. 'Be happy.'

Chapter 20

For the next three days Lily and the rest of the passengers aboard ship grew accustomed to a life on the waves, settling down into a comfortable routine which was built around mealtimes and the many activities on board. She grew used to seeing Captain Smith mingling with the passengers, the first-class ones, at least. His height, neatly trimmed white beard and solid figure would have made him an imposing man in any circumstances, but in his captain's uniform he was quite dashing in a somewhat stern sort of way. She listened to him talking to Mr and Mrs Gray one day and was surprised by his gentle speaking voice and mild manner and the patience with which he answered Edwin's stream of questions about the ship and his life as a sailor.

On the morning of the fifth day which was a Sunday, Lily attended divine service in the first-class dining room with Arabella, the girls and Adam and Nicholas. Much to Arabella's chagrin her husband and Edwin had made themselves scarce and gone to the gymnasium.

The ship's orchestra provided the music and on this occasion second- and third-class passengers were allowed in the first-class areas. Captain Smith took the service himself and as his calm tones led the assembled throng through the general confession and prayers, she found herself thinking she could see why he was a captain. He was the sort of man who would inspire confidence, whatever the situation.

Lily took the children to the promenade deck after lunch so that Edwin and the twins could play with their hoops and hobby horses while the two girls sat together and read the books they had brought with them. Arabella had another of her headaches and had retired for an afternoon nap. Lily wondered if the headache was anything to do with Mr Gray's ducking out of divine service and further compounding his crime by taking his son with him. Whether it was or not, when she brought the children back to the suite to change for their evening meal, the Grays had decided to have their own dinner in their sitting room once the children had been fed and were in bed.

'Take the rest of the evening off once the twins are asleep,' Arabella offered when Lily brought them all back from the dining room. 'And take the key with you so that you can let yourself in.'

Lily thanked her, but she didn't rush in bathing the twins. This was the time of the day she liked the most with the boys: their chatter as they sat either end of the bath, their naked, wriggling bodies when she lifted them one by one onto her lap to dry them, the sight of them in their pyjamas looking impossibly angelic in spite of whatever mischief they'd got up to during

329

the day. And most of all, the feel of them snuggled up either side of her while she read them their bedtime story, their curls damp from their bath and their eyelids drooping. They knew she loved them and they loved her, and every night she told herself that if she ever married – and that was highly unlikely now – she wouldn't give up such a precious time with her own children even if she could afford a dozen nursery-maids.

As usual, by the time the Grays tiptoed in to kiss the boys goodnight, they were half asleep, and once she had changed for dinner Lily left the suite after checking that her two small charges were sound asleep and saying goodnight to Edwin, who was sitting reading in his bed on the other side of the boys' bedroom.

She had more or less made up her mind she'd probably go back to the suite after her dinner, as the sea air was tiring, but once Tess discovered she was free for the evening she made Lily promise to wait for her. 'I'll get Miss Wilhelmina togged up in her best as quick as I can,' she told Lily. 'And tonight being special, it'll be two or three hours before she needs me again.' Since it was the last but one night of the crossing the first-class passengers would be dressing in their finest evening clothes for dinner, as was customary, as the last night was reserved for packing. 'We can go for a walk or visit the second-class dining saloon for the hymn singing.'

Tess was as good as her word, and once they'd made their way to the second-class dining saloon they sidled in at the back of the assembled throng. Quite a few of the hymns that were sung were about the dangers of the sea but Lily found them strangely comforting. Not so Tess. As they came to the line 'O hear us when we cry to Thee for those in peril on the sea', she nudged Lily in the ribs, muttering, 'Bloomin' cheerful, this lot are. You'd think they were wishing it on us.'

Lily couldn't help laughing even as she whispered back, 'It's asking the Almighty for protection, that's all.'

'Protection?' Tess's snub nose wrinkled. 'What does everyone else know that I don't?'

The hymn singing having come to a close, the two girls returned to their promenade. It was an extraordinarily clear and calm night but bitterly cold and the sudden drop in temperature had clearly driven all but the most hardy souls inside because there were few people about. They could hear the strains of music from inside the ship but otherwise it was quiet, even the breeze which had been present earlier in the day had died away completely. 'Isn't it smashing?' Tess's eyes were gleaming in the darkness. 'Look at the sea, it's as smooth as glass.'

'Tess, it's freezing,' Lily complained. 'Let's go into the warm.'

'Wait a minute.' Tess darted off, returning a minute or two later with two thick blankets the stewards usually tucked round the first-class passengers when they were sitting taking the air. Giving one to Lily she wrapped one round herself, cocoon fashion, so only her head was visible. Giggling, Lily did the same and they stood and gazed into the darkness for a little while, talking softly. Perhaps it was the ethereal quality to the night or maybe that Tess was so easy to talk to, but Lily found herself talking to another person about John for the first time in months. She didn't go into details, merely saying that there was someone she loved but had left for good in England. And then Tess told her of her own heartache, of a footman she had loved in Lady Lyndon's employ who had dallied with her affections and then upped and married someone else with no warning. 'I think Miss Graham's got it right,' Tess said soberly after they'd stood in silence for a few moments. 'She thinks all men are rogues and blackguards, intent on pillage and rape. She even takes a bath with her drawers on, you know.' They stared at each other before bursting into laughter, and a few minutes later, when Lily made her way back to the Grays' suite, she was aware of feeling better than she had in weeks.

Prudence and Belinda were asleep when she opened the door to the bedroom, their long fair hair carefully coiled round the strips of rags they used to make it curl in the morning. She stood gazing down at them for a minute or two. Prudence was nearly twelve now and quite a young lady, whereas Belinda at ten years old still struggled with decorum at times. But they were sweet-natured girls on the whole. She had heard horror stories of the way some young madams treated their servants but there was none of that in the Gray household. Both Molly and Bridget, and she herself, felt themselves part of the family. She had joined the household when the girls were very small and had watched them grow up, and seen Edwin and the twins born. All of her working life since she had left school at thirteen had been with this family. What would she do when Adam and Nicholas, the last of 'her' babies, grew up and didn't need her any more? Seek out another family and begin the process all over again? Forever caring for someone else's children till she was old and pensioned off, living in a couple of rooms somewhere with just a cat or two for company?

Surprised at the way her thoughts had gone, she shook her head at herself. She had felt more at peace when she had come back to the cabin but now she was all churned up again. She thought too much, that was her trouble. Sarah had always said that and her sister was right.

She felt too troubled to sleep and so she sat down on her bed fully dressed except for her shoes, after picking up a book from a pile Prudence had by her bed. It was called *Little Women* by someone called Louisa May Alcott and although she hadn't really expected to like it, within minutes the story had captured her and taken her mind off her troubles. She was deep into the book when, shortly before midnight, she felt a grinding, crunching jar and faintly heard a ripping sound, as though someone was tearing a long piece of linen. Her heart thudding, she swung her legs off the bed and glanced at Prudence and Belinda who were still fast asleep. Tiptoeing across the room she opened the door and checked on the boys, all of whom were sleeping, but as she came out of their bedroom she met Mr and Mrs Gray in their dressing gowns.

'Did you hear it?' Arabella had her hand to her throat. 'What was it?'

'I don't know, ma'am, but I'm sure it's nothing to worry about,' Lily said gently, seeing Mrs Gray was in a state.

'That's what I said.' Mr Gray's voice was over-hearty and he must have realised this because he moderated his tone when he said, 'I'll go and see what's what, Arabella. You go back to bed.'

'I'll go, sir. You stay with madam. I've been reading and haven't got undressed yet. I'll just put on my shoes and get my coat; it was much colder earlier than it has been.'

'Oh yes, Norman, let Lily go. Stay with me.' Arabella was clearly trembling and then her head tilted. 'Something's different. What is it?'

They all listened and then Mr Gray said quietly, 'The engines have stopped, dear. That's all.' He glanced at Lily over his wife's head and she obeyed his unspoken command, pulling on her shoes and coat and leaving the cabin. She made her way to the first-class promenade on the deck above on the starboard side, meeting more anxious passengers as she went.

As luck would have it Tess was one of the first people she saw; it appeared she, too, had been sent to find out what was what. Coming to her side, her face reflecting both excitement and apprehension, Tess said, 'It's an iceberg, we've hit an iceberg. I've just been talking to a gentleman who was leaving the smoking room when it happened. He said he couldn't believe his eyes at first because he saw what he thought was a full-rigged ship with her sails set right at the side of the ship. Mind, he'd been drinking. He was one of the guests at the party in honour of Captain

Smith tonight. So were Miss Wilhelmina and Lady Lyndon.'

Lily didn't care about Captain Smith's party. 'And he saw an iceberg?' she pressed.

'Aye, that's what he said. He realised after a second what it was and he said it was massive, towering up over the ship.' Tess was in her dressing gown and she was shivering violently in the freezing air, but she still said, 'Look, come and see this an' all,' as she pulled Lily to the forward railing of A Deck.

Lily's hand went to her mouth as she stared down into the forward well deck below. There were tons of ice, broken and splintered where it had been smashed from the iceberg as it had ground past the ship. Even as the two girls watched, some of the third-class passengers who had been berthed forward and who had come up on deck to see what was wrong began playfully throwing chunks of ice and handfuls of slush at each other. 'They don't seem too bothered.' Tess was smiling as she followed the antics of a group of young men playing football with a lump of ice. 'It can't be anything to worry about.' A steward hurried past and she caught hold of his arm. 'Has the ship been damaged?'

With a reassuring smile he shook his head. 'Everything is all right, don't worry. We will be on our way in a few minutes.'

As the man disappeared, Tess turned to Lily, smiling. 'I told you.'

'The ship's tilting.' Lily looked at the floor beneath her, her heart beginning to thump harder.

'What?'

'It's tilting. You must be able to feel it, it's lower towards the front of the ship.'

'The bow. It's called the bow and they say listing, not tilting.'

'Whatever it's called, it shouldn't be doing that.'

'Perhaps it's the weight of all the ice that's fallen on board. They'll clear that off in no time,' Tess said, but her voice wasn't so certain now. 'There can't be anything to worry about, lass. This is the *Titanic*.'

There were crowds of people milling about, variously attired in dressing gowns, fur coats, evening clothes, sweaters or pyjamas and slippers under greatcoats. Everyone was talking but from the snippets Lily could hear no one seemed to know what was happening or whether they were in any danger. One man said they'd lost a propeller blade, another that the jolt had damaged one of the engines and they were doing running repairs; there was little sense of alarm or panic. The *Titanic* lay motionless in the water under a sky where the stars seemed incredibly bright, the three functional funnels blowing off massive clouds of steam. Lily felt slightly reassured till the list under her feet got fractionally worse. She might know very little about ships and boats but she knew this wasn't right.

'I don't like this.' She looked at Tess. 'I'm going to tell my family to get dressed.'

'What, wake the bairns? They won't thank you for that if there's nowt wrong, lass. I'm going to find out for sure what's going on before I go back. Miss Graham'll have my guts for garters if I get 'em all up when there's no need, and you heard what that steward said.'

'Well, ten minutes has gone by and the engines haven't started again.' Lily's mind was made up. 'I'm going back.'

She left Tess still watching the third-class passengers kicking blocks of ice back and forth. When she went down the stairs the list was more noticeable and now her stomach was churning. Why hadn't she told John she still loved him before she had gone? Left a note with Sarah only to be given to him if anything happened to her? But she was being silly, nothing was going to happen to them. As Tess had said, this was the *Titanic*.

When she reached the suite Mr Gray was waiting for her and she told him what she'd seen and heard, adding, 'I think it would be wise to wake the children, sir, and get them dressed warmly.'

Arabella had appeared in the doorway to the master bedroom as Lily had been speaking. Now she said, 'No, I don't want them disturbed for nothing. You said yourself, Lily, that the steward didn't think there was anything to worry about.'

Mr Gray tightened his dressing-gown cord. 'I would prefer to hear what's what from an officer's mouth. Wait here.' He was back within a few minutes and his face was grim. Glancing at Lily, he said simply, 'Wake them.' And to his wife, 'Get dressed, Arabella, and we will all need to put our lifebelts on.'

'Oh, Norman.' Arabella had gone white. 'Is it serious?'

'Serious enough. Now come along, dear, no tears. You don't want the children to see you crying, do you? Be a brave girl.'

The children were remarkably good about being woken from a deep sleep. For some minutes all was bustle and activity. Lily chivvied the older ones along as she dressed the twins, putting several layers of their warmest clothes on. She made a game of it, smiling at their chuckles and hugging each little body once they were ready. Mr Gray came into the boys' bedroom as she was tying the twins' bobble hats under their chins, and under cover of the children's chatter, murmured, 'The officer I spoke to told me they've sent a call for assistance but he doesn't know how long it will be before help arrives. He seems to believe the ship is sinking, Lily, but I don't want Arabella worried at this stage.'

'Oh, sir.' Lily glanced at the twins. 'The children.'

'Would you take charge of Adam and Nicholas?' he asked quietly.

Lily nodded, glancing down at their little faces as her heart raced and fear turned her insides to jelly.

They were nearly ready when their own steward knocked on the door and informed them all women and children were requested on deck with their lifebelts on. Arabella blanched still further but after Mr Gray had shut the door, he smiled at his wife reassuringly. 'It's a standard precaution, Arabella, nothing more. We've hit an iceberg, that's why the ship has stopped. It will take them a while to get it going again, that's all.'

Lily looked from husband to wife and it struck her, not for the first time, that the reason their marriage was so successful was because Mr Gray babied his wife more than he had ever done his children.

The list to the ship was far worse now than when she had come back to the cabin, making walking difficult as they made their way to the boat deck where the lifeboats were, eight to port and eight to starboard. The girls were white-faced and silent but the twins took their cue from Edwin who seemed to think it all a great adventure. Ordinarily the boat deck served as the open-air promenade for first and second classes, the forward two-thirds of the deck being reserved for first and a third for second. Now it was crowded with passengers in varying states of dress watching groups of crewmen removing canvas covers from the lifeboats and getting them ready to launch.

As she watched them Lily wondered what was going to happen to the third-class passengers; there were none in the throng in front of her and she knew from what Mr Gray had said on the way to the ship that the staircases leading from the steerage upwards were kept closed and locked. But the stewards would see to them, she reasoned. They wouldn't just leave them in the bowels of the ship with no way of escape if the boat really was going to sink. Sink . . . John, oh, John. Why had she let Ralph part them? She should've told John about his brother, she should've told everyone.

They were at the back of the horde of people who had gathered on deck, probably because they had taken the time to dress the children although in spite of that the girls' teeth were clearly chattering in the icy air and the twins were hanging onto Lily's skirts and grizzling that they were cold. Only Edwin stood straight and tall beside his father. Some children who were only wrapped in steamer blankets over their pyjamas were already crying loudly, but the cold was such that it penetrated through the warmest clothing, none of which seemed adequate for the arctic conditions prevailing.

They got colder and colder as the crew finished preparing the lifeboats and then stood by them, apparently waiting for instructions. Slowly the atmosphere changed. The quips and jokes that had been flying back and forth at first died out as the tension mounted. Lily kept herself busy talking to the twins about this and that in an effort to distract them from the cold; it helped to combat the shivering that had taken hold of her. All around them people were murmuring that they wanted to go back to their cabins and they certainly didn't want to risk the icy water in one of those tiny boats. Why should they? they argued quietly. The ship appeared perfectly sound and the *Titanic* was unsinkable after all. Even the orchestra was playing in the first-class lounge; this was much ado about nothing.

It was evident Arabella had been listening to the grumbling. When, within the next minute or two, the officer in charge of the lifeboats on their side of the deck called for women and children, she viewed the half-hearted response with frightened eyes. Turning to her husband, she said, 'Everyone knows those boats are not safe. We would be exposing the children to greater danger in them than if they remained on this ship. It can't sink. You've told me a hundred times since we booked our passage it can't sink.'

'I was wrong.'

'No. No, you were not, Norman; you're just saying that now.'

As the officer shouted for more passengers from the crowd in front of them they watched a couple more women join those already in a boat. Someone in the front of the throng shouted for the new brides and grooms to go first, so a few young men joined the women. There seemed to be a great deal of confusion with seamen trying to prevent passengers' feet from getting snarled in the ropes and two men jumping into the boat when they clearly weren't young husbands, causing the officer to call for them to be thrown out. As several crewmen tried to haul them out, more men leaped in causing the women to scream as the boat tipped. Evidently the officer decided enough was enough because the next moment the boat was being lowered, even though it wasn't full. The progress to the water was not smooth, and Arabella watched in horror as first the bow dropped several feet, then the stern, then the bow again. Although the boat reached the water safely it was the last straw for Arabella and she burst into tears. Marshalling the girls and Edwin in front of her she said, 'Come on, we're going inside,' and marched off, leaving Mr Gray and Lily, who was holding tightly to the twins' hands, no option but to follow.

'You have to tell Mrs Gray what the officer told you, sir,' Lily said urgently, and he nodded, glancing at her briefly before increasing his steps so he caught up with his wife inside the ship.

'That's enough, Arabella.' He caught hold of his wife's arm and swung her to face him. 'You must get off the ship with the children because some time soon there won't be a choice in the matter. It is a case of leave when you can or go down with the ship. I'm sorry, m'dear, but there's no doubt about it from what one of the officers told me.'

Arabella stared at him wildly. 'I don't believe it, all this fuss is just a precautionary measure. Why are all the lights still on and the music playing? And no one is perturbed, not really.' The strains of 'Alexander's Ragtime Band' from the orchestra seemed to back up her declaration.

And then everything changed. A momentary flash and a loud whoosh came from the starboard bridge wing seconds before a cascade of stars burst high in the black sky accompanied by an ear-shattering bang.

'Fireworks, Daddy! Fireworks!' The twins were jumping up and down, their bodily discomfort forgotten. They'd seen fireworks at their father's parents' home in the New Year and the event had made a big impression on them.

'Now do you believe me?' Norman held his wife's horrified gaze and she nodded slowly. The *Titanic* was sending the distress signal asking for the help of any other ship in the vicinity.

Once they had retraced their steps to the lifeboats they saw the distress signal had convinced everyone the ship was in mortal danger. Now the air was full of goodbyes, wives clinging to husbands one last time before they stepped into the boats and children whimpering and crying for their fathers. Husbands were having to be firm with wives who tried to persuade them to climb into the boat, and sons with mothers for the same reason. The *Titanic*'s officers were adamant. Women and children only. It was now clear there weren't enough lifeboats for everyone and the slant of the deck grew steadily more ominous as people got into the lifeboats and they were lowered. Lily couldn't understand why they appeared half full. She had Adam and Nicholas in her arms and sensing Arabella was deliberately holding back she nudged Belinda and Prudence in front of her, saying, 'Go forward, that's it, keep moving forward.' What was Mrs Gray thinking of? she asked herself angrily as the children did what she said, Edwin following his sisters. The children needed to be got onto one of the boats. She turned, so far forgetting herself as to raise her voice to Mr Gray: 'You must get her into one of the boats, don't you see? The children must leave the ship. Mr Gray, you'll have to *make* her. There're hardly any boats left.' While Mrs Gray had been holding back she had noticed some women and children she hadn't seen before climbing into a boat which was partially lowered and was some feet down the side of the ship waiting for another boat beneath it to row away. They were almost certainly third-class passengers and while she was glad for them, the thought had struck her that if all the third-class passengers started coming to the boat deck they'd have little chance of getting the children away.

It was now over an hour and a half since the iceberg had accomplished its deadly work. As they neared the last boats the first panic rippled through the crowds waiting to get away and scuffles broke out. Lily watched as one young man threw himself over the rail into one of the boats and tried to hide under the seats among the women sitting there. The officer in charge drew his revolver, dragging the youth out and ordering him back on ship. Just seconds later another man tried the same thing but this time several men who had been putting their wives and children into the lifeboat before standing back, grabbed hold of the unfortunate individual and began to punch him about the head and chest.

The twins were clinging to her as tightly as frightened baby monkeys now, their arms limpet-like round her neck, and she tried to keep her voice steady as she kept up a flow of reassurance, explaining they were going to have a ride in one of the little boats. It would be nice, she told them. They'd be real sailors then and when they got home she was sure their mother and father would buy them sailor suits, they'd like that, wouldn't they?

They reached the lifeboat at last, but suddenly the woman in front of them who was being persuaded into the boat by her husband began to shriek and cling onto him. 'Don't put me in that boat, it will capsize, I know it will. I want to stay and take my chance with you.' The officer who was assisting the women into the boat tried to help the husband but even between them they couldn't prise her off and at last the husband admitted defeat and led his weeping wife away.

'I'm not going, either; not if you can't come with me.' Arabella stood stock-still as she stared at her husband. 'I've never been in an open boat in my life and I shan't be able to stand it without you.'

'Of course you will.' Norman took his wife into his arms. 'You'll have Lily and the children, Arabella.'

'I'm not going.'

'You must.' Sensing the officer's irritation Norman spoke sharply. 'You have to take care of the children.'

'Not without you.'

The ship's list to port had got much worse in the last few minutes. As Mrs Gray finished speaking they heard the officer from the bridge shout for everyone to move to the starboard side, and at the same time Prudence and Belinda began to cry and hold onto their mother saying they didn't want to go in the boat either. Lily looked desperately about her. It was clear the ship was doomed, and for the children to have any chance at all she had to get them into a lifeboat. As the passengers from the port side reached them she saw a familiar face and, forgetting all decorum, she yelled with all her might, 'Tess! Tess! Here!' Turning to the people behind her she said quickly, 'She's with me, please let her through,' and without any demur they did just that.

'Oh, lass, I was just about to get into the boat with Miss Wilhelmina when the officer said no more and I was to take the next one, and then we were moved over here—'

Lily cut off Tess's gabbling. 'You have to help me get the children into the lifeboat,' she said urgently. 'Mrs Gray's gone to pieces and Mr Gray' – she glanced across to where he was trying to reason with his wife who was clearly hysterical and had the three older children clasped to her – 'doesn't seem able to get through to her.'

Tess followed her eyes. 'She needs a good slap,' she said practically, 'but the gentry don't go in for that, do they?'

The officer had lost all patience. 'Get in,' he said sharply. 'There's no time to lose.'

The twins were hanging on to Lily for dear life and half strangling her in the process. 'Get in the boat,' she said to Tess, 'and I'll pass them to you, then I'll get the others.'

The officer bundled Tess rather unceremoniously into the lifeboat, but when Lily attempted to pass Adam to her friend the child began screaming so shrilly as he tightened his hold on her that the three of them nearly fell over the rail. Mr Gray had glanced across at the noise and as the officer said irritably, 'You'll have to get in, miss, and then I'll pass them to you one by one. They'll go in if they see you waiting in the boat,' her employer called, 'Get in the boat with the twins, Lily. We'll follow you in a minute.'

She glanced desperately at Edwin who had his face buried in his mother's waist and who suddenly appeared a very young child, and Prudence and Belinda who were sobbing uncontrollably. She felt like going and tearing them from their mother but with the twins crying and the officer shouting at her to do what he said right *now*, she had no other option than to kneel down and unclasp the toddlers' arms from round her neck. 'I'm going to get in the boat,' she said firmly, 'and this nice man is going to lift you to me, all right? But you mustn't struggle and wriggle like you did a minute ago. I'll be waiting for you and you must be good boys.'

She didn't know if they'd taken it in, they were beside themselves with fright, but the officer grabbed their hands in a vice-like grip and one of the men who was standing waiting to get his womenfolk into the boat behind her stepped forward and helped her climb over the rail and into the boat which was lurching slightly. Now Adam and Nicholas were frantic to get to her and the officer and the man who had helped her into the boat practically threw the little boys to her and Tess.

More women and children followed as another rocket shot up into the sky, but Edwin and the girls didn't appear. Lily shouted their names over and over again from where she sat with Tess, the twins held tightly in their arms, growing more distraught as the boat filled. Then the officer's head came over the rail and he shouted down to the two seamen who were manning the lifeboat that it was going to be lowered.

'You can't! You can't!' Lily stood up, but a big fat woman at the side of her pulled her down none too gently.

'Keep still,' she said tersely. 'Do you want to drown the lot of us? Whoever it is you're shouting for, they'll get the next boat.'

Shaking off the woman's hand, Lily cried, 'But there's still room in this one.'

The seaman nearest to her shook his head. 'If the boats are fully loaded before they're lowered the weight might cause them to buckle and break in the middle. This is as many as we dare take down. Once we're in the water we can take more on.'

'But that's ridiculous,' Lily said fiercely. 'No one is

going to get in once it's on the sea, you know that. And why make the boats this big if they can't be full when they're lowered? I don't believe that's true.'

'Don't ask me, miss. I'm just repeating what the officer told me.' The boat was jerking its way to the sea below as he added, 'Don't worry about your friends, they'll be all right.'

Lily said nothing, there was nothing *to* say, but she felt sick at heart. She should have made Prudence and Belinda and Edwin get into the lifeboat; how could she have left them on the ship? She hadn't meant to but it had happened in spite of herself somehow.

Seconds later the boat splashed into the water and immediately the two seamen began to row away from the liner. Lily hugged Adam to her and at the side of her Tess did the same to Nicholas, both girls trying to keep the little boys warm. Once clear of the ship and looking at it from the water it was clear to everyone on the lifeboat that the ship had only a short time left. They could hear crashes and bangs and then Tess clutched her arm. 'Look, another lifeboat's being lowered. The bairns might be in that one.'

Lily hoped so, oh, she hoped so. She was praying with all her heart, just one refrain, Get them off, God, please get them off. Get them off, get them off . . .

The slant of the ship was getting visibly steeper and to everyone's horror the *Titanic*'s huge propellers, still and motionless, slowly emerged from the black water. Tess was still gripping her arm and now she breathed, 'Oh, lass, I can't bear it,' as they saw desperate figures jumping and falling from the sinking vessel.

'Listen.' Lily tilted her head. 'It's a hymn.' Sure enough,

the faint sounds of an ancient hymn carried across the still water along with a series of dull booms as the ship went into her death throes. The tears running down her face, Lily held on to Adam with all her might as though through feeling him warm and alive his brother and sisters would be safe too.

The seamen had stopped rowing, now everyone was looking at the ship as the stern rose higher into the sky. The strains of 'Nearer, my God, to Thee' stopped abruptly and the noise from within the dying ship became deafening as she began to break under the terrible strain and everything movable inside her plunged towards the bow. The lights on the ship suddenly went out, plunging it into darkness, then flashed on again for one startlingly bright second, only to go out again for good. The stern rose till it was almost completely upright, a huge black shape to those in the lifeboats as it was silhouetted against the star-pierced sky. As it began to slip down into the dark, icy water a moan went through the lifeboat from the women who had husbands and sons or brothers still trapped on the vessel, a moan which was echoed by the other little boats dotted about the sea.

All night Lily had been thinking about John; with every breath, whatever she had been doing, one part of her mind had been calling out to him, but now her only thought was for Mr Gray and the others on board the liner. She didn't allow herself in these moments to imagine Edwin and the girls weren't safe in one of the last lifeboats to be launched, that would have been unbearable. They *were* safe, they had to be.

The end came quickly. Their lifeboat was some two

hundred yards from the ship and one moment they could hear those on board – husbands and wives, parents and children, brothers and sisters – calling out to one another, 'I love you,' and the next the vessel gathered momentum and went down into the depths. Within twenty seconds the ship had vanished.

Lily stared blankly where the ship had been. She had seen it with her own eyes but she couldn't take it in in the first heart-thudding moment. She was alive, the stars were still twinkling serenely in a black velvet sky, and hundreds of men, women and children had just died.

Chapter 21

Within moments it was all too horribly real. The *Titanic* might be sinking silently into a watery grave, but among the wreckage from the ship hundreds of people were struggling and splashing helplessly in the unimaginably cold sea. Some still had the strength to cry and scream for help as they clutched hold of whatever they could find to stay afloat; others were too injured or too cold to do more than gasp for their next breath.

'We have to help them.' Lily held Adam tight to her, trying to impart warmth into his shivering little body even though she herself was shaking and frozen to the marrow. 'There's room in this boat for more people, there's room in all the boats. We can't leave those people.'

'She's right.' Tess valiantly backed her up. 'They're drowning, we have to go back and pick up as many as we can.'

'No. With all those people they'll capsize the boat.' The fat lady at the side of Lily glared at them as everyone else remained silent. 'All that'll happen is that we'll all lose our lives and where's the sense in that?'

'We can't leave them,' Lily said again.

'And who are you to say what we should or shouldn't do?' The woman's voice was bitter as she took in the quality of Lily's hat and coat which Arabella had bought her for the trip to New York, along with the well-dressed child sitting on her lap. 'It's up to us all, the way I see it. Well?' She looked at the other women on the boat, most of whom had children with them. 'Are you prepared to risk drowning, you and your children, for the sake of them out there? They'll tip us up, you know that, don't you?'

'It might be your husband or brother or son we save,' Lily said passionately, glancing round at the other women.

'Ha, and what are the chances of that, out of all of them?' The fat lady had her arm round a child of six or seven, and now she said, 'My husband got me and our son on this boat to save us, not to die losing our lives in a useless attempt to save strangers. We'll be swamped if we go back, they'll pull us under.'

'We should do what we can.' Lily stared at the woman.

'Like they did what they could for us, you mean?' she bit back. 'In steerage?'

'What do you mean?'

'I'll tell you what I mean, my fine lady. No one came to take care of us and when they did it was too late. Locked in, we were. Forgotten. We were told that the officers and crew knew what they were doing and most of 'em believed it. Not my husband, God rest his soul. He wasn't going to sit waiting to die like a rat in a trap. He got me and our Norman out of there but only a few would come with us. The rest of them are still probably waiting to be told what to do in the dining saloon. They were having a prayer meeting when we left, praying to God to save 'em, but like my husband said, God helps them who helps themselves.' And with that she burst into tears.

Lily stared around helplessly. In a small voice, she said, 'Please, we must go back,' but no one would look at her and the two crewmen allowed the boat to drift on in the darkness. 'Leave it, lass,' Tess whispered. 'Whatever you say they're not going to try, they're too scared.'

Within an hour the rising swell had made two women violently seasick and several others, including Lily and Tess, felt distinctly queasy but Lily was too worried about the twins to dwell on how she felt. The cries from the people floundering in the water had long since faded away but she knew the sound of them would stay with her for ever; for the present, however, she concentrated on keeping the twins' minds off what they had seen and the vicious cold. As it happened, the twins were probably better off than most folk due to the fact she'd had the foresight to dress them in several layers. The fat lady's son had begun to cry from the cold some time ago, along with one or two other children, and everyone was shivering convulsively. One of the seamen had wrapped the sail around two small girls, and a lady in a fur coat farther back in the boat had taken someone else's baby onto her lap, enclosing the infant in the folds of the coat and talking to it in a soothing voice till it stopped wailing.

Most of the women wept quietly on and off as the first numbing shock of what they'd experienced began to wear off and there was little conversation except to the children. If another lifeboat came near one woman would call out to ask if her husband was on board but there was never the reply she wanted.

A big sturdy Irishwoman had been given the position at the tiller by one of the two seamen because they were both needed at the oars; when she became too cold to continue at this exposed point another woman, slight and delicate-looking and extremely well dressed, took her place without a word.

Perhaps it was the complete blackness of the sea but the night sky had never seemed so vast before or the stars so bright; there seemed to be a shooting star every few minutes. It seemed impossible, looking up into the tranquil heavens, that so many people had perished. Lily was glad of Tess's solid presence; for once her friend wasn't saying much but every so often they would reached out and squeeze each other's hand and Tess was doing her best to keep Nicholas warm.

Some time before dawn Lily saw what she thought was a flash of lightning followed seconds later by a dull boom. Others saw it too, one woman muttering, 'If it starts to rain it'll finish us off, we'll never survive being soaked in this cold.'

The seamen said nothing, but when another flash was seen and the sound came again they sat bolt upright. 'That's no thunder and lightning,' one muttered. 'That's a ship.'

'A ship?' A stir of interest moved round the grief-stricken women, the lady at the tiller murmuring, 'Thanks be to God, we're saved.'

Lily said nothing but she hugged Adam tighter as her heart raced. A ship. Someone was coming for them.

Dawn came with surprising suddenness. As a pale silvery glow stole over the sky they could make out a big ship on the horizon and other lifeboats, some close and some four or five miles away. Stretching from the northern horizon to the west was something which chilled Lily's heart; a huge unbroken sheet of ice with massive icebergs rising out of it.

The seamen rowed with purpose now, a brisk morning breeze producing waves that caused the two women suffering from acute seasickness more problems. As they lay in the bottom of the boat vomiting, too weak to lift their heads, the sky became a brilliantly clear blue, the sun sending arrows of golden light down into the water.

Lily could hear cheering echoing across the sea, even singing; other boats, like theirs holding all women and children who had lost their menfolk, were silent. Lily looked around the grief-etched faces as they grew nearer to the liner she could see was called the *Carpathia*. What she saw was a reflection of her own feelings. Unutterable relief that they were safe at last, that they weren't going to die, was only part of it.

At six o'clock they had reached the ship and one by one they were taken on board. Lily and Tess and several other women were able to use the rope ladders, the two women who had been so ill and a number of others were lifted on to the deck of the *Carpathia* in slings. The children were lifted up in mail sacks but such was their exhaustion they submitted like small frozen dolls.

Now the terrible fear Lily had been keeping at bay throughout the dark hours on the lifeboat wouldn't be ignored. After accompanying Tess and the twins to the dining saloon she swallowed the soup she was given scalding hot and, Tess having promised to keep the twins with her, she made her way back to the deck. As soon as she had come aboard she had ascertained Edwin and his sisters were not among the survivors already rescued, but that didn't mean anything, she told herself fiercely. There was a small fleet of boats still making their way to the *Carpathia*.

Someone brought her a blanket, someone else a mug of hot, sweet tea, but she wouldn't move from her post at the railing. As each little lifeboat came alongside she searched for the familiar faces, praying silently all the time. When one well-meaning passenger of the *Carpathia* tried to persuade her to go down to the dining saloon and get warm for a little while she nearly bit the poor woman's head off, but the same woman silently returned half an hour later with a bowl of hot soup and a crusty roll for which Lily thanked her. The woman pressed her arm and turned away, but not before Lily had seen the tears in her eyes.

By nine o'clock all the survivors from the *Titanic* were on board and Lily's vigil ended. Edwin and

Prudence and Belinda, along with Mr and Mrs Gray, were not among them.

Lily was not the only one beside herself with grief when that afternoon a brief service, a combined memorial for the lost and thanksgiving for those lives which had been saved, was held in the *Carpathia*'s main lounge. Seven hundred and five men, women and children were rescued from the boats; one thousand, five hundred and two people had gone down with the ship or died in the icy water after the *Titanic* had sunk.

One steerage passenger who had lost her husband, her two sons, and who had watched her baby daughter freeze to death in her arms before they were rescued asked the questions everyone was thinking. How could an iceberg sink a ship that had been declared to be unsinkable in just two hours, and why had so many people perished when the *Titanic* was supposed to be the safest ship ever built? And what was she going to do now? The woman clasped her remaining child, a small boy of five or six years old, to her. How was she going to be able to bear it?

Arms had reached out to hold mother and child and quiet sobbing had joined the woman's, but no one attempted to give an answer to the unanswerable.

Chapter 22

'I can't believe it. I can't believe that ship's been lost.'

John raised weary eyes to his mother. She had said the very same words periodically over the last twenty-four hours since learning of the disaster which had befallen the *Titanic*, but he wasn't irritated. He knew she'd always thought the world of Lily. *She had to be all right.* The physical sickness which had accompanied his hearing of the news was spent now, but terror and guilt still gnawed at his vitals. He should have gone to see her before she'd left, he'd known he should but pride had kept him away. *Pride* He wasn't going to let any woman reduce him to less than a man, he'd told himself; there were plenty of lassies who'd be only too willing to look the side he was on. Dear gussy . . . He groaned deep inside himself. He'd give the rest of his life for five minutes with her now.

The evening meal had been finished some time ago but no one had moved from the table. Harold sat puffing at his pipe, his mild eyes occasionally catching those of Robert who had been reading the same page of his paper for the last hour. Hannah was sitting by the side of John and every so often she patted his hand and even Larry hadn't said a word, doing his homework without griping for once. They were all stunned by the tragedy and concerned how it was going to affect John if Lily wasn't among the survivors.

The *Carpathia* wasn't due to arrive in New York till Thursday and although the wireless operators aboard the ship were doing their best to transmit the names of survivors to the White Star Line's New York office, it was a laborious task. Already the papers were reporting that Southampton was a city in mourning. Four of every five sailors aboard the *Titanic* had come from the coastal town and it appeared early reports were suggesting many of the eight-hundred-and-ninety-odd crewmen had gone down with the ship. Black cloth blotted out hundreds of windows and crowds had gathered outside the White Star Line's Southampton office all day awaiting the names which were posted as quickly as they came in.

'When do you think we'll know anything?' said Nora, bringing another of her endless pots of tea to the table and sitting down in her chair with a plump.

This was another question which had been asked incessantly and John gave his stock answer: 'I don't know, Mam, but Sarah'll let us know anything as soon as she hears.' Nora looked at her son and such was the expression in her eyes that John felt compelled to reach out and take her hand. 'Come on,' he said quietly. 'Pour that tea.'

Nora nodded, picking up the teapot and pouring six cups of tea that nobody wanted but which everyone drank without comment. Some time later Robert left to see his girlfriend and Larry went up to bed, leaving only John and Hannah and their parents in the kitchen when the back door burst open and the next moment Sarah flew in from the scullery. 'She's all right! Da's just been notified and he came straight round to tell us. She's safe, she's on the *Carpathia*.'

Ralph had followed his wife into the kitchen and as both Sarah and Nora burst into tears, clinging hold of each other, he stood silently in the doorway, his eyes on John who had gone white with relief.

'Oh, lass, lass.' Whereas Sarah's tears were diminishing, Nora was now sobbing as though she would never stop. 'I thought she'd gone, I did, and for us to have parted the way we did . . .' She looked at John through streaming eyes. 'I'd never have forgiven meself, never in a hundred years.'

John stared at his mother. What on earth was she on about? Standing up, he moved round the table and disentangled her from Sarah. Pushing her down on one of the hardbacked kitchen chairs, he crouched in front of her. His thankfulness in knowing Lily was safe made his voice very gentle when he said, 'Come on, Mam, don't cry. It's all right.'

'It's not all right. I should've known.' The relief that Lily had been spared and that she was going to have the chance to make amends had produced a kind of hysteria. 'I should've known, I tell you. She's a good lass, always was.'

John shook his mother's hands. 'Stop it, Mam.'

Harold had come to his wife's side, his expression showing he had no more insight into what was troubling her than John. He put his hand on Nora's shoulder.

'Oh, Harold.' Nora turned into her husband's body and as his arms went round her he shook his head at John, signifying his bewilderment.

It was a minute or two before Nora gained control of herself. Her giving way had shaken most of them nearly as much as the news about the *Titanic*. Nora was the rock of the family, the stalwart foundation on which they had all built their lives to a greater or lesser extent. All except Ralph. He alone remained unmoved at his mother's distress, his eyes narrowing as he sought an explanation for her garbled words.

Harold had actually made his wife a cup of tea and that alone showed the state to which he'd been moved. It was the first time in their married life he had so much as lifted a finger to do what he termed 'women's work'. His voice soft, he said, 'Here, old girl, get that down you and don't take on so. Whatever it is you think you've done, it can't be that bad. I know you better than most an' I'd stake me life on it.'

If he had but known it, his faith in her made Nora feel worse, not better. Sniffing loudly, she lifted her pinny and scrubbed at her face. Looking directly at John, she said, 'I went an' saw her – Lily, I mean – afore she went. You were miserable an' Sarah said she was miserable an' I thought I might be able to bring an end to it.'

John sat back on his heels, his face darkening. '*Mam.*'

'I know, I know. I knew you'd hit the roof, that's why I didn't tell you before.' She glanced at Harold. 'The same goes for you an' all. Least said, soonest mended an' all that. An' likely you're right. I wish I'd never gone, that's for sure. I've not had a minute's peace since.'

John was furious with his mother but he had to ask. 'What happened?'

'Things were said.' Nora swallowed hard. 'An' it wasn't till I had a chance to think that I realised Lily would never have got herself involved in anything like that but by then it was too late. She'd gone.'

Trying to control his anger and impatience, John stood up and drew a chair to him. Sitting down opposite his mother he took her hands in his as he leaned forward. 'Mam, start at the beginning. You went to see her, you say?'

'Aye. An' I can't rightly remember how we came round to it now but I got the feelin' she'd finished with you because she was worried about when you'd been worked over. I asked her if she was frightened she'd be got at next an' she said it wasn't that.'

Sarah had been standing by the table and now she said, sharply, 'Lily's never run away from anything and she wouldn't have left John for that.'

John motioned with his hand for her to be silent without taking his eyes off his mother's face. 'And?' he pressed quietly. 'What did Lily say?'

'She – she told me somethin'.'

'What?'

'She said I hadn't to say.'

'*Mam.*'

'For your sake, lad. Like I said, now I've had time to think about it I see she was fair scared out of her wits for you but at the time – well, I suppose I thought she'd been messin' about with some Tom, Dick or Harry an' caught her toe. I don't believe that now,' she added hastily as his face changed. 'Even before this with the *Titanic* I'd realised I was wrong, I swear it. But I didn't know what to do.'

'Tell me exactly what she said.'

Nora still hesitated till Harold spoke his wife's name. 'Nora,' he said. It was just one word but as husband and wife looked at each other, Nora seemed to sag.

And it was still with her eyes on her husband, she said, 'Lily knew who was responsible for the attack.' She was about to go on when the slightest movement from Ralph, who was standing behind his father, brought her gaze to her son. He returned her look, his eyes unblinking and now there was no movement at all in his wide, solid body. His eyes were cold, she hadn't noticed how cold Ralph's eyes were when he'd lived at home. In this moment, for the first time in her life, she realised she didn't know who her son was. He looked like the bairn she had raised to manhood on the surface but that was only the outward shell.

Dragging her gaze from his, she said shakily, 'She said she had to stay away from you an' then everythin' would be all right. Otherwise—'

'What?'

'Otherwise they would finish what they'd started an' this time they wouldn't stop at a beatin'.'

'Someone threatened her and you didn't tell me?' John asked incredulously.

'She said if I did an' they found out there would be an accident. They'd do for you an' make it look

363

like an accident. She thought the best thing was for her to go away an' then you'd be safe—'

Nora's words were cut off as John rose so abruptly his chair went skidding backwards. She waited for his wrath to burst over her head but he walked to the window, staring out into the backyard with his back to the room while he said, 'You should have told me.'

'She didn't say who it was?' Sarah asked in the silence which had fallen. 'She didn't give you any kind of clue?'

Nora looked at her daughter-in-law and shook her head. In spite of herself her gaze was drawn to Ralph once more but he had moved to sit down at the table where he was rolling a cigarette from the silver box he kept in his pocket. It was a fine silver box, just as his clothes were of the very best. Again the curdling in the pit of her stomach made her voice shake when she said, 'Whoever it was she believed they'd do what they said. I know that much. She was scared to death.'

'But – but I don't understand.' Hannah had never been very quick on the uptake. 'Why would someone tell Lily they'd hurt John if she went on seeing him?'

'The oldest sin in the world, lass,' her father said quietly. 'It started in the Garden of Eden when Adam an' his lady wife set their sights on somethin' that weren't rightfully theirs an' has continued ever since. Some folks'll do whatever it takes to get what they want, right or wrong don't come into it. Jealousy, envy, covetousness, call it what you will, it all boils down to the same thing in my book. Wantin' what you can't have.'

'You mean someone wants Lily?' Hannah began

and then stopped as John made a funny sound in his throat.

'I'll kill him.' He turned to face them, looking at his father as he repeated, 'I'll kill the sick so-an'-so.'

'But – but she's never said a word about anyone to me.' Sarah was looking from one face to another, her own expressing bewilderment and faint disbelief. 'I'd have known if someone was bothering her, I'm sure of it, and why wouldn't she tell her own sister?'

'Has anyone considered that this might be a lot of hogwash?' Ralph continued to put the finishing touches to his cigarette as he spoke, raising his head as he added, 'I thought she was desperate to go on this trip according to you, Sarah?'

'I never said desperate.'

'No? That's the impression I got.'

John didn't even appear to hear his brother. 'It all fits,' he said grimly. 'One minute she was fine and the next – aye, it all fits, looking back.'

'I'm sorry, lad.' Nora's voice was weak. She was fighting off a terrible presentiment, something so dark and deep she didn't dare face it. 'I should've said some-thin' but I was scared for you an', aye, angry with her at first. We – we didn't part right. An' then when I come to me senses an' thought about it she'd gone an' it seemed too late. You'll never know how I've regretted it since, never in a hundred years . . .'

It would have taken a harder man than John not to soften as his mother's face crumpled again. 'It's all right,' he said softly. 'I'm as much to blame as you. I should have trusted my instincts.'

'What about this pal of hers?' Harold looked at his

son. 'Would Lily have told this lass if someone'd been makin' a nuisance of themselves? Confided in her, like?'

'Not if she hadn't told me.' Sarah couldn't hide her indignation.

John said nothing to this. He continued to stare at his father as he said, 'It's worth a try.'

'I'll come along with you.'

'No need.' John waved his father's offer aside. 'You stay with Mam. I should nip and tell Ellen Lily's all right anyway. She called in to see me at work today to see if we'd heard anything and she was very upset.'

Nora had found herself staring at Ralph through this exchange but his face was deadpan. She was wrong, she had to be wrong and she was wicked, *wicked* to think such things about her own son.

What things? a different part of her brain asked her. She made no attempt to answer this, repeating instead that she was wrong, she was imagining things because she was all upset and was it any wonder? The last twenty-four hours she hadn't known if she was on foot or horseback. She still didn't.

When John had pulled his coat and cap on and was ready to leave, Ralph stood up. 'Where are you going?' Sarah asked her husband in surprise.

'John's right, Da needs to stay with Mam,' he said shortly.

'You don't need to come, man.' John's voice, too, expressed surprise along with gratitude for his brother's offer. 'You stay with Sarah; you must need to get back to the bairns.'

'It's all right, Da's with them,' said Sarah. She had

been relieved how civil Ralph had been with her father when he'd called to tell them about Lily. Her husband knew she saw her father because she couldn't stop the girls talking about their granda, but he'd made it clear he wanted nothing to do with him and that he wasn't welcome at the house. Perhaps this awful thing might be the first step to some kind of reconciliation between Ralph and her da? The thought didn't give her the pleasure it once would have. For the last year there had been no physical relations between them and he barely spoke to her except to snarl some order or other. Not that she would want him to touch her now, she hated him. She glanced across to where he was standing, his thick greatcoat and shiny leather shoes along with his hat – no cap, mind, she thought bitterly – proclaiming he was a man of means.

'We won't be long.' He had caught her look and, as ever, kept up the pretence that they were a happily married couple in front of other people. 'Soon as I'm back we'll get home to the bairns.'

Sarah nodded. She wondered what everyone's reaction would be if she spoke the truth and told him she didn't care how long he was, that if she never saw him again in the whole of her life it would be too soon. She became aware Nora was staring at her and she quickly forced a smile to her face. 'I'll make another pot of tea, shall I, Mam?' she said as the two men left. 'I'm sure we could all do with one.'

The night had a sharp nip in the air as John and Ralph walked to Crowtree Road after deciding not to wait for a tram, their main topic of conversation the *Titanic* disaster. Behind his brotherly façade, Ralph's mind was racing and he was calling his mother every name under the sun. Damned interfering old busy-body. It was typical of her she'd gone to see Lily, she couldn't keep her nose out of anybody's business. And that little scut, telling his mother what she had and presenting herself in the guise of a tragic heroine. He'd seen the look on John's face when his mam had babbled on about Lily giving him up for his own good; his brother wouldn't let hell or high water come between him and her now. But he was panicking here, nothing had really changed, he told himself in the next moment. Lily hadn't mentioned him by name when she'd talked to his mam, and there was no need for her to do so when John went to see her when she was home. She wasn't stupid, she knew as long as she did what he'd told her John was safe; she wouldn't open her mouth and she wouldn't risk his life by seeing him again.

But would his brother accept that? Ralph glanced at the man at his side. He considered John weak and lily-livered, why else wouldn't his brother come in with him with the dock business in the old days when he'd had the chance? But, like all spineless individuals, he had the capacity to surprise now and again. Like old Mick Duffy. Art had had Mick dancing to his tune for donkey's years before Mick had suddenly found the guts to stand up to him over the business of Doug Banks, just because his daughter was sweet on Doug. When the order had gone out to give Doug a concrete overcoat after he'd got too big for his boots,

Mick had flatly refused to do the job. Course, it hadn't helped Doug – or Mick, come to it. They'd both disappeared the same night, never to be heard of again. And he rather thought Lily might be John's Doug, in a manner of speaking. Well, they'd see, wouldn't they, but first of all he had to find out what this whore pal of hers knew. He didn't think Lily would have been so stupid as to mention anything, but you never knew with women. How would he handle it if she had?

His fingers slid inside his pocket where the knife he kept with him at all times was. It wouldn't be tidy, that was for sure, and Art didn't like things that weren't tidy.

He continued to muse over various scenarios till they reached Ellen's front door. The closed curtains in the front room glowed red; someone was home. Ralph felt the rush of adrenalin that always came when he was faced with a tricky situation. He liked the feeling, he could even say he was addicted to it – it gave him an edge when he needed it.

'John!' As Ellen opened the front door her hand went to her mouth as she saw John standing on the doorstep.

'It's all right, it's all right, she's safe. That's what I've come to tell you. She's one of the survivors.'

It wasn't till Ralph followed John into the hall that Ellen noticed he wasn't alone. As her eyes widened, John said, 'This is my brother, Sarah's husband. They came to tell us the news at home. Sarah's father was contacted by the White Star Line.'

Ellen nodded, still with her eyes on Ralph's smiling face. She waved her hand at the front room. 'Please, come in.'

369

It was the first time Ralph had seen Ellen close to and she wasn't what he had expected. He had seen her from a distance once or twice when he had followed Lily, but then Ellen had been in a lighted doorway and had been more of a silhouette. Now he looked at her pale creamy skin and delicate features, his mind adding up the cost of her stylish appearance and quiet tasteful clothes.

There was clearly money in her brand of whoring, he thought, following his brother into the front room which again struck him with its chic refinement. She had none of the coarseness of the whores he dealt with. He could see why a man would pay a bit for the pleasure though; she had something, did this one. Like Lily.

For her part, Ellen was completely taken aback that John had brought his brother with him. They were very alike, she thought, as she waved them towards the couch and offered them a drink. It was odd, because the impression she'd got had been that Lily didn't care for this particular brother.

'We won't sit down, Ellen, we're not staying.' John cleared his throat. 'I wanted to come and tell you about Lily, I knew how worried you've been, but there's something else. It's a little awkward.'

'Yes?' The two men were standing facing her and now she could see John was taller and leaner than his brother. When she included Ralph in her glance she saw he was not so like John as she had first supposed. The features were similar, the hair and the shape of the face, so what was it? And then she realised. John's eyes were a soft warm brown. Sarah's husband's were also dark but there was a density to the brown, a hardness that made them appear dead and cold. She had seen a picture of a shark once in a book about the predators of the deep; it, too, had appeared to have lifeless eyes. She couldn't imagine Lily's sister married to this man.

'Did Lily tell you why she was leaving Sunderland?'

Snapping her eyes to John, Ellen said, 'Yes, of course. She was going to look after the children on the trip, wasn't she?'

'But did she say why she agreed to go?'

Ellen's brow wrinkled. 'I'm sorry, I don't understand. It's her job to care for the Grays' children, so naturally—'

Ralph brought his hand out of his pocket. She didn't know. He had watched enough people trying to lie their way out of a tight spot to recognise the truth when he heard it. He touched John on the shoulder as he said to the elegant woman in front of him, 'It doesn't matter, does it, John?'

'What? Oh no, no, forget it, Ellen.'

Ellen stared at him a little bewilderedly before she said, 'What about the Grays? Are they all right?'

'I don't know. We don't know any details except that Lily is among the survivors but I should imagine if she's all right then so arc they.'

Ellen nodded. 'Bruce and I were very sorry how things turned out between you and Lily, John. I – I don't suppose this will make any difference to that?'

'Let's put it this way, Ellen. If she's not my wife by the end of the year it'll be over my dead body.'

Ralph moved from one foot to the other. 'We ought to get back.'

'Yes, yes, all right.' John smiled at Ellen. 'It's good news, isn't it?'

'The best, John,' she said, smiling back, but when out of politeness she let her smile include Ralph it slid from her face. She had said to Bruce that she felt Lily was frightened of this man and now she had looked into his face she could see why. She made herself hold out her hand and say, 'It's nice to have met you, Ralph,' but her flesh shrank in his grasp and she was glad he did not prolong the contact.

After they had left she went and sat on the couch, staring into the fire, but now her thoughts were not of Lily and John, nor even Ralph, but of Bruce. In her mind's eye she pictured his face, his long, scholarly, good-looking face, and his eyes. Kind eyes. Gentle eyes. She rocked her body from side to side for a few moments before sitting up straight again. His eyes had still held that kindly expression even when she had refused him again last night, for the umpteenth time. But they couldn't carry on like this. She had experienced a feeling of shame last night because even as she had told him she wouldn't marry him she had known she wanted him to keep trying. And that wasn't fair. She loved him but she would never be able to bring herself to marry him. She would cause him to miss out on a family, children, grandchildren, and what would he have in return? A relationship that was no relationship at all; a friendship that was a barren thing, unprofitable. He would grow old waiting for her to change her mind and one day his eyes would be luke-warm when they looked at her but by then it would be too late, he would have wasted his life.

Would she be able to bear that? She answered herself with a shake of her head. And she was under no illusions about herself; she knew why she was going to tell him their 'friendship' was over. It was cowardice. Cowardice because she didn't want to witness his love for her begin to pale and die; cowardice because she knew if she reached out and grasped what he offered it would be a wonderful life and she would spoil it with her fears and misgivings; cowardice because she would rather have nothing at all than take a chance and face whatever happened in the future.

She smiled grimly. All her talk about women's rights, all the suffragette meetings and rallies she'd attended, her being in control of her own life and livelihood – it was all a veneer. Underneath she was still the young, terrified, heart-sore girl who had wanted to die when she'd lost her baby. But she couldn't let anyone see that. While she pretended, she was safe. And she wanted to be safe, above all things she wanted to be safe, in a place where no one could hurt her because she wouldn't let them.

She rose slowly and walked across to stand looking down into the red and gold flames of the fire. She would tell him when Lily returned and that in itself was cowardly; she should tell him right away, tomorrow. But she would need Lily's friendship to weather the storm, it was as simple as that.

Chapter 23

When Stanley left his daughter's house once Sarah and Ralph were home, he knew he had to pay a visit to his ex-wife and tell her Lily was safe. Lily had put him down as next of kin but she had required her birth certificate for paperwork connected with the trip and had written to her mother asking for it, giving Geraldine a brief explanation. Although he felt Lily wouldn't necessarily expect him to inform Geraldine – especially because the certificate had been sent with no note or message from his ex-wife – when all was said and done, she was the lass's mother.

That's what Sally had said before he left the house. 'You ought to go and see her, Stan, she's Lily's mam. She has a right to know she's safe. She might be feeling awful about everything that's happened with the news about the *Titanic*.'

He doubted it. If Geraldine had mellowed at all, why hadn't she written a few words to the lass when she'd sent the certificate? That had been her chance to form some sort of contact again, or at least to try.

But he knew his Sally. She'd whittle on and on till he told Geraldine so he might as well get it over with. Not that he had any desire to see the woman he had spent half his life hating.

Did he still hate her?

Stanley considered the question as he made his way along the Queen Alexandra Road in the direction of Barnes Park. He would like to say no. Hate wasn't a pretty emotion and he agreed with Sally that it did as much harm to the bearer as it did the recipient. In all truthfulness, though, just the thought of Geraldine made his stomach muscles knot. She had gone out of her way to paint Sally as a scarlet woman during the divorce. He hadn't minded so much about the smear campaign Geraldine and her solicitors had levelled at him, likely he'd deserved some of the criticism he'd got, but Sally? And it had been nasty, spiteful. Geraldine had even written to Sally's stepchildren insinuating that he and Sally had been carrying on when their father was still alive. Fortunately they hadn't believed a word of it but they might have done.

The nature of his thoughts made his face tense and stiff by the time he reached Barnes View, one of the more select locations in Bishopwearmouth. When he'd first learned where Geraldine was moving to after the divorce he'd thought it would suit her brand of snobbery very well. His solicitor had told him her apartment was situated in what once had been a grand old house set in its own grounds. The original house had been converted into one- and two-bedroomed apartments and further buildings had been added to form a square featuring a communal garden in the centre.

Geraldine lived in apartment nine and the resident caretaker escorted him to her door and waited while he knocked. Stanley smiled grimly to himself. Little touches like this would appeal to his ex-wife; he could almost hear her describing the man to her friends as though his duties were those of a butler.

When Geraldine opened the front door she stared at him. For a moment he thought she was going to shut it in his face but then she glanced at the care-taker. 'Thank you, Mr Jenson,' she said coolly, before waving her hand at Stanley to enter.

He stepped past her into a wide hall, his feet sinking into thick carpet, and as she shut the door he turned to face her. She looked considerably older than when he'd last seen her, tighter, thinner, as though there was little moisture in her body. He hadn't expected that. She'd always held her age very well and had prided herself on her youthful appear-ance, spending a great deal on various creams and potions.

'Come through,' she said stiffly before he could speak, and once they were standing in a beautifully furnished sitting room with large windows and a pleasant outlook over the square of garden which was lit with strategically placed wrought-iron lamps, she surveyed him through narrowed eyes. 'Well?'

She had always been able to do this, catch him on the hop, and it annoyed him she still could. Knowing he was flushing a dull brick-red, he said, 'I thought you might be wondering about Lily.'

Her carefully shaped eyebrows rose. 'And?'

'I've heard she is one of the survivors.'

There was no change in the cold eyes, no spark of relief. 'I see.'

He thought of how Sally had reacted, how she'd clasped him and cried and gabbled, 'Thanks be to God. I told you, didn't I? I told you she'd be safe. Oh, thanks be to God.' Quietly, he said, 'Is that all you're going to say?'

'What do you want me to say, Stanley?'

'I'm not sure. Anything. That you're pleased, would be a start.'

She looked at him for a moment longer before walking across to the cream sofa and sitting down, crossing her legs and leaning back in the seat. He watched her mouth form into a button that aged her still further before it slackened and she said, 'Lily wrecked my life and you expect me to play the hypocrite?'

'What?' He stared at her. 'What are you talking about?'

'You would never have found the courage to go and live with that woman if Lily hadn't defied me over the business of this dreadful friend and caused me to say what I said. The scandal that's resulted means I'm ostracised by women who haven't an ounce of breeding; common individuals whose husbands happen to have risen in the world and therefore they think they are someone. You have no idea what I have had to put up with.'

'You blame your current situation on Lily?' he asked in amazement.

'Of course I do.' Her voice was dripping with resentment. 'Who else?'

'Me. You. Probably anyone but the lass.'

She glared at him, her green-flecked eyes reptilian in their coldness. 'I might have expected you to take that tack. You have never seen anything clearly in your life.'

He might have agreed with her once but all that had changed when Sally had come back into his life. From the moment on the bridge his vision had become crystal clear. They stared unblinkingly at each other for a moment, then he shook his head. 'And what about Sarah? You haven't contacted her since the day all that about Lily came to the surface. Do you blame her in some way too? Is that it?'

She shrugged her bony shoulders. 'Sarah is yours. She looks a Brown from the top of her head to the tips of her toes and she thinks like one too. Ralph Turner might think he's going up in the world but he only has to open his mouth to proclaim what he is, and Sarah chose him. She knew what an association with the Turners would do to our standing in the community but she went ahead nevertheless.'

Dear gussy. Her bitterness was consuming, it controlled and infected every part of her. She had two bonny daughters, granddaughters who could be the light of her life if she let them, and yet the poison had spread so completely she had actually chosen to cut them out of her life and live in embittered isolation.

Stanley found himself at a loss. He hadn't expected to feel sorry for Geraldine but now the emotion threading its way through his mind was one of pity. Whether something of this showed in his face he didn't know, but the next moment she had risen to her feet again, her eyes no longer cold but blazing with hatred. 'You've said what you came to say so I suggest you get back to your little trollop.'

He didn't fire back as he would have done only minutes ago. He looked at her, at her thin taut body which held none of the voluptuousness which had first attracted him, and her face, twisted with a bitterness which had cleaved lines into it like a tool carving granite. He guessed she spent much of her time in this luxurious prison, wearing expensive clothes that next to no one saw and waking up each morning knowing the day was going to be exactly like the one before.

He turned without a word and walked out of the room, but just as he reached the front door her voice came again in a low hiss. 'Every day I pray you and her will burn in hell, *every day*. And Lily too. Do you want to know what I felt when I heard about the *Titanic*? That justice had been done. But I might have known she'd survive.'

He swung round. She had caught him on the raw and now he spoke from the heart. 'Do you know what you are, Geraldine? Do you know why your fine friends cold-shoulder you and like to put the boot in? Do you? Well, I'll tell you. It's because they recognise, the same as everyone else, that you're an unnatural, mean-minded, vindictive woman who is incapable of genuine affection for anyone. My Sall is more of a mother to your two girls than you've ever been and they love her for it an' so do Sarah's bairns. Fair worship her, they do.'

'*Get out!*' She was beside herself with rage, hot colour blotching her skin as she stood in the sitting-room doorway looking as though she was going to spring at him with claws and teeth any moment.

'I'm going.' In contrast, Stanley's voice was quiet now, even gentle. 'And don't worry, I shan't be back. I'm going to my wife, to warm arms and a home that's like heaven on earth. And chew on this when you're praying your evil prayers; I don't think of you, lass. Not for a minute do you cross my mind.'

He ducked as an ornament from the small table in the hall flew across the space between them. Opening the front door with haste he stepped outside and closed it behind him. Flat nine was on the ground floor of the original house and he hurried across the tiled floor of the entrance lobby, pulling open the door and exiting the building with a feeling of deep relief. He felt more shaken than he would have liked; his hands were trembling as he stuffed them in his trouser pockets and began to walk briskly away. Rows had been commonplace when he had lived with Geraldine but the last years with Sally had made him forget how unnerving such scenes were.

He shouldn't have said what he did. When he came to a part of the street which was in darkness, being between street lamps, he stopped and wiped his face with his handkerchief. In spite of the cool night he was sweating.

He should have said nothing and just got out of the place, that's what Sally would have wanted. Instead he'd allowed Geraldine to get to him with what she'd said about Lily. Stuffing the handkerchief into his pocket, he began walking again. He'd meant every word, mind. He nodded to the thought. It was funny, but for some months now he'd begun to wonder if he'd blown Geraldine up as worse than what she was; guilt could do that. And he *had* felt guilty about her on the quiet, not that he'd ever admit that to Sally.

And now? He stretched his neck, squared his shoulders and began walking again. Now he felt as though something had sloughed off him. His footsteps quickened and by the time the cottage came in sight he was almost running. He was going home, to his love.

PART SIX

May 1912 – Breaking Free

Chapter 24

Lily stood with the twins' hands held tight in hers as the *Carpathia*'s captain finally advised them they could leave the ship. They had sailed into New York harbour on a cold, misty night accompanied by driving rain, lightning and the rolling booms of thunder, but their welcome had not matched the weather. Thousands of people were standing in the April rain to meet the ship, and a fleet of steam launches, ferry boats, tugboats and yachts sailed to greet them. The mayor of New York and several high-ranking officials led the procession in a large tug, and as the *Carpathia* was spotted every boat in the harbour saluted the ship with their steam whistles, bells and sirens.

Less welcome were the waiting reporters, some of whom had climbed aboard the boats and then managed to jump onto the pilot boat. Without any regard for the passengers of either the *Titanic* or the *Carpathia*, they proceeded to shout questions by means of their megaphones while their photographers took flashlight pictures. It wasn't till the *Carpathia*'s captain made it clear that no reporter would speak to the *Titanic*'s survivors till they were off his ship that the melee calmed down, and then the *Carpathia* steamed past the Cunard pier to the White Star dock to return the *Titanic*'s lifeboats to the shipping line. It was some time before the ship was able to make her way back to the Cunard pier where the canopied gangways were manoeuvred into place, and then the *Carpathia*'s original passengers were the first to leave.

Lily had been amazed at the furore, and as she had cuddled the twins she'd thought back to the last few days. The weather had been sunny but bitterly cold, and all the *Carpathia*'s passengers had put themselves out to try and make the voyage more comfortable for the stunned survivors of the *Titanic*. They had provided clothing and toiletries, welcoming folk into their cabins when spare berths were available and sewing warm garments out of steamer blankets for the women and children. Most of the survivors had slept in makeshift dormitories, and even those who had been offered a berth in a proper cabin usually made their way back to the other survivors as soon as they were up. They needed to be with those who had gone through what they had, it was as simple as that. Even though the normal distinction between master and manservant, mistress and maid, still held, it was different somehow.

Lily had said her goodbyes to Tess after dinner; both girls knew it was unlikely they would meet again and had shed tears at the parting. The indomitable Lady Lyndon was planning to tour America as she'd intended so she could keep an eye on her wayward daughter;

there was no question of her returning to England till the unsuitable suitor was well and truly out of the picture. Many other passengers, like Lily, were going home as soon as it could be arranged.

It was after ten o'clock by the time Lily led the twins down the gangway where the solid mass of reporters were waiting. The little boys were tired and fretful but to her relief the Grays' relatives were waiting and immediately whisked them away in a fine motor car. The thrill of riding in an automobile for the first time was enough to keep Nicholas and Adam cheerful till they reached their destination, which turned out to be a magnificent three-storey house approached by a tree-lined drive in a quiet part of Lower Manhattan.

Not much was said that night, but in the morning after her first proper night's sleep since the *Titanic* had gone down Lily told Mr Gray's uncle and aunt exactly what had happened. They were visibly upset, but promised to relay the details to the Grays' relatives in England, and also let Lily's father know she was staying in America for a short while. It had been agreed that the twins would spend a week or two in the United States while they recovered from their ordeal, and then Lily would escort them home. She privately felt very concerned about what would happen to the little boys then. Arabella's parents had died some years previously but Mr Gray's were alive and very much landed gentry with power and influence. She knew from little things she had picked up while working for the Grays that Arabella had not liked her husband's family, considering them cold and distant.

She had to all intents and purposes been the children's nanny rather than a nurserymaid and Arabella had treated her accordingly, but she had a niggling worry that Mr Gray's family would not take this into account when they made their decision about the little boys' future. They needed her, she told herself as the days crept by. Now more than ever. She was the one, solid, dependable fixture in a world which had been turned upside down. If Mr Gray's relatives let her, she would do anything, go anywhere with them, but would they? The little boys had always been closer to her than to their own mother, but would that be considered? They had reacted quite differently to the loss of their parents, brother and sisters. Adam had become very clingy, panicking and crying if she was out of his sight for a moment, but Nicholas had suddenly started having one tantrum after another and only she could handle him when he started.

A full investigation as to how one thousand and five hundred men, women and children could be left on the decks of a sinking liner – and this against a background of only four passengers in the last forty years having lost their lives in the North Atlantic – had begun the day after the *Carpathia* had arrived in New York. It was understood that a great many witnesses would be called throughout the inquiry, some of whom would be passengers, and Lily was thankful she would not be one of them. She had her hands full with Adam and Nicholas and as far as she was concerned everything else was secondary to the little boys' welfare.

By the time Lily and the boys left for England the newspapers seemed to share the general opinion that

Captain Smith had allowed himself to be pressured into sailing the *Titanic* too fast with inadequate precautions for an area where icebergs were known to be, and the White Star Line was being criticised for the insufficient number of lifeboats on board. The inquiry was by no means over, however, and it seemed likely it would continue for weeks yet.

Lily had had sleepless nights worrying over how the twins would react to boarding yet another liner, but to her great relief they appeared relatively unconcerned as long as she was in sight and sound twenty-four hours a day, which she made sure she was. She had also had John constantly on her mind. She had told herself over and over again that nothing had changed, that the reason she had ended their relationship still applied, but something *had* changed. If she had died that night he would always have believed she didn't love him enough and the thought was a torment. Added to this was an overwhelming sense of guilt and shame that she hadn't saved Edwin and the girls. She heard them calling to her every night in her dreams, and she awoke shaken and distraught. She should have grabbed them from their mother and father and manhandled them into the boat. She had known Mrs Gray had gone to pieces and Mr Gray had been more concerned about her than about getting the children off the ship; she should have *done* something. But she hadn't and now it was too late.

She played the last frantic, confused minutes on the *Titanic* again and again in her mind, and each time her actions appeared more heartless. Prudence had been on the verge of burgeoning womanhood and

Belinda was sweetness itself, and Edwin . . . always trying to appear older than his years and with a little strut to his walk, but unable to get to sleep at night without his Mopsy, a little bedraggled toy rabbit with one ear and a missing tail. He'd had a passion for animals, had Edwin. Anything small and helpless in particular . . . And so it had gone on.

When they docked in Southampton the twins' grandparents were waiting for them. Lily had seen them before, once when they had visited Mr and Mrs Gray one Christmas and again when they had visited after the birth of the twins. They had not deigned to notice a nurserymaid on those occasions and for a moment she thought they weren't going to this time either. When both little boys refused to take the hands of the tall, forbidding-looking servant woman they had brought with them but clung to her instead, their grandmother clicked her tongue impatiently. 'Bring them to the carriage,' she said imperiously to Lily as the coachman saw to their meagre luggage. 'You will travel with Burns in the second carriage.'

This presented another problem. Once the twins realised Lily was not going to climb up beside them they began to howl but this time their grandparents were having none of it. With one little boy being held in his seat by his stiff-faced grandfather, and the other pinned by his grandmother, the carriage trundled away, leaving Lily no choice but to do as she had been told. Visibly shaking, she climbed into the smaller and less ornate carriage beside the other woman who eyed her haughtily.

'Do they always behave like that?' she asked by way

of introducing herself. 'The master and mistress won't take kindly to such displays of temper.'

Any feeling of intimidation fled. 'They're frightened,' Lily said hotly. 'Surely that's obvious? They've just lost their mam and da and brother and sisters; of course they want to be with me. They've been through a terrible ordeal and they're only babies.'

The woman looked into the slanted furious green eyes. Her gaze narrowing, she said coldly, 'I'm Nanny Burns and you are merely a nurserymaid so I'll thank you to keep a civil tongue in your head.'

Aware she had almost certainly made an enemy, Lily forced a calmness she was not feeling into her voice when she said, 'Do you know what is going to happen to the twins now?'

'They will live with the master and mistress of course.'

'And — and me?'

The woman gave a small, hard smile. 'That's not for me to say.'

Terribly afraid that her worst fears were going to come true and that she would be separated from her babies, Lily pushed aside all pride. 'Please,' she said quietly, 'if you know, tell me.'

The woman drew herself up with all the dignity her position warranted. 'You'll find out soon enough. The mistress wants to see you directly after lunch and you'll be told what's what then. Till then you can keep your questions to yourself.'

It was not a pleasant journey.

The Grays' country estate was situated on the outskirts of Newcastle. The sun was shining brightly as the carriage passed between two huge iron gates and on to the gravel drive, glinting on the windows of the enormous house in the distance which had a stone terrace with a pillared portico and a massive stone lion either side of the wide steps.

As they neared the other carriage which had drawn to a halt, Lily saw a lady, whom she presumed was the housekeeper, dressed all in black and a regal-looking man who appeared to be the butler come to meet their master and mistress. 'I'll need to see to the young masters; you stay in the carriage, it'll take you to the kitchen,' Burns muttered, opening the carriage door without waiting for a reply. Lily just had time to see Adam and Nicholas alight, their faces red and swollen from crying, before the carriage was on the move again.

For the rest of the morning Lily felt she was caught up in a nightmare. When she entered the enormous kitchen after the carriage had deposited her in a stone-flagged courtyard, it was to find a cook and two kitchen maids busy at work. The cook told her to take off her hat and coat and put her small bundle of clothes, that the Grays' relatives in America had given her, under the hardbacked chair she was to sit on. This had been placed to one side of the biggest range she'd ever seen, but apart from being offered a glass of water she was not spoken to again before lunch. She tried to make conversation several times, but it was clear the other servants had been instructed not to speak to her.

At midday more servants joined the ones in the kitchen, but when the cook gestured for her to join them at the long scrubbed kitchen table no one spoke directly to her although Lily felt everyone was looking at her. There was a large joint of ham and another of

He allowed a full ten seconds to tick by before he said, 'You are the nurserymaid,' in a tone which did not require affirmation. Lily stared at him. He had a red bulbous nose and small eyes and she couldn't see anything of his son in him at all. 'Would you care to explain how the nurserymaid got herself into a lifeboat when my son and his wife and three of our grand-children perished?'

Lily felt sick, faint. His words were a reflection of the words she had been asking herself ever since the accident. 'I – I thought your relatives in America had sent word –'

'You do not expect me to believe that ridiculous story that my son's wife would so far lose control as to endanger her own life and that of her family?'

Lily stared blankly at him. 'It's true,' she said bewil-deredly. 'Mrs Gray was upset and frightened of getting into the lifeboat; they didn't appear very safe.'

'But you got yourself into one.'

'Yes. Yes, I did, but I thought Mr and Mrs Gray and the bairns were going to follow me.'

'Follow *you*?' Norman Gray's mother's voice was icy. 'Do you normally lead your betters, girl?'

'It – it wasn't like that, ma'am. There was so much confusion and a line of folk waiting to get off the ship. Mr Gray told me to take the twins and they would follow.'

'I've never heard such nonsense.' Mr Gray senior glared at her. 'And if you repeat this wicked story I'll have you locked up, do you hear me? Not content with abandoning the children under your care you are now intent on maligning my son and his wife.

I've no doubt that you saved your own skin at the cost of my grandchildren.'

'No, sir, no. The twins—'

'Just happened to be in the same lifeboat as yourself, which gave rise to this wild tissue of lies. But you will have no opportunity to indoctrinate them into believing such falsehoods in the future. You will leave this house forthwith, and if I hear so much as a whisper of this story outside these four walls you will rue the day you were born. Do I make myself clear?'

'But – but the twins. They need me—'

'They most certainly do not, girl. Who on earth do you think you are?' The twins' grandmother stood up, outrage in her voice and manner. 'In my father's day you would have had the dogs set on you for such presumption.'

Lily stared at the couple looking at her with such disdain. These cold-blooded, *unnatural* people were the boys' grandparents and they had the full weight of the law, not to mention their wealth and influence behind them, and they were going to take her babies. 'I spoke the truth when I said what happened,' she said, her voice shaking with a mixture of pain and anger, 'and you know it. Deep inside you know it. There is no reason for me to make up a story, the truth is terrible enough as it is. And the only thing I've done is to make the decision to get the bairns off the boat rather than leave them to die with the rest of the family. Mrs Gray was never going to get into a lifeboat, I see that now, but Mr Gray thought he could make her. He should have made the other children come with me but he didn't. It's not my fault.'

'How *dare* you.' Mr Gray's father looked as though he was about to have a seizure and his wife had sunk down onto the chaise longue again, half swooning. It was clear to Lily that neither of them had ever been spoken to in such a way by a servant.

'Oh I dare, sir. I dare. And I can see now why Mrs Gray felt like she did about you.'

'*Get out.*' He pulled on a bell rope as he spoke.

'You are going to break your grandchildren's hearts. Don't you care about them?'

The door opened as she spoke and the young footman stood there, his wide-eyed stare taking in the scene in front of him. 'Get this scut out of the house,' Mr Gray senior ground out. 'And give instructions that if she sets foot on the estate again she is to be horsewhipped to within an inch of her life.'

Lily stood there, sick of heart. They wouldn't let her see Adam and Nicholas again one last time, it was useless to ask. Nevertheless, she said, 'Can I say goodbye to them?'

'Get her out *now.*'

When the footman touched her arm Lily turned, walking out of the room and into the sunlit hall. There she paused, and as the young man looked at her inquiringly, she said desperately, 'If you get the chance, will you tell the twins I love them and I didn't want to leave them? Please, would you?'

'It'd be more than my life's worth.'

'Please? They are bright little boys. If you make it clear they mustn't repeat what you said, they won't tell.'

'I dunno, lass.' He rubbed his mouth uncomfortably. 'I can't promise anything.'

She was going to cry and she couldn't, not in this house. She had to wait till she was outside. 'They've just lost their family, I don't want them to think I didn't care about them. I've looked after them since they were born.' She gulped hard. 'And the nanny, Burns, she didn't seem to be a sympathetic sort.'

'You're right there.' He lowered his head close to hers. 'Look, I'm walking out with one of the house-maids and she's a good sort. She does upstairs, likely she'll see to the nursery and might be able to say something.'

'Thank you.' It was the best she could do. As he nodded at her and turned to lead the way to the kitchen, she stopped him in his tracks when she said, 'I'm not going that way.' Walking to the big studded front door she pulled it open, ignoring his startled demand she come with him, and stepped into the fresh air.

Amazed by her own temerity she walked down the wide stone steps, the blood thundering in her ears. The gravel crunched beneath her feet as she walked down the drive and she didn't hurry, stopping twice and searching all the windows on the first and second floors for two little faces. When she reached the iron gates which were still wide open she turned a last time, praying with all her heart she would catch a glimpse of the boys. There was nothing.

Outside the gates she walked for a few yards before leaning against the high stone wall which surrounded the grounds. The memory of Adam's and Nicholas's red, swollen faces would haunt her till the end of her days, she knew it would. Last night they had insisted on sharing her bed, snuggling and giggling against her while she had told them a story, their thumbs in their mouths and their small dimpled hands touching her face now and again in the loving way they had. And what had she brought them to? They had trusted her and she'd had to leave them with their grandparents and that awful woman. They would think she had abandoned them.

She moaned in her throat, an agonised cry escaping her and then she collapsed on to her knees on the grass verge as the tears came. All restraint gone, she began to wail; for Adam and Nicholas, for Edwin and Prudence and Belinda, for Mr and Mrs Gray, for those poor people who had been screaming and crying for help in the icy water, for herself -- she had a mother who didn't even like her and a da who wasn't really hers, and for John. Oh, John, John . . .

It was a long time before she gained control of herself, and then she continued to sit on the grass with her back against the stone wall and her eyes shut as the sunlight played over her face. A great weariness had enveloped her. She knew this estate was somewhere on the edge of Newcastle and she had to make her way to Sunderland before nightfall, but none of that mattered. She felt as though everyone she had ever loved had been taken from her and in this moment she didn't care if she lived or died. It had to be something the matter with her, she told herself woodenly. Everything she touched turned to ashes. She was a jinx, a curse on anyone who cared about her. It would have been better all round if she had never been born.

She was brought out of the orgy of self-pity by the sound of a horse clip-clopping along the country lane.

Opening her eyes she saw a farm wagon coming towards her. She continued to watch the horse and cart but without moving; she felt she never wanted to move again. Perhaps she would sit here for ever, just fading away.

The horse drew to a halt on the road below the grass verge and the driver, an elderly weatherbeaten man with a white beard and clay pipe in his mouth, looked over to her. 'Owt wrong, lass?' he said after some moments, his gaze taking in her tear-stained face and tangled hair where she had run her hands through it in an agony of despair.

Lily stared at him. 'I'm – I'm all right.'

'Aye, an' I'm a monkey's uncle, lass,' he said with no attempt at humour. 'Tisn't the place for a young lass to be, out here all alone. Where you makin' for?'

Her head was aching and she felt nauseous, likely because she hadn't eaten since first thing that morning. Still without moving, she said, 'Sunderland.'

'Oh aye, well, you're in luck the day. I 'appen to be goin' that way meself. Come on, climb up into the back of the wagon, there's nowt but bales of hay in there.'

She stared at him for a moment more and then reached for her hat, stuffing it on over her mop of curls before picking up her coat and the small bundle of clothes at her feet.

And it was like that, sitting with her legs hanging over the edge of the wagon and her nostrils full of the scent of sweet-smelling hay, that she made the journey home in the dappled sunlight of the May afternoon.

Chapter 25

John felt sick with a mixture of excitement and fear as he knocked twice on the Grays' kitchen door. Excitement, because since Sarah had got word to him that morning at work that Lily was home the blood had been singing through his veins like hot mulled wine; fear, because in spite of all his brave words the possibility that he might not be able to convince her they had to be together terrified him. But he mustn't show that, he told himself for the umpteenth time. He had to appear strong and resolute.

He prepared himself for the first hurdle of getting past Bridget or Molly. In the months he had courted Lily he'd got to know the sisters a little and felt they liked him, but he knew they were somewhat protective of her. Not a bad thing, he conceded, except in the present circumstances. Only it wasn't Bridget or Molly who opened the door.

When he saw her standing there his whole stomach jerked as though he had been punched hard and the fine words he had been rehearsing all afternoon went straight out of his head. He stared dumbly, shocked at the change in her. She had always been slender but now she looked ill, the pallor of her skin giving the impression that her eyes were too big for her face. It took him a moment or two, but then he said softly, 'Hello, Lily.'

She opened her mouth but no words came out, and after another moment, he said just as softly, 'May I come in and talk to you?'

He had expected opposition so when she stood aside and pulled the door wide for him to walk through his heart leapt before he immediately cautioned himself: steady, steady. Allowing him in was a courtesy, it didn't necessarily mean anything.

Molly and Bridget were sitting at the kitchen table when he walked in. 'Well, hello, lad.' Molly smiled warmly at him. 'Fancy seeing you the day. It's been a while, hasn't it?'

'Not by my choice, Molly,' he said quietly. He nodded at Bridget who smiled back before glancing at Lily who had followed him into the kitchen. He turned to face her. She was clutching the back of one of the kitchen chairs and staring at him as though he was an apparition. 'How are you?' he said gently.

He watched her wet her lips before she shrugged. 'Not – not too bad.'

Molly made a sound in her throat that suggested otherwise. 'They've taken Adam and Nicholas away, the master's lot, and won't let Lily see them again. Cruel it is, wicked. And they've given us notice to be out of the house by the end of the week.' She hoisted up her ample bosom with her forearms. 'Had someone in a couple of days ago, they did, making a note of everything in the house as though we were going to steal something. I told him, I'd as soon as take the gold and silver out of a church as steal from the Grays, God rest their souls.' Her cheeks burning with remembered indignation, she added, 'There's a cup of tea in the pot if you want one, lad.'

'Thank you.' He didn't think he'd be able to swallow anything but he wasn't about to refuse an excuse to stay.

When Molly had poured him the tea, Bridget touched her sister's arm. 'I thought we were going to carry on with packing up the silver in the dining room,' she said quietly.

'What?'

'The silver.' This time Bridget put more feeling into her voice and after glancing at Lily's bent head and John, who hadn't taken his eyes off her, Molly said, 'Oh aye, the silver.'

Once they were alone, John, aiming to take some of the tenseness out of the situation, forced a laugh. 'I take it tact isn't one of Molly's strong points?' Then he quickly added, in case she thought he was criticising her friend, 'Bless her.'

They were both still standing but as he spoke Lily sank on to a chair as though her legs couldn't hold her any longer. Without looking at him, she said, 'You shouldn't have come.'

'I disagree.' The seconds screamed by and when he realised she wasn't going to speak, he said, 'My mother told me what you'd said to her the day she came to see you, Lily.'

Her head shot up, her eyes widening as colour stained her cheeks. 'She shouldn't have!' It was fierce and the first sign he'd had of the Lily he remembered. 'She had no right to do that.'

'She had every right. She cares about me and she cares about you and, like me, she feels we should be together. Whoever this person or persons are, you can't let them come between us. You must see that?' She didn't answer and again he ended the long pause by saying, very softly, 'I can't imagine what you went through on the *Titanic* and I'm heart sorry about the Grays and the older bairns, but I nearly went mad when I thought you were lost. That I'd lost you. I'm not going to let anything or anyone separate us again, Lily, so you might as well get used to the fact.'

'If your mother told you what I said then you know it's not as simple as that.'

'You mean about this person threatening to beat me up again? It won't happen. I'll be ready for them this time.'

'Don't be so stupid!' She jerked to her feet. 'It won't be like that.'

'It's a man, isn't it? Someone who wants you? What's his name?' And when she shook her head wildly he reached out and took her by the shoulders, holding her tight to him when she struggled. 'Tell me his name, Lily, and then let me deal with it like you should have done in the first place. I can't live without you, it's as simple as that. These last months I've only been existing, not living, and I'd rather be dead than carry on like this.' As she raised shocked eyes, he grated, 'You might look at me like that but it's the truth.

If I've got to live my life without you simply because some sick so-and-so has frightened you to death, then I'd rather be out of it.'

'Don't — don't say that.'

'I mean it. I look round at other couples, friends, family, all of them, and none of them have got what we've got. You know it, too. I want to marry you, Lily. I want to have bairns and a house where we shut the door and it's just us, no one else. I want to sit at work knowing I'm coming home to you and that we'll eat together, laugh together, sleep together.' His voice had thickened and now he raised her chin, saying, 'Don't cry. I've just proposed to you and you're supposed to say yes please, John.'

She gulped. 'You don't understand.'

'I understand we love each other and that's all that matters. Everything else, *everything* else we'll sort out.' His mouth came down on hers, and he kissed her as he had never done before, without restraint, almost devouring her. As he felt her respond he lifted her up in his arms and sat down on a chair with her on his lap where he continued to kiss her till they were both gasping for breath. When he eventually raised his head he kept her tight within the circle of his arms. 'We're going to be married and soon,' he said firmly. 'Say it, say you are going to marry me.'

'John—'

'Say it, Lily.'

He felt the fight go out of her. In a whisper, she said, 'I'm going to marry you.'

'Soon.' He kissed her nose. 'Say it.'

'Soon.'

'I want to look after you. I know you won't forget what happened on the ship but I'll try and help. Any time you want to talk about it or cry, I want you to do it with me. Can you tell me about it, or is it too difficult?'

'No.' She shook her head. 'I want to tell you.' Slowly she related all that had happened, right up till the moment she had been forced to leave Adam and Nicholas and come home alone.

'You did everything you could and more for all the bairns, you have to believe that,' John said gently as he dried her tears. 'It wasn't within your power to physically drag the older ones away from their parents and if you had stayed the twins would have perished too.'

'But you didn't see their grandparents, John, and the nanny. I can't bear to think of them in that place.'

'Then don't.' She was at the end of her tether and no wonder, John thought grimly. And he hated adding to her distress but he couldn't put it off any longer. 'You know I need to know his name, Lily,' he said very softly.

As she went to pull away, his grip tightened. 'I promise you I'll take care of it, but you have to tell me.'

She made a small defensive movement with her head. 'I can't.'

'Lily—'

'I can't,' she said again, brushing her hair from her damp face. 'I don't know his name.'

He stared at her searchingly but the green eyes were still glittering with the tears she'd shed and he couldn't read anything in her face. 'You must do.'

'No.' She shook her head. 'There was a letter after

you were hurt saying what would happen if we carried on seeing each other. They knew every detail of that night so I knew it was real.'

'I'm sorry, my love, but I don't believe you.' When she didn't answer him, he said questioningly, 'Lily?'

'Please, John, leave it at that. If – if another letter comes I'll keep it and show you and we'll get the matter sorted properly. You're right, I should have done that in the first place but I was so frightened for you I wasn't thinking straight. Will – will you trust me?'

'Of course I trust you.' As she fell against his chest he held her close again, but his face was thoughtful. He had no doubt she knew who it was who had threatened him, but she thought she was doing the best thing in keeping it from him and he didn't under-stand that. One thing was for sure, she was in such a vulnerable state he couldn't push her for a name till she had recovered a little. It would be too brutal. She had promised to marry him, that was enough for now and he could take it a day at a time. He still felt at bottom that someone with a grudge against him for trying to better himself had had him worked over, and another bright spark who'd had his eye on Lily had taken the opportunity to play silly devils and frighten her into finishing with him.

He frowned, his guts twisting at the thought of his Lily being intimidated by anyone, and especially the type of scum who would play such a filthy trick as this. But he'd get the name from her in due course. For the next little while she had enough on her plate looking for another job and sorting out where she was going to live.

This last thought prompted him to say, 'Have you any idea where you're going to live when you have to leave here?'

Lily shrugged. 'Da and Sally have said I can stay there but I don't know. I – I would prefer not to live with them. Not that I didn't get on with Sally when I met her, I did, but it would seem . . . strange. I'll see, anyway. Molly and Bridget have got work together in a big house in Roker where they'll live in. It will be different to here, it's a large guest house over-looking the promenade, but they're happy to be together so they'll be all right.'

John didn't say it, but he wasn't interested in the sisters. 'You could always stay at ours, you know. Mam would find room for you somewhere.'

'I'll see,' she said again, and then as they heard the noisy approach of Molly and Bridget in the hall outside she stood up, smoothing the hair from her face and smiling weakly as she said, 'They'll be as pleased as Punch when we tell them, they couldn't understand why I said we couldn't see each other any more.'

He hadn't either, and he knew he still hadn't got to the bottom of it yet. There was a reason she was keeping this man's name from him, something more than the fact that she was afraid of what he would do when he confronted the swine, he felt it in his bones. As the door opened he stitched a smile on his face, putting his arm round Lily's shoulders and responding to the sisters' squeals of surprise and effu-sive congratulations with all the right noises, even as his mind worked on a different plane altogether.

Chapter 26

Nora was on tenterhooks. When John had bounded into the kitchen earlier like an excited puppy she had known immediately Lily was back, even before he had shouted the news to her as he'd torn off his shirt and pulled on a fresh one. He had been in and out of the house in three minutes flat, and ever since she had been in turmoil. She didn't know what was worse, the lass accepting him or refusing him again. The latter meant he would be crushed so badly he might never rise from it, but the former . . . She sat down with a plump at the kitchen table as her stomach turned over. She had had to pay a visit down the yard four times since he'd gone and she knew the attack of the skitters wasn't due to anything she'd eaten.

Her eyes unseeing, she stared across the kitchen. She had known this day would come, the day when she would have to face up to the fact that one of her sons was twisted in his mind, that he was bad, unnatural. Oh, she knew they all thought she'd been blind to Ralph's sideline at the docks and then the reason for his sudden elevation to owning his own boatyard, but she wasn't daft. She'd chosen to close her eyes to it because she'd known she couldn't influence him one way or the other and he'd follow his own road. He always had, even as a bairn. And he'd had Sarah, she'd reasoned. A good wife and two bonny bairns to keep him on track even if he did sail too close to the wind.

When had she first realised there was something wrong with the marriage? That he wasn't treating Sarah right? She pressed the corners of her eyes at the bridge of her nose between her middle finger and thumb, trying to clear her thoughts. She should have done something then, brought the subject up with Sarah and found out what was what.

But no, she answered herself in the next moment. How could she have done? She couldn't have meddled in their affairs, put herself between man and wife. If Sarah had wanted to tell her anything she'd had plenty of opportunities over the years.

But you knew the lass wanted to talk to you.

She stood up abruptly, walking over to the range and banging the big black kettle on to the hob. Aye, she had, she had. And if she'd taken the bull by the horns and not fooled herself that everything would work itself out, Ralph might not be responsible for half killing his brother.

No! No! Again she denied what she felt to be the truth. She might be on the wrong track here and doing the lad a terrible injustice.

And what about the stuff she'd discovered in the last days since she had seen Ralph's face in the kitchen the night she'd told John what Lily had said? Ralph had done himself no favours when he'd given Wilf Wright the elbow some months back because Wilf had disagreed with him over something or other. Not that Wilf had spoken to her but his wife had been more forthcoming when she had made it her business to go and see her one morning. Maggie hadn't known what the cause of the falling out had been, but it would have had to be something really bad, she'd said, for her Wilf not to be able to stomach it and cut off the gravy train that was Ralph. He was scared to death of Ralph, Maggie had revealed, since he'd got involved with Art Shawe and some of the other criminals who ran the East End. So scared he'd not told her much of what went on, but a wife knew, nonetheless, didn't she?

Aye, Nora had agreed. A wife knew.

The boatyard was just a front, of course. Maggie had spoken as though Nora was fully aware of this. And the bit of handling they'd done in the early days had turned into full-scale smuggling and other things besides; she didn't like to think what was stored in there some nights. And of course since Ralph had had the rooms built over the warehouse floor . . .

What? Nora had asked. What did she mean?

Looking straight into Nora's eyes, Maggie had said, 'Look, lass, I know you're his mam and all, but I don't hold with a man doing the dirty on his wife with the types that hang round the docks, not if she's a decent body like Ralph's wife is. Neither did my Wilf and that didn't go down too well with Ralph either. He said some of the goings-on he heard talked about by Art's lot when Art and your Ralph and their pals had the lassies in fair turned his stomach, and he's no prude, my Wilf. I used to rate your Ralph in the old days and to be fair it's him that's made it possible for us to get our own place, all bought and paid for, but that aside, there're lines you don't cross, in my opinion. Do you know what I mean?'

Nora did know what Maggie meant, and when she had finally left the smart little terrace in South Durham Street she'd had to lean against a wall for a moment and take deep steadying breaths.

The kettle was singing and now Nora made herself a pot of tea and took it to the table. She'd always trusted her instinct over her bairns when they were small, and it was that same instinct that was telling her now that Ralph had arranged to have John beaten up, that he wanted his own wife's sister. That was why Lily wouldn't give her the name of the man who had threatened her, because it was Ralph, and the lass had known it would blow the family sky high.

She was still sitting there when Harold and Robert came in from the union meeting they had attended, Larry hot on their heels, sensing dinner was nigh, and Hannah following a minute later.

She had sliced a big slab of stottie cake to go with the hodge podge and dumplings that had been simmering for a couple of hours when the door opened and John walked in. Turning from the range where she was preparing to dish up, she knew immediately what Lily's answer had been. His face radiated it. It didn't need him to come over and lift her right off her feet, swinging her round once before he set her down, saying, 'She's said yes, Mam! She said yes.'

412

'Ee, give over.' She made herself smile broadly as she extracted herself from his arms, pushing him as she said, 'I'm in the middle of dishing up so sit yourself down with the others and tell us what happened before you do yourself an injury. I'm no wisp of a thing like Lily.'

'You're grand.' He didn't do as she said, his face straightening as he caught her arms and said again, 'You're grand, I mean that. But for you going to see her we might not have got this sorted because she'd never have told me herself.' He kissed her, his face smiling again as he added, 'We'll be sure to call the first bairn after you, Mam.'

'That'll upset the apple cart if it's a little laddie.'

Under the laughter her sally brought forth from John and the others she pretended to give her attention to the dinner, but her bustling demeanour hid the feeling of dread his words had caused. John was right, but for her having gone to see Lily that day they'd be none the wiser as to why the lass had called it off. But she *had* gone, and now her lad was in danger. But could she be sure it was Ralph? Could she?

The hilarity at the table somehow made her suspicions even more improbable and yet she felt she was right. All through dinner and for the rest of the evening Nora put on such a good show that not even Harold suspected anything was wrong, but inwardly she was crying out the whole time: God, give me a sign, show me, let me know. I'll never ask you for anything else in the whole of my life, but just do this one thing. Give me a sign.

*　　*　　*

413

When she called round to see Sarah the next morning and saw her daughter-in-law's black eye, she knew she had her sign. She had woken up feeling she had to see Sarah, not necessarily to ask her anything about Ralph but just to talk to her, to gauge how she was, how things were. The minute she'd washed the break-fast dishes she'd taken off her pinny and put on her coat and hat, leaving the house before nine.

She'd walked in the back way as she always did, calling Sarah's name, but the kitchen had been empty. It had been a moment or two before Sarah had answered her from upstairs, and when she had finally come into the room Nora had taken one look at her swollen face and said, 'Oh no, hinny, no. Not that.'

'I – I walked into the back door.'

Nora looked at the woman she loved like a daughter. She looked tired and ill, even old. The gaiety had gone, it had been gone for a long time if she thought about it. Without choosing her words, she said softly, 'It's him, isn't it? Ralph? He's done this and something tells me it isn't the first time he's hurt you. I'm right, lass, aren't I?'

Sarah stared at her, her eyes wide, and then as her face slowly crumpled Nora reached out and drew her into her arms. 'There, there, hinny,' she said sooth-ingly. 'Don't cry, lass. He's not worth it. He's me own, but he's not worth it.'

It was two hours later before Nora left the house, and by then she knew a great deal more about the workings of her son's mind. She didn't like to think that she and Harold were responsible for raising such a man, and several times as Sarah had unburdened herself she'd wondered where they'd gone wrong. They'd brought Ralph up the same as the others, hadn't they? They'd fed, clothed and housed the lot of them and made it a point never to make fish of one and fowl of another.

But none of that mattered for the moment, she told herself, clearing her mind and focusing on the thing Sarah had said which had disturbed her the most. The black eye was apparently the result of Sarah telling Ralph she'd let John know her sister was home. Ralph had gone fair barmy, Sarah had sobbed, but then the slightest thing provoked him these days.

Aye, but this was no slight thing to Ralph. Nora's mouth was set in a grim line. With hindsight she could see various pointers leading to this day, and it must have started years ago. She could remember when he'd got drunk at his wedding and he and his pals had started singing that song, 'I love a lassie, a bonny, bonny lassie, she's as pure as the lily in the dell.' They'd got too raucous and she'd gone across to put a stop to it and he'd shaken off her hand, and none too gently. She and Harold had got him outside in the hopes he'd sober up a bit and he'd been muttering the lines of the song to himself. On and on he'd gone, swearing and cursing, until Harold had gone to the horse trough and come back with a bucket of cold water which he'd tipped over his head. She hadn't thought anything of it at the time but now . . .

Would he really do for John? Her answer to herself was a low moan in the base of her throat.

She would have to talk to him, tell him she knew. She imagined the look of scorn on his face. But she could threaten she would go to the police and tell them what he'd said to Lily and that he was responsible for the attack on John.

No, no, that wouldn't do. They would demand some sort of proof and she had none if Ralph called her bluff. And she wouldn't put it past him. No one would tell Ralph Turner what he could or couldn't do, his mother least of all.

She couldn't stand back and do nothing, though. Her thoughts propelled her along the back lanes and by the time she got to her own back door she was sweating profusely and feeling, as she put it to herself, right bad. Both Harold and Robert had picked up a shift at the shipyard that day and so the kitchen was quiet as she mashed a pot of tea. By the time the teapot was empty she was feeling better but no nearer to solving what had become an unsolvable problem.

It was on Saturday morning, the day after John had helped Lily move her things to Ellen Lindsay's house where she was going to stay for the time being, that Nora awoke in the early hours and knew what she had to do. She'd known it all along in the deep recesses of her mind, she admitted, lying quietly beside Harold who was snoring softly. Ever since the chat with Maggie Wright. She just hadn't been able to face the thought of being the means of sending her own son along the line. He had been such a bonny babe, Ralph, and Harold had been over the moon at having a boy. Not that he hadn't loved their Cissie but she knew he'd been a bit disappointed she wasn't a boy.

She lay staring up at the ceiling, wondering how she was going to let the police know about the boatyard and its contents. She couldn't go into the police station herself. If this went wrong Ralph mustn't find out it was her who had shopped him. He had to think it was one of his dubious colleagues who had done the dirty on him.

She would have to write a letter. The trouble was, she wasn't much good at reading and writing, having only had the odd week of schooling here and there. Her mam and da had been hard pressed to put food on the table, let alone find the pennies needed for schooling for their offspring. Nevertheless, she'd have to do her best. She could get one of the bairns playing in the street near the police station to deliver the note if she slipped them a ha'penny.

She lay watching the pitch blackness give way to grey light as she planned what she was going to write, and once she could pick out the battered wardrobe and chest of drawers the room held, she quietly slid out of bed and got dressed.

How could she be sure Ralph would have stuff stashed away when the police called? she asked herself as she made her way downstairs to the kitchen. She couldn't, she'd just have to hope and pray he did. After putting the kettle on the hob she stood at the kitchen window looking out into the yard. If someone had told her a few weeks ago that she would be hoping her son would be locked up for a long, long time she would have laughed in their face, but John had to come first. Holding herself tight round her middle she stood swaying slightly, the tears trickling down her face and into the collar of her faded blouse.

Chapter 27

Lily was awake early too. She was lying on a put-you-up at the side of Ellen's studio couch. It wasn't nearly so comfortable as her bed had been at the Grays', but it wasn't this which had had her tossing and turning for most of the night. She had been the same since she had promised John she would marry him.

Carefully turning over so she didn't wake Ellen, she lay staring at the wall. The last three days had been hectic as she'd helped Molly and Bridget clean the Grays' house from top to bottom. The sisters had been adamant not a speck of dust would greet the Grays' representatives when they came to take over, and although Lily hadn't seen the point of the three of them working themselves to a frazzle to clean a house that was just going to be put on the market, she had done her bit. But now her time was her own. Her heart began to pound and she brought her knees up as though she had a physical pain in her abdomen. Today she would have to go and see him.

The thought of facing Ralph and her worry about John had to some extent cushioned the worst of her agony of mind about the twins although she still had moments when all she could do was cry, but she could do nothing to influence the boys' grandparents. She could, however, try to talk to Ralph one last time before she told John the truth. If Ralph would see reason there would be no cause to put Sarah in what would be an impossible position, break Nora's heart and bring about a split in the family, the repercussions of which would be endless. She knew John would believe her, but what about the others? She had seen families that were forced to take sides and it was horrible, but the most important thing, the terrifying thing, was that she didn't know if she could trust Ralph even if he agreed to leave John alone.

She'd know when she spoke to him face to face. Whatever he said, she'd know. She closed her eyes for a moment, as the thought of seeing him made her flesh creep, and then she sat up, quietly swinging her legs to the floor.

As silent as she had been, Ellen stirred, her voice low as she said, 'Lily? Are you all right?'

'I can't sleep. I was just going to make myself a hot drink.'

'I can't sleep either, I'll come with you.'

Once in the kitchen they sat facing each other. This room, like the front room, had Ellen stamped all over it, from the white-painted walls and light blue cupboards to the gaily painted crockery in the dresser. 'I'm so glad you are back with John.' Ellen reached across the table and squeezed her hand. 'But I have to tell you something. I've decided to finish with Bruce once and for all, Lily. It − it can never work and it's not fair to him to keep him hanging on.'

'Oh, Ellen.' The spectre of Ralph faded into the background. 'Are you sure?'

'Absolutely sure.' As the kettle began to boil Ellen stood up and walked across to the hob. 'I've decided to move back down south, not straight away, I'll stay for the wedding.' She turned and gave Lily a smile. 'But nothing can change my mind now. It's the right thing to do.'

'When are you going to tell him?'

'Today or tomorrow, soon.' The slim shoulders straightened. 'I'm going to train as a nurse, I want to do something useful with my life. That way, when I end up as an old lady with just a couple of cats for company, it won't seem such a waste.'

'He loves you very much, you know.' Lily had to say it even though she knew her friend didn't want to hear it. 'And with Bruce you could be a wife and mother. Think about it some more, Ellen. Please.'

Ellen shook her head, her mouth faintly tremulous as she said, 'I can't, Lily. I can't waver now. More than anything else I need peace of mind and I'll never have that while I live close to Bruce. I − I love him too much.'

A deep sadness enveloped Lily as her friend turned away and began to see to the tea tray. She knew Ellen and Bruce loved each other and there was a fiercely maternal streak in Ellen. Ellen had spoken about waste and this decision would lay waste to two lives because Bruce was a one-woman man. If he couldn't marry

Ellen he would never marry, and he was made to be a husband and father more than any other man she knew — except John. Oh, why was life so complicated? Sarah was deeply unhappy — she knew she was, even though her sister had made light of things when she had talked to Sarah on returning home. Ellen and Bruce should be together and there was still this huge shadow hanging over John, a shadow she had inadvertently caused simply by loving him. Ellen's husband had been a vile man and yet he was still ruining her life even though he'd been dead for years. Why was it that the innocent suffered and the bad people always seemed to win? It wasn't *fair*.

She was still thinking along these lines later that morning when she turned into the road that bordered the wharf, sawmills, engine works and boatyards that stretched along the banks of the river. The May morning was warm and sunny, but this only served to make the smell of fish more overpowering. A group of black-clad fishwives were busy gutting fish as she passed, their shawl-covered heads turning towards her for a moment or two before they concentrated on their grisly task once more, the cobbles slimy and bloody beneath their boots.

Lily breathed a little more easily once she was past the women but still the stench of the East End, a distinctive composite of the industries lining the river, fish and poverty, made her feel slightly sick. The labyrinth of alleys and narrow courts where families of eight or nine lived in one room and shared an outside tap and privy with twelve or more other houses, made the smell of animal and human waste an offence to the nostrils on even the coldest winter day in some areas, and this was one of them.

She could see Ralph's boatyard in front of her. It was similar to others she had passed except that there were small square windows in the upper part of it as though someone had made this into a living area. His name was painted in large letters along the front of the wooden building and a high solid fence made of black timber surrounded the whole with a gate set into it. It was to this gate she walked, and when she was outside it she peered through the wooden slats into the boatyard. It was packed with piles of wood, chains, anchors, several small boats and all the para-phernalia one would expect, but as far as she could see no one was working. She waited for a few minutes and then shouted, 'Hello! Is anyone about? I need to see Ralph Turner.'

Almost immediately a door opened in a small structure set to the side of the boathouse. A large rough-looking individual with a pockmarked face and a nose that had clearly been broken at some stage in his life came towards her, and for a moment the desire to turn on her heel and run was overwhelming. Controlling the emotion with some difficulty, Lily called, 'I need to see Ralph Turner.'

'Aye, you said.' He reached the gate but made no attempt to unlock it. 'An' who might be callin'?' he asked with mocking civility.

Holding herself straight and stiff, Lily glared at the man. 'His sister-in-law,' she said coldly.

'Oh aye, his sister-in-law, is it?' His eyes moved up

and down her with insulting thoroughness and it was clear he didn't believe her. 'Well, Ralph is a mite busy at the moment. You'll have to come back later.'

She couldn't. She would never have the nerve to go through this again. 'I need to see him now,' she said a little more loudly. 'Please tell him I'm here.'

'Now look, lass. I'm tryin' to be polite, all right? He can't be disturbed, even for a pretty little piece like you. Come back in an hour or two.'

In answer Lily shouted at the top of her voice, *'Ralph Turner! I need to see Ralph Turner! I know you're in there!'*

'Shut up.' The man's voice was a growl now.

'I won't, I want to see him. *Ralph Turner! Ralph Turner!'*

Swearing darkly the man began to unlock the gate. 'If you want to do this the hard way, that's all right by me.'

Frightened and poised to run, Lily's flight was arrested by the door to the boathouse opening and Ralph and another man appearing in the yard. It was this man who called, 'What the hell is going on, Alf? They'll hear her in Newcastle.'

'I'm sorry, Mr Shawe, but she won't take no for an answer. I told her Ralph was busy.'

'I want to talk to Ralph.' As Ralph and the thin, ferrety man came nearer, Lily stood her ground. 'I'm not going till I do.'

She could tell she'd caught Ralph off guard; he looked nervous, uneasy, and when the other man turned to him and said, 'I've told you before, you keep the tarts in their place,' Ralph's voice had a whine to it when he said, 'It's not like that, she's family, the wife's sister.'

This answer seemed to please the man still less. Looking at Lily, he said, 'Get yourself home, lass. Anything that needs to be said can be said when he's not working.'

'No, it can't. Not what I want to say, anyway.'

The man had been about to turn away, his hand on Ralph's arm. Now he swung back and looked at her afresh. 'I'm not asking, lass. I'm telling.'

She felt goose pimples break out on her flesh. He was a small man, a half-pinter as her da would say, but there was something about him that was chilling. Nevertheless, she knew if she didn't speak now she'd never come back and she didn't want Ralph coming to find her. 'It will only take a minute but it's important,' she said with a firmness she didn't feel. 'If – if you don't want the police round here.' She didn't know why she added that last bit except that she was desperate. 'I – I need to warn him.'

The cold eyes narrowed. 'What does that mean?'

'I – I can only talk to Ralph. It's his business.'

He stared at her for some moments then turned abruptly, saying over his shoulder to Ralph, 'Two minutes and then get her out of here or Alf will. Understand?'

'Aye, aye, course, Art. I'm sorry, man.'

Art had clicked his fingers at the other man, much as one would summon a dog, and as they walked away, Ralph said under his breath, 'This had better be good, I'm warning you.'

Aware it had all gone wrong, Lily stared at Sarah's husband. The other man had been slight and foxy-looking but immaculately dressed, and his thinness had carried the impression of whipcord strength. In contrast, Ralph looked bloated and greasy, none of the good looks that had first attracted Sarah to him remaining.

'John and I are going to get married and nothing you can do will stop us,' she said tightly. 'I want your word you will leave John alone or I'll tell everyone it was you who set up the attack on him. I mean it.'

He stared back at her, his eyes unblinking. 'Is that it?' he hissed softly. 'You've come here and put me in the mire with Art for that?'

'Do I have your word you won't hurt John?'

He called her a name she hadn't heard before but which she knew was bad, before he ground out, 'Like I said before, if you love him, you'll stay away from him or his blood'll be on your hands.'

'I'll go to the police.' She was trembling. 'I'll tell them what you told me.'

'And even if they believed you, what do you think they could do?' He'd noticed she was shaking and his voice was low, thick, when he added, 'You can't fight me, Lily. I've got all the aces. Whatever you say and do, you can't win. Do you really want to marry him knowing that one day, maybe a month or a year or five years from now, he won't come home? Is that what you want? I couldn't live like that meself.'

It was no use. She had been hoping for a change of heart, for a miracle, but deep down she'd known what the outcome of this visit would be. But she'd had to try. She turned away, aware of the man Art and his henchman standing in the doorway to the building watching her. She had only gone a few steps when Ralph's voice came to her, soft and holding a coil of silky laughter. 'Keep looking over your shoulder, lass, if you go ahead with it. That's all I'm saying. But you can't be with him all the time, can you . . .'

Ellen was out when she got back and Lily was glad of this. It gave her time to compose herself. Once Ellen returned she told her everything, starting with the day Sarah had got married when Ralph had cornered her in the club's yard.

'Oh, Lily.' Ellen was white-faced and horrified by the time she had finished talking. 'I knew it, I knew there was something wrong but I didn't know what. I felt you were frightened of John's brother but then I told myself I was imagining things. You must tell John and the rest of the family.'

'But what about Sarah? Oh, I know things are not right between them and haven't been for years; she told me she hated him not so long ago, but he's still her husband and the girls' father. She won't be able to stay with him when this comes to light and—'

'Lily, from what you've told me she'll be thankful for the excuse to go.'

Lily nodded. Ellen was right. Anyway, regardless of what happened in the future, she had to speak out because she couldn't bear to leave John again. It was as simple as that. She should have told him before, she saw that now. She had been stupid to let Ralph blackmail her.

'When will you tell John? I presume you'll tell him first and then you'll face the rest of the family together?'

Lily nodded again. 'He's calling here at eight o'clock and we were going to the picture house but I'll say

I want to go for a walk instead. I'll tell him then. I suppose we'll have to go and see Nora, it would be better if she came with me to see Sarah. Oh, Ellen.' Lily shook her head wearily. 'This is going to hurt so many people.'

They talked for most of the afternoon by which time Lily had developed a throbbing headache. When Ellen pressed her to go and lie on the studio couch and take a nap while she prepared a light dinner, Lily didn't protest. She felt exhausted, emotionally and physically, but better for having shared the burden with Ellen.

She didn't expect to fall asleep, she'd had in mind just to lie quietly and shut her eyes to relieve her aching head, but when she came to, she realised she must have dropped off. She lay in the half-world between sleep and consciousness wondering what had roused her, and then she saw him. Ralph was standing behind her and as she opened her mouth to scream he sprang forward, clamping his hand over her mouth as he hoisted her off the couch.

Her feet were dangling, her back against his torso and his big hand still fastened over her mouth and nose so tightly she could barely breathe as she struggled frantically. He was holding her as easily as a child would hold a rag doll, speaking in an eerily quiet voice, words which her whirling brain couldn't make sense of. 'Thought you'd do the dirty on me, did you? Sending in the law to poke and pry. And course it would have to be one of the times when the place was packed full to bursting. But you didn't reckon on me not being there when they arrived; lucky I went out on a spot of business this afternoon, eh? Crawling over the yard, they were, when I come round the corner.'

She was making sounds in her throat but they were too stifled for anyone to hear her.

'Wanted to get me locked away, didn't you? I know, I know. I saw it in your eyes earlier. And they could throw away the key as far as you're concerned. But I'm cleverer than you think, I've got enough stashed away to be all right once I leave here. Not that you'll be around to know or care. You've been a thorn in my side too long, I see that now. But you've got something about you, that's the thing. I'm damned if I know what it is because you're as thin as a lathe with no figure to speak of, not like Sarah. Now Sarah's what I call a woman, something to get hold of. I haven't played fair with Sarah, but then you know all about that, I'm sure. Know about a lot of things, don't you, Lily? Lady Lily. By, I used to think you were as pure as the driven snow, the lily in the dell. But this lily needs gilding, that's for sure. Aye, and I'm just the man for the job.'

She struggled again, trying to call Ellen's name, and his grip tightened. 'It's no use calling for your fine friend. She tried to warn you I was here and I couldn't let her do that, now could I? Still, what's one whore more or less?'

Twisting in his hold, she managed to kick out, causing him to stagger slightly, but then he hauled her across the room, grabbing her hair and releasing the hand across her mouth but only long enough to bash her forehead against the wall.

The blow was enough to stun her, and as she

desperately fought to remain conscious he flung her roughly on to the couch. His hands tearing at her dress, he ripped it from bodice to waist. As her hands came up to claw at his face he hit her again with the flat of his hand across the side of her face so that her neck felt as though it had snapped. The next thing she knew he had crouched over her and forced his cotton neckerchief into her mouth, tying the ends behind her head.

He was too strong for her. He was going to rape her.

The horror of the situation lent strength to her arms. With an animal-type moan she gave an almighty push, at the same time bringing her knees up as hard as she could into his groin. It was this which caused him to yell out, the push had barely registered on the big solid body above her, but as she tried to roll aside he yanked her back and brought his fist straight between her eyes.

Panting, he sat astride her. Dimly, through the faintness the blow had caused, she heard him mutter, 'On no, you don't get away, not now, not till I decide I'm finished with you. And then you'll be going on a little journey, the same one your whore friend went on a few minutes ago. I've even brought the paraffin for the funeral pyre. Impressed? By the time they dig you both out of the ruins they won't know what you died of. It was a knife in the ribs for your pal in case you're interested.'

When she felt his hands on her breasts she tried to flail but her strength was gone, and then he was hoisting her dress up to her thighs. Dizzily she screamed out for John but only in her head; with the gag choking her all that emerged was a strangled groan.

And then it was as though a giant hand had picked Ralph up and catapulted him off her. She felt his weight go from her and heard the thud as his body hit the floor, but as she struggled to sit up, terrified he'd leap on her again, her blurred streaming eyes made out the figure standing there. Ellen was holding one of the heavy brass candlesticks that sat on the mantelpiece over the range in the kitchen, and her other hand was pressed against her side, covered in blood. Her blouse, skirt, everything was red. Even as she watched, Ellen crumpled slowly to the ground but now the whirling in her head was taking her down, down, and she was powerless to resist it.

Aeons of time later, or perhaps it was only minutes, Lily became aware of voices and sounds. She couldn't move, it was as though her limbs were weighted down, but she wasn't unconscious either. When she felt arms about her the terror that it was Ralph made her try to flail, but it was as though she was in the dream she'd had since the *Titanic* had sunk; the dream where she was one of the poor souls drowning. As she tried to swim and reach the lifeboats her arms and legs wouldn't move. And then Bruce's voice said, 'Ssh, ssh, you're safe now, it's all right. Can you hear me, Lily? You're quite safe.'

She wanted to tell him she wasn't safe, that none of them were, that any minute Ralph might spring out and attack them again, but she couldn't. Just as she sank into the darkness again she tried to form John's name but it was nothing more than a sigh.

Chapter 28

For the next five days Lily lay in the Sunderland infirmary oblivious of where she was or what was going on around her. Afterwards she had vague, misty memories of her hand being held and kissed, of John's voice, soothing and soft, talking to her endlessly and arms holding her up while warm liquid was trickled into her mouth, but it was phantasmagorical, shadowy. She was content to stay in this half-world because she was tired, so very tired, and the pain in her head became unbearable if she attempted to move or speak. And then, on the morning of the sixth day, she awoke to bright sunlight spilling across her starched counterpane and a broad northern voice saying briskly, 'And how are we this morning, Miss Brown?'

Opening her eyes, she saw a rosy-faced nurse looking down at her. 'Could I have a drink of water?' she asked faintly.

The nurse's professional bustle suffered a hiccup. 'Oh my goodness, you're back with us. I must get Sister.'

She shut her eyes again, the sunlight was piercing and her head felt tender but the terrible gnawing pain had gone. She opened them once more when a soft voice said, 'Miss Brown? I'm Sister Randall. How are you feeling?'

'Better, I think.' The question that had been there in the dreams the whole time surfaced. 'Ellen? Is Ellen all right?'

'Miss Lindsay is out of immediate danger but still poorly. I'm sure it will do her good to know that you are feeling better.'

Lily nodded, a great weight lifting from her, and went back to sleep again.

After that her progress was rapid. By visiting time at six o'clock she was sitting up in bed, washed and with her hair tied back with a blue ribbon by one of the nurses, having been moved from the small side room where she'd been since she'd been brought in. She was now in a main ward. She had been told that the blow to Ralph's head had killed him instantly, that Ellen had been able to talk to the police and explain everything and that the whole affair had been the talk of Sunderland for days. She had also asked for a looking-glass and seen the result of Ralph's brutal treatment. Her whole face was black and blue and her forehead was lacerated through coming into violent contact with the wall. Her nose, the sister assured her, was not broken, only swollen and sore. Lily hated to think what a broken nose would look like in that case, because the massive blob in the centre of her face bore no resemblance to the one she remembered.

But the marks and abrasions would vanish in time, the kindly sister had assured her, and her friend would recover from her injuries in a few weeks. It could all have been a lot worse, she had finished brightly. One had to look on the bright side in these situations.

Lily thought of how John must be feeling, and Nora and Harold, and Sarah and the bairns. Their brother, son, husband, father, had been labelled a maniac and a dyed-in-the-wool villain to boot. Ellen had nearly lost her life because Ralph had definitely intended to kill her, there was no doubt about that. And all because she, Lily, 'had something', as he'd put it. Well, she wished she hadn't. She had said as much to the sister who had patted her hand gently and then done the unheard-of thing of sitting on the side of her bed. 'You're very low at the moment, my dear, but when you're feeling better you will see things differently. I'm much older than you and one thing I've learned in life is that people are not always as you would wish them to be. This man, your brother-in-law, chose the path he took; you were not responsible for that. If you want to apportion blame, you could say it's your sister's fault for marrying him in the first place, but you wouldn't be so silly as to think that, and quite right too. He was, quite simply, my dear, a bad man. If it's any comfort I had a word with his mother when she visited you and she sees things very clearly. She has been greatly concerned about you,' she added, standing up and straightening the counterpane. 'Everyone has.'

But now it was visiting time and the sister had told her with a smile that John was always the first one through the door. Today was no exception. As the doors swung open and she saw him come towards her, her throat became blocked and her eyes full of tears at the look on his face when he saw her sitting up. If ever she had doubted his love for her – and she hadn't – it was there in his face for everyone to see.

'Oh, Lily, Lily.' He bent down and put his arms around her, holding her so tightly it hurt the bruises on her body but she didn't care. She wanted nothing more from life but to be in his arms. 'I've been out of my mind with worry, my love. They said you just needed time, but . . .' His voice broke and then he pressed his lips to hers, his hands coming to gently cradle her battered face. 'I couldn't live without you, I mean that,' he muttered, tears streaming down his face. 'And when I thought that fiend might have hurt you . . .'

She knew what he meant and she was quick to reassure him. 'He didn't, Ellen was in time.'

'I know.' He sat by her bed, taking her hand in his and tracing each finger softly with his own as he said, 'What you must have lived under for so long and all because of my brother. I'm sorry, I'm so sorry.'

It came to her that they were all going to feel like this – herself, John, Nora, Sarah – but the sister was right. Ralph and Ralph alone was responsible for what had happened and they all had to get that clear in their minds because, like it or not, the tittle-tattle that would follow this scandal wouldn't be pleasant. There would be those who'd say there was no smoke without fire, that she must have been carrying on with Ralph, leading him on to make him think he could behave like that. And no doubt all the old rumours about Ellen would come to the fore again, besides a lot more about them all. She knew how the old wives gossiped over their backyards, and what they didn't know for sure they made up. But they'd weather it. She reached out and lifted John's face, looking into his beautiful brown eyes. 'It's not your fault, it's not my fault, it's no one's but his. And he's paid for what he did.'

'Not enough.' He clasped both her hands in his. 'It was too quick, too easy.'

'Don't, John,' she said softly. 'Don't let him change you and make you bitter. I've seen what that's done to Ellen. And I'm not being holier than thou when I say bitterness only consumes and mars the vessel that contains it, it's the truth. You have to let it all go and remember the good times, like when he used to look out for you when you were boys. Probably if he'd been able to do what he'd intended I might feel differently, but he didn't, and this' – she extracted one of her hands and touched her face – 'will soon be gone.'

He made no response for a moment. Then he said quietly, 'I'll try.'

'That's good enough for me.' She smiled, loving him.

'I was going to give you this on Saturday, I'd got a special meal arranged as a surprise.' He reached into his jacket pocket, drawing out a small velvet box which he placed in her hand before kissing her.

'Oh, John.' The bright green emerald was surrounded by tiny diamonds and the stone flashed green fire as she lifted it out of the box.

435

'To match your eyes,' he said huskily, taking it from her and slipping it on to the third finger of her left hand. 'And I promise you this, I'll make you happy, Lily. I don't intend to be a junior accountant for ever. We'll have our own house, not a two-up and a two-down, but somewhere with a garden for the bairns to play and on the edge of town. And a motor car. They're the up-and-coming thing, motor cars. I'll give you everything you've ever wanted.'

'I have it,' she said simply. 'I've got you.'

Four months later, on a mellow September day that carried the lingering scents of honeysuckle and meadow-sweet on the balmy air, Lily walked down the aisle on Stanley's arm to meet John. The reception was an informal affair in the garden of Stanley's and Sally's house, with children running round and everyone partaking of the excellent buffet lunch which Sally, Nora and Sarah had worked hard to prepare. It was a happy day, a day of laughter and light and love, and as Lily sat by her new husband at the long trestle tables she looked down the row of faces that were so dear to her.

Nora and Harold were content to sit close together and watch their children and grandchildren enjoy themselves after all the trauma of the last months. Lily's grandparents were there too; so frail now, but enjoying a new lease of life since they had come to live with Stanley and Sally two months ago. Sarah looked younger and happier than she had in years, and Imogen and Felicity looked pert and pretty in their pale green bridesmaids' dresses as they chattered away to Molly and Bridget.

And Ellen. Her dear, dear Ellen. As Lily caught her friend's eye, Ellen smiled. Raising her glass, she silently toasted her, mouthing, 'Be as happy as I am,' before turning to her husband as Bruce whispered something in her ear. Bruce had been quite unabashed at making the most of the opportunity to catch Ellen at her most vulnerable, persuading her to marry him when she was ill and fragile in her hospital bed, and then whisking her down the aisle a month later so that she had no opportunity to change her mind. They had come back from a week's honeymoon surrounded by a radiant glow that made everyone who was with them smile, and only the day before Ellen had whispered to Lily that she was sure she was expecting Bruce's child.

'You look as bonny as a summer's day, lass.' Stanley, on Lily's other side, hadn't been able to stop grinning all day.

She smiled, resting her fingers on top of his for a moment. She couldn't imagine how she had ever thought of this man as anything other than her father.

'He's right, as always.' John didn't kiss her, but brought her other hand to the side of his face. It was one of the loving little things he did often and which never failed to touch her.

She had so much. She let her gaze wander over the tables and garden again, packed with relatives and friends. She felt loved, really loved, and it was precious.

Just for a moment her thoughts touched on the woman who had borne her, the woman who right now was probably sitting in her cold, beautiful apartment in her fashionable clothes, alone, eaten up with bitterness and hate. She had written to her mother to invite her to the wedding when her father and Sally had said they didn't mind, but had never received a reply.

'I love you.' John put his arm round her, pulling her close. His love and care encased her and the shadow was gone.

'I love you.' She lifted her face for his kiss. 'So much.'